# Shadow Sun Unification

Book Five

of the

Shadow Sun Series

By

Dave Willmarth

Prologue


Rajesh looked out the window of his office at the factory floor below. More than a hundred of his people were down there, working to create his most valuable and profitable commodity. Outside the walls, thousands more were harvesting the materials his factory workers needed to do their job. His thoughts drifted back to the early days, when this building had just been a shelter for himself and his family. Before they figured out how to make it work for them.

A brief knock at the door interrupted his reverie. "Come in."

"Good morning, Rajesh. I have the weekly reports here." An older man wearing a pristine white shirt and pants entered the room, extending a ledger.

"You will address me as Earl Rajesh, please. I should not have to keep reminding you of this, uncle."

"I changed your diapers when you were little, Rajesh. Be glad I do not address you using your nickname from back then, Stinky." The old man grinned at his nephew, setting the ledger down on the desk before him. "In formal settings I shall use your proper title. But here and now, with just us two, you are my dear Rajesh."

Rajesh sighed. His uncle Agni was irrepressible, and he supposed he wouldn't want it any other way. The old man had stayed by his side and supported him without fail since the earliest days of the apocalypse. Taking the ledger, he gave it a quick scan, his eyes moving down to the bottom line.

"Sales have been good. We are very close, I think, to being able to expand again."

"And maybe this time you will become a prince!" Agni waved his hands in the air with a flourish, then bowed gracefully, grinning the entire time.

Rajesh shook his head. "I wish there were some kind of wiki or instruction book that spelled out exactly what it will take. That Allistor person achieved the title months ago! I dislike being second, and will *not* tolerate being third. We must expand as quickly as possible, so that I am next to achieve princedom."

Agni nodded his head. "The researchers have been monitoring the open market via the kiosks, and we are still the only ones selling our product. Eventually, there will be no more of it to scavenge, and every human on earth will be your customer."

Rajesh chuckled, shaking his head slightly. "I never gave it much thought before our world as we knew it came to an end. This new world, it presents many opportunities. Who would have ever guessed that I, a simple accountant and virtual game hobbyist, would become the Toilet Paper Prince of Earth?"

"Toilet Paper Earl." Agni corrected his nephew, his smile wide as he held up one finger. "Perhaps you would reconsider contacting this Allistor? He is, after all, the only one who can tell you how he achieved the title of Prince."

Rajesh scowled. He had already refused this suggestion from his uncle more than once. He had no idea what type of man Allistor was. How would he respond to a competitor? Would he assist Rajesh in achieving the next rank? Or would he lash out in jealousy, attempting to take Rajesh's holdings for himself?

"There is too much risk, uncle. Continue to gather information about this man as best you can. Should we find accurate intelligence that he is good and honorable, I will seek him out. Otherwise, it is best not to show ourselves. We will continue to sell our toilet paper via anonymous trade accounts, and buy weapons and armor the same way."

"What about our new neighbors? Surely they will have more information on the prince."

"The jelly creatures?" Rajesh raised one eyebrow at Agni. "Do they even speak?"

"The System called them *gelatinous* when we used *Identify* on them, not *jelly*. I imagine they must communicate, somehow." The old man looked thoughtful. "If you would lift your orders not to interact with them, I could find out…"

"The only person who has *interacted* with them screamed for a full two minutes before he was engulfed and dissolved. You wish to tempt that fate yourself?"

The old man shook his head slightly. "Gupta was a fool. He did not even try to communicate. He simply charged into their midst as soon as they emerged from that cave, hacking and slashing like a madman, shouting about loot."

Rajesh thought it over for a long moment. Finally, he nodded slightly. "You may attempt communication." He held up a finger, much like his uncle had earlier. "But not you, personally. Choose someone less important, and instruct them on what to do. And make sure no one else is nearby. Gupta nearly caused a panic among the peasants with his screams."

The old man bowed his head slightly, and exited the office. Rajesh returned his gaze to the factory floor, drumming his fingers on the arm of his executive chair.

## Chapter 1

Allistor sat on the roof of a recently cleared high rise not far from Invictus Tower. His crews of beastkin, and lower leveled humans from among the recent recruits, had been working hard to clear structures in an expanding zone around their home. There were a hundred groups now, each taking a building at a time, working their way outward from his tower across lower Manhattan.

Escorted by battle droids, the groups were earning decent experience killing the remaining monsters that had spawned during Stabilization. Allistor had given them all a repeatable quest to clear and claim each building, providing significant experience and klax even if they did not encounter monsters. They were learning to fight together as teams, and the loot they were gathering was useful for several crafts, from leatherworking to alchemy.

As with each of the other buildings, Allistor had just used the City tab on his interface to begin repairs of the building he stood upon. This one would take about eighteen hours for the mostly superficial damage to repair itself. He hadn't bothered to change the footprint. It was previously an apartment building, and would continue to serve as one going forward. Allistor did choose to upgrade the elevator, and place an anti-aircraft turret on the roof, which is why he was up there.

And since he was alone and isolated, he decided to experiment with his dangerous new spell. His mentor had warned him not to fail in the casting, and to be far from any innocent bystanders, especially the old elf himself, just in case.

Daigath had recommended he begin with a small object, and one that would easily accept enchantment. So Allistor chose a small emerald from a looted bag of gems. If the enchantment worked, he could have the stone set into a ring, or a bracelet, or even just sewn into his armor somewhere.

Allistor set the emerald down atop an old HVAC exhaust housing, and focused his attention on it. He took a moment, again on the advice of his mentor, to study the gem carefully. To take in its color, the cut of its many facets, and to remember its weight in his hand. Keeping all of that in mind, he cast *Dimensional Manipulation.*

He could feel the magic of the spell as it was pushed into the emerald. It felt sort of slippery and twisted, and Allistor could almost see the tear in his reality that was being created inside the gemstone. At the same time, he felt a pull. As if his body and soul were being dragged toward the rift. It was only a slight tug, easily resisted for the few seconds it took for the spell to complete.

### *Spell Level Up! Dimensional Manipulation +1*

Allistor lifted the stone and held it in his palm, casting *Examine.*

### *Enchanted Emerald*
### *Item Quality: Uncommon*
### *Enchantment: Void Storage; Capacity Used: 1/50*

*This gemstone contains a single compartment of Void Storage. An item stored in this pocket dimension will be reduced to .01% of its normal weight. Item will be preserved in the state in which it was deposited. Living organisms will perish, but be preserved in the same condition.*

Allistor tossed the little gem up in the air, then caught it. "Yesss! Who can make secret compartments for hiding important stuff? This guy!" he pointed to his own chest with his thumb. Taking a moment to read the description more carefully, he mumbled to himself. "So, the weight reduction is very cool. It means I could carry ten thousand pounds of gold, for example, and it would only weigh a pound. And the capacity thing..."

He stared at the bit that said he'd used one out of fifty, or two percent of the gem's capacity. "Pretty sure this means I can turn this into a fifty-slot storage item. But can I just cast the spell again now and add another slot? Or did I need to add all the slots at once? If I try to re-cast it, will this thing explode?"

Thinking back to all the old sci-fi stories he'd read and watched, it seemed to him that when one dimensional abnormality or rift encountered another, the results were catastrophic. Sure, it was all fiction. But now Allistor knew that much of old Earth's fiction was based on fact, created as a sort of primer for Earth's inhabitants to help them adjust to their eventual induction into the Collective.

"Better ask Daigath before I try again on this one." He returned the gem to his inventory ring, holding his

9

breath as he did so. He had no idea how stable his new device was, or whether it would react badly to being stored inside another. When nothing happened, he let loose the breath with a relieved sigh. Pulling another emerald of similar size from his inventory, he decided to try again, with two slots.

This time he held the gemstone in his hand as he studied it. When it came time to cast the spell, he imagined the emerald with two storage slots, side by side. He felt more resistance to the magic as it entered the emerald, and this time the pull felt stronger as well. Gritting his teeth in determination, he narrowed his focus and pushed harder.

Much to his surprise, a window popped up on his interface in the middle of the casting. It displayed an image of the emerald, and some numbers.

**Common Emerald**
**Enchantment In Progress: Void Storage**
**Capacity: 50 compartments; Mana Cost: 1,000/compartment**
**Mana Available: 15,400; Maximum Available Compartments: 15**

Allistor's total mana pool was currently at sixteen thousand. And though he hadn't checked, he assumed that the previous spell had cost him one thousand mana for the single slot. He'd regenerated a bit of mana since then, but he was still limited to fifteen slots by his current mana pool. Which didn't matter, because he doubted he could manage that many on his second ever attempt at the enchantment.

*Let's try ten slots.* He thought to himself. As soon as he thought the words, his intent was manifested by the spell. The emerald began to glow with a silvery-black pulse, and the pull on Allistor's physical being actually caused him to lean forward slightly. A moment later the glow faded, and the slightly warm gem sat calmly in his palm. He felt a little lightheaded after the rapid drain of nearly two thirds of his mana pool, and used his empty hand to steady himself against the exhaust housing. After a short rest, he used *Examine* on the gem.

> ### Enchanted Emerald
> ### Item Quality: Uncommon
> ### Enchantment: Void Storage; Capacity Used: 10/50
> *This gemstone contains 10 compartments of Void Storage. Any item stored in this pocket dimension will be reduced to .01% of its normal weight. Item will be preserved in the state in which it was deposited. Living organisms will perish, but be preserved in the same condition.*

Proud of himself, Allistor tested the gem. He pulled several random items from his inventory ring and set them atop the housing, then one by one placed them into the emerald's slots. He chose a couple large items, like a fomorian spear and shield, just to make sure they'd fit okay. And they did.

Allistor quickly emptied all the items from his new creation and returned them to his ring, then headed downstairs. He wanted to show off his creations to

Amanda, Lilly, Michael, and Ramon! And he needed to visit Daigath to ask a few questions.

*****

Instead of his squire William, who was usually waiting for him when he returned to the tower, L'olwyn was waiting for Allistor in the tower lobby when he arrived. William was at the Silo, as he had been practically every hour of the last few days, watching the dragon eggs with Daniel. There had been several false alarms, the eggs vibrating and wobbling, but no hatchings as of yet. The young boy was determined to be there for the first of them.

Allistor motioned L'olwyn toward the sitting area, and when both were comfortably seated, asked, "What's up?"

"I have finalized the trade agreement terms with Queen Xeria's factor, Allistor. I thought you would wish to review the terms before executing the agreement."

Allistor nodded. "I would indeed. But I think maybe that's a discussion for a larger group. As I mentioned before, I don't know much of anything about trade, and would like some more experienced eyes than mine on this. No offense to you, L'olwyn. I'm sure you did a wonderful job."

"Indeed." The elf's dry response was as stiff as when he'd first arrived on Earth. Allistor felt a twinge of regret for offending his analyst, but he believed in what he'd just said. He had advisors for a reason, and was not too proud to admit when he needed them.

"How about we discuss it over dinner? We'll have food brought up to the conference room. You can provide the other analysts and Harmon with copies for them to review between now and then."

"Of course, sire." The use of the title, rather than his name, was a clear sign that L'olwyn had taken offense. Allistor would have to find some way to make it up to him.

L'olwyn departed without another word, and Allistor decided to stop in the kitchen to make dinner arrangements. To his surprise, Meg was nowhere to be seen when he stepped through the kitchen door. Instead, he found Sydney and Addy preparing several dozen sandwiches, humming a quiet duet as they worked. He waited for them to finish before speaking.

"Hey ladies! That was a very pretty tune. The usual buffs?"

Addy shook her head. "We're experimenting with different songs, different intentions as we sing, hoping to figure out new buffs. Like, how cool would it be if your wedding cake gave a *Charisma* buff?" She grinned at him.

Allistor pictured an entire ballroom of humans and aliens, all of them just a bit more charming than normal.

"It would certainly make things interesting!" he chuckled. "I was looking for Meg…"

"She's at Luther's Landing today. Amanda and Nancy, too." Sydney looked sad as she added, "Making sure the folks there are okay after... George."

Allistor felt a twinge of pain himself at the mention of his old friend's death. It had only been a few days. "Ah, gotcha. I'm glad she's looking out for them. I should probably visit there myself." He paused, forgetting for a moment why he was in the kitchen. When he remembered, he added, "I'm having a dinner meeting up in the conference room this evening. Can you girls make sure the staff sends up food for... let's say ten people? Nothing fancy. These sandwiches would be fine." He smiled at them as both girls nodded.

Wishing them good luck with their experiments, he left the kitchen and headed for the teleport pad. A few moments later he arrived at Ramon's Citadel on Governor's Island. Allistor was barely five steps from the pad when Max came bounding over to greet him. He spent a few minutes playing with the enthusiastic mutt, his heart lightening a bit as he wrestled with Max and watched the carefree mutt sprint around the open space.

Before long, Ramon's voice came to him through Nigel. "I'm in the crafting lab if you need me."

"Just the man I was looking for." Allistor responded. "Be there in a few. Max needed some lovin'." He petted the dog one more time, then headed for the old fort where Ramon and his people created copies of all the spell scrolls. Max happily followed along, running circles around Allistor as he walked, and barking occasionally, letting Allistor know he wouldn't be opposed to a treat.

True to his word, Ramon was sitting at a table in the lab, several sheets of paper in separate stacks in front of him. Most of them were blank, and looked to be standard old-world copy paper rather than scroll parchment.

"Hey, buddy. Whatcha doin?" Allistor shook his friend's hand.

"I'm actually working on some new skills." Ramon answered without looking up. He was folding a piece of the copy paper. Allistor watched as it began to take the form of a classic paper airplane.

"Uh, didn't you learn to make those airplanes in first grade, like the rest of us?" Allistor teased.

"Yup! But not like this…" Ramon completed the last fold, staring at the paper plane for a moment before picking it up and launching it into the air. It floated in a lazy circle, coming around and zeroing in on Allistor.

"Well, it works…" Laughing, he reached out to catch it gently. But the moment his hands touched the paper, it exploded! Allistor's hands went numb, and frost formed on both of them, stretching all the way to his elbows. "What the hell?"

"Ha! Told you." Ramon beamed at him. "Don't worry, I only put a few points of mana into the spell. The frost will fade in a minute or so." They both watched Allistor's hands, and the frost began to melt almost immediately. Allistor wiggled his fingers, which seemed to speed the process.

"I visited my class trainer the other day, and opted for a cool class specialization." Ramon began to explain. "It's called *Paper Sorcerer*. I can create enchanted items with paper, and control them. Like the plane, or a paper golem. Watch this." Ramon grabbed another sheet of paper and quickly folded it several times, creating a four-pointed star that was several layers thick. It resembled one of the Asian throwing stars Allistor had seen in old movies. After closing his eyes for a moment, Ramon flicked his wrist, sending the paper star spinning toward a metal trash can about ten feet away. The projectile struck the side of the can, and erupted in a tiny fireball, sending the trash can careening across the floor. "That was just twenty mana." Ramon grinned at Allistor.

"That's... *awesome!*" Allistor shook the last of the frost off his hands, then patted Ramon on the shoulder. "Very cool."

"Glad somebody thinks so." Ramon shook his head. "Last night I made a lil paper golem, 'bout the size of a gingerbread man. I sent it upstairs with a message for Nancy, nearly made her pee herself. She's still mad at me." Ramon hung his head.

"Ha! She'll get over it. Maybe you can make one to be the ring bearer at your wedding." Allistor winked at him. Ramon just chuckled.

"Oh! You're not the only one who can do cool stuff, my friend. Check this out!" Allistor retrieved the emerald with ten slots in it, holding it out in the palm of his hand.

Ramon picked up the gem and *Examined* it. A moment later, his eyes widened. "Dude! You can make storage devices!" He looked down at the gem, then back at Allistor.

"Just small ones for now. But as I level up the spell, I could make some pretty cool stuff."

"This is already cool! You could sew this into your armor, and even if somebody knew to steal your storage ring, you could have backup gear in here." Ramon held the gemstone up close to his face and peered into it. "I can... almost see some kind of darkness in there."

"That's probably the dimensional rift. I could feel it pulling at me when I cast the spell. Which is why I'm going to take things slowly. Master Daigath warned me that failure in casting this one could kill me. And maybe everyone around me."

Ramon quickly handed the emerald back to Allistor. "Yeah, don't go around creating black holes all willy-nilly, dude." He looked at the stone in Allistor's hand with a bit of fear evident on his face.

Allistor grinned. "And don't you go making any giant Stay Puft marshmallow golems out of paper. Can't have one of those things rampaging through the city..." Both men chuckled at the visual from one of their favorite old movies.

"How's the scroll production going?" Allistor changed to business.

"We're making several hundred scrolls per day now. But it'll still take us months to make enough just for everyone you've already recruited to get the basic three scrolls. At the rate you're going, we'll always be behind. The direct teaching is helping a lot, though. Nancy and the others have been setting aside three or four hours per day, traveling to the different settlements, teaching as many as they can. It seems there's a limit to how many people you can teach in a day. It drains the teacher's *Stamina* and mana a little bit each time they share a spell. And it has to be done one person at a time."

"Maybe the class trainers will help?" Allistor ventured, mainly to himself.

"Oh, they've been a tremendous help!" Ramon got enthused again. "I mean, we're all getting spells and skills we never dreamed of. I'd say, on the average, those of us who've been to our trainers are nearly twice as strong as we were before. In terms of survival, I mean. But the trainers are focused on class skills, not the basic spells we want everyone to have. A lot of the classes don't have any kind of healing ability, for example."

Allistor nodded, his mind already working the problem.

"We need to increase the number of people who can teach the healing spells to others. Pass the word. I want everyone walking around casting the heal spell on each other at random. Or on the chickens, cows, random birds flying by, whatever. I want everyone working to level up their heals so that they can teach it to others. Because it's not just Invictus citizens I want to teach. We're about to set out to find other human communities, and I want to be able to teach them. I want a thousand people who've mastered *Restore* and *Mend* who can walk through a portal or get on ships and teach a whole community in a day."

Ramon's look turned mischievous. "Same daily training with Flame Shot?"

"Ha!" Allistor shook his head. "No, I don't want folks burning everything down. But everyone could walk around shooting light globes into the air."

"I can picture that causing a few incidents as well." Ramon's expression didn't change. Allistor was about to ask what he meant, when he felt something bump into his butt. Turning around, he found a light globe floating there.

"Well played, dork." Allistor chuckled. "But I think practicing *Light* should be pretty harmless." He paused for a second, then added, "But not after like, 8pm. I don't want to keep people's children up past their bedtime. And let people know that we'll pay them for their time when they teach others."

*"Pardon the interruption, sire. Master Daigath has requested your presence at the Wilderness Stronghold."*

Both men, and everyone else in the room, looked up at the ceiling when Nigel's voice rang out. There were a few looks of alarm, caused by the realization that the AI had interrupted a conversation, rather than waiting to notify Allistor when he was through talking.

"Thank you Nigel. Please let him know I'm on my way." Allistor was already headed for the door.

As soon as he left the building, he increased his pace to a jog, quickly reaching the teleport pad. The moment he appeared at Wilderness, he found Daigath waiting for him in the courtyard.

"Good morning, Allistor. I have several bits of news that I wanted to relay immediately. I apologize if my request interrupted something important."

"Not at all, Master Daigath. What do you have for me?"

"First, I have been informed that Harmon's orcanin have completed their search within the fomorian complex. They did not locate the remains of a Matron in the rubble. It is still possible that she was completely destroyed by one of the bombs."

"But it could mean that she's out there somewhere, looking for payback."

Daigath shook his head. "A Matron, especially one who has lost her Patron and Scion, would normally not risk a rash act of vengeance. She would bide her time, rebuild her clan until she was strong enough to claim revenge. This would normally take decades, but for creatures so long-lived, it is not such a burden." Allistor sighed with relief, which was short-lived.

"But to reclaim her clan's Ancestor Orb? For that, a Matron would take nearly any risk. She cannot rebuild her clan without the relic." Daigath shook his head. "Every day you retain ownership of that relic, it presents a real threat to you and yours."

Allistor had been walking them towards the eating area, and his mentor's words caused him to sit without realizing it. He placed both hands flat on the table in front of him, sliding them back and forth as he thought.

"I've been wondering about something. You said I'm not powerful enough to use the relic, and won't be for many years. But *you* can use it." He raised both hands as Daigath opened his mouth to object. "I know, you've already told me you don't want the orb. Or the power it could give you. And that's not what I'm offering you." Allistor got back to his feet and paced back and forth, his hands now clenched behind his back.

"I recently learned that it's possible to create dungeon cores, rather than wait to discover a dungeon and take control of it. Master Longbeard explained to me about how emperors often use dungeons to train their people." He stopped pacing and turned to face the ancient elf.

"What if you were to use just some of the orb's power to create a few dungeon cores for us to seed Orion with? We could place the dungeons near our existing settlements, where they could be protected. And since I control who gets to settle on the planet, and where, we could also control who gets to use the dungeons."

Daigath shook his head. "I won't use the relic, even for something as innocuous as that. But I have made contact with several entities who have expressed interest in the relic. And by *interest* I mean that several powerful factions are offering trades that will make even an emperor as wealthy as you blush." The ancient Battlemage smiled slightly. "And I'm sure you could have a few dungeon cores thrown in with whichever offer you accept."

Now Allistor was curious. "What kind of trades? Ships? Klax?"

Daigath shook his head. "I have promised to let them make their offers, and attempt to persuade you to accept them, in person. Five factions, including your friends the Or'Dralon, are awaiting invitations for an audience."

Allistor was slightly nervous, again. Representatives from five obviously powerful factions coming to see him. Which meant a day or more of formal audiences, with all the protocol, and risk, that affairs of state involved.

"How... would we do this? Private meetings? Or a public auction sort of situation? Will we need to host a formal dinner?"

Daigath smiled. "Well, this is a rare occurrence, and I am not aware of any particular protocol. If it were me, I would call them all together and allow them to present their offers publicly. It would create an instant competition between the bidders, and drive up the price.

Still, one must be careful in any dealings with such powerful entities."

"Would you be there with me?" Allistor was definitely scared, now. "I don't have any idea what they'll be offering, or what the value would be once I'm told what it is."

Daigath favored him with a fatherly smile. "Yes, I will stand at your side. As will Harmon. And no one has a keener eye for the value of things than him. I suggest you have your four analysts attend, as well. Once the final offers are made, it is acceptable behavior for you to take some time to discuss them with your advisors. Wise rulers don't make rash and unconsidered decisions." Patting Allistor on the shoulder, he added, "As for protocol, as the host and the seller of such a valuable commodity, you may make the occasion as formal, or informal, as you like. Though I recommend making some of Lady Meg's delicious food available, if only to put the bidders in a better mood."

Allistor relaxed a bit. "When do you suggest we do this?"

"As soon as possible. The sooner that relic is gone from here, the safer you will be. The Matron, if she lives, likely has a connection to the orb, and may be able to track it. And as I mentioned before, even if the Matron has perished, there are factions that will not hesitate to crush you in order to obtain that relic. All of the bidders have declared themselves available at your earliest convenience. I would recommend tomorrow."

Allistor sighed. "Better to just rip off the bandaid, right? Please set it up as you described, with all of them presenting their offers tomorrow at midday. We'll serve lunch... where do you think we should do it? I don't exactly have a throne room."

"You should correct that as soon as you can." Daigath smiled. "A noble should have a place for formal gatherings. But for now, the weather is gentle, and the group should not be large. Three or four representatives from each faction, I would think. The courtyard between your building and Harmon's should serve nicely. L'olwyn has worked wonders on the sunken garden, and tables could be set up for dining. This location also allows Harmon's troops to watch over the proceedings unobtrusively from nearby, should their assistance be needed."

"We can manage that. Thank you, Master Daigath. I'll go break the news to Meg."

Allistor was turning to head back to the portal when he remembered he had questions.

"Master, about the *Dimensional Manipulation* spell..." he produced his first two experiments and showed them to Daigath. "I wanted to ask you about this first one that I created. It only has one slot, though the gem shows it has a capacity for fifty. Can I go back and add more slots? Or will it... you know, explode?"

Daigath chuckled. "For now, your skill level is insufficient to go back and increase the storage capacity. You'll find, as a general rule, it is much harder to modify an enchanted object than it is to create it in the first place.

At your current skill level you would be unlikely to cause an explosion. You would simply fail in the casting. Once your skill level is above ten, you should be able to go back and modify this to increase the capacity. It will be easier to modify your own enchantment than it would be for you to modify that of another enchanter." The ancient elf looked at him and winked. "In case you were having any grand visions of increasing the capacity of your storage ring."

Allistor nodded. That thought had actually occurred to him while he'd been daydreaming about the spell's possibilities. Though he'd been thinking more about the storage devices on the *Phoenix* than his own ring.

"Inside the gems, there's a sort of darkness, like a tiny rift or black hole. And when I created those, I felt a sort of... physical pull. Are they dangerous?"

Daigath shook his head. "Because your spell level is still very low, these items are slightly more vulnerable than your ring, for example, which was created by someone much more advanced in the skill. Should these encounter a nullifying element, the enchantment could be broken, the containment element of the spell disrupted. It would then cause an implosion that would be catastrophic within a small area."

Allistor gulped, suddenly regretting just tossing his emeralds into his storage ring.

Daigath chuckled. "Do not worry. The odds of you encountering a nullifying element strong enough to disable even your first attempts here are almost beyond reckoning." He held out his hand, and Allistor handed him both emeralds. "Still, just so you won't lose sleep the night before you host such an important event, I will modify these for you."

The old elf put his free hand over top of the one that held the emeralds, closed his eyes briefly, and there was a soft glow that leaked between his fingers. When he removed his hand, Allistor quickly *Examined* the gems. Both of them were now fifty-slot storage devices.

Impressed, Allistor accepted the gems back. "Thank you, master. You're right, I was considering throwing these into the lake before going home." He grinned at Daigath. "I'll hold off on more experiments for now."

Daigath motioned toward the teleport pad. "I'll return to Invictus with you now, and assist L'olwyn in his preparations. I'd also like to have a word with Harmon before the auction."

Chapter 2


Back at the Invictus Tower, Allistor stopped to see if Amanda was back in her infirmary. She was sitting at a work station, studying something under a microscope. Moving in close, he peered over her shoulder, trying to identify what was on the slide.

"Back up a bit, buddy. My fiancé could walk in at any minute." Amanda spoke without looking up from the microscope. "He's kind of a big deal around here."

"I think I could take him." Allistor grinned at her back. He placed a hand on her shoulder, rubbing with his thumb. "How are the folks at Luther's Landing?"

Amanda sighed, still looking through her scope. "They're still mourning, obviously, but I think they'll be okay. They're already starting back to work today. We're all getting too used to losing loved ones."

Allistor grimaced. That was an ugly truth that he didn't want to examine just then. So he changed the subject. "Whatcha lookin at?"

This time she did raise her head, turning to smile at him. "Skin. Specifically, some of my skin. I've found something interesting, but I'm not sure it means anything." She motioned for him to take a look as she rolled her chair to one side. He leaned down and placed his eyes in front of the appropriate lenses. What he saw didn't mean much to him. A bunch of cells all clumped together.

"Okay, keep watching, I'm going to cast *Restore*." Amanda cast the spell, and watched Allistor's face.

In the microscope, Allistor saw the cells begin to vibrate. They rubbed against each other, moving more and more quickly for several seconds, before slowing down again and eventually growing still.

"What was that?" He raised his head to look at her. "I mean, I know it was a heal spell. But what was the activity I saw?"

"That skin is from a small piece I sliced off my arm about five minutes ago. In theory, nothing should have happened when I cast a heal on it. It's just dead flesh, disconnected from my body, from any blood flow to keep it viable. But it still tried to react to the healing magic. If you were able to count the cells before and after the spell, you'd find that new cells have been created." She took a pair of tweezers from the table and lifted the half-inch wide section of skin. When she held up her arm, Allistor could see the still bloody section she'd sliced the skin away from.

Using the tweezers, she laid the skin back in place on her arm. "This skin should have been dead by now, but…" She cast *Restore* again, and they both watched as the sample melded itself back into place, meshing with the surrounding flesh until neither of them could see a hint of the wound. Amanda's arm looked untouched.

"So… what? You're part zombie now?" Allistor was a little creeped out.

"Dork." She shook her head. "I'm not sure what this means. We already know we can't heal the dead and bring them back to life. We've tried and failed often enough." She paused, thinking of some of the friends they hadn't been able to save. "And that skin should have died quickly once removed. But casting heals on it about once per minute seems to have kept it viable long enough to be reattached. Re-assimilated. Whatever. It might be just because it's a small piece of a very simple organ…" Her voice faded as she got lost in thought.

Allistor was starting to get excited. "Are you saying you've found a way to resurrect people?"

"What? No." She shook her head, coming out of her thoughts to answer him. "At least, not yet. But maybe if I follow this line of experimenting? I just don't know. I mean, even with old med tech, we were able to bring someone back after being dead for as long as twenty minutes, in the right conditions. Mostly drownings that happened in very cold water. The body temp was lowered, and decay was slowed. Though in many of those cases, there was significant brain damage."

She sighed, picking up a tablet to make some notes. "I mean, in theory, if we could use the motes to repair or replace decaying cells, we might be able to rez someone who was very recently dead." She paused, both her writing and talking, closing her eyes. After a moment, she shook her head again. "Then again, there might just be some immutable law imposed by the System that prevents it. I think I should go speak with my trainer." She set down her tablet and got up from her chair.

"Sounds like a good idea. How awesome would it be if we never have to lose anyone again?" Allistor was smiling broadly.

"Not so fast, buddy. Don't you think if resurrection was possible, we'd have heard about it by now? Wouldn't Harmon have brought back some of his dead troops? I mean, the Collective has been around for many thousands of years. I can't be the first one to try chasing this."

Allistor's excitement faded, the cold chill of logic quenching it quickly. She saw the disappointed look on his face, and patted his cheek with one hand. "I'll speak to the trainer. Maybe it's like in the games? It's restricted to certain classes? Or only priests of certain gods can do it? We'll see."

Allistor just nodded. "Listen, Daigath has arranged for several powerful factions to come here tomorrow around lunchtime. We're going to auction off that orb, just to be safe. So pick something nice to wear. I'm thinking we keep things informal, so no need for a fancy dress. But let's look pretty, anyway." He pulled her in and kissed her gently.

She gave his butt a little squeeze, and smiled at him. "Right. I can look pretty. You... not so much. Going to trade the orb for another planet?"

"I don't think so..." It was his turn to get lost in thought as visions of space fleets and dungeon cores flashed through his mind. "I mean, we still have more of Earth to secure, and I haven't really done much of anything with Orion yet. I don't need more real estate. I need resources that will make us stronger."

"Like a big old battle cruiser with laser cannons the size of subway tunnels and a transporter system?" She grinned at him, them planted a quick kiss. "I'll let Meg know about the visitors for lunch tomorrow. You go find L'olwyn and find out about etiquette for this kind of gathering. I'll join you after I've spoken with our healy trainer." Amanda hugged him and gave him a quick kiss as she passed on her way out the door.

Allistor headed upstairs, asking Nigel to gather the analysts in their floor's conference room, send a message to Harmon asking him to join them for dinner, and notify the kitchen to send up the food he'd requested earlier. By the time he exited the elevator, all four of his alien analysts were seated and waiting.

"Good evening folks. I've got food coming up shortly. I know it's a bit early, but we have a lot to discuss. In addition to the trade agreement information that L'olwyn has shared with all of you, we need to discuss what kinds of items we might accept in trade for the fomorian Ancestral Orb."

Eyes widened, mouths dropped open. Longbeard coughed and pounded his chest with one hammerlike fist. Even the reserved minotaur took in a surprised breath, leaning back in his chair. Longbeard was the first to speak.

"Ye plan ta trade the artifact? With whom?"

"I plan to hold an auction. Tomorrow. Master Daigath believes the faster we dispose of it, the safer we'll be."

"He is correct." L'olwyn found his voice. "In addition to the possibility of the clan's Matron coming to retrieve the orb, it is possible that another fomorian clan, or some powerful faction of another race, would attempt to seize it. We are not yet strong enough to resist an attack from such unscrupulous entities."

"I agree. And there are representatives from five powerful factions coming here midday tomorrow for the auction. Daigath recommended setting up tables in the courtyard near your sunken garden, L'olwyn."

The elf bowed his head. "Master Daigath spoke with me just a short while ago. I shall see to the details."

Allistor grimaced. "We're not ready for a formal event yet, so let's make this as casual as possible without being offensively simple?"

"Understood, Allistor." L'olwyn smiled.

"Alright, while we wait for Harmon, is there any other Invictus business you'd like to discuss?"

Selby raised her tiny gnome hand. "I wanted to thank you for granting us access to the trainers. My next level of spells would have cost me close to a million klax on my homeworld. The faction that controls the planet charges steep prices for non-members." The others, all except Longbeard, nodded in agreement.

"You are most welcome. If we're going to grow Invictus and become powerful enough to stand on our own, even against unscrupulous factions that might target us, I need all of you to grow as well. Don't forget, you are welcome to join as many of the raids as you like. And hopefully soon we'll have a dungeon or two that we can level in."

Longbeard shook his head. "We been usin' the satellite to survey as much o' the planet's surface as we can. The complete survey will take another three days at the level of detail we've set. But so far, we've no' located any sign o' dungeons."

Droban cleared his throat. His deep, sonorous voice added, "But that doesn't mean they're not there. Dungeon entrances are often underground, or within structures, and undetectable to satellites."

"So I've been told, thank you." Allistor looked up to see Harmon approaching the door. He raised a hand in greeting as the orcanin entered and took a seat. "Thanks for coming, my friend. As I was just telling everyone else, we're holding an auction tomorrow for the orb. Once we're done discussing the trade agreement with Queen Xeria's people, I'd like to discuss potential auction proceeds."

He nodded at L'olwyn, who touched a few holokeys on the table before him. An image appeared above the table in front of each of them.

"As I assume you all have read," the elf paused to give Allistor a stern look, assuming he hadn't read the material. "We have reached what I believe to be an equitable agreement with the queen's factor. We will initially provide resources in the form of livestock, fish, and other consumables to help them rebuild their reserves before the next hatchings. In return, they are providing one thousand saplings of the tree you expressed interest in, as well as five thousand vials of hatchling blood, and ten tons of chitin harvested from the recently deceased araneae. The chitin comes in various sizes and thicknesses. The queen's factor wished me to inform you that the hatchling chitin is soft and flexible, yet still tough. Suitable for reinforcing the leather armor you seem to favor."

Allistor frowned. "Can we afford enough livestock to feed millions of hatchlings?"

Droban shook his head. "We can not. But we can afford the number of cattle and antelope specified. As for the fish, the quantity outlined in the agreement requires approximately one full day's worth, or one sixth of our fishing fleet's current production per week. Our resources are merely a supplement to their own, and the recent number of hatchlings was far in excess of the norm."

"Good enough, then. Anybody have any objections, or anything to add?"

No one spoke up, so Allistor concluded that bit of business. "Good then! L'olwyn, I want to thank you for your efforts on our behalf, and for your patience. I still have so much to learn, and at least for now, I'm going to proceed with caution on most things having to do with dealings with other species."

The elf bowed his head in acknowledgement of the compliment, but didn't speak.

"Alright, now let's discuss the auction. Master Daigath apparently has received some indication of what the factions will be offering, but has agreed not to ruin the surprise." He paused as Harmon chuckled. "I have been told that in the few times such an item has surfaced, it has been traded for items of great value up to and including an entire planet."

The others nodded, either taking in the information, or already aware of it. "I'm of the opinion that we don't currently need another planet. I haven't yet done much with the one I already own, and I have plans to claim a much bigger chunk of Earth before we're done. Anyone here think I'm misguided in that thinking?"

Most of the heads shook in a negative motion, and only Longbeard spoke. "I'd just say that ye shouldn't disregard the offer of a planet offhand, should one be made. Let us determine its value first, and weigh it against other offers. Ye could always turn around n trade the planet to another, rather than take charge of it yerself."

"A good point, and one that didn't even occur to me. Thank you." Allistor nodded. He looked toward Harmon next. "Before we get into the wish list, Daigath told me there were five factions attending the auction, including the Or'Dralon. Which brings up two questions. Do we need to worry about showing favoritism, or not showing favoritism, to a particular faction? Like, will a sore loser wipe us out just for spite?"

Harmon shrugged, as if the idea of having a city blasted out from under him wasn't at all disturbing. "Anything is possible, I suppose. But such an event is unlikely. If you were here alone and attempting this on your own, then you'd be right to worry. But with Daigath and myself here, any misbehavior would carry dire consequences. And the factions he has invited are not known for rash, irresponsible actions."

Allistor thought back to the day the Or'Dralon nearly vaporized the *Phoenix* on its maiden voyage, and wasn't sure he agreed with Harmon's assessment. But he let it go. "Thank you, Harmon."

Turning back to the others, he began. "Now, for the list. The one thing I know for sure we want is some dungeon cores. And some badass combat and transport ships. Colony ships? A fleet of ships of various configurations, I guess. But I want even factions like the Or'Dralon to have to think about the cost of attacking us in the future."

Droban cleared his throat, then offered. "You should think bigger, Allistor. You could demand ships as payment for the sections of Orion you're auctioning off. If it were me, I would demand something more along the lines of a ship manufacturing facility. Either an existing portable one on an asteroid, or the construction of one on Orion. Then you can not only manufacture your own fleets, but you'll potentially create jobs for thousands of your immigrant citizens."

"I like it!" Allistor thumped a hand on the table. "Good thinking, Droban!" Allistor began taking notes with pencil and pad. "Think big." He muttered as he wrote the letters in large print at the top of the page.

Longbeard chuckled. "This be a bit like givin a wee child a million klax and sendin' em shopping. How many candies and toys can they use? No offense, Allistor. But the value o' this orb be so much more than we be prepared to make proper use of... if there weren't so much danger attached to it, I'd recommend ye hold it fer ten years until Invictus be large and powerful enough to absorb this windfall properly."

Allistor caught Harmon nodding along. He blushed slightly, embarrassed by the truth of it, even though he knew he shouldn't be. By all accounts he'd already achieved a tremendous amount of success in a short time.

"Alright, I can accept that. But there *is* much danger, and we need to do the best we can here in a very short time. So let's get creative, and see if we can't find a way to maximize our benefit and still make proper use of the auction proceeds."

The group talked, and ate, and talked some more until Allistor eventually called a halt for the evening. The number and range of possibilities had become too much for him to process.

"I think we have a good idea what we're looking for, and what we feel we don't want or need. Let's take the night to process all of this, and keep it in mind tomorrow when we're considering offers. Thank you, everyone. And sleep well."

*****

Morning brought a bustle of activity. The moment Allistor woke, Amanda and Lilly descended upon him with a new set of clothes for the auction. He barely convinced them to let him take five minutes to shower before trying on the outfit Lilly had created. By this time she had his measurements, at least until he leveled up some more, and there was no need for any adjustments. Allistor stood in front of a full length mirror and inspected himself.

"I look good. Damn good." He grinned at Lilly, who just snorted. The outfit was vaguely martial, but not formal, and it accentuated his muscular build quite nicely. The pants and jacket were both black with silver accents, and there was a silver-grey silk shirt with a priest's collar under the jacket. On the left jacket breast was a pin with the Invictus symbol on it. Altogether the outfit was simple, yet elegant.

In contrast, Amanda appeared wearing a silver silk gown that hugged her every curve. The gown extended all the way to her ankles, with a slit on the left side that reached just above her knee. The front of the gown was cut in a deep v lined with diamond chips that accentuated her cleavage. Around her neck was a silver choker with yet more diamonds, and a tiny version of the Invictus pin at the front.

The moment she appeared, Allistor gave a wolf-whistle and started trying to get Lilly to leave and give

38

them a little alone time. As Lilly threatened to poke Allistor with a handful of sewing pins, Amanda blushed slightly, and gave a soft, throaty laugh. "Cut it out, perv. Plenty of time for that later. We've got a lot to do today."

With an exaggerated sigh, Allistor nodded and left Lilly to fuss with Amanda's dress. He found Daigath waiting for him in their sitting room, along with a cart filled with breakfast.

"Good morning, Allistor. I apologize for the intrusion, but Lady Lilly assured me you wouldn't mind. I trust you slept well?"

"Heh. You are always welcome here, master Daigath. And who can sleep with five superpowers about to show up at my door, argue over who gets to take home a powerful prize, and potentially decide they hate me if they lose?"

Daigath shook his head. "I have chosen older, more established factions that are stable and unlikely to lash out over petty differences. The most volatile of the five are the Or'Dralon, whom you have already had dealings with. There are two dwarven factions attending the auction, both powerful and honorable. The Stardrifter and Lighthammer clans. Their focus is on exploration, crafting, and manufacturing, not conquest. They seek out new resources, new materials, new designs to learn and improve upon if they can."

Daigath paused to take a bite from one of Meg's pastries. "Mmmmm. Were Lady Meg not already spoken for, I would ask that woman to bond with me." He shook his head with regret, then got back on topic. "The fourth faction is led by an old friend of mine. A mages' guild known as the Azure Order. They are a multi-race organization dedicated to researching magic and the origins of the universe. Though they do possess a cadre of battlemages and other martial capabilities, they use them mainly for dungeon delving for rare resources, and defense of their own assets."

"Battlemages. Trained by you?"

Daigath nodded, taking another bite chewing slowly before answering. "A few of the founding members. I have not seen them in several millennia."

Allistor took a breath, shaking his head. He often forgot just how old Daigath was.

"The final faction are a race I don't believe you have encountered yet. They are the Arkhon, more commonly known as technomages. An elder race that mostly keep to themselves, they specialize in the art of combining science and magic, of imbuing technology with enchantments. The artificial intelligences like Nigel and your ship AI's are the result of their experiments. As are the portals you use at each of your properties. Though they have long since surpassed those achievements. Most have gone into seclusion, focusing entirely on their craft. They once fought a war against the fomorians, when both races were young. They remain mortal enemies, and of all the factions I have invited, they will be the most eager to obtain the orb."

Allistor was fascinated by all the insight that Daigath was providing. He found himself wanting nothing more than to sit with the ancient elf and discuss the history of the universe. In particular, he wanted to question him more about the Ancient Ones. But there were more urgent items on his calendar for the day. And a question had just occurred to him.

"Harmon's not bidding? He has an empire behind him, surely he has the resources?"

Daigath shook his head. "He cannot participate. For one thing, were he to outbid the elves, they might find a way to consider it a breach of their treaty. And because of his close ties to you, there would be a perception of favoritism should he win, or accusations of collusion."

"Collusion?" Allistor didn't catch on immediately.

"Less scrupulous sellers have been known to use allies at auctions to drive up the bids."

"Oh, right. Collusion. That never even occurred to me." Allistor nodded.

"And to answer your question, I will be at your side during the auction, but we have engaged a professional auctioneer to both conduct the auction and determine the value of any bid items where there is a dispute. The Grandmaster of the Ethereal Auction House is another old friend of mine, and was happy to volunteer his services for such a rare event." Daigath grinned down at the pastry in his hand. "Though I did promise him a quantity of Lady Meg's choice edibles."

Allistor's fears of the night before still lingered. With so many powerful factions on their way to his home, he felt like a mouse hosting a herd of cats for lunch.

"Are you concerned at all about the losers retaliating against us in some way?"

"It is unlikely, Allistor. They will sign peace accords provided by the Ethereals before being granted access to the portal. This is standard procedure when multiple potentially opposing factions attend an auction. In addition, I have personally made it clear to each faction leader that any action taken against you, or Invictus, will also be taken as personal attacks by myself and Harmon. Put those thoughts out of your mind. This is a chance for you to safely participate in, and learn from, an event with some of the most powerful factions in the Collective attending. Focus on gaining knowledge, and listen more than you speak. Be a polite and genial host, and try to enjoy the day. You are about to be handed immense resources and power, after all." Daigath took another bite of the pastry, leaning back in his chair and closing his eyes as he savored what smelled like an apple cinnamon tart.

Allistor took the opportunity to eat some eggs and bacon himself, trying to picture in his mind how the auction would proceed. Where before he'd had visions of aliens throwing insults at each other, and at him, now his vision was of a more sedate and polite experience. His shoulders relaxed slightly, and he took a few deep breaths.

"Thank you, Master Daigath. For all you've done."

Swallowing the last bite of his breakfast, Daigath got to his feet. "If you're ready, we can check in with L'olwyn down in the courtyard. Preparations were nearly complete when I passed by before dawn. I think the setting will do nicely for our purposes today." He paused for a moment, then with a rueful grin he took several more pastries from the tray and deposited them in his inventory.

Allistor quickly shoveled down the last of his eggs, and grabbed the two remaining slices of bacon as he got to his feet and followed Daigath to the waiting elevator. The bacon was gone by the time they reached the ground floor lobby. There was a small crowd awaiting him, including his four analysts, Ramon and Nancy, General Prime, Harmon, Lars, and Gralen. He motioned for them to tag along as he and Daigath proceeded out the back doors into the courtyard between the Invictus tower and Harmon's building.

Allistor could hardly believe his eyes. The concrete had been completely covered with a deep green material that resembled astroturf. Except that instead of rough plastic, the material seemed to consist of millions of soft blades of grass. Allistor actually knelt down to run his hand across it. As the blades shifted under his palm, a faint scent of forest and flowers reached him.

"This is wondrous, whatever it is. Can we just leave it here from now on?"

"Certainly, Allistor." L'olwyn replied as he motioned toward the sunken garden. "Please, take a look."

Allistor did as requested and walked across the spongy green surface to the garden. Every plant in sight was looking vibrant and healthy. Some even seemed to glow with a sort of aura around them. The hundreds of different scents seemed to blend together into a calming, peaceful odor, encouraging Allistor to take several deep breaths. He heard the others behind him doing the same, and turned to see smiling faces.

Daigath complimented his fellow elf. "It's lovely, L'olwyn. You clearly have a gift with the chemistry of flora. I would welcome your input on my own garden, should you have time."

"I will certainly make time, thank you, honored elder." L'olwyn bowed deeply.

By the time they'd finished walking the garden, Allistor felt more relaxed than he had at any time since the apocalypse. They moved to a group of round tables that had been set up near the garden. Here was where Meg would serve lunch before the auction began. Across the courtyard a low stage had been erected, just large enough for a podium and a small display table. In front of the stage were thirty or so ballroom chairs in three rows arranged in a half circle around the stage. Allistor recognized that the arrangement would allow each of the visiting factions to have a few front row seats. There was also a row of ten chairs behind the stage for Allistor and his advisors.

"This all looks perfect!" Amanda declared as she joined them, getting a wave of compliments on her dress from the gathered friends.

"Almost as perfect as you." Allister pulled her close to his side with one arm and kissed her cheek. "Thank you, everyone, for putting this together so quickly. This is going to be a big day for us!"

"Prime, please secure this courtyard. No one other than this group and kitchen staff in or out without express permission from me, starting now." Allistor motioned toward the tables, and the group went to take a seat.

For the next three hours, they discussed the auction, the protocol, and general Invictus business. Ramon lightened the mood a bit by setting a paper golem that looked like a gingerbread man on the table and directing it over to dance on Amanda's hand. Then it crossed the table randomly to give high fives to Allistor and Ramon before attempting to climb inside Longbeard's beard.

Daigath repeated the information on the factions that were attending the auction, and a few folks asked questions. Ramon was particularly interested in meeting the Arkhons, though Daigath warned him they were not normally very sociable.

L'olwyn spent some time with the humans, warning them against standing too close, touching any of the visitors, or making any sudden movements. He also attempted to obtain promises that they would limit their conversations to short phrases like, "It's an honor to meet you." Or "Welcome to Invictus, please enjoy the refreshments."

There was a brief ruckus when Sam tried to join them, and Prime's droids wouldn't let him past the door.

When Allistor waved him through, the old man grumbled his way across the courtyard and took a seat, producing a bottle of goblin brandy and some glasses.

"Thought maybe everyone could use a swig before the big event!" he proceeded to pour and pass around shots.

"Got a glass for me?" A small voice called from the lobby doors. Allistor and the others turned to see a bald gnome in a grey robe waving from between the legs of a battle droid.

Daigath leapt to his feet and strode over to welcome the visitor. "Prime, this is Grandmaster Igglesprite of the Ethereal Auction House. Please allow him access."

Prime looked to Allistor, who was already nodding and getting to his feet along with all the others. Daigath shook hands with the gnome, then led him over to the table. "May I present today's seller, Allistor of Invictus, Planetary Prince of Earth , Emperor of Orion."

The little gnome hopped up onto a chair before bowing at the waist toward Allistor. "My pleasure, Prince Allistor."

"Welcome to Invictus." Allistor started to offer a hand to shake, then jerked it back when he remembered it wasn't proper. Instead he inclined his head slightly as L'olwyn had instructed. "And thank you for coming here today to help us."

"I never miss an opportunity to see my old friend Daigath. And…" he passed a hopeful gaze over the empty table. "There was mention of a talented chef?"

Chuckling, Daigath took the seat next to the gnome and produced a couple of the pilfered pastries from breakfast. Handing one to Igglesprite, he set his down and poured a glass of goblin brandy for his friend, then waited as he took a bite. The gnome's eyes rolled up, and he licked his lips. "You spoke true, my friend. This is a wonderment!" He took another bite, his eyes twinkling. "Worth the trip!"

Amanda laughed, wanting to hug the cute little gnome who had started rubbing his belly. "Meg will be out shortly with lunch, but we can bring something else now, if you'd like."

"No, no. This will hold me over, for a little while, at least." He smiled at her, then popped the last of the pastry into his mouth and chewed slowly. When he'd washed it down with a gulp of brandy, he looked around. "Might I see the item in question?" Allistor produced the orb, carefully handing it to the gnome, who set it on the table in front of him. His eyes unfocused as he *Examined* the orb, and his head began to nod.

"Yes, yes. This is a rare piece, indeed. Definitely fomorian, containing…" His eyes widened and he looked at Daigath. "Containing nearly two thousand Scion entities."

Daigath shook his head. "I had assumed it to be from a lesser clan, maybe half that many souls."

Igglesprite produced a round base from his inventory and set it on the table, then set the orb upon the base, preventing it from rolling around. "This may cause some consternation among the bidders, as the value is

47

higher than anticipated." He looked thoughtful for a moment. "The five factions you've invited all have more than sufficient assets to meet the likely value, but I doubt they will be liquid. Are you willing to accept some form of deferred payment to make up the difference?"

Allistor nodded, having already discussed this possibility with his advisors the night before. "We are, with a sufficiently binding agreement."

The gnome nodded once, satisfied. "Very well, then. Here is our standard agreement. Have your people review it, and we can execute after lunch. Then we'll see how badly our galaxy's elite want this item!" His infectious grin made everyone laugh as he produced a paper document and handed it to Longbeard when the dwarf extended a hand. The four analysts retired to another table to huddle over the agreement terms.

They all shared another round of goblin brandy as Allistor introduced everyone else. Igglesprite had already met Harmon, and the two of them exchanged good-natured barbs. "Igglesprite, good to see you again. Have you grown a few millimeters?"

"Only under my robe, you big clumsy oaf. I'd show you, but I don't want to make you jealous!"

Meg and the kitchen staff were just wheeling out several carts laden with food when Nigel's voice rang out. *"Sire, the Or'Dralon faction have requested permission to access the portal."*

Chapter 3


Allistor and company met the representatives from Or'Dralon at the teleport pad. He stood front and center with Amanda on his right arm, Daigath to his left, and Harmon next to Amanda. The rest of his group, the analysts, Ramon and Nancy, and the others were arrayed behind them.

The first to step off the pad was a familiar, if uncomfortable, face for Allistor. It was Commander Enalion, the elf that almost blasted Allistor out of the sky on his first trip into space. Behind him were two more elves, one much older and distinguished looking, and a young female.

Enalion bowed his head to Allistor, then bowed much more deeply to Daigath. "Prince Allistor, Honored One, thank you for your gracious invitation."

Daigath pressed his lips together in an attempt to avoid smiling. He looked to Allistor and nodded slightly while the elf was still bowing.

"Welcome to Invictus, Commander Enalion. And thank you again for sparing my life in our first encounter." Allistor answered.

Enalion cleared his throat, seeming slightly uncomfortable as the elder elf behind him raised an eyebrow. Stepping forward, he too bowed his head to Allistor, then to Daigath, then to Harmon.

"Greetings, Prince Allistor, Master Daigath, Emperor Harmon." He focused his gaze on Allistor. "I was not aware that my great grandson had met you previously, Prince Allistor."

Enalion looked even more uncomfortable, and was about to speak when Daigath took over. "High Lord Eragin, it has been too long. I trust you have been well?"

"I have, Honored One. The family thrives, and I find myself less and less involved in faction business each year. These days I spend most of my time gardening, and playing with the little ones." He smiled. "Though I could not miss an event such as this, or a chance to see my old mentor once again."

The head of the Or'Dralon faction motioned for the female to step forward. "This is my great, great granddaughter, Melise."

The elfess stepped forward. She was wearing a nearly-translucent silk dress that left very little of her form to the imagination. When she bowed, it covered even less. Amanda's grip on Allistor's arm tightened, and he thought he heard a slight growl from her.

"It is an honor, Prince Allistor, Honored One, Emperor Harmon." Her voice was quiet and silky smooth, almost musical.

Daigath beamed at the young elfess. "You are as lovely as one would expect from such an illustrious bloodline, my dear!" He offered his arm before Allistor had a chance to respond, for which Allistor was relieved. "You quite closely resemble your great, great grandmother. You know that I had designs on her, before Eragin here stole her heart..." The elfess giggled musically as Daigath led her, and the others, away from the teleport pad and out to the courtyard.

Amanda held Allistor back as the others departed. "I suppose that show was for you?"

"Show?" Allistor asked innocently.

"That dress. Or lack thereof. They might as well hang a piece of meat in front of a hungry wolf. I thought they would wait until after we were married before trying to force another wife on you."

Allistor shrugged, doing his best to sound uninterested in the incredibly beautiful elfess. "Maybe that's just elven fashion? Either way, *you* are the one for me. You're the one I'm in love with. You're the one I'm going to unwrap that dress from tonight." He gave her a gentle kiss, and she made a non-committal grunt, squeezing his arm slightly.

"Good answer."

They were about to follow the others when Nigel announced the next arrivals. Allistor gave his approval, and a pair of dwarves appeared on the pad. They stepped forward in unison and bowed at the waist.

"Good day, Prince Allistor, Lady Amanda. We be Drolor and Crump o' the Stardrifter Clan. Thank ye fer invitin' us to this event."

"Welcome to Invictus, and it is our pleasure to have you here." Allistor smiled at the dwarves, who both wore functional-looking leather gear from head to toe. Having seen the dwarves arrive, Longbeard came striding back across the lobby to gather them up.

"Drolor, Crump! Good to see ye!" He actually hugged both of the dwarves, clapping them on the back. "Come right this way, and I'll show ye to the food!"

With a laugh and a nod toward Allistor, the three dwarves departed. Allistor and Amanda waited near the pad, assuming the other bidders would arrive shortly. Harmon and Daigath returned after a minute or so, chuckling with each other. Amanda cleared her throat and looked at Daigath.

"I don't suppose the great great granddaughter is some kind of expert on ancient orbs?"

"Ha!" Harmon snort-laughed.

Daigath smiled sympathetically at her. "I'm sorry, Lady Amanda. It seems my old friend hoped to include her as part of Or'Dralon's offer, securing ties to Allistor here as well as securing the orb. I've just quietly let him know that now is not the time. It seems Enalion failed to pass on to his elder more than just the report of your previous incident."

Amanda looked over the elf's shoulder toward the courtyard, where the young elfess was distracting the Stardrifter dwarves. "I noticed Enalion didn't greet Harmon, either. What's his problem?"

Harmon followed her gaze. "There are a number of elves who still view us as nothing more than slaves, who resent our freedom. Enalion ignores me in protest of that freedom."

"Then I would say Or'Dralon has already lost their chance at the orb." Allistor growled. "The question is, do we send them home now, or allow them to waste their time bidding?"

Harmon shook his head. "Do not be hasty, my friend. They are powerful, and possess great wealth. Theirs might be the bid you seek. And at the very least, they will push the others' bids higher for you. Please don't risk offending them on my account. I am used to their snubs, and they mean little."

Daigath nodded. "Listen to Harmon. My old friend Eragin would not have purposely offended you. He clearly was not aware of your reluctance to take on another bride at this time. Remember, multiple marriages are commonplace nearly everywhere in the collective, and he would see the offering of Melise as a compliment to you. Throwing that back in his face would be a grave insult. As for Enalion, I believe his failure to inform his lord, and to recognize Harmon, will go badly for him later today."

Amanda squeezed Allistor's arm gently, and gave him a small nod. If she was willing to let it go, so would he. "Fine. Thank you both, for calming me down."

*"Sire, the Azure Order representatives have requested access."*

"Thank you, Nigel. Please invite them over."
Allistor took a deep breath as they all turned to face the
teleport pad once again. A group of three appeared on the
pad, the one in front stepping forward and bowing. She
was tall, at least eight feet, with a small torso and extremely
long, willowy limbs. Her neck was at least two feet long
and was capped by a small head with very large eyes. Each
of her hands sported just two fingers and a thumb. She
wore a tight-fitting black silk outfit that appeared to be one
long cloth wrapped around her limbs and torso dozens of
times.

"Greetings, Prince Allistor, Emperor Harmon,
Honored One. We thank you for the invitation to attend
your auction." She stood straight and turned to face
Allistor. "I am Omidia, Grandmaster of the Azure Order."

Allistor bowed his head slightly in
acknowledgement, suddenly unsure of who outranked
whom in this matchup. "Welcome to Invictus,
Grandmaster. It is a pleasure to meet you."

"Omidia!" Daigath stepped forward and embraced
the mage. "It has been too long, my dear. How are the
children?" The old elf led her and her fellow mages off the
pad and toward the courtyard.

Almost immediately, Nigel reported the next
pending arrivals, and two dwarves from the Lighthammer
clan appeared. Both dwarves bowed at the waist and
greeted their hosts politely, reporting their names as Gurin
and Lonrin. Allistor welcomed them warmly, having
grown a fondness for the dwarves in general. "Welcome,

Lighthammers. There are refreshments in the courtyard just through those doors. Please, help yourselves before the elves eat it all." He winked at them, causing them to chuckle as they moved to do as he suggested.

The last of the bidding factions arrived just a minute later.

"*Sire, the Arkhon representatives are ready to teleport.*"

"Thank you Nigel. Go ahead."

There were just two of the Arkhons on the pad, and they stepped forward in unison. Neither of them bowed, and to Allistor's surprise, Harmon offered them a deep bow instead.

"Greetings, Ancient Ones. May I present Prince Allistor of Earth, Emperor of Orion, and his betrothed, Lady Amanda."

The two beings, who were dressed head to toe nearly identically in a sort of scaled attire that looked like alligator hide, but with softly glowing blue circuits worked throughout the surface, bowed their heads slightly toward Harmon, then Allistor. Neither of them spoke, so Allistor cleared his throat.

"Welcome to Invictus, Ancient Ones. We are honored to have you here with us today. If you'll accompany us out to the courtyard, we have some refreshments for you to enjoy before the auction begins." He motioned as gracefully as he could manage toward the lobby doors, and Harmon led the way. The Arkhons followed, their movements smooth and graceful, not making a sound.

Allistor and Amanda brought up the rear, except for Prime who followed unobtrusively. All of them followed Harmon to the refreshment tables, where Allistor smiled to see that all the dwarves had built heaping plates of food and were sitting together, exclaiming over the various tastes of Meg's creations.

He watched the Arkhons with great interest as they perused the offered refreshments and loaded plates with a few samples. Their armor, if that's what it was, appeared to be almost alive, the glowing circuits pulsing as power seemed to circulate through it. Both of them were nearly as tall as Omidia, but with much hardier frames. When they took seats at a table by themselves, the armor that had also covered their faces opened up much like a helmet's faceplate, and they began to taste the food.

Allistor was distracted from his observation when Melise cleared her throat from behind him. Both he and Amanda turned to find the young elfess offering an embarrassed smile. Allistor couldn't help but notice that she was breathing slightly more heavily than before.

"Please pardon the interruption." Her voice was truly musical, and Allistor found himself ready to pardon pretty much anything. "I feel I must apologize on behalf of my family. My lord Eragin and I were not aware of your… matrimonial customs. I hope my presence here does not offend you?" She took a deep breath and bit her bottom lip, her eyes widening slightly, hopefully.

Amanda sighed, looking down at Melise's dress, then pinching Allistor's arm. "You are lovely, Lady Melise, and I am sure you intended no offense by coming here. It was gracious of you to apologize, but unnecessary. Come, tell me about this dress of yours. Allistor clearly approves, and I might want to have one made for myself." She quickly steered the elfess away from Allistor, much to his regret. As they walked away, he heard her say, "Nigel, would you ask Lilly to join us, please?"

A moment later Harmon's great paw clapped him on the shoulder and turned him toward the food and drink. "Best leave them to their own devices, my friend. What we need is a good stiff drink before the bidding starts!"

Allistor didn't argue, and with visions in his mind of Amanda wearing Melise's dress, he turned and accepted a double shot of brandy from the beastkin bartender.

After half an hour or so of socializing and food tasting, Igglesprite climbed up behind the podium and called the bidders to their seats. Allistor and company filled the seats behind the auctioneer as the faction representatives arranged themselves. Allistor was surprised to see that the dwarves distanced themselves from each other after sharing a meal, placing themselves on opposite ends of the front row of seats. The Archons took the center, with the Or'Dralon and Azure Order on either side of them.

"You've all been informed as to the rules of this sale, and signed the appropriate agreements. As of this moment, we begin the auction of the Ancestral Orb seized by Prince Allistor from the fomorian clan that he engaged here on Earth." Igglesprite produced the orb and held it aloft for a moment, then placed it into its base on the nearby display table. "The orb is considerably more powerful than previously estimated. You may approach and examine the artifact if you desire. I will begin the bidding in five minutes."

The only one who rose and stepped forward was one of the Arkhons. Igglesprite stood protectively near the orb as it leaned close and appeared to sniff the artifact. When it reached a finger forward, the gnome shook his head, and a force field appeared around the orb. "I'm afraid no touching is permitted, Ancient One." he said quietly and respectfully. The Arkhon grunted, withdrew its hand and straightened, returning to its seat.

Igglesprite, seeing that no other bidders wished a closer examination, approached Allistor at his seat behind the stage. "Any last minute changes to your instructions, Prince Allistor?"

Allistor looked to Daigath, who just smiled and shrugged. Looking back to the gnome, he replied, "Um, drive the price up as high as you can?"

"Ha! Indeed, indeed." The gnome grinned at him, then at Daigath. "This is going to be fun!"

*****


The bidding only lasted for about twenty minutes, but by the time it ended, Allistor was sweating. His pulse was pounding, and he kept looking to Harmon and Daigath, waiting for them to react somehow. He was doing his best to follow their lead and maintain a poker face, but the sheer immensity of the wealth and resources being offered up was getting to him.

The final bid, submitted by the Arkhons, silenced all the others and effectively ended the bidding. There were murmurs from the other factions, but none advanced another bid. Igglesprite called three times for any additional offers, then slammed a gavel on the podium.

"Bidding is now officially closed. Our seller and his advisors will now take a few minutes to consider your offers. Please take your leisure, walk the garden, and enjoy the refreshments." One of the dwarves from Stardrifter snorted in amusement, well aware that there was already a clear winner among the offers.

Igglesprite removed the orb from the display, slid it back into his inventory, stepped down from the stage and motioned for Allistor and company to follow him. He led them back into the lobby, and Allistor directed them all over to the sitting area. Prime stationed several of his droids in a line across the lobby, cordoning off the area and keeping any prying ears away. Igglesprite spoke a few words and wiggled his fingers, and a translucent bubble appeared over the seating area. He took a seat on one of the sofas, produced a flask from his inventory, and took a long swig. Then another. "Well, now. That was certainly entertaining!"

Allistor's heart was still racing. He didn't even understand what the final bid was, what it meant, or why the other faction representatives had so clearly been surprised by it. But the other bids... he was about to be obscenely wealthy. Still, he had to ask before he could make an informed decision.

"Someone, please tell me what the Arkhons just bid, and why you all nearly wet yourselves?"

Daigath raised a hand before Igglesprite could respond. The gnome just sat back and took another swig, smiling happily.

"The Arkhons final bid was a pair of eternity gates." He turned in his seat slightly so that he was facing Allistor directly, and leaned forward as if about to tell a secret. "Eternity gates are technology developed and manufactured solely by the Arkhons. In the twenty millennia since they were invented, the gates have been tightly controlled. They are prohibitively expensive, even these wealthy factions only having a small number each. The Or'Dralon, for example, possess eight of them, last I heard. Harmon here has... five?"

Harmon nodded. "Nearly bankrupted the empire when we purchased the first set. But they were absolutely worth every hardship involved in obtaining them."

Allistor took a guess. "They're some kind of instant travel? Like a controlled wormhole?"

Daigath tilted his head slightly. "Very similar, yes. The eternity gates actually fold the space between them when connected, allowing a ship to pass nearly instantly from one to the other. The time required for travel from gate to gate varies based on the distance between, but the variance in real time is calculated in milliseconds."

"In real time?" Amanda asked.

"They are called *eternity* gates because though the physical transport time is short, sentient beings experience a prolonged mental sensation during the transfer. Your body may move light years in an instant, but your mind perceives the journey as having taken much longer. Anywhere from minutes to days, sometimes longer. It is said that the first volunteer to test the gates, a young Arkhon, never returned. Or rather, his body returned, but his consciousness was lost somewhere in the null-space between gates for all eternity. For a race such as theirs, this is a tragic loss. Hence the name."

Harmon added, "We slow our ships to a crawl before entering the gates. It has been found that the faster your ship is moving when it enters the event horizon of a gate, the longer the mental effects last. The best theorists, outside of the Arkhons, who aren't talking, believe that the speed causes some kind of backlash in the magic-tech hybrid operational mechanics of the gates. No one knows for sure, because anyone caught tampering with the gates, trying to reverse engineer them, has their gate immediately confiscated. If they own other gates, those are shut down. Permanently."

Allistor absorbed that for a moment. "Okay, so the gates are valuable, and rare. But do they do me any good if I don't have a fleet a ships to send through them?"

Longbeard chuckled. "Please, allow me?" Daigath nodded, and Longbeard stroked his beard for a moment, gathering his thoughts. "Ye remember we told ye that ye could use the proceeds from auctioning off bits o' yer other planet to purchase ships, or trade ships fer land?"

Allistor nodded, starting to see where the dwarf was going. But his eyes widened and his pulse quickened a bit at Longbeard's next words.

"Ye park one o' them gates in orbit around Orion, and ye increase the value o' the land there at least tenfold! Orion becomes a trading hub overnight. No longer a small out o' the way rock with decent agricultural potential. Ye could buy or trade a dozen fleets o' ships fer what you'd earn." The dwarf winked at Harmon, adding, "And Harmon here, with his space station already in orbit, would make a pile o' money as well."

"Damn." Sam added his two cents.

Allistor shook his head. "Shouldn't we at least discuss the other offers? I mean, there were a lot of the things we said we wanted – planets with valuable resources, asteroids with minerals, dungeon cores, and at least two fleets of ships, including some warships that would help me defend both Earth and Orion…"

Droban the minotaur spoke, his deep voice catching everyone's attention. "We can certainly entertain and discuss the other bids, Allistor. But ownership of the gates puts you in a position to afford all those other items on your own, and in a relatively short period of time. In addition, I believe I can safely say that none of the other factions would be offended were you to accept the Arkhons bid. In fact, I believe that were you to accept one of the other bids, that faction would immediately turn around and trade the orb to the Arkhons, claiming the gates for themselves." He paused as the others nodded in agreement. "I would, however, suggest that we take a moment to discuss *why* such a bid has been offered."

Selby agreed, her tiny gnomish voice the next to be heard. "He's right. The orb is certainly valuable, and the Arkhons can probably make the best use of it, other than possibly the Azure Order mages. But by my estimation, they are vastly overpaying."

Daigath mused, "The Arkhons have long been enemies of the fomorian race. It may be that obtaining such an orb and its secrets will assist them in their fight. Then again, it may just have increased value as a trophy, or a lure that might allow them to kill or capture the clan's Matron."

Igglesprite shook his head. "The Arkhons value their privacy. I would not want to be the ones to ask them why they want the orb." He hiccupped, then took another swig and passed the flask to Selby.

"We have another problem with that bid." L'olwyn observed. "I do not know what value the Ethereal Auction House might put on those gates, but we would need to pay them their percentage out of Invictus treasury funds. And I'm not sure even you are that wealthy, Allistor."

Igglesprite shook his head. "We would be willing to work out some accommodation. Say, an allotment of land on Orion once you've placed a gate there, and free access to the gates for our own ships, in peep... preprit...perpetuity." He grinned, patting his clothes and looking for his flask. Selby didn't hand it back.

Daigath smiled affectionately at the gnomes, then turned back to Allistor. "Unless I miss my guess, the other factions have been spending the last several minutes preparing alternate bids to present to you. Not for the orb, but for something similar to what Master Igglesprite has just suggested. A piece of Orion, or whatever planet you choose to host a gate, and access to the gates. That is how you will obtain your dungeon cores, warships, and such."

Allistor took a deep breath. Amanda squeezed his hand and smiled at him, nodding her head. He looked around at the group. "Anyone disagree? Or have anything else to add?"

Ramon grinned at him. "As one of your bestest buddies, I'd like you to put me in your will, Emperor Moneybags." Nancy smacked his arm, but she was smiling when she did it.

"Anything *useful*?" Allistor shot Ramon a finger.

When nobody spoke, he looked at Igglesprite, who was now half asleep with his head on Shelby's shoulder. "Master Igglesprite, we accept the Arkhons' final bid of two Eternity Gates, with a couple conditions. They will deliver and install them at locations I determine, and agree to maintain them."

Igglesprite sat up, nodding his head. "That is all standard, and will be automatically included in the final agreement. They would in fact insist on maintaining the gates themselves, as they forbid anyone else from even examining them closely. Let us return to the others and give them the news. I have a feeling you've got a long day of negotiations ahead of you." He winked, one whole side of his face bunching up and his mouth contorting with the effort.

It turned out that Daigath was correct. The moment Igglesprite completed the auction by announcing the Arkhons as winners, the other factions requested meetings with Allistor to discuss alternate agreements. Allistor agreed, asking them each to remain in the courtyard while he and his advisors met with them individually. One by one the faction representatives moved into the lobby and sat with the Invictus group. Daigath and L'olwyn did most of the speaking with the Or'Dralon and Azure order, while Longbeard took the lead with the dwarven factions. Some of the offers overlapped, but Allistor approved them anyway. As far as he was concerned, there was no such thing as too many ships, or too many dungeon cores. The new offers didn't include any planets, but there was still a mining asteroid offered by the Stardrifters. They even agreed to tow it to a stable orbit near Earth, for ease of mining.

The loot from the day's negotiations included a total of six dungeon cores, each of a different type. Allistor hadn't even known there *were* different types a few days ago, and he was excited to try them out. Invictus would shortly have a large fleet of ships, including twenty warships ranging in size from huge fighter carriers to smaller battleships and drop ships for land invasions. There were ten brand new colony ships, each of them roughly twice the size and capacity of his captured goblin ships, and twenty cargo haulers that the Lighthammers agreed to modify with heavy shields and weapons before delivery.

Eragin considerately excluded both Melise and Enalion from his discussions, leaving them out in the garden while he negotiated. Before they began, he asked Allistor to relate his version of how he'd met the commander. Allistor explained about it being their first trip into space, and how his gunner had been targeting random items, accidentally targeting Enalion's ship. He purposely made the elf commander sound more accommodating than he had actually been, in the interest of future relations. Then Daigath made a point of letting the high lord know that Allistor's unwillingness to accept a second bride in the near future had been related to Enalion personally.

"My apologies, Prince Allistor. I was not informed of any of this, and I fear my actions this day reflect that lack of knowledge. I meant no offense."

Allistor resisted the urge to shrug, instead leaning forward and placing his hands on his knees. "No apologies necessary, High Lord Eragin. I am a relative child trying to fill the shoes of a prince and emperor, and have made more than my share of mistakes. I look forward to a long and friendly relationship with Or'Dralon, and with you."

The old elf smiled, saying, "Very gracious of you. And toward that end, let us see if we can't reach an agreement!"

The high lord secured a large swathe of land on Orion, as well as the only national park in Vermont, which was about 650 acres. Allistor was happy to include it, as it bordered on the forest the commander had already secured for his faction. In return, Allistor received a mutual defense pact with the Or'Dralon on both planets, a veritable mountain of crafting materials that would help his people level up their skills, an unaligned dungeon core, and a small space station to be placed in orbit above Invictus City. The space station could be used to dock up to a dozen of his ships, as well as host several merchant shops, restaurants, repair bays, medical facilities, hydroponics bays, guest quarters, and housing for a thousand staff. It was also easily expandable.

When it was all over, Orion would be sporting a branch of the Azure Order, Strongholds or Citadels built by the Or'Dralon, Lighthammer, and Stardrifter clans, several new dungeons, and an eternity gate. In addition, the Lighthammers were entering into a joint venture with Invictus to restore the planet's damaged gravity lift. Though there weren't sufficient mineral resources to justify the expense, with the planet about to become a trade hub, and secure orbital storage space being limited and therefore expensive, having a way to cheaply transport large quantities of goods to and from surface warehouses now made fiscal sense.

The dungeon cores excited Allistor as much as anything else. Between the four factions, he would soon have an insectoid-based core that would generate monsters that dropped chitin and other valuable crafting components. Also slime-based, and plant-based cores that would produce mostly alchemy ingredients, a mineral core in which not only would the element-based monsters drop valuable minerals from iron to mithril, but the cleared dungeon could be safely mined for additional minerals for twenty four hours before it was repopulated. The fifth dungeon was a combat core, the kind Emperors used to train their troops. It featured staged arenas of increasing difficulty where large groups and combat units needed to work together using battlefield tactics to kill opposing groups and level up. The final core was unaligned, meaning it could be programmed to become a specific type of core, or could be planted and left to randomly become any one of a hundred types.

After sending all the factions home with newly executed agreements, which took well past dinner hour, Allistor and Amanda thanked everyone for their help, and retired to their quarters. Allistor had obtained a list from Longbeard of all the known dungeon core types. He and Amanda cuddled on the sofa as they went through each one, discussing the potential benefits and weighing them against the others. There were elemental dungeons of air, water, earth, and fire, as well as obscure types like puzzle dungeons, and several that featured skill challenges.

Allistor especially liked one that featured cooking skill challenges, joking that Meg could be their tank.

There were cores specifically for melee types, and casters. One that stood out, called a paladin core, challenged those who wished to become servants of one god or another, testing their faith and courage as well as whatever skills their chosen deity favored. Amanda pointed it out, reminding Allistor that paladins and priests in games often had divine spells that allowed them to resurrect dead companions.

With the adrenaline of the day fading, the two of them finally gave up on the list, leaving the decision for another day. Allistor set down the list and scooped Amanda into his arms, carrying her toward the bedroom. "Now... does this dress have a zipper, or buttons, m'lady?"

*****

Several hours later, with Amanda snoring softly next to him, Allistor lay awake worrying about the future. Pulling up his character sheet, he mumbled to himself as he reviewed the numbers. "I need to get stronger. We all do."

| Designation: Emperor Allistor, Giant Killer | Level: 55 | Experience: 7,200,000/57,000,000 |
|---|---|---|
| Planet of Origin: UCP 382, Orion | Health: 72,000/72,000 | Class: Battlemage |
| Attribute Pts Available: 0 | Mana: 16,000/16,000 | |
| Intelligence: 25 (29) | Strength: 10 (18) | Charisma: 12 (16) |
| Adaptability: 8 (10) | Stamina: 13 (20) | Luck: 8 (14) |
| Constitution: 22 (27) | Agility: 15 (21) | Health Regen: 2,200/m |
| Will Power: 25 (33) | Dexterity: 7 (11) | Mana Regen: 1,400/m |

Chapter 4

Allistor was midway through breakfast in the main dining hall when Bjurstrom came running up. "Got a problem, boss."

"Who and where?"

"Well, we did like you asked, and started sending small teams to each of the parks that shows as having trespassers. The satellite scans have helped a lot, showing us right where they're camped or have built homes. Most of the time we've found individuals or small groups, some families and such. They've either agreed to leave, relocate to one of our strongholds, or taken the oath in return for being allowed to stay where they were. Having a big spaceship land nearby, and high level humans accompanied by battle droids march into their area, has discouraged them from fighting, mostly. Others were convinced with food and decent weapons."

"But not now." Allistor guessed.

"We've got one group that won't listen at all. Not far from home, too. They opened fire as soon as our people got in range, nearly killed one of the noobs. They painted *Screw Allistor* across the gate of an old-school wooden palisade, and refuse to speak to anyone. Best guess, there are ten of them in there." He paused. "Do you want us to just take them out? They did try and ambush us."

Allistor shook his head. "Take me there. Let's see if we can resolve this peacefully." He picked up his still half-full plate and followed the airman to the teleport pad. A moment later they were in the Warren, walking toward one of the *Juggernauts*. Bjurstrom climbed into the driver's seat, and Allistor took shotgun. As he got in, he noticed three others sitting in the back, cleaning rifles or munching on snacks. They all smiled and waved in greeting.

Bjurstrom drove them almost due south for a short distance along the same road on which Allistor had first found Helen. It wasn't long before they entered the Medicine Bow National Forest territory. A notification flashed up on Allistor's UI that trespassers were inhabiting his property.

They turned down one dirt road, then another, and Bjurstrom was just slowing when a bullet pinged off the vehicle's windshield. He slammed on the breaks, then reversed about fifty yards before coming to a halt. "Seems like they've moved out from their shelter a bit, probably hoping for a lucky kill."

Allistor used the vehicle's loudspeaker to call out to the trespassers. "Whoever you are, this is Allistor. I'm not here to hurt you, I just want to talk. There's no reason we can't work something out here."

Another bullet bounced off the vehicle, this time right in front of Allistor's face, and a voice drifted through the trees. "Screw you! You're the greedy bastard who owns every park in the country! You don't need this place! Go away!"

Allistor tried again. "Yes, I own all the parks. And I keep getting this annoying notification about you trespassing here. Come talk to me, and we can sort this out so I don't have to keep hearing about you."

"We killed one of you already! Leave now, or you're next!" This time the bullet struck the hood of the *Juggernaut*, then the windshield, before zooming off into the trees.

"I don't need this shit." Allistor said to the people inside the vehicle. "How far is their compound, or whatever it is?"

"About half a mile up the road." One of the men in the back offered. "We were part of the first group to come here."

"Alright, drive. Fast. Make this asshole sniper run to catch up to us. Maybe somebody at the compound is feeling more reasonable. If you catch sight of the sniper, shoot him. He thinks he already killed one of us, and doesn't mind killing more."

Bjurstrom floored the accelerator and the vehicle shot forward. There was another single shot that struck the left side as they passed the sniper's position, then nothing for the minute that it took them to cover the distance to the palisade. More shots rang out, and an RPG raced toward them, missing the moving vehicle by less than a foot and exploding into a tree behind them. Allistor wasn't worried, he knew from experience that even an RPG impact wouldn't do more than scratch his *Juggernaut*. He had them stop about fifty yards out, and tried the loudspeaker again.

"This is Allistor. I'm here to talk. Please stop shooting."

More shots rang out, and a man stood up from behind the wooden poles that made up the wall. As soon as Allistor saw his face, he cursed loudly. The man shouted, "I know why you're here! You want to finish the job! You want to kill me and all my friends!"

Bjurstrom looked to Allistor. "Friend of yours?"

Allistor shook his head, trying to remember his name. He was frankly shocked the man had survived. Last time he'd seen him, the man was badly beaten, broken, and walking into the wilderness unarmed. He couldn't recall ever hearing his name.

"You! You're a Lakota. Standing Bear's nephew!"

"That's right! And you're here to try and kill me again!" The man's voice was whiney even as he shouted the accusation. Allistor pulled his sniper rifle from inventory and opened his door, setting the rifle down by his leg.

"What? You lying little shit! It was *you* who shot *me* through that closet door after you were caught waiting to ambush me! And I didn't lay a hand on you! It was your uncle and your own tribesmen who beat you and banished you!"

"Because you told them to! You bribed them!"

"I'm the one who *kept them from killing you*, you moron! And I came here today to talk to some strangers about trespassing. I had no idea you were here, or even still alive. And frankly I couldn't care less. Put down your guns and come out here, let's talk this out."

He got out of the vehicle and stood behind the open door, casting *Barrier* in front of the door to help stop any incoming rounds. Within seconds, the whiner lifted his rifle and fired. Allistor held his ground, even though the round shattered his *Barrier* spell and plinked into the window in front of him.

"Alright, that's it. You're a dead man. I'm through giving you chances!" Allistor growled through the loudspeaker. "The rest of you, you can still live. Send that little shit out here, or shoot him yourself, I don't care which. When he's dead, we can talk about your living situation!"

Allistor sat back in his seat, lifting his rifle as the crowd behind the wall began to mumble, and the chief's nephew began shouting and cursing at them. Allistor calmly raised his rifle, set the forestock in the crook between the vehicle door and frame, and sighted through the scope. After a single deep breath, he pulled the trigger.

The annoying whiner's head exploded, silencing all the others inside. Allistor put down the rifle and stood up, speaking once again through the loudspeaker. "The rest of you, minus the sniper that's somewhere behind us, I have nothing against. If you'd like to come out and speak civilly, we can come to some kind of arrangement. On the other hand, if you fire at me again, you're all dead. I'll give you one minute to think it over."

Looking to Bjurstrom, he said, "Use the *Juggernaut's* sensors. I want to know when that sniper walks up, and where he is. You three in the back, dismount and spread out in the woods. If you see him before I get him, put one in his chest."

The three didn't hesitate, exiting the back door and quickly fanning out into the underbrush. Allistor figured if the sniper had run to follow them, he should be arriving any minute. Bjurstrom checked the sensor display and shook his head. No sign of him yet. Allistor was hoping he'd show up, and he could shoot the man himself. Save his people that burden. Killing fellow humans, even murderous assholes, wasn't easy to live with.

"We're sending someone out to talk!" A new face appeared atop the wall, an elder man with snow white hair. "Please don't shoot."

"Come on out! I've already told you, I mean you no harm." Allistor stood behind the door once again, watching as the gate opened and a woman strode out. She had her hands up and was dressed in blue jeans and a flannel shirt, the unofficial uniform of the territory. As she got closer, Allistor could clearly see both fear and determination on her face. He waited until she was within a few feet of the vehicle before speaking again. "Don't worry, you're safe. Now, let's start again. My name is Allistor, what's yours?"

She hesitantly lowered her hands as she replied, "I'm Diana. Why are you bothering us?"

"Short and to the point. Okay… I'm not here to bother you, I'm here to help you. Maybe." He looked behind her at the wooden palisade. "You're obviously not doing too well out here, and you're squatting on my property. If you and your people would be willing to become citizens of Invictus, you could improve your situation considerably."

"And your way of helping us is by killing an innocent man? And what for? For a small piece of land that's like nothing compared to all that you own?"

Allistor glared at her, his temper and blood pressure both rising. She actually flinched when he moved his hand to run it through his hair.

"You know what? Screw you, lady. Innocent man? You heard him admit to trying to kill me before. And you actually saw him shoot at me. Then you walk all the way out here to throw a bullshit accusation like that at me?" He turned to Bjurstrom. "Call in one of the ships. Let's just flatten this place and move on, I'm done wasting my time here."

"No! Wait!" She took a step forward, her eyes wide. "You can't just kill us all!"

"Why not? You've tried to kill me and my friends here more than once now. You've refused my offer of help. Should I just leave you here to continue hating me and potentially try to kill more of my people? I don't know how you folks survived this long, but you're clearly too stupid to continue. Go back and tell your people to send out any children you have in there. I'll spare their lives. You have about ten minutes."

Tears rolled down her face, and her shoulders slumped. "Please, no. They sent me out here to talk to you. I don't want to be the one that gets everyone killed. Please."

"Then cut the shit. If that was some kind of negotiating tactic, it was stupid. I don't feel the least bit guilty for killing that asshole, so that wasn't going to help you. Listen to me carefully. You have nothing in there that I need, or want, except your lives. I want you to live, and thrive. But not if you're all out to hurt me or mine because you believed some line of bullshit that guy fed you."

She lowered her head, shaking it slowly back and forth. "Please come inside and talk to the others. I'll guarantee your safety." She looked up at him, and he considered for a moment before nodding. Just as he was stepping out around the vehicle door, a single shot rang out, and a bullet tore through his upper arm, spraying the inside of the window with blood. Diana dropped to the ground, and two more shots rang out in rapid succession.

Allistor cast a heal on himself, as did Bjurstrom. A voice called out, "We got him boss! You okay?"

"I'm fine, but maybe next time shoot the sniper *before* he shoots me?" Allistor grunted, watching as his flesh mended and the bleeding stopped. In a quieter voice, he said "Get up, Diana, before your people think we shot you."

When she was on her feet and waving back at the wall that she was okay, he asked, "You going to hold that killing against me, too? Or should my people have let him finish me off?"

She looked stricken, and didn't answer right away. Allistor was getting angrier, when she finally spoke. "That was my brother-in-law you just killed. But no, I don't blame you. He had to have seen you talking to me. He risked my life, shooting at you."

Allistor had to force himself to say, "I'm sorry for your loss. Are we still going inside to talk?"

Diana just nodded and turned to walk back. Allistor followed a few feet behind, and Bjurstrom drove the Juggernaut behind them. The other three carried a body out onto the trail, set it down, then followed at a distance. Allistor recast his *Barrier*, just in case.

The gate opened to let Diana and Allistor through. It wasn't quite wide enough for the vehicle, so Bjurstrom remained outside with the engine running, ready to smash his way inside if necessary. To his surprise, Allistor found many more than ten people gathered inside the walls. There were closer to forty, at least a dozen of them under the age of ten, and another dozen or so teenagers.

The man with the white hair that had stood up on the wall stepped forward. "My name is Ozzy. I guess you could say I'm the leader around here."

"Now that whatshisname is dead?" Allistor pointed to the corpse still laying near the base of the wall, half his head gone.

Ozzy shook his head. "He wasn't our leader, he was just loud and persistent. Had half our people believing his story."

By the looks on the faces of the teenagers, Allistor thought he knew who the believers were. He stood and faced them, speaking loudly enough for all to hear. "Listen to me. That man was banished by his own uncle from the Lakota tribe stronghold in Thunder Basin. They were trespassers on one of my parks, just like you. I went to visit them, gave them hunting rights, and established an alliance with them. I gave them food, and weapons, and a way to earn more through bounties. I established an Outpost not far from their Stronghold, and we were just finishing a celebratory dinner when this asshole snuck into my Outpost and hid in a maintenance closet, intending to ambush me." Allistor watched the faces, and most were not changed.

"I gave him a chance to come out peacefully, but the moron shot me through the door with his shotgun. His uncle and tribesmen were going to kill him, but my girlfriend convinced them to let him live. So they beat him within an inch of his life, and sent him away." A few of the faces showed some doubt, so he pushed. "You heard him a few minutes ago. He didn't deny it. He just claimed I bribed them to do it. Which I did not. He was already a pain in their ass, as I'm sure he was a pain in yours!"

This time most of the heads in the compound nodded.

"The man outside, Diana's brother-in-law, took several shots at me before we got here, and you all saw or heard him try again just now. Diana was standing right next to me. We killed him in self-defense."

Again most everyone nodded, including Diana. "It's true. He fired at Allistor first. Hit him in the arm." Allistor held up the arm with the bloodstained shirt.

"Now, I'm going to assume that the rest of you held no more than the standard grudge against me, the one caused by the constant trespassing notifications. And that's why I'm here. I have built an entire nation of survivors just like you. Folks that have held on through the first year, survived monster spawns and cold, disease, hunger, all of it. You are true survivors, and among the last of the human race. I'm here to invite you to join me, join the citizens of Invictus. You take an oath not to harm me or your fellow citizens, and you can live among us in real strongholds. With running water, heat and air conditioning, and plentiful food. I have strongholds from the west coast to the east coast, from Toronto on down to the Caribbean, even one over in England now. And I have taken possession of a whole other planet called Orion. You take the oath, you can live in any one of those places."

"And if we want to stay here?" One of the teenagers asked.

Allistor looked around. The compound was crowded, dirty, with a large central fire pit and a well pump to one side. "I suppose we could turn this into an Outpost so you have power and water, but I really think you'd be happier at one of the other places. I can send a ship to pick you up and show you our closest Stronghold, or take you all the way to England if you want."

"How do we know you're not just going to kill us when you've got us separated?" Another teenager asked, sneering as he spoke.

Allistor was starting to lose his patience again. "What's your name, you rude little shit?"

"Aaron!" the kid spat the name at him.

"Aaron, I could have killed all of you, right here, right now. I could have dropped a bomb on your compound, or frankly, I could walk in here and kill you all single-handedly..." He drew his knife, cast *Dimensional Step* on himself, and appeared behind the teenager. Grabbing his hair with one hand, he pulled his head back and pressed the knife to the kid's throat. "And you wouldn't be able to stop me."

The others gasped as the kid wet himself, and Allistor had to quickly pull the knife away to avoid actually cutting him. He let go of the weak-kneed kid and walked back to Ben and Diana. He shouted, putting some rage into his voice. "I could have wiped you all out without ever wasting my time coming here in person, and no one except these folks would have known!" He glared at the teenagers, most of whom were watching Aaron cry in a muddy puddle of his own urine.

Ben shook his head. "Alright, you've made your point. I don't think you needed to be so rough on the kid."

"I've learned the hard way to weed out the assholes, or they come back to bite me." Allistor pointed at the dead man by the wall. "He clearly still thinks I'm lying, though I have absolutely no reason to do so. It would have been faster and easier for me to just take you all out. And believe me, I had a busy day planned. I didn't need this distraction. But you're all human, and human lives are important to me. I'll give him one chance to take the oath. If he refuses, I'll give him food and a weapon and send him away, mark him as hostile to Invictus."

"I'll take your oath." Diana stepped forward. "I've had enough of this place." She held out her arms, and two of the small children ran to her. "My kids and I will take the oath and go back to civilization."

Ben stepped forward as well, then most of the others, including all of the small children. Some of the teenagers joined them, but half a dozen stayed near Aaron, who was still sitting in his own filth.

Allistor was about to speak again when one of the holdouts grabbed Aaron under his arms and lifted him up. Keeping his distance, he took hold of one arm, and a second kid took hold of the other. They practically carried him forward, and had nearly reached the others when he braced himself and tore free of them.

"Screw you, dude! He was right about you!" He pulled a knife from a sheath at his back and hurled it at Allistor. The knife sailed past Allistor without him even having to move, and his people all raised their guns, aiming at the kid.

Allistor calmly addressed him. "I'm gonna chalk that up to you being a teenager, and angry because I just made you piss yourself in front of your friends. So take a deep breath, calm down, and think. You want to end up alone out there?" He pointed toward the wall. "With the wolves and the bears and whatever monsters are still out in those woods?"

His friends had backed away from him as soon as the guns went up, and he now looked left and right to see that he'd been abandoned. The kid who'd helped him stand mumbled, "Don't be a dick, man."

Allistor continued. "I'll give you a few minutes to think while I set up an Outpost here." He opened his interface and selected the appropriate tabs, eliminating the wood walls and expanding the footprint, including the usual utilities, security, and sensors. There were gasps from the crowd as everything went translucent and the ground beneath them seemed to disappear. When he was finished and had pushed the button, there were more surprised sounds as the Outpost took shape around them. Instead of a simple wooden enclosure with some tents and lean-tos, there were now high stone walls with stone buildings inside.

Allistor looked at Aaron. "You've had a few minutes to calm down now. This is just a small example of the comforts you can enjoy if you join Invictus as a citizen. Can you get over yourself and swear the oath? Or do you want to take a hike?" Allistor saw a sneer appear on the kid's face, as did most of the others. They backed away.

"Before you say you'll take the oath, thinking you can just freeload off me, you need to know that you *will contribute* or be thrown out. And if you take the oath and break it... well the few people who have done so have died horribly. The System takes oaths seriously, and punishes oathbreakers."

The sneer disappeared from the obnoxious kid's face. Allistor waited patiently for a full minute, staring at the kid. The others watched, still at a distance. When the kid still didn't answer, Allistor shrugged.

"Fine. The offer is rescinded. The rest of you are welcome to join us. Aaron is, as of now, an enemy of Invictus." He turned to one of his people. "Get me a backpack, fill it with food, his knife, and a .45, without any bullets. When we leave here, give him a box of rounds."

He turned back to Aaron, whose face had gone white. "This outpost is off limits to you, as is this entire park, and every park or property I own. If one of my people encounters you after today, they will shoot on site. Everyone here is a witness, I've given you several chances, even after you tried to kill me. You're just too stupid to live." Allistor looked around, but none of the crowd spoke up for the kid.

Needing a little space, he turned his back on the now crying teen and walked over to the security pedestal by the new metal gates. A quick touch of the pad, and the gates opened. Bjurstrom drove the Juggernaut inside the much more spacious new compound, and got out.

"Please administer the oath to everyone except the little asshole over there crying. He's KoS after today."

"Oh, shit." Bjurstrom looked from Allistor to the kid and back. "What'd I miss?"

"Tell you later. Let's get this done. Nigel, please ask Kira to send a ship out here to pick these people up. They're to be transported to the Warren to start with, then they have permission to travel the teleport system like any other citizen, assuming they've taken the oath."

Bjurstrom had already gathered the crowd together, and Allistor grinned despite his foul mood when his friend made a show of having them all take a knee and raise their right hand while they repeated the oath. The lights swirled around them, and Nigel dutifully reported that all but Aaron had sworn. The kid was over to one side, one of Allistor's men handing him a pack full of food. Allistor watched as he was forcefully led to the gates and escorted out. When he'd disappeared into the woods, one of them set a box of .45 shells on the ground near the gate, then stayed with it to make sure the kid didn't claim them too soon and try to shoot someone.

Allistor and Bjurstrom left the other three to organize and supervise the new recruits, letting them know that a ship would arrive shortly. He knew he hadn't handled things well, and that these people had mainly been bullied into joining him. He'd let the Lakota outcast, sniper, and Aaron get to him, along with his resentment at having to waste half a day on this type of issue when he had a whole kingdom to run. That in itself bothered him a little. He should always have time to save more than three dozen people.

But now he was running a kingdom of tens of thousands, and an entire planet. A planet that was about to become a heavily populated trade hub. And here on Earth he had hundreds, if not thousands of human settlements to reach out to.

Bjurstrom tried to coax him into talking on the way back to the Warren. He could have waited with the others and just driven the vehicle onto the ship, been back to civilization faster. But he wanted some time to think, and a quiet car ride through the forest was as good a place as any.

Eventually, he asked. "Why haven't you taken a Stronghold of your own and started building a community? You're more than qualified."

"Nah, boss. Not what I'm made for. I do have a Stronghold, and claimed my ten acres. But I'm letting a family live there and farm it. It's not like I need moolah, after getting my share of the gold depository loots. Eventually, when I'm done running around saving the world, I'll retire there and let them feed me and change my diapers. But until then, it's the pirate's life for me!" He grinned.

Allistor snorted. "Alright, well… if you ever change your mind and want a Citadel like Ramon and Nancy have, it's yours. You've more than earned it. Maybe Dover Castle?"

"Ha! Only if you make me a knight. You should be a knight if you live in a castle."

"Alright, fine. I dub thee Sir Bjurstrom, Knight of Invictus!"

To their mutual surprise, a blue light swirled around Bjurstrom, and a moment later he nearly ran the vehicle off the road from laughing. "You just really made me a knight!"

"Oh, shit. Well, cool!" Allistor grinned to himself. "Young William is going to be *very* glad to hear about that! His dream is to become a knight."

"His dream right now is to successfully bonk you on the head." Bjurstrom countered. "Followed closely by having his very own dragon to ride." He snorted. "And you know McCoy and some of the others are gonna want to be knighted as well."

Allistor chuckled, his mood improving. "We'll make them do some ridiculous test or trial, first. I'll let you think it up. Nothing too dangerous, just embarrassing. By the way, does being a knight come with any kind of bonuses?"

Bjurstrom pulled to one side and stopped the vehicle, then unfocused his eyes. "Says it's a subclass, and yeah, it has its own skill tree. There are honor points that earn you skills, and... hey! I can take on a squire of my own, and give him quests. If he grows up to be a knight as well, promoting him earns me a huge amount of honor points."

"Alright, well I think we'll be creating a large number of knights and squires in the near future!" Allistor gave him a fist bump, and Bjurstrom got the vehicle moving again.

After a few minutes of silence, Bjurstrom cleared his throat. "Hey uhm… boss?"

"Yeah?"

"About that super sexy elf girl that was hanging around the tower yesterday."

Allistor tensed up. "What about her?"

"Well, the scuttlebutt is that the elves brought her here to try and marry you. But that you're not going for it?"

"Well, for once the scuttlebutt is correct. Why?"

"First of all, are you crazy? Did you *see* her? She's pure fun on two legs!" He chuckled as Allistor scowled at him. "Second, you think there's any chance she'd be interested in a real, honest to goodness knight? I mean, since you won't be starting a harem?"

Chapter 5

Allistor didn't wait for the newcomers to reach the Warren Stronghold. Shortly after he arrived, Nigel alerted him to a new issue.

*"Sire, squire William requests to speak with you immediately."*

"Put him through please, Nigel."

"Allistor! It's happening!" The boy's voice practically squeaked with excitement. "They're hatching! Like, really hatching this time! I can see a foot pushing through that one over there!"

Allistor grinned at the boy's enthusiasm. A moment later Daniel's voice came through as well. "This is not a drill, boss. We're about to have a bunch more mouths to feed."

"I'll be right there!" Allistor ran toward the teleport pad, not even needing to speak as Nigel anticipated his needs, transferring both he and Bjurstrom to the Silo the moment they were atop the pad and holding still.

From the Silo pad they ran to the elevator and took it all the way to the bottom level, where they'd fought the mama drake what seemed like eons ago. The moment the doors opened, both men dashed down the corridor at speeds that even pre-apocalypse Olympic sprinters would have been pressed to match.

Entering the cavern through the huge circular door, they found Master Daigath along with dozens of Silo and Citadel residents gathered around Daniel and William, watching as the eggs wobbled and rolled about, several of them beginning to come apart as their inhabitants pushed free.

"Allistor!" William was jumping up and down. "Look! Baby dragons!"

"Baby *drakes*." Daigath corrected the boy with a smile. "These are drakes, a lesser cousin of the dragons. They look very similar, though they do not grow nearly as large. Dragons are intelligent beings, creatures born of magic. An elder race, even older than the elves, and respected by all. Drakes are barely capable of understanding basic communication, and their magic is typically limited to the element into which they are born. Fire drakes breathe flames and are resistant to heat. Frost drakes are the opposite. Water drakes can breathe underwater, and so forth."

William looked slightly disappointed for about three seconds before his enthusiasm swept him away again. "They're busting out of their eggs! Look how tiny they are!" He pointed at a few from the nearest cluster.

Altogether the humans had found thirty four eggs after they'd defeated the female drake. The group watched, mumbling and exclaiming to each other as the eggs hatched. Tiny snouts and limbs of various colors pushed through the thick shells, widening cracks and forcing them to break apart. Behind Allistor, more and more citizens were coming through the door, with Helen and Amanda joining him after just a few minutes.

"They're SO cute!" Helen clapped her hands together and started toward the nearest of them. Daigath reached out a hand, holding her back.

"They are going to be extremely hungry when they emerge, and not at all picky about what, or who, fills their bellies. I suggest you start gathering all the meat you can, and toss it over to them. Once their bellies are full, you may approach them with reasonable safety."

Instantly everyone in the crowd who had food in their inventory began tossing out chunks of raw meat, jerky, cheese, even granola bars. One airman sheepishly rolled several hard-boiled eggs toward the little drakelings.

The first of the little ones to fully escape from his shell bleated out a complaint, shaking its head, then its entire body, like a dog emerging from a pond. Its tiny, leathery wings flapped on either side of its body, which was covered in blood red scales much like its mother. Then its nose went up in the air, and it turned with laser focus toward the growing pile of food on the ground. Stumbling slightly, the newborn half-walked, half-hopped over and snatched up a chunk of canid meat, raising its head high and swallowing it whole. There was a visible lump that progressed down the drakeling's throat before the meat reached its belly. A moment later it let out a much happier sounding honk before grabbing another bite.

One by one the drakelings made their way to the food, some with chunks of shell still stuck to them.

Adorably, a green one was wearing a shell hat as it wobbled over and pushed through its siblings to get at the food. Another still had a large section of shell stuck to its belly, and used it as a sort of sled, pushing with its stubby rear legs and sliding across the cavern floor.

There were several different colors of drakelings, and Daigath called them out as he pointed. "The white are frost drakes. Green are forest, blue are water, the red are obviously fire. That little yellow one over there is a sulfur drake, they spit acid. The brown ones are earth drakes, and the black one is thunder. They are rare, and can create storms at will."

"Just like Allistor!" William beamed up at his guardian.

Helen was watching the furthest corner, and pointed to a drakeling that was obviously smaller than the others, and waddling much slower toward the food. Its scales were a luminescent silver hue. "What about the silver?"

"Ah, yes." Daigath smiled. "Silver drakes are quite rare. They are always female, psychic, and often possess illusion magic. All drakes can communicate telepathically with other drakes and dragons, but silvers can speak to the minds of other sentient beings."

When the slow-moving silver reached the throng of drakelings mobbing the dwindling food pile, the others ceased their pushing and shoving and gave way, clearing a path. The silver made her way through and almost daintily scooped up one of the boiled eggs, swallowing it shell and all before grabbing a large chunk of jerky. Flopping down on her belly, she placed one forepaw atop the hunk of meat, which was nearly as large as her tiny head, and began to gnaw on the other end, making happy-sounding grunts and growls as she chewed.

The others gave her some space, resuming their battles for access to the food on either side of her. The observers continued to toss whatever they had in their inventories, while Daniel, who had been anticipating their need to feed as he cared for the eggs, pulled a seemingly endless supply of beef, canid, elk, and lanx meat from his storage.

Being smaller than the others, the silver finished her first meal sooner. Her little belly full, she looked around the cavern and honked questioningly. Not seeing a mature drake, she noticed the gathered crowd of humanoids and shrank back slightly.

William took a step forward, then got down on one knee. He held out a hand, and began speaking softly to her. "It's okay little one. We won't hurt you. Me and Daniel, we've been taking care of you! Keeping your egg warm while you grew."

Most of the crowd gasped as the little drake seemed to recognize the boy's voice. First her head tilted to one side, an obviously curious expression on her face. Her already large eyes widened, and she belted out a happy little honk before jumping to her feet and hopping quickly toward William.

Allistor was stepping forward to protect the boy when Daigath reached over and held him back. "Just watch. The boy will be fine."

The silver flapped her wings as she hopped, unable to fly but catching enough air to extend the small hops into longer jumps. When she was within a few feet of the young squire, she folded her wings flat against her back and wobbled forward, crashing into William and knocking him backward. She was less than half his size, but her momentum pushed him onto his back. Hopping up onto his chest, she plopped down on her belly and began licking his face.

"Ugh! Quit it!" William tried to protest even as he laughed. The concerned adults in the room relaxed a bit, and watched with smiles as the boy began to wrestle with the little silver. He rolled onto his side and dumped her off, then reached out to tickle her belly. Snorting, she lifted her wings a bit to give him better access, then extended her neck over his shoulder as if hugging him.

"That is the cutest thing ever!" Dawn gushed from somewhere in the group. Amanda and Helen where holding onto each other, both of them smiling and crying at the same time.

The one-on-one cuteness was short-lived, however. As the other drakelings filled their bellies, they began to follow the silver, intent on getting in on the shenanigans. Allistor pictured William being buried by a mob of little lizards, and panicked.

"Uhhh… guys? Everybody pick a drake and intercept it. Distract it."

The humans all happily obliged, stepping forward and calling out to the little ones, waving hands, making smoochy noises, even holding out more treats and waving them around. Bjurstrom produced some kind of squeaky toy and moved to one side, squeaking it at one of the black drakes. He noted the questioning looks from the others, just shrugging. "Don't judge me because I came prepared."

Unfortunately for him, the squeaky toy got the attention of four of the little drakes, and he was quickly mobbed as they all tried to grab it. "Help!" he held it high above his head and laughed as the determined little monsters tried to climb him. Helen and Dawn rushed to his rescue, Amanda not far behind.

For the next fifteen minutes, the humans engaged the little drakelings, eventually separating them and distracting them with treats, scratches, wrestling, and lots of baby talk. Daniel even engaged one of the yellows in a game of tug using a short piece of rope he'd pulled from his ring.

Allistor, who had left the drake wrangling to the others, watched with a wide smile on his face. He noted that the silver had somehow gotten herself back onto William's belly and appeared to have fallen asleep, the boy happily stroking the side of her neck.

Bjurstrom and the black drakeling were playing fetch with the squeaky toy. He would toss it into the nearby pool of water, and the little fella wobbled over to the edge, diving into the water where it immediately became much more graceful. It would disappear under the surface, emerging under the toy like a great white snatching up a seal, giving it a few good squeaks as it turned and swam back to the edge. When it returned with the toy, Bjurstrom had to wrestle it free of the tiny jaws, the drakeling growling and twitching its tail.

Amanda joined Allistor, placing her arm in his as they watched their people bond with the cute little monsters. Helen had, unsurprisingly, chosen a green forest drake to play with. She was sitting on the floor, legs crossed, with the drakeling on its back in her lap. She alternately rubbed and scratched its belly, being rewarded with a sort of purring sound and lazily waving feet. The end of its tail twitched occasionally, slapping against the floor.

Over near the door with his yellow drakeling, Daniel let out a disgusted groan, then laughed. When the others turned to him, he shook his head. "Damned thing just farted. Master Daigath was right about the yellows being sulfur drakes. That's just nasty." He waved a hand in front of his nose, but was grinning as he did so.

Allistor turned to Daigath, who was sitting on the floor with a green drakeling climbing up onto his shoulder. As it wrapped itself around his neck, the old elf tickled under its jaw.

"Looks like you've found a new friend." Allistor smiled at the old elf.

"For now, yes. Though I won't bond with him. I've had many bonded companions over the millennia, and outlived them all. Drakes are not as long-lived as dragons, or elves. Though they will likely outlive some of you humans. Being part of the System, your lives will be greatly extended, but I'm afraid I don't know for how long."

Allistor became concerned. "What happens if a drake bonds with one of my people, and that person dies?"

Daigath shrugged, disturbing the sleepy drakeling, who honked in complaint. He petted its head and made soothing sounds for a moment, apologizing. "One of several things. It may decide to take another bond. Or wander off into the wild and live out its life alone. Some have been known to simply perish along with their bonded, having lost their will to live. Others have gone berserk and tried to kill anything and everything in sight. Some of those were able to be calmed, others had to be put down." He paused for a moment as if remembering a particular incident.

"Bear in mind, bonding with drakes is not a popular practice. They are volatile, and often difficult to control. They are rarely trainable, and don't serve a purpose in most cases. Some are used as guard beasts, protecting estates that can afford to feed them. Generally though, they are more trouble than they're worth."

Goodrich, who was feeding bits of a chocolate bar to a white drakeling, overheard. "I'm totally bonding with this one!" He nodded at the white, offering another chunk of chocolate on his open palm, which the tiny creature daintily took by wrapping its tongue around it. "You said the whites are frost drakes, right? I'm gonna train this one, and have ice cold beers and sodas for life!"

Daigath and the others within earshot laughed, and the elf nodded his head. "You may indeed have success with training it to perform such simple tasks, like using its magic on command. Especially if you begin your training early." He paused as the little white chirped a demand at Goodrich, who quickly broke off another bit of chocolate. "It will be a week or so before they'll be able to use their magic. Until then, they will eat almost constantly, only pausing to sleep when their bellies are full. And I'm afraid their food consumption will only increase as they grow larger, until they are full grown. At which point they may only need to eat every month or so."

Allistor imagined that thirty or so growing drakes could put a strain on their food supply. He'd have to either detail some people to make sure they were all fed, or put the responsibility on the people they bonded with.

Daigath noted his thoughtful look, and grinned. "Do not worry. Drakes have strong survival instincts, and are excellent hunters. Once they've grown into their magic, they'll be able to hunt for themselves, killing bugs, small mammals, fish, birds, whatever presents itself. They'll have to be taught right from the start that small humans are not food. And I recommend keeping them away from your chickens and rabbits."

Helen, always thinking ahead, asked, "What about breeding them? Can we use this flock to create more?"

Andrea chimed in. "Hell yeah! Drake-mounted air corps!"

Daigath looked around at the nearly three dozen little monsters. "Generally among each generation an alpha male and female will emerge. In this case, the silver will almost certainly be the alpha female, and the matron of the group due to her increased intelligence. Whichever male emerges as the alpha of his gender will be subservient to her. While any of the males and females may mate, only the eggs of the alphas will be allowed to mature."

McCoy spoke up from near the back, where he was petting a crimson drake. "So, if the others breed, we can make drake egg omelettes. Imagine the kind of buffs we'd get from those!"

Eventually, the drakelings all drifted off to sleep, and Daniel called for everyone to clear the room and let them rest in peace. Eight of the drakelings woke when their chosen human tried to leave, and began to whine and honk loudly, refusing to be left behind.

"Those have bonded already. You should either remain with them here, or take them away with you." Daigath advised.

William's little silver was one of those who'd bonded, not to anyone's surprise. Also Bjurstrom's black, Goodrich's white, Helen's green, Daniel's yellow, along with two blues and a red that had adopted humans. The folks who hadn't been chosen grumbled a bit, and asked to come back to try again. Allistor left that up to Daniel, with Daigath to advise him.

Taking his squire, who was now cradling the little silver like a newborn in his arms, Allistor and Amanda made their way back to Invictus tower. The moment they got back to their quarters, Syd and Addy mobbed the little boy and his sleeping drakeling. The three of them went off to his room to "create a nest for her", the girls already demanding a chance to go bond with drakes of their own. Amanda promised they could go first thing in the morning, and advised them to bring along plenty of snacks.

"When you get there, try singing to them." Allistor advised. "But be prepared to be mobbed."

*****

Hel watched with satisfaction as the human prince mercilessly killed yet another human who opposed him, then intimidated the others in a small settlement. She was developing a fondness for the man, and saw great potential in him. During his short tenure within the Collective, he had excelled at navigating the newly imposed System, thriving beyond all expectation. He had made powerful friends and allies, and defeated powerful enemies. The rewards for which now included a pair of eternity gates.

Breathing out in a long sigh that caused the mists to briefly part in front of her before filling the void again, she waved her tentacles in a languorous manner that among her people was an expression of regret. Yes, she was growing fond of this Allistor. But that would not stop her from killing him, framing her father for the crime, and bringing Odin's wrath down upon him.

Loki had come to her not long ago, ranting about the human. Unaware that Hel had witnessed Baldur's threat against him, and his directive to protect the human, Loki had pressed his daughter to find a way to eliminate Allistor without the deed being traced back to her, of course. Aware that he was counting on her rebellious nature and almost pathological need to disobey her father, Hel had walked a thin line with her response.

She could not simply agree to her father's request, or he would have been instantly suspicious. At the same time, outright refusing to eliminate the human, when her father was surely aware of her previous actions against him, would raise alarms as well. The two of them had played this game for ages. Punch, and counterpunch. Scheming and plotting against each other, and sometimes together against a common foe. The truth was, Loki would be suspicious of her no matter how she responded.

So she went on the offensive, attempting to distract him. She'd first tossed him a tiny sensor device she'd only just found in her rooms. One of the three that Loki had managed to keep hidden up to that point. Loki was long past being ashamed or incensed by the discovery, but she still enjoyed letting him know that she'd bested him again, and he disliked the enjoyment she derived from it. Hel added a few jabs that she knew he would feel. Despite his need to protect the human now, he still despised Allistor.

"Two eternity gates, father. The human is indeed impressive. Barely more than a year since his induction into the Collective, and starting with almost literally just the shirt on his back, he has accomplished great things. Given a century or so, he might even surpass your own accomplishments!"

Loki's tentacles twitched briefly, and the mist around him rippled with barely restrained frustration. "He got lucky. The orb practically fell into his lap, and he only picked it up because he nearly tripped over it. A hairless monkey picking up a shiny new toy as he crawled about in the mud."

"A very valuable shiny toy." Hel exuded satisfaction at being able to push her father's buttons. "His new planet will benefit greatly from the gate he places there. Already he's leveraged that opportunity to create great wealth and power for himself. Space station, dungeon cores, the ability to raise the skills and levels of his entire populace. Not to mention the new alliance and defense pacts! All of this makes acting against him anonymously an order of magnitude more difficult."

"I have faith in you, daughter." Loki transmitted pride and encouragement through the mists to her. Hel felt no falsity in any of it. Her father was, after all, the trickster, the god of deception. "I would eliminate him myself, but Baldur is watching me more closely than ever before. He does not currently suspect you of wanting to harm the boy, though, being aware of the assistance you provided in the form of that void titan scroll."

Hel adopted an innocent stance, her tentacles hanging loosely at her sides. "I have no idea what you mean, father." Did he think her a fool? Admitting to violating the non-interference directives on a planet still in Stabilization would result in her instant destruction by the System.

"Of course, of course." Loki turned toward the door. "In any case, should the young prince come to grievous harm in the immediate future, I would be willing to reward you accordingly."

As the door closed behind her departing father, Hel shook her head. How surprised would he be when she not only fulfilled his request, but did so in a way that ensured he would be blamed? As she moved toward her encrypted communications console, her thoughts turned to imagining just how Baldur would execute his promised vengeance.

*****

Agni walked into his nephew's office moving as fast as his old bones could carry him. Which, since the apocalypse, was much faster than previously. He'd reached level eighteen, and found that putting three of his attribute points into *Constitution* and one into *Agility* had made him feel thirty years younger, at least.

"Rajesh. I have news of the prince!"

His nephew looked up from his desk, where he'd been reviewing his most recent market reports, wondering why his increased sales and accumulated wealth had not allowed him a new title. "What is it, uncle? And will you ever learn to call me Earl?"

"No." The old man grinned at his nephew. "And our short wave radio operators have been picking up some chatter about Allistor. It seems he is using spaceships to send out teams of his citizens. They are claiming new lands, and seeking out settlements like ours and trying to recruit them to join him."

Rajesh grew alarmed, and his voice went up in pitch. "Armed takeovers? How dare he?"

"No, Rajesh. Calm yourself." The old man shook his head, taking a deep breath and sitting in one of the soft chairs across from his nephew. "I apologize. I should not have rushed in here and alarmed you. He is not taking them by force." He paused, then restated. "Not the settlements occupied by humans, anyway. He has forcibly taken a few places that were infested with monsters. But one cannot hold that against him, yes?"

Rajesh took a moment to process the information. "No, one cannot complain about killing monsters. But if he is not using force, how is he taking the other settlements?"

"He offers friendship, and protection. His people bring food, weapons, and stories of thriving communities within his lands. They offer the chance to train one's class skills, to get stronger. Some have joined, others have established alliances."

"No threats?"

"None that we have heard about so far. And he certainly *could* threaten. His people are all reported to be much higher level than ours, some of them over level forty, all of them above thirty. The reports regarding their armor, weapons, spells… with the power they possess we could not prevent them from just taking your holdings if they wished it."

Rajesh's eyes widened. He was among the highest-leveled of his own people at thirty two. Most of his fighters were between level twenty and thirty, and the average of his general population was around level ten. Despite his uncle's assurances, he felt his gut clench in fear.

"Rajesh, calm yourself." Agni saw and recognized the look on his nephew's face. "We must reach out to this prince, and propose an alliance. That is assuming you do not wish to simply join him as part of his kingdom. It may be that serving as a noble under him would be more profitable than becoming a prince on your own…"

Rajesh was already shaking his head. "I *will be* the next Prince of Earth!" he slammed his hand down on the desk.

"Fine, fine…" Agni patted the air between them, a calming gesture. "But let us at least make contact and request a meeting. Better to approach him now from a strong position as a fellow noble, than to wait and be 'saved' by his wandering recruiting teams."

Rajesh leaned back in his chair, thinking hard. When he didn't respond for several minutes, Agni tried again.

"Allistor is rapidly expanding his territory. Right now, he is motivated to be friendly and accommodating to those settlements he encounters. But should you wait too long, he might achieve whatever his goal may be, and lose that motivation. Lose his inclination to be friendly." Rajesh was young, and prideful. Agni had hoped he wouldn't have to reveal the stick, that the carrot would be enough to sway his nephew. But he was convinced that an alliance with Allistor was what was best for their people, and would do what was necessary to make that happen.

Rajesh closed his hands into fists, and the visible muscle movement along his jawline told Agni that he was clenching his teeth. But after a moment he relaxed and took a few deep breaths. "Very well, uncle. Please reach out to this prince. Send him greetings from Earl Rajesh and request that he join us for tea, or a meal, at his convenience." His voice was flat, emotionless. This worried Agni.

"I will see it done, nephew." was all he said as he rose and left the office. His heart thumped in his chest, and he was filled with a feeling of dread. The only other time he'd seen Rajesh behave in such a way, the boy had led a raiding party against some slavers who had killed his betrothed in a raid of their own. Though it cost Rajesh nearly half of his force, not one of the slavers had been left alive. Agni would need to find a way to calm his nephew, to alter his state of mind, before the more powerful prince arrived.

Chapter 6


Allistor felt like a zookeeper. Standing in the middle of the Wilderness Stronghold, he took in his surroundings Next to him was Helen, then Amanda, with her bear companion Fiona. William, Sydney and Addy were gathered around Fuzzy, who lay on his back nearby, his feet batting gently at four baby drakes who were happily 'attacking' him. There was a red drakeling that had bonded to Sydney, Helen's green, and Addy's was a blue. William's silver, the alpha female of the recent brood, was sitting atop Fuzzy's chest, watching him intently and snapping at his tongue every time it escaped his mouth. Allistor was slightly concerned that if she actually managed to clamp her jaws on it, either she or Fuzzy might be hurt.

They'd come to Wilderness in part to see Master Daigath, and to let the drakelings hunt small critters in the forest. But with the unruly little drakes, Allistor was beginning to second guess that decision. He was imagining having to chase them all through the woods, drakes and kids alike, when Amanda took his hand.

"Look at our little family." She beamed at him.

Allistor couldn't help but smile back at her. They'd had a few more discussions over the last couple days regarding the kids and potentially adopting them. L'olwyn had offered up the idea of making them official wards, giving them the protection of being part of the royal family without placing them ahead of any future biological heirs in the line of succession. Amanda planned to bring up the subject with the kids today, while they had some alone-time in the forest.

Things had been hectic in the days since the orb was auctioned. While awaiting the delivery of the first eternity gate, and some of the promised goods from his new allies, Allistor had sent four groups out on the *Bellerophon*, *Opportunity*, and two of the goblin colony ships, to locate and make contact with other groups of survivors in Europe, Asia, Africa, and Australia. He'd filled their cargo bays with gifts of fresh fish and other food, plasma rifles, and crafted gear that his own people had mostly outgrown, but would be upgrades for most other humans. He'd also sent along a few class trainers, a healing, melee class, and casting class with each ship. Reports so far were that most groups were friendly and receptive. Except for two that had attacked his people on sight. One of those was eventually calmed and agreed to talk peacefully. The other group was left alone for the time being.

Allistor had spent many hours closeted with his advisors, working out the details of what lands the auction participants had chosen, what other lands he wanted to make available at auction, what and who he wanted to place on his new space station that would hover above Invictus City, where they might place their new dungeon cores, and a thousand other details. Amanda had contributed to many of those discussions, as had several of his core group.

News of the pending eternity gate at Orion spread quickly through the Collective. A new gate was an uncommon event, and a new gate owned by a fledgling emperor was unheard of. Factions were sending representatives with great haste, expecting to take advantage of Allistor's inexperience to gain both profit and power.

The morning after the hatching, the girls had indeed gone and sang to the little drakes, earning bonds for each of them. About half of the drakelings had now bonded with one of Allistor's people, and part of the reason he was on his way to see Daigath was to ask about the remainder. If they didn't bond, something would have to be done with them.

As they rousted Fuzzy and the drakes to begin their hike to Daigath's home, Helen fell into step next to Allistor. Her green drakeling took station upon her shoulder, wrapping its tail around her neck for stability, then huffed contentedly. She absently stroked its side as she spoke to Allistor.

"The dwarves at Lightholm contacted me this morning. They say they'll have the volcano at Yellowstone stabilized in a week or so. They've also passed along two requests."

"Requests?"

"First, there are approximately ten thousand more dwarves who'd like to join us here on Earth, and at least double that number that would like to live on Orion. That's besides the Lighthammer dwarves who will be working on the gravity lift, and the Stardrifters who will be living in their Citadel on the planet as well."

Allistor grinned. "I don't see any reason why we shouldn't welcome them. Dwarves are good people, and generally fun to have around."

"Which brings us to the second request. They'd like permission to establish a second Citadel at Yellowstone, and significantly expand Lightholm, to make room for the additional arrivals."

"That's an easy one. Lightholm is theirs to expand as they see fit. And of course they can create a second Citadel. As long as they use their own resources. You already knew I'd say yes, so why bring this to me...?" He paused, seeing the look Helen was giving him. After a moment, he realized why. A grin appeared on his own face. "Hold on a second."

He opened up his UI and selected the tab labeled Vassals. After a few clicks, he watched as Helen's eyes widened. Waving at Amanda to get her attention, he nodded his head toward Helen. When Amanda saw Helen's mouth hanging open, she gave him a questioning look.

By way of answer, he said, "Congratulations, *Countess* Helen! In case you aren't aware, that's the female equivalent of the noble rank of Earl. And I've promoted Longbeard as well, so now he can create that second Citadel without you."

"Congrats!" Amanda hugged the surprised former park ranger. "It's about time Allistor recognized your hard work and loyalty."

Allistor looked at his feet as both women glared at him for a moment, then chuckled at his discomfort. "Thank you, Allistor." Helen's smile grew warm, as did the look she gave him.

"You know what this means, right?" Amanda happily queried. She waited a moment for Helen to raise an eyebrow before finishing. "Handsome men, elves, dwarves, maybe even orcanin will be lining up trying to bag themselves a Countess of Invictus!"

Helen rolled her eyes and groaned. Looking to Allistor, she grumped. "You did that on purpose! Take it back!"

"Ha! No chance." Allistor gave her a one-armed hug and resumed following the bears toward Daigath's home. "And I feel I should point out that it probably won't be just the handsome ones."

He could hear the two women muttering to each other as he moved ahead of them, picking up his pace a bit. If he didn't stay close to the bears, they'd likely wander off to harvest berries and such. Once they were away from the cleared area outside the gates and following the trail through the forest proper, the baby drakes perked up. There were a thousand little sounds of chirping birds, insects, rustles in the leaves and bushes. Their hunting instincts kicked in, and they began to peer around, sniffing the air and making tiny growly noises.

When they came upon the small creek crossing, Allistor called a halt. "Let's stop here for a bit. The bears can catch a few fish, and the drakes can do a little hunting.

Kids, make sure you keep them close by. And you stay where we can see you."

While Fuzzy and Fiona happily splashed into the rocky creek, quickly joined by the blue drakeling, the others leapt from their humans' shoulders and flapped clumsily down to the ground where they began nosing through the undergrowth. The little blue darted gracefully through the water, at home in his element. He snapped up several minnows in the shallower water before rolling over onto his back to sun his full belly on a wide flat rock. Despite being full, when Fuzzy flung a two-pound fish onto the bank a few minutes later, the little blue waddled over and sniffed at it. He was about to take a bite when Fuzzy growled a warning. Immediately the drakeling was back in the shallows, snapping at more minnows, acting innocent. Addy giggled happily at her pet's antics, moving to sit on the bank and calling to it.

There was a high-pitched scream and a tiny yelp of surprise as Helen's green, having spotted a small wiggling bit of fluff, bit down on a bunny's tail, causing it to react. Both critters were frightened, the bunny leaping out from under a bush and away, even as the drakeling tumbled backward ass over teakettle. Helen snort-laughed, walking over to the little green and picking her up. "That one was a little too big for you right now, pretty lady. But don't worry, in a few weeks you'll be gobbling up bunnies as a light snack."

Five minutes later the group continued onward, the humans picking their way across the stones to the other side of the creek, the drakelings with full tummies falling asleep on their shoulders or in their arms. It didn't take them long to reach Daigath's home tree, where he and Netsirk the dark elf druidess greeted them all.

"Welcome!" Daigath got to his feet, opening his arms wide and indicating several sections of tree roots that had fashioned themselves into chairs arranged in a half circle. "Please, make yourselves comfortable. And congratulations, young ladies, on your new bonded."

They took a moment to introduce the elves to the new pets, then set them down where they could snooze comfortably on the grass and leaves. The druidess gathered up the girls and William, tempting them into following her. "I happen to know where there are several blackberry bushes ripe with the sweetest berries. Would you like to help me pick some?"

As the kids drifted away, Allistor looked to Daigath. "Sorry to just barge in on you, but we have some questions, if you don't mind?"

"Of course not, Allistor. What can I do for you?"

Helen took the first one. "About the drakes. Nearly half of them have not bonded with anyone yet."

Daigath nodded. "It is likely that at least a few of them will not bond. Some will be more feral than others, even among the bonded."

"Do we just kill the ones that refuse to bond? Or maybe sell them? Is there a market for drakes somewhere?"

Daigath nodded his head. "That is your choice. You can choose to kill them now and be done with them, set them free, or find a way to raise them as livestock. When they reach adulthood you can harvest a good deal of meat, hide and other useful parts. I'm afraid there's not much of a market for baby drakes. As I mentioned before, they're considered a nuisance in most places."

Helen offered, "We could maybe take them to Orion, set them free somewhere that isn't inhabited. Let them grow up, then hunt them for xp and materials." As a former park ranger, part of her job was husbanding the various species dwelling within her territory. Life and death were simply the normal cycle that every creature must follow. It didn't bother her to hunt and kill predators that might later become a nuisance.

The idea struck a chord with Allistor, and he closed his eyes for a moment, trying to focus on the barely formed thought Helen had inspired. The others went silent, until Helen asked "Are you in pain, or just thinking? Because on you, it's the same face either way."

Allistor shot her a finger, causing the others to chuckle as he chased the thought down. When he finally grasped it, he had a whole new question for his mentor.

"Master Daigath, as you know, I have an unaligned dungeon core. If we were to take the unbonded baby drakes into the dungeon, would they... I don't even know how to say it. Would they bond with the dungeon core, I guess? Would they become dungeon monsters that could be killed and respawn?"

The ancient elf nodded his head thoughtfully. "There is such a thing as a dragon core, though I know of only three in existence. I have never heard of a drake core, but it should be possible. I'm not one hundred percent positive I know what you mean by *respawn*, but I think I grasp the idea. In a dungeon, the enemies you defeat are regenerated using the core's energy and resources, and reborn, usually at the same level at which they perished. Dungeon inhabitants level up by killing those who enter, or feeding on each other, if no visitors appear for long periods of time."

"Resources?" Allistor asked. He had a feeling he knew the answer, but didn't want to waste the chance to obtain knowledge from Daigath.

"Dungeon cores use what is around them to power their dungeons, and their growth. Initially, newly formed cores harvest the soil, stone, minerals, flora and fauna in the vicinity of the core to create their first chamber. That chamber then acts as a collector for ambient mana, drawing it in from a limited area around the core. As the core grows larger, the draw becomes more efficient, and both mana and resources are harvested from a larger area. Cores gain experience just like any of us, by killing living creatures. To begin with it may just be worms and insects, algae and moss. But unlike us, the core can also absorb and make use of one hundred percent of the corpses. Breaking them down into mineral components or biomass that it can use to create its inhabitants."

He looked at Allistor, then over at the snoozing drakelings. "The cores that you've received are already powerful, having developed a dungeon that was then conquered. Those that defeated the dungeon harvested the core, and sold or traded it. Once you place them in their new environment, they will quickly recreate their dungeons, with a bit of modification from using local resources. For example, if a core is placed near some natural underground structures and tunnels, it may use those rather than expend the energy to create new ones. Plant or animal based cores may modify its inhabitants roster to include the local resources, rather than whatever was native to its previous world. All except for the unaligned core, of course. That one did not grow on its own, but was created artificially, and given significant power during that process."

Allistor shook his head. "It just occurred to me that we had significant trouble killing the mother drake when we found her. I'm not sure I want to send my people into a dungeon with eight or ten of them, even if they only have to face one at a time. Maybe have one as the final dungeon boss or something. I need to think about this some more."

"Wise decision." Daigath patted his shoulder.

Thinking of losing his people to a gaggle of drakes in a dungeon reminded Allistor of another question he'd been wanting to ask Daigath. "Master, Amanda has been studying the motes closely, and is working toward finding a way to resurrect our people when they're killed. It occurs to us that if resurrection were possible, we'd have heard about it by now. Harmon would have revived some of his lost troops, or something. We can't be the first to think of this, or attempt to find a way."

The old elf just stared at Allistor, his face impassive, waiting.

Allistor took that to mean he was waiting for an actual question, so he continued. "Is it possible to resurrect someone who's just been killed? I mean, we here on Earth could do that to some extent using our science, not magic. For example, someone who's heart stopped could be revived using electric shocks, at least for a little while after their death."

Daigath nodded once, a satisfied look on his face. "It is good you asked. There are rules within the System that pertain specifically to this topic, the first of which is that the information I am about to pass on to you can not be volunteered. One has to ask the question, first."

Amanda practically shoved Allistor aside as she stepped closer to Daigath, laser focused on his words.

"The short answer is yes, resurrection is possible. But only in very limited circumstances, and at significant cost." He smiled as Amanda leaned in his direction, balancing on the balls of her feet, her eyes wide. "The first thing you need to know is that not everyone can cast the required spell. It takes a great deal of mana, generally more than anyone under level one hundred can produce. It also requires mastery of several advanced healing magic spells, again something that only high level individuals have accomplished. The nature of the spell requires that the caster bind their own life force with their target for a short while, effectively lending a spark to rekindle that of the deceased. This carries a significant risk, as each time this sharing takes place, there is a chance that the healer's life force will be completely drained into their target. Especially if the deceased is a similar level, or higher level than the healer."

Amanda sat down on the ground, thinking hard. After a moment, she nodded once, and said, "It's population control, right? If the System allowed every healer to resurrect dead friends, no one would ever die. The natural order of things would be thrown out of whack, and overpopulation would put a strain on resources."

"Exactly right, my dear. When the Collective was young, when I was young, there was no risk to the healers. One still had to build up a massive mana pool, and master the necessary spells. But once those goals were achieved, they were free to revive others as often as they liked. There was a time limit, of course. Bodies had to be revived within a solar day of their death. Wealthy houses, guilds, and factions spent great amounts of wealth to level up healers to the point where they could resurrect the dead. But the System took note of what you just surmised, and a correction was made. The life force sharing factor was added, and many of the healers became unwilling to risk their lives to resurrect others. Among those still willing, many perished. The houses and factions that supported them began to forbid them from resurrecting anyone except nobles, or even the most elite like emperors or house elders. As I said before, it required a significant investment to create a healer capable of resurrection magic, and the factions protected that investment."

Amanda was about to ask another question when Daigath's eyes lifted to the sky behind the humans, looking back toward the Stronghold.

"Either your Stronghold is under attack, or they are trying to get our attention." He nodded toward Wilderness, and the others all turned in unison to see several fireballs arcing into the sky.

"Shit!" Allistor took off at a run, the other adults not far behind him. All except for Netsirk, who called out that she would watch over the kids and hatchlings.

With their improved physical forms, all of the humans were able to keep a rapid pace as they dashed through the woods, Allistor cursing at himself for not having a radio in his inventory. He could have simply called in via a relay through one of the droids at the Stronghold instead of having to take the time to run back from Daigath's clearing. Always having Nigel around, or a droid nearby, it hadn't occurred to him to grab a radio.

Allistor crossed the creek at a run, leaping far out into the water, placing one foot on a rock about midway across, before a second leap took him the rest of the way to the far shore. The others stayed with him, though Amanda was lagging behind slightly. She'd put fewer points into her physical stats, and was having to work hard to keep up. Daigath, by comparison, seemed to be holding back to keep pace with the humans and bears. His breath came easily as he moved almost silently through the forest next to Allistor.

Before they even reached the gate to Wilderness, the moment they were within Nigel's range, he spoke to them.

*"There is a large group of humanoids attacking the Warehouse Outpost in Laramie, Sire."*

"Put me through to the Outpost and the Stadium, on loudspeaker!" Allistor continued to run on through the gate, the others right behind.

*"Go ahead, Sire."*

"This is Allistor. Tell me what's happening!"

"Allistor, this is Cindy! I'm at the Warehouse." Allistor remembered her, the former prisoner that had requested to remain at the Outpost the day he and his people had freed them from Barden and claimed the property. "It… it sounds crazy, but we're being attacked by zombies! Like, really a lot of them. They've surrounded our walls and are trying to get in!" Her voice sounded half hysterical.

"Allistor this is Bob at the Stadium. We're already loading up trucks to head over there. When we couldn't reach you, I called Gralen and asked him to bring his ship over from Cheyenne. It'll be there in a few minutes."

Allistor ran toward the teleport pad. "I'll be there in thirty seconds, Bob. Wait for me. Cindy, can you hold for ten minutes?"

"We're… we're okay right now. There are only ten of us here, so we're spread a little thin. The gate is holding, but they're stacking up against the wall, climbing over top of each other!"

Allistor didn't answer right away, as at that moment Nigel transported them from Wilderness to the Stadium. As soon as he arrived, he headed toward the line of trucks that were being loaded up. "Cindy, that place used to have a lot of supplies. If they're still there, find something flammable. Oil, gas, booze, whatever. Start pouring it over the walls onto the zombie piles and then hit them with flame!"

"Already on it, Allistor! We've got the kids running to find some right now."

Allistor and company leapt onto the back of the nearest truck, and the Stadium's gate opened. The first truck in line squealed its tires as the driver accelerated out the gate and down the road toward the Outpost. Allistor held on as his truck did the same. A squad of about a hundred battle droids sprinted out the gate alongside the vehicles, matching their speed. The one closest to Allistor began transmitting. "Allistor this is Gralen. I'm five minutes away."

"Gralen! Good. You'll get there right before we do. Start blasting the enemy off the wall! Focus on the spots where the pile is nearing the top. If you have any battle droids with you, drop them inside the walls to help with the defense!"

"I've got twenty here on the ship. They already have orders to protect the residents, and to carry them away if necessary."

Allistor found he was leaning forward, willing the truck to move faster. The drivers were already speeding, moving as fast as they could on the cleared city streets between the two properties. They all had friends or family at the Outpost. As they rounded the last corner and the Outpost came into sight, Allistor cringed. It was one thing to think 'zombies' in your head, but quite another to actually see them.

There were thousands of them.

Quite literally, they were the walking dead. Reanimated human corpses in differing stages of decomposition from recently dead and mostly intact, to skeletal remains with a few tatters of skin and muscle holding them together. Some were on fire already, stumbling around and making a high keening sound that was part scream, part wail, and one hundred percent unnatural. They moved slowly, Allistor estimated about half the normal walking speed of a human. Some dragged broken or dislocated limbs. Others crawled or dragged themselves toward the walls, significant parts of their bodies missing altogether.

Even from fifty yards away, the stench hit the humans like a brick wall as they approached.

"Oh shit, that's awful." One of the men in the truck bed with Allistor said as he covered his mouth and nose with his free hand. Allistor barely heard him, already starting to channel his *Storm* spell as soon as the truck got into range. As he waited for the storm to build, he saw several others had cast Erupt, causing stone spikes to shoot

123

up from the ground into the mob of undead. But other than one that took a spike through its skull, none of the zombies went down. Several that were securely impaled simply struggled in place, reaching toward the wall in front of them. A few more spikes shot out from the wall, but the undead simply used them to pull themselves higher.

As Allistor's lightning bolts began to fall upon the undead, he heard Bob shout, "Stop wasting mana on spikes! Physical damage won't help! Did you guys never watch a movie? Use fire! If you have to shoot, shoot them in the head! Melee fighters, cut off their heads! Don't let them scratch or bite you!"

Allistor's spell was only moderately effective. The lightning bolts were stunning large groups of the undead, causing them to freeze up and, in many instances, fall over. Several rolled back down the pile they'd just climbed. And while he could see many of the corpses were scorched by the lightning, they were not catching fire. He let the spell continue for about ten seconds, then stopped channeling. Instead he began targeting the highest concentration spots and calling down *Flame Shots* as rapidly as he could. Several of his people were doing the same, flooding the area directly in front of them with fireballs and columns of fire. The trucks began to fan out, circling around the perimeter as the occupants mowed down the mobs.

More undead were still moving in from the surrounding streets toward the Outpost, and Allistor winced as he saw one of the pickup trucks collide with three of the slow-moving zombies. The impact caused the passengers in the truck bed to lurch forward, one woman falling over the side. Immediately, two of the walking corpses literally fell upon her, their rotting bodies covering her up as she screamed in terror. Two other survivors hopped off the back to pull the zombies off of her as the others refocused their attacks on any approaching undead, covering their friends. Others cast heals as the bloodied woman scrambled away to safety.

Gralen's *Opportunity* came rushing in over top of the Outpost, the guns on its underside already blasting away. It hovered over the interior for a moment, and a score of battle droids leapt out of the open cargo bay. Then Gralen piloted the ship a short distance out beyond the walls and began circling the structure, plasma guns blazing away at the undead below. The heated plasma rounds burned through the corpses like a hot knife through butter, leaving large holes in the piles that quickly collapsed under the weight of the dead bodies above.

Allistor's assigned communication droid stayed at his side as the others waded into the fight, firing plasma rifles with two of their four arms, spreading out along with the vehicles and focusing on any enemies that approached, protecting the humans rather than the Outpost.

"They're inside! Oh my god, they're in here with us!" Cindy's voice screamed out of the droid's body just a moment before Allistor heard multiple screams from inside the wall. "The children! Protect the children!" she sobbed. Allistor remembered she had a son named Jeremy that had been with her at the warehouse. His blood ran cold, and he leapt from the back of the truck, sprinting toward the wall. He drew his sword as he ran, cutting heads or legs or arms

125

off any walking corpses from behind as soon as they were within reach.

He needed to get in there. To get past the thousands, maybe tens of thousands, of walking dead that surrounded the place.

The moment he thought he was in range, he focused on a spot atop the roof of the nearest building visible above the wall, and cast *Dimensional Step*. In the blink of an eye he was stumbling across the roof, having been moving at a sprint when he arrived. It took a few seconds to stop and steady himself before he could turn and rush to the edge of the roof and look down.

Undead were streaming out of the building below him. Two of his people were already down on the ground, several biting and clawing mobs on top of each of them. Others were being scooped up by battle droids who were retreating toward another building as they and the unencumbered droids blasted away at the stream of zombies emerging from the warehouse. Allistor looked up, spotting Cindy and three others still atop the wall, facing inward and ignoring the threat outside as they fired at the zombies dogpiling the two humans on the ground.

Allistor tried casting heals on each of the two humans, but they were already gone. Second by second, pieces of them were being bitten and ripped away from their bodies. He shouted "Cindy! They're already gone! Get off that wall and down to the other building! Get behind the droids!"

He saw the woman look over at him, her face mostly blank, her stare uncomprehending, even as she continued to blindly fire a plasma rifle toward the two dogpiles. Another of the survivors atop the wall grabbed her from behind and began pulling her toward a ramp that led down into the courtyard. Two of the droids had secured the ramp and were keeping it clear for the humans to descend.

Allistor called a Flame Shot down atop one of the piles, then the other, burning the zombies and his dead citizens to a crisp. He heard Cindy wail as she was dragged down the ramp, and a moment later plasma bolts began to flash past him. He looked up to see Cindy firing at him, the blank look on her face replaced with one of anger and pain. One of the droids snatched the weapon from her hands as it scooped her up and began to run toward the others.

Allistor looked down at the smoking piles of corpses, and in his mind replayed Cindy's message about the children looking inside the buildings for something flammable. His heart wrenched when he made the connection, realizing that Cindy's son Jeremy must have been one of the two killed below.

"Nigel, what happened? How did they get in?"

"*A significant force has tunneled up from below, emerging inside the warehouse, sire.*" The AI's calm tone aggravated Allistor. "*I was unable to detect them until they entered and began to move around in the building.*"

"What? Why?" Allistor shouted at Nigel as he called down another Flame Shot on the stream of undead still emerging from the door below him. "Never mind! We'll figure that out later. How many are you detecting inside the building now?"

*"Two hundred and eighty three, with more still emerging from below, sire."*

Allistor checked his interface map, and saw a mass of red dots clustered below him, some winking out as the undead were destroyed by the droids, others winking into existence as they emerged from the hole in the floor. He gasped when, to his horror, he saw a single green dot indicating one of his people still inside the building. They were near the northwest corner, and though the vast majority of the dots were moving away toward the open bay door and the courtyard, half a dozen red dots were slowly advancing toward his citizen.

"There's someone trapped inside!" He shouted down to the droids. Immediately, six of them set out at a run toward the zombie-infested warehouse. Plasma rifles firing in two hands, a third hand swinging and stabbing with their staff weapons. Allistor called down a massive *Flame Shot* in a column that cleared dozens of the corpses from the doorway just ahead of the charging droids. The two lead droids spun their staffs horizontally and held them in two hands, effectively turning themselves into battering rams, plowing into the tightly clustered bodies and shoving them to either side. Allistor saw one of the following droids reach out with a free hand and snap a zombie's neck as it tried to regain its feet, while others simply stomped on spines and skulls as they disappeared into the building.

Allistor was about to drop down and follow them inside when more than a dozen of the corpses got back up and turned to follow the droids even as more began to push outward through the door, causing a log jam in the doorway. There was no way he could get through them. He called down another Flame Shot as he watched the half dozen green dots that indicated the droids advance across the building floor on his map. The small number of red dots that had been approaching his trapped citizen were much closer now, and the droids' progress was being slowed.

A few seconds later there was a muffled scream from inside the building, and the lone green dot winked out, turning grey.

Allistor roared in frustration, angry at losing another person when the droids were so close. Angry at himself for not being able to help enough to make a difference. He watched as the six green dots below him turned and began to make their way back toward the door. Their progress was slowed even more, and Allistor imagined they were swarmed with zombies.

A shout to his left caused him to turn toward the other building. The remaining seven humans were atop the roof, having been carried up by the droids. Several of the droids took up station next to them, while the others remained on the ground in the courtyard, mowing down the walking corpses that emerged from the warehouse Allistor stood upon.

"Gralen! I need you to pick up the people on the roof! Nigel, order the droids in the courtyard to get up on the roof and join them! And tell the droids beneath me to climb up here to this roof if they can't make it out the door!" He cast two more sets of fireballs down at the enemy below as Gralen's ship swooped down to hover inches above the other rooftop. The people boarded, two of them supporting Cindy, and the droids followed. A moment later the remaining droids from the courtyard popped up onto the roof and into the ship before it lifted off, moving toward Allistor. He continued to burn the undead below as they emerged, calling out to his AI.

"Nigel, I want you to open the gate!"

Nigel didn't answer, but Allistor saw the heavy metal double doors swing inward, allowing a crush of undead to tumble inside. Like a giant wave breaching a sea wall, the creatures piled over top of each other in their rush to get through the choke point. Allistor saw that his people outside were panicking, massing their fire attacks at the gate, unaware that Allistor had invited them in.

"Nigel, give me loudspeaker, top volume!" he called out as he saw the roof hatch open nearby and a droid arm emerge from below. He waited a moment, then shouted. "Hold your fire! Hold your fire on the gate! Let them through! Herd the others around and push them through, or let them climb over! I repeat, let them in!"

He watched as his peoples' attacks at the gate slowed, then stopped. A moment later undead heads appeared in two places atop the wall, and bodies began to spill over. A quick check showed two of the droids on the roof with him, another emerging through the hatch. He stepped up onto Opportunity's ramp and waited for the remaining droids to join him. They were all intact, but covered in blood, slime, and rotted body parts. While he waited, he asked, "Gralen, have you got any bombs on board?"

"Just one, Allistor. Left over from the power plant. It is one of the conventional bombs, I believe you call bunker busters?"

"Perfect. Get some altitude while we let these things pile inside. When I give the word, drop the bomb on the warehouse, directly over the highest concentration of enemy bodies. That has to be where they're coming up out of the hole. All of you who are outside in the trucks, as soon as you're out of targets outside the walls, back off and give the all-clear! I want you out of range of the blast. Let any stragglers on through for the bomb to deal with."

Allistor watched as the ship rose higher, more and more of the scene visible with greater altitude. He saw thousands of unmoving corpses piled up against the outside of the wall, as well as scattered across the ground further out. There were still hundreds of them drifting in from even further out, those who moved too close to his people were being cut down, while others were allowed to stumble past the trucks toward the gate.

He listened to Cindy sob and wail somewhere behind him as he waited. More of the creatures were emerging from the warehouse, but he was now out of range for spell casting. Still, he pulled several of Meg's napalm grenades from his ring and dropped them, aiming for the area just outside the door. The first landed on the roof, but splashed a good portion of its contents where he'd wanted. He adjusted slightly, then dropped three more, coating the area with the volatile liquid. Pulling a flare from his ring, he lit it, then dropped it, smiling as he saw the entire area burst into chemical flame. More undead stumbled out of the doorway only to burst into flames as well.

"Nigel, close the gate!" He called out. The gates closed, and the truck crews continued to retreat, though there were still a few dozen of the walking dead outside the walls. "Gralen, drop it!"

Allistor watched the undead burn at the warehouse doorway, unable to see the bomb drop from the belly of the ship. A few seconds later the building erupted in flame, pieces of debris and bits of animated corpses flung outward from the building.

One of the droids standing next to Allistor started transmitting a voice as he watched the mushroom cloud of smoke and flame rise from the building.

"Uhhh… boss? This is Bob. We've got a uhm… we got a corpse here waving a white flag. It's holding a piece of paper. This is creepy as hell. Should we just waste it?"

Allistor was angry, and his first impulse was to tell Bob that yes, he should burn it until it was nothing but a pile of ashes. Helen's voice replied before he could form the words. "Take the paper. Carefully. Then kill it."

Allistor took a few deep breaths, trying to calm himself. About a minute went by, then Bob's voice came across the radio again. "It's a note. A note to you, Allistor."

"What does it say?"

There was a sound of paper being ripped, and Bob began cursing quietly. Then, in a louder voice, "It says, 'Bet you wish you let your bear kill me when you had the chance.' And it's signed 'Kyle.'"

Allistor's mind reeled, trying to make a connection. "Kyle?"

Bob filled him in. "It's that little shit that you banished the day we killed Barden and his people. He was the one that refused to take the oath, and clubbed Fuzzy on the head."

Allistor remembered. He had banished Kyle after the surviving former prisoners at the warehouse had voted to let him live. It was a punch in the gut. Twice in recent days he'd been attacked by men to whom he'd shown mercy. And this time it had cost at least three lives.

"Gralen, take us back down, please. Drop off the droids, then use your guns to finish off any of the undead inside the walls. Destroy every building if you have to. Bob, you and the ground crews, take out any stragglers you

133

see outside the walls. See if you can figure out what direction they're coming from. We're going to find this Kyle, and kill him."

Even as the ship descended, Allistor heard a grimly enthusiastic reply. "Roger that, Allistor. He's gonna die slow."

Allistor turned and walked over to Cindy, who was being comforted by one of the other survivors. She sat on the floor of the cargo bay, hugging her knees and rocking back and forth. Crouching down, he reached out and took her hands in his. "I'm so sorry."

"I don't want to hear you're sorry!" She lashed out at him, the venom and rage in her voice making him lean back and release her hands. Tears poured down her cheeks from red, puffy eyes that glared daggers at him. "My little boy is gone! You were supposed to keep us safe! Why are you still alive and Jeremy isn't?" She lowered her head onto her knees and sobbed.

Allistor stoically took the blows, understanding Cindy's words to be a reaction to her loss. He did his best not to take it personally. He wanted to tell her that he'd arrived as quickly as he could. That there had been nothing he could do to save Jeremy. But he also knew that she wouldn't hear him.

Backing away slowly, he got to his feet and moved to another small group of survivors. One among them was a man with a face he recognized as being a former prisoner at the warehouse. He approached the man, a grim look on his face. "I know we lost Jeremy. Who else?"

The man swallowed hard, then took a breath. "Two more kids. Teenagers. We had given them quests to help out around the warehouse, to help level them up." He tried to take another breath, but it was ragged, and tears began to form in his eyes. "We sent them in there to find some liquid fuel when the zombies started piling up on the walls. We sent them in there to die." His voice was a hoarse whisper by the time he finished the sentence.

Allistor put a hand on the man's shoulder and squeezed. "You can't think like that. Believe me, I know. There was no way you could have expected them to come up through the ground in there. None. That building should have been a safe place, a fallback for when the enemy breached the wall. You were being overwhelmed, and needed every adult body on the wall with a weapon. Sending the kids was the right thing to do."

The man didn't look convinced, but nodded his head in acknowledgement of Allistor's words. At that moment he and everyone else that had been inside the Outpost leveled up.

The ship stopped moving underneath them, and the guns went quiet. Gralen's voice came over the intercom. "No more targets within the walls, or the immediate area outside, Allistor."

"Thank you Gralen. Please take these folks back to the Stadium. Give me thirty seconds to hop off before you go. And keep an eye out for more of these things. We still need to find out where they came from."

Allistor took one more look at Cindy, once again being held by one of her fellow survivors, then moved to the edge of the ramp and jumped. He cast *Levitate* on himself, the spell taking effect when he was about halfway to the ground. Slowly he maneuvered himself to where he saw Bob with Helen and the others, descending as he went. When he touched down, he saw the nearby corpse still holding its white flag, a large hole in its head.

Helen was first to report. "Two of the trucks are headed off that way." She pointed. "Most of the undead seem to be coming from that direction."

Bob added, "I should have guessed. Greenhill Cemetery, the old city cemetery is up that way, literally a stone's throw from the Stadium. It's the one with the potter's field where they buried unclaimed or indigent bodies for more than a century."

Allistor shook his head. "That could be... tens of thousands of bodies." He looked around at the fully dead corpses piled around the wall and in the gate. "We killed a lot here, but there could be a lot more. How are they coming to life? Is this some new twist from the System? Are all the dead on Earth coming to life?"

Daigath stepped forward, his voice a low growl. "No, Allistor. This was the work of a necromancer. One who revives and controls the dead."

"Seriously?" Allistor's eyes widened. "Friggin necromancy is a real thing, now?"

"It is a class, like any other. One that is certainly less common or popular than most others, and frowned upon on nearly every world, as most have respect for their dead. I myself consider it an abomination. Most of those that embrace the necromancer class are worlds that thrive on slavery. They purchase live slaves, work them to death, then employ necromancy to bring their corpses back and put them to work doing simple tasks like swinging a mining pick or carrying things. They retain a certain amount of basic memory from their previous lives. Especially repetitive tasks. And you don't have to feed or house the undead."

"So has a human become a necromancer? Or did one of them come here as a settler?"

Daigath looked off in the direction Bob had indicated for the cemetery. He frowned, and produced a beautiful wooden sword from his inventory. It resembled the dagger that Harmon had shown him, the one crafted by Daigath himself.

"Let us go and discover the answer to your question."

Chapter 7


Hel looked up from her work at the faint chiming sound that drifted through the mist to her left. It was her communications console letting her know that her message had been retrieved, and a response was incoming. Drifting over to the console, she used three of her tentacles to press the complex series of holokeys that unlocked that particular channel. A moment later the nervous face of a human appeared in front of her. From his end, he was not seeing her true image, but a representation of a female elf, instead.

"Report, human."

"I did as you said! But it didn't kill him. Barely killed anyone! And now I think they're hunting me!"

"Calm yourself, fool. Of course they're hunting you. Did you expect them to just accept an attack and cower before your might? Especially after you sent Allistor that ridiculous note, revealing your identity and taunting him? Where is your master?"

His face began to turn red with anger. "The lich is where he always is, in some graveyard raising more minions. We lost nearly all of the last group in the attack."

"Should you not be assisting him?"

"Did you hear me?" he exploded. "I'm being hunted! We need help! I need to get away from here to someplace safe! Someplace where we can rebuild our army even larger than before."

Hel made her species' equivalent of a disgusted face, her tentacles twitching in annoyance. Yet she kept her voice calm. "Yes, yes. This is as expected. Your master and I have already formulated plans for just such a contingency. Neither of us had much faith in you or your ability to successfully command the force you were given. Alas, we work with the tools that we have. Go and report to your master, tell him that I have said *the time is come*. He will know what to do."

Without waiting for a response she disconnected the link to Earth. The fool human had annoyed her more than enough since she began to follow his progress on the day Allistor banished him. In the beginning he showed a slight degree of promise, and a great willingness to adopt a class that most rejected out of hand. She had recognized a usable tool, and arranged for him to receive just enough assistance to survive the stabilization on his own. Now he had made himself useless to her, except maybe as bait. Still, he had served his intended purpose this day, putting yet more pressure on Allistor, while making an attack that would look like an attempt to bait him into a deadly situation.

Which in turn would further anger Baldur and Odin, and put even more pressure on her father.

And the lich had his instructions, which he would follow without fail. She had the ultimate leverage over him, after all. In a small compartment below that same console was a box containing the lich's phylactery. Should he fail her in any respect, the lich knew she would smash the stone that held his soul, ending his existence. From what the half-witted human had said, the lich was already hard at work replacing the forces that his incompetent apprentice had thrown away. She had watched the battle, even smiled when the undead forces exploited the weakness she had pointed out and emerged in the center of Allistor's Outpost. His direct interference prevented the bloodbath she had hoped for, but the end result was... satisfactory.

*****

Allistor and company had delayed their trip to the cemetery in order to loot and clear all the corpses from the Outpost, burning them where they lay. The stench was overpowering, and many humans lost their breakfasts onto the streets and sidewalks.

The warehouse under which the undead had dug themselves access was now gone, Nigel absorbing and recycling whatever the bomb had not destroyed. While they worked, Allistor asked, "Nigel, how did they dig into the compound without you detecting them?"

Daigath spoke before the AI could answer. "I'll take this one, Nigel. The AI, at its current level, has a significant sensor array and detection capabilities. Unfortunately, the sensors are keyed to detect things like heat, movement, and life energy. The undead do not possess life energy, nor do they produce a heat signature. Nigel was only able to detect them via their movement, and only once they'd broken through the floor and that movement was visible to his sensors. It is an unfortunate gap in his capabilities, and one only an individual familiar with the intricacies of the System would know to exploit."

"So you're saying Kyle had help."

Daigath gave Allistor a look that made him feel like he'd grown a second head. "I should think that would be obvious, Allistor. Even you, the highest level among the Earthlings that we're aware of, do not possess enough mana to raise so many undead in such a short period of time. There were at least ten thousand raised corpses here."

Allistor shook his head, feeling foolish. "Of course. Thank you, Master Daigath." He paused for a moment to access his UI. "I've just started repairs on the Outpost. We'll leave some droids here to guard the place, and alert us if there's another attack. I think it's time we head over to the cemetery."

They piled back onto the trucks, and Bob directed the lead vehicle toward their goal. Gralen had taken the *Opportunity* high into the sky and was moving to observe the ground ahead of them, ready to warn of any large groups of undead heading their way. The cemetery was close enough to the Stadium that Virginia had called a few thousand citizens to stand atop the walls and provide cover for Allistor and his team as they entered the grounds.

The cemetery was overgrown, having been neglected since the apocalypse. The grass was taller than many of the headstones, though little of it was left. Everywhere they looked, graves had been disturbed. Not dug up, like someone had recovered the bodies. Each one looked as if its occupant had burrowed its way out.

Allistor had decided to leave the vehicles outside the gate, and his people walked onto the cemetery grounds in groups of ten. There was a shrill whistle from atop the Stadium wall to the east, and Bob looked up with a smile to wave at Virginia, who was blowing him a kiss.

The group moved north and west, deeper into the cemetery. The groups were spread out, but only about twenty feet apart. They all stepped carefully, not wanting to fall into an open grave, or fall victim to something emerging up from the deep grass. Tensions were high, and no one spoke a word as they moved.

Eventually they reached the midpoint of the property, where a narrow paved road ran east-west across from end to end. At the center was a wide circle with a couple of abandoned vehicles still parked. Within the paved circle was a grassy area that featured a majestic old oak tree. Allistor was about to continue north, when he heard a muffled shout. His head, and every other head in the group, snapped toward the direction of the sound. A moment later one of the group that was closest to the tree called out, "Over here!"

Allistor and the rest converged on the sound, shortly finding themselves gathered around the large oak tree at the very center of the cemetery. The crowd parted for him as he approached, and moved a bit farther back when they heard him begin to growl at what he saw.

"Kyle. You sick piece of shit."

There in front of him was the man he'd banished from the warehouse. He was a year older, and had gained some weight, but it was the same man. Only now instead of an insolent smirk and angry gaze, Kyle's face held a look of sheer terror. He was bound to the tree with a length of barbed wire wrapped several times around his ankles, legs, torso, and neck. Whomever had secured him there had pulled the wire so tight that it cut through his clothes and into his skin in several places. His mouth was stuffed with filthy rags that smelled as if they'd been pulled directly from a corpse's wardrobe. Gazing at Allistor, the man struggled briefly, but his efforts only served to cause the wire to bite more deeply into his flesh. Eventually, he stopped struggling and sagged against the tree, blood dripping from several deep cuts and gouges. He tried to say something, but the rags in his mouth made the words unintelligible.

Without even thinking about it, Allistor *Identified* the man.

> *Kyle*
> *Human Necromancer*
> *Level 22*
> *Health: 3,492/9,000*

Allistor motioned toward Bob, who stepped forward and punched the man in the jaw, causing his head to slam against the trunk of the tree. Shaking his head, Allistor said, "I meant pull the rag out so he can speak. But good shot."

Smirking, Bob reached forward and used his pocket knife to snag a bit of the filthy rag and drag it out of Kyle's mouth. Kyle's face was blank, his eyes glazed after the double blow to the head a moment earlier.

"Looks like whoever your friends are, they got sick of your bullshit, Kyle." Allistor motioned toward the barbed wire. "That looks really uncomfortable."

Kyle shook his head, a little bit of focus coming back to his eyes. He spit several times, attempting to get the taste of corpse juice out of his mouth. "Water."

"Nope." Allistor shook his head, removed a water bottle from his inventory, and took a long drink before putting it away again. "You like to play with dead bodies, so we'll just let that taste linger for a while. You just killed three of our people, Kyle. Three *kids*! You have to pay for that."

"I didn't take your stupid oath! You have no authority over me! No authority to punish me!" Kyle screamed at him, his voice raw. He once again strained against his bonds for a moment, then whimpered in pain. More blood soaked into his clothing.

"He's right, you know." Helen stepped up next to Allistor, taking a moment to spit in Kyle's face before continuing. "We don't have any particular right to punish him. In fact, I don't think we should do anything to him. I vote we leave him just like this, watch him bleed out slowly, or die of thirst, whichever comes first."

"Or maybe something will come along and nibble on him." Bob added, a malicious grin on his face. "I'd be happy to sit back and watch." Several of the others murmured in agreement.

"No! You can't leave me like this!"

Allistor shook his head. "Kyle… you just said I have no authority over you. Someone clearly thought you deserved to be bound to this tree. Presumably so that we'd quickly find and kill you. Why'd they'd do that?"

Kyle's mouth clamped shut, and he glared at Allistor, hatred plain in his eyes.

"Come on, Kyle. Speak up. We know you didn't raise an army of undead all on your own. Tell us who helped you, and where they are, and maybe I'll cut you loose. Give you a little drink." Allistor retrieved the water bottle from his ring again, holding it up and shaking it slightly so that Kyle could hear the water sloshing around inside.

The man continued to resist for about half a minute, still just glaring at Allistor and the others. But eventually, he caved.

"It was the lich. Sent here by some elf woman. He found me a few days after you kicked me out, taught me the necromancer class, helped me level up. He's the one that raised the army, not me. I can only raise and control two or three corpses at a time! Now give me some water!"

"Not so fast, Kyle. Where is the lich now? And how many more undead has he raised?"

"He left! He tied me up like this and left me here! Said he had orders to go back east. Orders from that damned elf woman! He has others raising corpses somewhere else. She told him to leave me like this, I know it!" He growled in anger and pain. "He... he had about a hundred corpses with him."

"What level is the lich, Kyle?"

"What? I don't know! Too high for me to be able to see. He had enough mana to raise corpse after corpse without stopping for days."

There was a sharp intake of breath from Daigath. The old elf immediately stepped forward. "Did he use any kind of object to channel his spells? A staff, or a stone of some kind?"

Kyle spat again, a nasty glob of discolored spittle landing near Allistor's feet. "He carried a staff, yeah."

Daigath nodded, seeming relieved. He turned and walked away from the tree, passing through the crowd. Allistor turned from watching him leave, facing Kyle again.

"How do you get to be such an obnoxious ass that even an undead murderer can't stand you?"

"Water! You promised me water!"

"No, I said *maybe* I'd cut you loose and give you a drink. And I've decided not to. We're going to leave you right here to face the fate you've earned. I'm curious what will happen. I mean, the motes will keep trying to heal you, and gravity will keep causing that wire to cut deeper into you, once your legs give out and can't hold you up anymore. So maybe you live long enough to die of thirst? Or even starvation? The energy that the motes need to heal you has to come from somewhere, right?"

Amanda stepped forward and was reaching for Allistor, but Helen turned to face her and blocked her path. The ranger shook her head, a grim look on her face. Amanda froze for a moment, trying to decide whether to take on Helen to save Kyle's life. With a sad nod of her head, she stepped back.

Meanwhile Kyle had started to cry, begging for his life. "I'm sorry, okay! I was angry that you kicked me out! It's all your fault, man. If you had just let me stay there where it was safe…"

"MY FAULT!?" Allistor roared at him, balling his fists and stepping forward as if to strike the man. "You refused to take a simple oath not to harm your fellow survivors. That was all you had to do! Just not be a dick and victimize others. But you couldn't make that promise. How is that my fault!?"

"You could have let me stay without the oath." Kyle hung his head, his voice weak.

"Obviously not, you murdering little shit! First chance you got, you killed Jeremy and a couple other kids! You remember Jeremy? He never hurt you, or anyone else!" Allistor cast *Mind Spike* in his rage, causing Kyle to scream and struggle against his bonds. Which in turn did more damage to his flesh.

"Allistor!" Amanda scolded, this time stepping past Helen, who didn't try to stop her. She cast a heal on Kyle, causing many in the crowd to grumble angrily. In less than ten seconds Allistor's spell wore off, and Kyle slumped against the tree trunk. Many of his wounds had closed, but gravity cause more to appear as the wire took his full weight.

"Just kill him, Allistor. Quickly." Amanda took his hands and held them up against her heart. "He deserves a slow death. Nobody is arguing that. But what will it cost your soul to let him die like this?" She flicked her gaze over his shoulder at the crowd behind him. "What will they think of you?"

The woman who'd fallen off the pickup and almost been killed by the undead spoke up. "It'd be fine with me… let him rot here!" Amanda watched in dismay as most of the others nodded or spoke words of agreement. She felt Allistor tense, and he pulled his hands away.

"I should have let Fuzzy kill you last year." Allistor's face was dead calm as he addressed Kyle. "How many other people have you killed since then? How many humans would still be alive if I hadn't shown mercy?"

Kyle opened his mouth to speak, but never got the chance. Almost faster than anyone could follow, Allistor had his sword in hand and swung it at Kyle. The blade thunked against the tree trunk, embedding itself in the wood as the man's severed head rolled free. Allistor levered the blade out of the wood, producing a rag to clean the blade as he turned his back to the headless corpse and walked away.

"I know some of you are angry, but when you calm down later, you'll understand." There were mixed emotions in the crowd as they parted for him.

Bob was the next to speak. "Alright folks, let's go. Somebody loot him, then leave him for the scavengers."

Helen did just that, a surprised look appearing on her face as she examined the loot notifications. A moment later she called out. "Hey, guys. Come back. Everybody needs to loot him. Right now."

One by one each of them touched the still bound body, a few of them kicking the head instead. Each person's eyes unfocused, and a few of them cursed as they read their loot notifications. Allistor was the last of them, having turned around and come back. When he looted Kyle's body, he understood. He received a small amount of klax, which he ignored, and two other things that made him raise his eyebrows.

The first was a spell scroll labeled *Repel Undead*. He set it aside to give to Ramon, making a note to tell him that reproducing this one would be a priority. The second notification was the one he assumed the others were reacting to.

*Quest Received: Ditch the Lich*
*Quest Difficulty Level: Hard*
*You have engaged the undead minions of a high level necromancer, and learned that he plans to*

*raise even more on orders from a powerful unknown third party. This presents a threat to your citizens, and potentially the planet itself. Locate and destroy the lich and all its minions.*
**Reward**: *Variable experience based on number of enemies defeated; Increased reputation with all light factions.*

Allistor shook his head. "It's always something." He was just starting to make progress in uniting the remainder of the human race, and the System throws another obstacle at him. "Alright guys. We need to clear this place. I want this cemetery burned to ash. Every square inch. Get a few thousand people out here, let them practice their Flame Shot spells. Form a line and burn this place down. Send patrols down every street, through every building for a quarter mile in every direction. Burn those down too, if necessary." He paused as he noticed a significant look from Daigath. "Don't burn the trees if you can help it. And be wary of traps."

No one argued as they made their way back to the trucks and loaded up. One of the nearby droids had transmitted his orders, and by the time the vehicles reached the Stadium gate, people were already forming up inside the walls. The teleport pad was flashing every few seconds, volunteers from other properties coming to help. Allistor watched as a long procession of several thousand citizens walked out the gate and turned toward the cemetery. He climbed to the top of the wall and watched as his people moved down the various streets until they surrounded the cemetery. Then every other body began moving forward, casting fireballs and columns of fire as they went. The others remained where they were, half watching the progress in the cemetery, the other half turned to face outward to watch for incoming threats.

About two thirds of the grounds were blackened ash when progress stopped. Those who'd been doing the burning retreated back to the streets, switching places with the watchers, who in turn walked through the ash and began burning the still green areas. The first group had run out of mana, and someone had wisely rotated them out. Turning to Virginia, who was back atop the wall watching over Bob below, he said. "Please find out whose idea that was, and let me know? They deserve a promotion, whoever they are."

She smiled at him. "Of course, Allistor. And…" She paused as if unsure whether to continue, then went for it. "You did the right thing out there. Ending it quickly, I mean." She stepped forward and gave him a warm hug, which for some reason made him want to cry. But he held it in, taking a few deep breaths before disengaging.

"Thanks, I appreciate that. How's Austin doing? Getting into trouble as usual?"

Her face fell, and she shook her head. "He's crushed. Those were friends of his that died today. He would normally have been there with them, doing daily quests for experience, but one of the hunters offered to take him along this morning. They went to Pelican Bay to harvest a few feral hogs. Probably saved his life."

"I'm glad he wasn't there." Allistor patted her shoulder. "And I know I don't have to tell you this, but keep him safe, Virginia. Austin and those like him represent our future."

*****

While Amanda and Helen followed Daigath home to retrieve the kids, bears, and drakelings, Allistor stopped at Ramon's Citadel to deliver the new scroll. He gave Ramon and Nancy a brief report on what happened, and Nancy immediately left to go comfort Cindy, who had worked with her and George in the greenhouses over the winter.

As Ramon took the scroll and read it, Allistor tried sharing the lich quest with him. When he was successful, he began to look through his UI, searching for something. A minute or so later, every citizen of Invictus received the quest. Allistor had no way of knowing where the lich would appear next, and he wanted to make sure that all of his people benefitted from its death.

"This is a cool spell. Creates AoE light magic damage against undead. The first level spell covers a twenty foot circle. Double that, plus a damage bonus, for paladins and priests of any light god. It'll take about an hour to make each copy of this one." Ramon offered, bringing Allistor's focus back to him. "Most of my people aren't advanced enough to make it yet."

152

"Right. Then let's focus on making sure the raid leaders get the scrolls first, along with each Stronghold leader, and all of our inner circle. I need at least two or three people at every property to know this spell, just in case."

"I'll get right on it, boss. Who needs sleep, anyway?" Ramon sat down and got to work, calling for his assistants to bring him specific types of paper and ink. Allistor left him to it, heading back to Invictus Tower after a brief game of fetch with Max. The dog's simple joy at chasing and retrieving the stick helped to lighten Allistor's heart a bit, banishing the echoes of Cindy's hurtful words. Before stepping onto the teleport pad, he rewarded Max with a large canid steak from his inventory.

Back at Invictus headquarters, he stepped off the pad to find Longbeard and Harmon chatting with Igglesprite in the tower lobby. They all got to their feet to greet him as he approached.

"Allistor!" Harmon clapped him on the shoulder. "Master Igglesprite has returned with good news."

The little gnome, who had stood up on his chair rather than hop down before greeting Allistor, grinned happily, raising his ever-present flask in salute. "The eternity gate is being installed in orbit around Orion as we speak. It should be functional in two days. The Arkhons wished me to pass on their assurances that the second gate is ready and waiting for you to select its installation location as well. Will you be placing it here?"

Allistor shook his head. "Thank you, master Igglesprite. And no, not here at Earth. We're not ready for that kind of traffic. Maybe never will be. The space station is probably more than enough for now."

"Ah, yes. Your new space station, along with a significant portion of your military vessels, will arrive by the end of the week. Several of the cargo and colony ships are already in orbit above both Earth and Orion, as you requested."

Longbeard added, "We took the liberty o' providin' skeleton crews on each ship from among dwarven and beastkin citizens with the proper experience. Members o' Gralen's and L'olwyn's ship crews be supervisin' the recruitment. I think a few o' them hope to be made captains themselves."

Harmon cleared his throat. "Several of my people have volunteered as well. To work on the ships or space station. While they do not wish to become citizens of Invictus, they are bound by my oath to you, and you can trust that they will not betray you."

Allistor motioned for them all to sit as he did so himself. He still couldn't get used to people standing in his presence. "Thank you, all of you. And of course your people are welcome, Harmon. You have shown me that orcanin value honor, maybe even as much as dwarves." He smiled at Longbeard, who snorted.

"Have the Arkhons taken possession of the orb?" He asked the gnome, who took a swig before answering.

"Aye, they have indeed. But fear not, they will still honor their bargain with you. We have no knowledge of them ever failing to meet the terms of a trade agreement. Or ever failing to enforce them. I remind you again not to tinker with the gates in any way."

"Understood. No poking our noses into Arkhon tech. Loud n clear." Allistor smiled at the gnome, who hopped down from his seat.

"You should really get some gnome-sized furniture around here." He mumbled, adjusting his robe. "Right! I'm off to visit my old friend Daigath. He says he has some fancy new brandy to share. Which way is his home?"

"Just instruct Nigel to send you to the Wilderness Stronghold. From there, any one of my people can escort you."

"An escort won't be necessary, but thank you. And good day to you all!" The ancient gnome gave a friendly wave before toddling off to the teleport pad and disappearing.

Allistor raised an eyebrow at Harmon. "Should I be worried that he'll get lost in the woods?"

"Ha! No need to worry. Igglesprite has more tricks up his sleeve than possibly any living being within the Collective. He's likely got a ring full of teleport scrolls and such."

Longbeard cleared his throat again. "If ye have time, we should discuss in more detail yer incoming ships, staffing, and such."

"Sure, now is good. Do you want to do it here? Or head upstairs and include the others?" He looked over at Harmon. "Oh, and in case you haven't heard, we have a lich necromancer here on Earth. He and his apprentice just attacked one of our outposts with several thousand animated corpses. The apprentice is dead now, but he told us the lich was heading east."

"I did hear." Harmon growled. "My people consider necromancy to be among the worst of crimes. The dead should be honored, not defiled and abused. Any assistance you need in eliminating this lich, we will provide."

"Thank you, my friend." Allistor followed Longbeard, who was already heading toward the elevators. "It seems we're going upstairs. Nigel, please ask the kitchen to send up snacks for a dozen people? Nothing fancy."

*"Of course, Sire. And please allow me to apologize for my failure to detect the undead intruders this morning."*

Allistor stopped dead in his tracks, his mouth open, staring up at the lobby ceiling. The AI's apology surprised him. After a moment, he closed his mouth. "No need to apologize, Nigel. Daigath explained to me that whomever sent that lich to earth and ordered the attack was aware of your inability to sense the undead, and exploited it. It is no fault of yours. In fact, would an upgrade to your next level increase your ability to sense them?"

There was a slight pause before Nigel answered. *"I'm afraid that ability is still several upgrades away, Sire. But thank you for inquiring."*

Though he knew that Nigel felt no emotions, Allistor still felt a need to reassure the AI. "Well, let us take care of the first of those upgrades right now." He stepped off the elevator and opened his UI as he walked into the conference room. Taking a seat, he selected his custom-made *Nigel* tab and keyed up the next upgrade. The resource and population requirements had been more than met, so all that was required was two billion klax. He only hesitated for a second before confirming the transaction. As always, Allistor was disappointed that the System provided no fanfare with the upgrades.

"There you go, Nigel!"

*"Thank you, Sire. Your generosity knows no bounds."*

Allistor's other analysts began to file into the conference room and take seats, apparently summoned by either Longbeard or Nigel. As he was about to update them, L'olwyn spoke first.

"Your dungeon cores have all been delivered, Allistor. Lady Melise delivered the unaligned core from Or'Dralon personally a short while ago. She seemed... quite disappointed that you were not available." The elf's face was stiff as stone, but Allistor noted the twitch of a smile trying to break free. When Selby snorted, and the others chuckled, the elf finally succumbed and allowed a small smile to spread across his face. For a moment, anyway.

Longbeard saved Allistor from having to respond. "Right, then. First order o' business be yer new space station. When it's delivered, there'll be a few days o' work settin' it up like ye want it. There'll be a crew o' Stardrifter dwarves here to make sure it's all runnin' properly, and to make any modifications."

"Modifications?" Allistor asked.

Droban nodded. "I have been in communication with them over the last day or so. These are the base schematics for the station. It can be modified, within reason, at no extra cost. And more extensive modifications can be ordered at a discount from normal cost if you have them done now, while their technicians and supply ships are already here." The minotaur touched some holokeys in front of him, and a three-dimensional hologram of the space station appeared above the center of the table. It wasn't what Allistor had expected. The stations he'd seen around Orion were basically a long cylinder with several wheels of various sizes surrounding it, connected to the central core by spokes that served as access corridors or conduit runs. Some part, or all of the station, spun around the axis to generate artificial gravity.

But this one looked... imposing was the first word that came to Allistor's mind. As it turned and spun above the table, Allistor thought it looked like the designers had taken the old Earth universal biohazard symbol and made a three-dimensional version, then spent a little time adding some badassness.

There was a small rotating central ring that resembled a sort of barrel, out of which grew three larger rings in a trefoil pattern, but with their outer edges open, and coming to a point on each side of the gap. The three large rings intersected the center barrel and connected to each other in the middle. Along the outer edges of the rings were what looked like a series of docking bays for large ships, mixed in among open cargo bays that smaller vessels could fly directly into. Various towers and globes grew up from the surfaces of the outer rings, both upward and downward, and everywhere Allistor looked there were windows of every shape and size.

"At the moment, the station is in this standard configuration. It features housing units of various sizes, from barracks rooms to luxury suites, that will accommodate approximately twenty thousand. The central hub contains the engines, control center, and most of the engineering and maintenance facilities, along with offices, storage, some housing, and dining space. In an emergency the hub can be separated from the larger rings and become self-sufficient for a short period of time." Droban pushed a button and the larger rings broke apart, separating from the barrel.

"Each section of the outer rings can also function as what amounts to a life pod, if they remain structurally intact. Individual sections can be sealed off and jettisoned in the event of a catastrophic breach or security concern. The larger rings host most of the housing units, as well as cargo bays, docking and repair bays, and the merchant quarters. That is a literal term, by the way. One quarter of each of the rings is designed for shops, restaurants, and various entertainment venues. The towers that you see on the outer rings are mostly residential, and can be used as privately owned residences or hotels. The domes are hydroponics, large greenhouses designed to provide fresh fruits and vegetables to the dining facilities."

As Droban spoke, different sections of the hologram glowed green and enlarged for everyone to see. Allistor was having a little trouble determining the scale of everything, so he asked, "Droban, what are the dimensions of that hydroponics dome?"

After a brief pause, the image of the dome grew larger, and there was several lines with symbols. "The diameter of the dome is approximately two hundred feet, making the floor area of the dome approximately thirty one thousand square feet. About half of that area is actual growth bed space. Each dome accommodates four levels of growth beds, giving you a total of approximately one and a half acres of soil. The current configuration features four domes per outer ring, for a total of twelve."

"Is that enough space to grow food for twenty thousand people?" Allistor had no idea.

Harmon cleared his throat. "It's not quite that simple. The station would primarily be provisioned from here on the surface. The domes are meant to be a supplement, providing fresh herbs and consumables, as well as serving as a source of oxygen, and a filtration system. Some portion of the station's waste is treated and used for fertilizer, as well. In a pinch, one might grow enough food to feed the entire population for a short time. But in the event that the station is for some reason cut off from surface supplies, it is likely that a large portion of the population will have abandoned the station."

As Allistor nodded, Droban added, "There is also this option." A new, much larger dome appeared directly above the top of the central barrel. When it zoomed in, the interior of the dome looked like someone had cut out a small section of forest and flown it up into space. The central area was a grove of tall trees, surrounded by open meadows and scattered shrubs. Droban pushed another button, and some kind of four-legged animal appeared, scattered around the meadow and grazing.

"It can be used to raise livestock!" Allistor clapped his hands together. "That's awesome!"

Harmon chuckled. "That is quite an expensive modification, and the growth of the flora within the dome can take some time."

Allistor relaxed some. He had an entire planet on which to grow crops and trees, and a good chunk of Earth as well. Maybe a good deal more of Earth before he was done. "Alright, so maybe we don't really need that. How about defenses?"

Longbeard took over. "There be a small swarm o' tiny sensor and defense satellites that hover 'round the station at a distance. The station itself comes with weapons turrets on each o' the pointy bits ye see, as well as several

161

on the rings' surfaces, above and below.  A total o' thirty two."

"Is that enough to defend against an attack?"

Harmon shook his head.  "That depends on the attack.  It would fend off pretty much any single ship attacking the station.  Or a small group of raiders with four to six ships.  But a full military attack fleet would take or destroy the station in minutes."  Harmon grinned at him.  "For your purposes here, it should be fine.  You have ships to assist in defense, or you soon will.  And you have allies here on Earth with mutual defense pacts that would discourage all but the most powerful factions in the Collective from attacking your station.  And even those factions would need an extreme motivation to do so.  Going to war with you and your allies would be no small thing, Allistor."

Allistor felt slightly uncomfortable at that statement.  But he shrugged it off and continued.  "Cool!  So we're good with defense.  And we can grow enough food.  Is housing for twenty thousand enough for the staff, merchants, and visitors to live comfortably?"

"It is… if the crews of the ships that are docked for repairs remain aboard while they're in port."  Harmon offered.  "But if the ships are badly damaged and life support is down, for example…"

"Gotcha.  So we need to increase the housing, and maybe set aside some as reserved for ships' crews.  Maybe a couple more of those tower hotel thingies?"

Longbeard chuckled. "Aye, one additional tower per ring would be more than enough. Though it be unlikely that every ship at dock would be that badly damaged at the same time. One tower, modified into a crew quarters design with small rooms and bunk beds, would do."

Allistor thought about that scenario for a moment, then shook his head. "Let's assume that the station is going to expand in the future. Better to add extra accommodations now than to wait until we need them. They can always be closed off and shut down so they're not a power drain, right?"

Longbeard just nodded, smiling.

"Alright so let's put an extra tower with the standard hotel configuration on each of the outer rings. I assume that's like… a majority of small single rooms at the base, with the top few floors being larger fancy suites?"

"Something like that, yes." Droban confirmed. "Except the suites are on the lower levels, where there is more available floor space, they are less likely to be damaged, and in case of emergency the escape route is shorter."

"Damage! I didn't ask about shields. This thing has to have shields, right? To guard against tiny meteors and such?"

"Yes, there are several shield generators that combine to create what is effectively a bubble around the entire station."

"Well, let's increase the shield capacity. Like, a secondary system in case part of the standard system fails. Before Earth was moved, there were thousands of satellites orbiting the planet. I don't know how many of them made the trip with us, but there could be all kinds of space junk floating around out there, circling the earth at thousands of miles per hour. Or, you know, giant alien space bugs, or whatever." He grinned at the others.

His grin disappeared when they all nodded, like giant alien space bugs were a real thing to worry about.

Chapter 8


Rajesh stood on the roof of his factory building. The tallest and largest of the buildings within his territory. Next to him his uncle stood quietly, leaning slightly forward and squinting at the figure below. The two of them were observing as one of Rajesh's peasants walked slowly and with great hesitation across an open field. On the opposite side of that field was the area claimed by the slime creatures.

"Tell him to go faster. We don't have all day." Rajesh commanded. "We need to know if the jelly creatures can communicate."

His uncle sighed. "Gelatinous. Not jelly." he replied before speaking into the handheld radio. Both men saw the nervous peasant jump when his radio spoke to him. He turned his head back to look at the observers on the roof, stumbling slightly in the tall grass. The unfortunate *volunteer* did as he was told, moving slightly faster toward the line of shrubs that concealed an upright maintenance entrance to the city's network of storm drainage tunnels.

Rajesh snorted in derision when the man began to frantically wave a stick with a white cloth tied to one end. "They're aliens, uncle. The white flag will likely have no meaning to them. For all we know, they may consider that fool's gyrations to be a hostile act."

Agni nodded solemnly at his nephew's statement. "I explained that to him. But the flag makes him feel a little less nervous, and he insisted on taking it along. I could not refuse him."

Both men watched as their emissary reached the shrub line, slowing to a standstill and leaning forward to peek through the greenery. A few more hesitant steps, and he was passing through the shoulder-height shrubs. Now all they could see of him was his head as it moved slowly toward the concrete structure. He took a dozen more steps before halting suddenly.

"There!" Rajesh pointed, his voice excited. "One of the jellies is emerging!"

The man on the ground froze, his white flag held out in front of him shaking slightly as terror gripped him. The gelatinous being facing him did not approach, remaining just inside the five-foot wide tunnel opening. Standing about waist high in a roughly cubic form with rounded corners, its body quivered slightly. Sunlight reflected off of multiple objects within its form. Agni raised a set of binoculars, trying to make out details.

"The creature's body contains... several bones. A small skull, probably a rat. And some kind of silver sphere near its center."

Not caring in the slightest, Rajesh commanded. "Tell him to make contact. Speak to it!"

Agni dutifully relayed the message, speaking softly into his own radio, not wanting the peasant's radio to emit any harsh sounds that might trigger an attack. "You're doing fine. The creature is not approaching. Take a deep breath, and try speaking to it."

The man's head nodded briefly, and he lowered the white flag. Agni and Rajesh were much too far away to hear anything, but they could see him hold out his free hand as he appeared to speak to the creature. After nearly a minute with no response from the gelatinous being, Agni spoke into his radio again.

"Try tossing it a piece of the meat we gave you. Toss it close, but try not to hit it. We don't want it to think you're attacking."

Again Rajesh snorted, this time chuckling to himself. "Meat attack."

They watched as the man reached into a bag hanging from his shoulder. He extracted a lump of meat and carefully tossed it underhand toward the creature. The meat landed less than a foot in front of it, and Rajesh clapped his hands. "Well done!"

They watched as the creature's body trembled once, then began to slide forward, its lower surface undulating much like a snail's body as it moved to engulf the meat. All three men stared as the offering was slurped up into the creature's body, where it immediately began to break down, the digestive enzymes within the gelatin working quickly.

Encouraged, the man didn't wait to be given instructions. He produced a second chunk of meat and tossed it over to the creature. Unfortunately, his aim this time was not as precise. Agni gasped and held his breath when the treat actually struck the front surface of the creature's body and stuck there. The impact caused a reactive ripple through the gelatinous substance, and the creature's core flashed from silver to red in an instant.

Even as the meat was absorbed into the body, the creature elongated its form, extending itself upward until it stood as tall as the man it faced. The body began to lean backward, and the emissary took a retreating step of his own, dropping the flag and raising both hands in front of himself. Agni imagined the man was speaking placating words, apologizing whole-heartedly for accidentally striking the creature.

"What is it-?" Rajesh didn't finish his question as both men witnessed the creature's response. The upper portion of the elongated body snapped forward, the base remaining in place. A glob of the creature's flesh shot across the distance between it and the unfortunate man it faced. The man had no time to react, other than to raise his outstretched hands slightly to protect his face. The flying glob struck both hands, which did manage to block some, but not all, of the substance. The remainder passed between and struck the man's lower face, neck, and chest.

There were several seconds of stunned silence, the man looking at his hands, then down at his chest, before the flesh began to melt and the screaming started. He turned to run, his hands frantically swiping at the slime on his face and chest, though all he was doing was smearing it around, spreading it further. He stumbled through the shrubs and several yards into the field before his screams turned into a wet gurgle as the acidic substance ate into his throat. A few steps further, and he fell silently, facedown in the tall grass. Rajesh and Agni watched as his body twitched a few times, then went still.

Agni cursed loudly as both men's eyes returned to the creature that had just killed their emissary. It had not left the concrete area between the tunnel walls. Two similar creatures had advanced to either side of it, and all three seemed unwilling to move further out of the tunnel, despite the enticing meal laying just a short distance away.

"That fool!" Rajesh stomped one foot like a petulant child, an action his uncle had seem him repeat often as he grew up. "You specifically told him *not to hit* the jelly! Incompetence! I'm surrounded by incompetence!"

Feeling shaken himself, Agni tried to calm his nephew. "I'm sure it was not intentional, Rajesh. The man was terrified. And he paid dearly for his mistake."

"Get me another volunteer! One who won't piss himself in the face of danger." Rajesh demanded, stomping toward the door that would lead him back downstairs.

Agni shook his head, despairing at the uncaring attitude of his Earl. After a few deep, calming breaths, he spoke quietly into his radio again. "Three of you, go and retrieve the body. Move slowly, and keep your eyes on the creatures. If they advance, you retreat." He paused, looking at the location where the body had fallen, unable to see it in the tall grass. "And wear gloves. Take a plastic tarp to wrap him in. Don't touch any of the contaminated areas if you can help it."

*****

Allistor took Amanda's hand as they both watched the viewscreen on the bridge of the *Phoenix*. Both of their mouths, along with those of the rest of the humans on the bridge, hung open in awe. They were approaching Allistor's new space station, and though some part of him had known it would be large, the actual scope of the structure hovering in orbit above Invictus City was mind-blowing. The towers that he'd discussed with his advisors during their design session dwarfed his tower down in the city. The main central hub of the station had to be a mile long, or longer. And the partially forested green area inside the dome at the top end was enormous, looking like a small island floating in space.

Kira was guiding the ship toward one of the gigantic rings, a small section of which had opened at their approach to reveal a shuttle bay. The opening had looked tiny from a distance when it first began to open, but now that they were about to pass inside, Allistor could see that there was room for three or four ships the size of his *Phoenix* in this space.

Harmon, seeing the look on his friend's face, laughed aloud. "This is just one of dozens of shuttle bays on the station, Allistor. And each of the rings has the capacity for a score of ships to hard dock on their exterior, for passenger and small cargo transfer through the airlocks."

Amanda squeezed his hand tightly at the mention of airlocks, and Allistor turned to see her eyes were wide, a hint of perspiration on her forehead and upper lip. "You okay, my empress?"

Her eyes met his, and she shook her head. "I'm... I dunno. The idea of walking around in that place just... Allistor it's basically a giant tin can surrounded by a vacuum."

Allistor nodded, trying to find words to reassure her, when Harmon helped him out. "Lady Amanda, I have spent a great many years living aboard stations like this one. They are built to protect and preserve the lives within. There are multiple layers of safeguards in place, should a vital component fail, including force fields, pressure doors at every section juncture, reserve oxygen supplies, and constant monitoring by the controlling AIs. You feel comfortable enough here on this ship, do you not?" He waited for her to ponder for a moment, then nod. "Well you are just as safe aboard the station."

Amanda took a few deep breaths, and her death grip on Allistor's hand loosened. "Thank you, Harmon. I'll be fine, I think. Just never expected to, you know, walk around a city in space before. Takes a little getting used to."

"Are there gonna be any damned giant spiders walkin around in there?" Meg broke the tension with her anti-bug attitude. "Cuz I can't be held responsible if a friggin bug pops out at me from some side door or something." She held up one of her grenades, which Sam promptly confiscated, blowing his love a kiss when she glared up at him.

"Ha! No, Lady Meg. The station is only sparsely inhabited at the moment. The work crews that are finishing up the last of the modifications are mainly dwarves. There are a few other races mixed in, but none that should give you... pause." Harmon smiled at her. Meg just grumbled quietly in return.

"And speakin o' dwarves," Longbeard pointed toward the screen. "Our greeting party has arrived." They all turned toward the view screen, which showed a small contingent of dwarves entering the shuttle bay in front of the ship.

Longbeard led the way as all but the bridge crew headed to the lower deck and the exit ramp. Allistor followed, still holding Amanda's hand. Right behind them were William and the girls, along with Meg, Sam, Ramon, Nancy, Chloe, Michael, Gene, Harmon, Helen, and the remaining three alien advisors. Fuzzy and Fiona had opted to stay on Earth, Fuzzy showing Allistor a mental image of the woods around Daigath's home. Allistor had instructed Nigel to teleport the bears to the Wilderness Stronghold, and back, when they were ready. In the cargo bay was a small contingent of citizens that were coming along to get familiar with the station's facilities and operations. This included several of Gene's engineers and mechanics, three of their best gardeners, two of the reserve bridge crews in training, and a score of others.

Stepping off the ramp onto the shuttle bay deck, Longbeard strode forward and shook hands with the lead dwarf of the welcoming party. After a few claps on the back and some mumbled greetings, Longbeard cleared his throat, and spoke in a loud, formal tone.

"Master Engineer Cogwalker o' the Stardrifters, I present to ye Planetary Prince Allistor o' Earth, Emperor o' planet Orion, His fiancé Lady Amanda, and their advisors!"

Allistor inclined his head to the exact degree that L'olwyn had coached him to on the flight up, while the dwarves all bowed at the waist. "Welcome, yer highness, to yer new station. She ain't got a name yet, but I'm sure ye'll be resolvin' that soon enough."

"Thank you, Master Cogwalker. For the welcome, and for your hard work in preparing this incredible structure for us." Allistor answered. "And now that formal introductions are complete, please just call me Allistor." He grinned at the dwarf as somewhere behind him L'olwyn sighed with despair.

"It'd be my honor, Allistor." Cogwalker bowed slightly a second time. "And my pleasure to give ye the guided tour o' this place. Where would ye like to start?" He motioned toward the double door leading into a wide corridor.

Allistor looked unsure, glancing at Amanda, then Gene. "Well, I think we will split up, if you don't mind. Gene here and his people would love to see the engineering sections and the inner workings of this place. And while I'm sure it's fascinating, I'm afraid I'd be lost in all the technical jargon. Michael and a few others would like to see the crafting facilities first." He motioned toward his people, and Cogwalker immediately detailed a couple of his dwarves to escort them as requested.

"As for the rest of us," Allistor looked up toward the ceiling. "I guess we'll just start at the top. Does this place even have a 'top' and 'bottom'? Or is it like a ship, where you have fore, aft, port, and starboard?"

The dwarf chuckled briefly. "Aye, the answer is yes, to all o' that. When navigatin' a station such as this, ye have upper and lower decks, or up and down. We orient direction based upon the location o' the central hub. So if ye be facin' the hub and walkin, yer movin *inward*, or '*in*'. Facin' out into space, yer movin '*out*'. Lateral direction be a bit harder to get used to. Again, they be oriented on the hub. *Port* be to yer left as ye face the hub, also known as *spinward*. And *starboard* would be to yer right." He paused, waiting for Allistor and the others to indicate their understanding before he continued. "Each section be numbered and labeled to help ye navigate. And the AI can give ye the most direct route to yer destination if ye ask."

To demonstrate this last point, he led them out of the shuttle bay into the adjacent corridor. The walls were a good twenty feet apart, the ceilings just as high. Once they'd all gathered around him, he spoke to the AI. "Matilda, can ye show us the way to the habitat dome?"

"Certainly." A voice that sounded much like a female dwarf replied. "Please follow the flashing blue lights to the nearest tram. Welcome, Emperor Allistor and company. It is our pleasure to serve you." The dwarf pointed at the floor where a series of flashing blue lights led down the corridor and around a nearby corner.

"Thank you, Matilda?" Allistor raised an eyebrow at Cogwalker, who coughed and looked slightly embarrassed.

"Eh, Matilda were a lass I knew in me younger years. It be just a temporary name until ye choose one more to yer liking."

Amanda poked Allistor with her elbow. "I think Matilda is a wonderful name." Allistor just nodded his head, not really caring either way.

The dwarf cleared his throat, blushing slightly, changing the subject. "If ye'll follow the lights, we'll head to the tram. It be the fastest way to the central hub, where we can take a lift up to the dome." He motioned for Allistor and Amanda to take the lead, falling in behind them next to Longbeard.

It was a short stroll around the corner to the waiting tram, which looked like a set of three bullet train cars connected to each other. The cars were luxuriously appointed, with comfortable seats upholstered in some type of leather. The walls were an elegant shade of dark green

175

with a pattern that suggested ferns and trees. The windows were tinted, and several blank viewscreens were scattered around each car.

"Very comfy." Meg said as she bounced up and down on one of the seats. They'd all loaded into the nearest car, and there were more than enough seats for everyone. Sam took the seat next to hers, leaned back and stretched out his legs.

"These cars are better appointed than most." Cogwalker explained. "The bay you landed in is the VIP shuttle bay. This is where your wealthiest and most important visitors will normally land and enter the station."

"VIP, that's me!" Sam agreed happily.

A moment later the doors closed, and Matilda warned everyone to take a seat before the trams began to move. Allistor quickly found out why the windows were tinted when the car moved out of its station and into the tube that extended from the hub out to the ring where the shuttle bay was located. The tube was mostly clear glass or plastic, with a metal framework, and as soon as they left the station the light from both suns struck the cars.

"Ooh, it's beautiful." Sydney murmured, looking through the windows out into space. Below them was Earth in all its blue, green, and white glory. And above the horizon was their new star-filled sky. The ride was mostly quiet as they all took in the glorious sights, which included an impressive lightning storm on the planet below. In less than a minute the tram slowed down again, and the doors opened. More blue lights led Allistor and friends into the hub. They crossed another wide corridor, a short distance beyond which was a bank of elevators. The blue lights led them to a specific elevator, the innermost of the set. As Allistor approached, the doors opened on their own, and everyone boarded. The size of the lift car surprised Allistor. With more than twenty beings in the car with him, there was room for at least that many more. He could have parked an ambulance inside the thing.

The moment the doors closed, the lift began to rise. There were no floor indicators, but Allistor got the impression of great speed. Which made sense, since they were going *upward* roughly a quarter mile to get to the habitat dome at the tip of the hub.

In what seemed like no time at all, the lift came to a stop. As the doors opened to reveal the habitat within the upper dome, audible gasps escaped from most of the people behind him. Amanda squeezed his hand tightly, and to his left, William mumbled "Whoa!"

Allistor stepped out of the car, his eyes drifting upward from the vast meadow in front of him to the tall trees in the near distance, all the way up to the clear dome above them, and the stars beyond. There was a moment of dizziness as his mind struggled to process what his eyes were taking in. He blinked a few times, focusing on a cluster of stars that were brighter than the others, and taking a deep breath to steady himself. "That's... wow. This place is amazing. Beautiful!" he lowered his gaze again, taking a deep breath of air that had the clean, earthy smell of nature. "How is there already a grove of full grown trees?" He turned to look at their dwarf tour guide.

"There be a gaggle o' druids here with me team, helpin ta set up all yer habitats. At least, the basics required fer oxygen production and minimal food crops ye requested." He paused to motion to one side of the dome. "Walk with me, and I'll show ye."

The others turned to follow Cogwalker, and Allistor noted that the elevator was housed in a simple square metal structure that protruded up through the center of the grassy meadow. The dwarf was headed directly toward the dome's perimeter, he and the others leaving a trail in the tall grass. Motion off to his right caught Allistor's attention, and he saw a head pop up above the grass. The creature wasn't one he recognized, with a wide head, oversized eyes and a small nose that protruded outward slightly above an extremely wide mouth. When the creature noticed his gaze, it waved a tiny hand and smiled, revealing a large number of very sharp teeth. It nodded its head slightly, causing two large, almost winglike ears to flap in Allistor's direction.

"Uh, hello there." Allistor called out, raising his own hand in greeting. Hearing his voice, Cogwalker halted and turned, following Allistor's gaze.

"Ah, here be one o' the druids now." He waved the diminutive creature over.

As its head bobbed above the grass in their direction, Harmon whispered, "The druid is a griblin. A mixed race, half gremlin, half goblin. Much more intelligent than your average goblin, with a natural gift for tinkering and magic from their gremlin bloodlines."

"Aye, they be hardworkin' and handy to have around." Cogwalker agreed. "There be more'n a score o' griblins here on the station. About half be druids, the rest o' them workin on the engineering crew."

When the griblin arrived, it bowed deeply at the waist, its face plunging into the tall grass which tickled one of its ears, causing it to twitch. When it spoke, its voice was high-pitched, reminding Allistor of old-time cartoon chipmunks. "Greetings, great Emperor! I am Gimble, druid of the Stardrifter clan. It is a pleasure to serve you."

"Greetings, druid Gimble. And thank you for your hard work. This place is... wonderful." Allistor's smile was wide and sincere. He turned his head and motioned toward Nancy, Chloe tagging along as she stepped forward. "Nancy here is a druid as well. I'm sure she would love to ask a few questions if you have a moment?"

Gimble the griblin bowed to Nancy and then to Chloe, who was slightly taller than he was, before giving her a friendly wink. "It would be my pleasure. And are you a druid as well, small one?"

"I'm bigger than you!" Chloe grumped, causing Nancy to blush, but eliciting only a chuckle from Gimble. Realizing what she'd done, Chloe lowered her eyes. "I'm sorry. That was rude. I'm Chloe, and yes, I'm a druid just like momma. I can make stuff grow really fast! Watch!" She focused on the grass in front of Gimble's feet and cast a growth spell. Allistor heard the girls behind him start to quietly hum at the same time, using their magic to boost Chloe's spell.

Almost instantly the grass began to sprout upward while transforming into a flowering plant that gave off a pleasantly sweet scent. Gimble took a step back so as not to be overwhelmed by the quickly growing plant, his eyes shining. "That is lovely, young Chloe. What do you call it?"

Chloe bit her lower lip, her look of pride becoming one of uncertainty. She glanced up at her mother, who just smiled and nodded. "Umm... I don't know? This is a new one. Sometimes when Addy and Sydney help me with my magic, the plants don't come out like I want them to."

Gimble nodded. "That is to be expected. Spells like yours are controlled in part by the nature of the plant you select. In this case, simple grass. But the spell also incorporates your intent for the target. Anytime more than one person participates in the spell, unless you have already clearly coordinated your plan, the varying intents of the participants involved combine to create variations on the original. In this case, a lovely and fragrant mutation of the grass." He paused, and his face wrinkled as he frowned. His gaze included the two teenagers as well as Chloe. "But you must be extremely careful when you combine your talents, young ones. The variations of your uncoordinated wills can just as easily create a dangerous, even deadly mutation."

When he saw Chloe's lower lip tremble and tears begin to form in her eyes, his face softened. "Now, we must find a name for this lovely creation of yours." He looked around at the surrounding field. "And we must protect it from the herbivores that will soon roam this meadow. I imagine they would find it most tasty!" He smiled at the girls as he made a show of waving his tiny hands over the new plant. The soil beneath it rose up, creating a mound about two feet high. The griblin reached into a pouch at his side, removing several seeds which he sprinkled onto the mount around the plant. "What would you like to name it?" he asked as the seeds burrowed into the soil and disappeared.

Chloe looked at the sisters, who both nodded at her to indicate she should choose the name. Biting her lower lip once again, her face became a picture of concentration as she watched the druid cast another spell, this time over the seeds. Within seconds, the seeds sprouted, and thin root tendrils emerged from the soil. Each rose up until they were slightly taller than Chloe's new plant, with offshoots branching out to the left and right even as they thickened. In less than a minute the growths had reached out and entwined together to form a sort of short fence enclosure around the mound. Allistor saw it was just tall enough to keep hungry cows from reaching the sweet-smelling flowers within.

Chloe's eyes widened. "That was neat! I could use that spell to make more bunny houses!" She turned her eyes to the griblin. "Can you teach me that spell?"

"Of course, young Chloe. But first things first. The name?"

The little girl's gaze went from the druid to the mound. Her eyes lit up, and she beamed at the griblin.

"It's a Gimbleflower!" She gave a happy little hop and clapped her hands. The others all smiled as well.

"I think that's a wonderful name." Nancy patted her daughter on the head.

Gimble bowed his head slightly, his wide smile once again revealing very sharp teeth. "I am honored to have such a lovely creation bear my name. Thank you."

Cogwalker cleared his throat, catching Allistor's eye and nodding his head toward the elevator. "There be much to see today…"

Allistor looked at Chloe. "Maybe you and your mom would like to stay here and speak with Gimble for a bit, while the rest of us continue the tour? You can catch up with us later."

"Yes!" Chloe impulsively hugged the little druid, who stiffened in surprise for a moment, before chuckling and returning the hug.

"Good enough. Master Cogwalker, please lead the way." Allistor and company turned and followed the dwarf back toward the elevator. He couldn't resist staring up through the glass above at the stars as he walked. The view of the vast expanse outside the dome was amazing and intimidating at the same time, and he quickly developed a slight sense of vertigo as he walked. Stumbling a bit, he lowered his gaze and focused on the dwarf ahead of him. Looking to Amanda, who was still holding his hand, he saw her gaze firmly locked on the ground under their feet. "Not digging the wide open sky?"

"No." Her response was terse, and he wisely chose not to question her further. Instead he simply squeezed her hand a bit tighter and led her into the elevator behind their guide.

Once they were in the lift, Cogwalker offered, "The upper sections o' the main hub, those above the rings, be mostly operations spaces. Power generation, engineering, fabrication, storage, and the like. The outer sections of each level also include housing for the station's workers, as well as staff amenities like cafeterias, bars, mercantile spaces, exercise facilities, and the like."

Amanda spoke up first, much relaxed now that they were back in the enclosed elevator. "Can we see one of the staff sections? Maybe tour a standard living space?"

"O' course, milady." Cogwalker rattled off a level and section number for Matilda, and the elevator began to move. In mere seconds it came to a stop and the doors opened. Cogwalker once again led the group out.

"This be a mid-level staff section. The quarters be a mix of sizes, from single occupant to family cabins." He pointed at doors to his left as they walked down a corridor, indicating the outward side. "They all have viewports. Folk like to watch the stars, or the planet below, and the ships comin' and goin'." The dwarf stopped in front of the next door and put his hand on a panel, causing the door to slide open. He motioned for Amanda to lead the way.

The interior of the cabin was sparsely furnished. She stepped into a room that was approximately twenty feet wide by twenty deep, with two windows on the far wall.

Just below the windows was a sitting area with a cushioned bench and two matching chairs. To her left was a dining table and six chairs. The dwarf peeked his head in, then nodded once. "This be a family unit. Based on the size o' the table, probably three sleepin' rooms."

Amanda advanced further into the room, making room for Allistor and the others. She saw a doorway to the right, and began to explore. There was a short hall with two bedrooms along the outer wall and a bathroom opposite. All three rooms were small and functional. The bedrooms had fold-down beds attached to a side wall, as well as a small desk, chair, and closet. Each had a single viewport in the outer wall. A third, larger bedroom with its own bath sat at the end of the hallway. This one featured a larger free-standing bed in the center of the room, nightstands on either side, two closets, and a larger desk with a comfortable-looking chair.

"It's not fancy, but it seems comfortable enough." Allistor observed.

Amanda nodded, leading back to the main room so others could follow through. "With the common areas and amenities close by, they really only have to use this space for sleeping and... homework for the kids. That kind of thing." She crossed the main room to the opposite side, and found a small kitchenette setup. "They can even cook here if they want to."

"Aye." Cogwalker nodded. "Folks livin' and workin' on a crowded station need a comfortable space o' their own to decompress. Space be a valuable commodity on a station, but we learned long ago that packin' folk in like sardines causes problems." He motioned toward the soft bench under the windows. "And o'course these just be standard staff quarters. For those that clean, cook, and keep this place runnin'. Quarters for merchants, paying guests and VIPs be more spacious and better appointed."

The tour moved on through the staff area, quickly touching on one of the cafeterias, a small market section with half a dozen shops, even a gym with a small swimming pool. Cogwalker then led them back to the elevators and down to what he called the *main level*.

"This be level zero, or the main level. It aligns with the center level of the outer rings, including the shuttle bay ye landed in. This be where the main marketplaces, administrative offices, banks, and the best entertainment venues be located." He walked them into a gigantic promenade that seemed to go on forever. There were actually three levels, the upper two having open walkways and balconies above the main floor.

"So… VIPs come into one of the fancy shuttle bays, take the same short ride on the tram that we did, and it funnels them right into all the places they can spend their money." Meg observed. "I like it!"

Harmon laughed. "A woman after my own heart, Lady Meg! I have already secured a space for my own mercantile…" He paused as he looked around, then pointed. "Right over there. Location is everything, after all. And you might notice that there's a prime location for a restaurant right next door. I was hoping you might be interested in opening a business of your own. And not just because I'd enjoy having access to your delicious food a few steps away!" he chuckled as she rolled her eyes at him. "I'm betting you could convince Allistor to allow a deep discount on the rent..."

"Ha! I've got enough work already, feeding all the wayward souls Allistor's been gathering into that tower down there." She paused, then looked at Sam, who winked back at her. "But maybe I could come up here once in a while... you know, on special occasions? And train a staff to work here full time."

"Blasted orcanin!" Cogwalker mumbled under his breath, reaching into his pocket and handing something over to Harmon. When Allistor raised an eyebrow at the dwarf, Cogwalker shook his head.

"Harmon here already had me set up that space with a very specific kitchen layout. Bet me that Lady Meg here would agree to open up a top tier restaurant. Said her food will have customers traveling from distant sectors just fer a taste."

Harmon grinned like a madman, thumping the dwarf on the back. "I even had him expand the footprint, and stocked the freezer and pantry myself. Both are dimensional storage spaces, by the way. So you'll not be running out of supplies on crowded nights." He licked his lips as he put one hand on his belly. "Would you like to take a look?"

Meg chuckled at the orcanin, who was twice her size, putting her hands on her hips and looking up at him.

186

"I'll not be opening any fancy schmancy black tie restaurant full of snooty customers! Everyone will be welcome, and prices will be affordable!"

Harmon bowed his head slightly, then waved her toward the restaurant space. "As you command, Lady Meg."

They all followed her a few steps down the promenade and into the indicated space. There was a spacious foyer with a host's podium and several soft benches just inside the door. Beyond that was a cavernous wide open space with a horseshoe-shaped bar in the center. The open area was empty of any furnishings, as were the walls. Sam whistled as he took it all in, and Meg was unusually silent.

"Depending on how you set it up, there is space for as many as a hundred tables of varying sizes. You need only decide how you want it set up, and it shall be done." Harmon spoke quietly. Meg stepped toward the bar, spinning around in a full circle as she walked. Allistor could see her picturing table placements and a room full of customers. Finally she turned back to Harmon.

"You could fit our entire diner in here, two or three times. Show me the kitchen. It better be huge if you expect me to feed this many people without making them wait all night!"

"For your food, they would wait without complaint. But I think you'll find the kitchen to your liking. I modeled it after your kitchen in the tower." Harmon pointed toward the double swinging doors located behind the bar area. Meg just grunted and stomped her way through.

She got maybe three steps into the kitchen before stopping, forcing Sam to halt right behind her, where he promptly got smacked in the behind by a swinging door. They both looked around the oversized kitchen with its multiple ovens along one wall, and more than a dozen stovetops with six burners each. There were fryers and wide griddles, and prep space galore.

When Meg didn't speak up right away, Sam turned around and gave a thumbs-up through the window in the swinging door to the crowd still waiting on the other side. Eventually, Meg turned back as well, speaking absent-mindedly to them, not meeting anyone's gaze.

"Y'all go on ahead with your tour. Sam and I are gonna poke around in here for a while. Maybe make some lunch for when you're done…" Her voice drifted off as she turned back around and headed toward the walk-in freezer door. Addy and Sydney volunteered to help, charging into the kitchen and almost smacking Sam with a door again.

"Oh, you're in for a treat." Harmon said to Cogwalker. "If these girls are helping, the food will have some interesting… enhancements."

Allistor added, "If you could contact some of your people and get some temporary tables in here, I'm sure Meg will make enough to feed your entire staff."

"Aye! I can do that!" the dwarf spoke briefly into his comms, grinning the whole time. Then he asked "What would ye like to see next?"

"Maybe one of the residential towers on the outer ring?" Amanda asked. "Or... where would we stay while we're here?"

"The answer be the same fer both!" the dwarf clapped his hands. "We configured the tower nearest your landing bay to serve as yer royal residence. I can take ye there now." He turned away from the promenade and headed back toward the exit, and the tram tube beyond.

Amanda began to follow, taking Allistor by the hand and pulling him close. "An entire tower, just for us? No way!"

Allistor shrugged. "They take the whole nobility thing pretty seriously. Seems like a tremendous waste of space to me, but it wouldn't surprise me."

Overhearing, Cogwalker explained as they stepped into the tram car and it began to move. "Your private tower be smaller than most o' the others. The top several floors be your actual residence, offices, and other private spaces. There be room below that for staff, important guests, and such. And some o' the space be taken up by emergency systems. The whole tower be a self-contained safe zone should there be a problem. Power generation, water and oxygen supply for a month, food storage, armory, and so on." He paused as the tram stopped and began leading them down the corridor. "There's even a system o' maneuvering thrusters, in case ye need to separate and distance yerself from the station. And two small weapons batteries fer if ye need to defend against an attack. Though that be extremely unlikely."

As he finished speaking, they rounded a final corner just about a hundred steps or so from the landing bay. There was a short corridor with transparent walls that ended at a huge round door. "Now that's an impressive hobbit hole." Ramon mumbled.

"Looks like the entrance to a bomb shelter or nuclear silo." William added. "You could walk an elephant through there!"

Allistor agreed. The door was at least sixteen feet in diameter, taking up most of the twenty foot height of the corridor. And it looked like it weighed several tons. "Why so big?"

Cogwalker coughed into his fist, looking slightly abashed. He looked at Harmon, who took over.

"As a head of state, and owner of this station, you may find yourself entertaining a wide variety of species as your guests. Some are… larger than others. And a few require enclosed habitats transported atop hoverpads like the ones we rode when we met the queen. This tower was built to accommodate as many different scenarios as possible."

"I'm getting an elephant!" William thrust a fist in the air. "Gonna walk him right through the front door."

Amanda patted him on the head. "No elephant for you, young squire. But there's lots of room for your

190

*dragon* to grow, and still fit through the door." She grinned down at him as his eyes widened.

"Yessss!" the elephant was immediately forgotten. "But they're drakes, not dragons. Daniel says mine still might get big as a bus!"

Cogwalker cleared his throat, looking questioningly at Allistor. "The young lad has a pet drake?" Allistor sighed. It seemed there was no keeping that particular secret, no matter how hard he tried.

"We killed a mama drake who left behind a bunch of eggs. They've just recently hatched, and several of our people have bonded with hatchlings. William here was one of the first." He looked down at his beaming squire. "But we can discuss all of that later, over a meal. Let's get on with the tour, shall we?"

Just as he finished speaking, the massive round entry door in front of them began to roll to one side, revealing yet another griblin stepping through toward them. This one was wearing a tool belt and vest full of pockets and loops, each one filled with tools and gadgets of various sizes and shapes, clearly marking the griblin as one of the Stardrifter engineers. The little creature smiled and waved at Cogwalker before noticing the rest of the party. Upon recognizing Allistor, its eyes widened, and it immediately stopped walking, bowing low at the waist.

"Greetings mighty Emper-"

The griblin engineer never finished the greeting as it exploded in a bright white flash and a pink mist. The explosion was followed by the sound of screaming metal, screaming people, then the howl of rushing air. Allistor, having been nearest the blast, was knocked backward even as he was peppered with shrapnel, pieces of bone and metal gadgets from the griblin's vest lodging in his skin. Standing right behind him, Harmon was also knocked backward, but his bulk cushioned Allistor's fall. Momentarily blinded by the flash, Allistor heard more screaming, and blinked several times, moving his head back and forth as he blinked away spots caused by the flash. His eyes cleared just in time to see Amanda, who was crouched low and hugging William against her for protection, get pulled by the rush of air escaping through a newly blasted opening in the side of the corridor. He leapt forward, using every bit of strength his improved body possessed as he reached for them. William screamed as he and Amanda were sucked through the ragged hole in the wall, Allistor's reaching hand just a foot or so away. He continued to lunge toward them, but a flash of blue light registered in his still spotty vision right before his hand slammed into something solid, his head impacting it a fraction of a second later. The sound of rushing air ceased immediately.

An emergency force field had activated, sealing off the breach and preventing him from passing through. Allistor heard Cogwalker cursing loudly even as he himself screamed at the barrier in front of him.

"Noooo!"

Without thinking, he focused on the quickly retreating bodies and cast *Dimensional Step*, instantly finding himself in the vacuum of space. The cold bit at him, and his vision faded as his eyes began to freeze. Unfortunately, while he had appeared right in front of the spot Amanda and William had occupied when he cast the spell, he hadn't taken into consideration the fact that the momentum of being pushed out the hole was still moving them away.

Amanda's last act as she succumbed to the effects of exposure to space was to shove William away from herself, thrusting the boy back toward Allistor even as it sped up her own momentum in the other direction, sending her body spinning away. As Allistor's eyes froze over completely, he felt William's small body impact his hands. Latching on even as his fingers froze, he pictured the corridor and cast *Dimensional Step* again. An instant later he vaguely felt himself falling, then lost consciousness.

Chapter 9

Master Daigath was sitting on a branch of his new home tree, both hands on the trunk and his eyes closed as he communed with the tree's spirit. Each day the tree shaped itself a bit more in order to conform to the druid's desires. Daigath provided a nearly limitless supply of energy in the form of mana to feed his new friend's growth. Already it had widened its trunk to nearly triple it's original girth, which had been considerable to start with. The tree had also hollowed out large sections of its interior, opened knotholes to serve as windows, and was currently forming a staircase that wound around the exterior of its trunk from the ground up to the first level of Daigath's habitat.

The ancient elf smiled at the tree, sending it thoughts of warmth and gratitude. And though the tree was not yet as fully sentient as his previous home tree, it was growing closer.

A distant roar interrupted the druid's communion with his tree, the sound causing his eyes to pop open as it rang out loud and long. It was a sound that Daigath recognized all too well.

He hopped off his branch, using his magic to ensure a soft landing on the ground some thirty feet below. The moment he touched down, the elf dashed toward the source of the sound, which was now being repeated, and accompanied by a second, louder roar. With the ease of millennia of practice, and the natural agility of his race, Daigath rushed through the underbrush and dodged around trees without slowing in the least. It took him less than a minute to reach his destination and confirm his suspicion.

In a small open area next to a blackberry bush, he found Fuzzy and Fiona, both with muzzles and faces smeared with berry juice. The bears sat on their haunches, heads lifted toward the sky as they roared in anger and grief. Each roar ended in a sort of pained whine, sounding much like an injured dog. The ancient druid recognized what these sounds meant, having heard them before when a bonded companion lost their master. Regardless of the species of the grieving companion, the nature of the sound was always the same.

For an instant, Daigath feared that Allistor had perished. A quick check of his UI revealed that his agreement with the human was still in effect, which told him that it was instead Amanda who had died, severing her link to Fiona. Fuzzy's grief was for both the loss of a beloved friend, and sympathy for Fiona.

Daigath began to whisper words to Fiona, holding both hands in front of him in a calming motion as he slowly stepped closer. He knew from experience that bonded companions that survived their masters often lost their will to live, and perished themselves. Others lost their sense of self and went wild, sometimes injuring or killing those nearby. He finished his whispered phrase, and Fiona was enveloped in a soft green glow. Her roar of grief faded, and her head lowered as she fought to keep her eyes open, to resist the sleep spell Daigath had cast upon her. But the druid's magic was more than a match for the distressed bear, and she slowly succumbed. Her head drooped, then her body rolled to the side until she lay on the ground next to Fuzzy.

"She'll be alright, Fuzzy." Daigath took the final steps to reach the bears, laying a hand on Fuzzy's head and scratching one ear. He instantly felt the tension begin to leave the massive grizzly cub. "It is no small thing to lose your bonded. She'll need some time, and you should remain close by her side." The bear's answering growl was one of sadness and agreement. "Stay here and guard her while she sleeps, my young friend. Maybe hunt something for her to eat when she wakes? I shall go and learn what has happened."

As Fuzzy chuffed and nodded his massive head, Daigath turned and resumed his run, this time heading for the Wilderness Stronghold.

*****

Nancy and Chloe were sitting in the grass not far from the upper habitat's elevator housing, chatting with the griblin druid when alarms began to sound. Wide-eyed, their gazes flitted around the enclosure before both turned toward Gimble. "What's happening?" Nancy asked, concern in her voice.

"I do not know." Gimble raised one hand and pressed a button on a bracelet. His eyes widened, and he hopped to his feet. "There has been an explosion! We must get you both to a safer place. Come." He began to run toward the elevator, motioning for the two humans to follow. He called out "Matilda! We need the elevator, right now!" as he ran. The little creature moved surprisingly fast for having such short legs. Nancy was just getting to her feet and reaching to pick up Chloe, when Gimble disappeared in an explosive cloud of red mist. There was a moment of stunned silence as Nancy's hand moved without conscious thought to cover her daughter's eyes. Then Chloe began to wail. "Gimmmble! NOoooooo!"

Nancy's legs went weak, and she fell to a sitting position in the tall grass, clutching her sobbing daughter against her chest. Though both she and her daughter had seen more than their share of violence and death in the past year, she was having trouble processing what just happened. One moment the kindly old druid had been chatting with them in this pristine and serene meadow, happily discussing nature magic and fawning over Chloe. The next moment he was just… gone.

She was still sitting there, clutching Chloe tightly, muttering that everything would be okay, blinking in confusion and shock, when the elevator door opened and several dwarves emerged with weapons drawn.

The first dwarf took one look at the scattering of blood and biomatter just in front of the doors and began to speak into his own wrist device as two others quickly charged toward Nancy and her sobbing child, holstering their weapons as they moved. "Are you hurt?" the closest of them called out as he ran.

Nancy, shook her head slightly. "N...no. We're okay. But Gimble. He... he just disappeared. It was..." her voice drifted off as she replayed the explosion in her mind.

The first dwarf helped her to her feet as his companion gently took Chloe from her. Both dwarves quickly inspected their respective human, looking for any signs of injury. Fortunately, the griblin's speed had put him far enough from Nancy and Chloe that only a scattering of blood droplets had reached them.

"Let's get you somewhere safe. Can you walk?" The dwarf began to urge Nancy toward the elevator as his colleague carried Chloe gently ahead of them. When Nancy stumbled in the tall grass, the dwarf simply scooped her into a princess carry and began to run with her.

*****

Meg, Sam, and the girls all froze when the restaurant floor beneath them shuddered, and alarms sounded throughout the promenade. The dwarves who had been carrying in tables and chairs dropped their burdens in unison and checked their wrist communicators. Even as Meg was shouting "What the hell's going on!?" four of the dwarves dashed toward the humans while the others drew weapons and headed out of the restaurant.

"Please, there has been an incident. An explosion and hull breach." A female dwarf called out as she approached Meg. "We need to escort you all to a safe location nearby." She motioned with her hands for the four of them to move toward the back exit. Even as the humans began to follow, the other three dwarves took up positions surrounding them. They had only taken a few more steps when a second explosion, this one much nearer, sent a vibration through the promenade. The lead dwarf kicked open the rear door and stuck her head through, drawing her weapon as she checked the walkway in both directions. "All clear, let's go. Hurry, please!"

Throughout the station, Stardrifter dwarves were rounding up their human charges and escorting them to safety. Their wrist communicators were updating them in real time with shocking reports of griblins exploding in several locations within the station. At least one of the humans had been killed, and several others injured.

The dwarves cursed quietly as they worked to prevent further casualties, some taking charge of the humans while others took weapons to hand and began to hunt for their griblin clansmen. This was a dark day for the Stardrifter Clan, one that would bring great dishonor.

*****

The first thing Allistor was aware of was the sounds of crying, mixed with a chorus of voices. Some were shouting, others cursing or issuing commands. Next came excruciating pain. Every part of him hurt, from head to toe. When he took in a ragged breath, even his lungs registered searing pain. It was as if his whole body was on fire.

Which wasn't far off. He had in fact been frozen. Even as several healing spells washed over him, his nerve endings were waking up and screaming in protest over the abuse. They couldn't tell the difference between thawing and burning, and just then neither could Allistor. He let out a groan of pain, and attempted to open his eyes, but they didn't respond.

"He's awake!" Allistor heard Helen's voice cry out, half shout, half sob. He felt hands on his shoulder and chest, and the sensation made him scream. The sound that escaped his half-frozen throat was more of a strangled moan, but it was enough to make his point. He felt the hands quickly lift away from his body. Despite the pain, his lips twitched briefly when he heard Helen's next words. "You friggin idiot! What were you thinking? You should have died out there!"

The moment the words registered, he remembered. His heart began to race, and he struggled harder to open his eyes. "Amanda?" he managed to croak. Immediately, all the voices around him went silent, only the sound of crying remaining. He heard Helen sob again, and his heart sank into his stomach.

"She's... gone. There was nothing we could do, Allistor. I'm so sorry." There was a pause as she broke down, crying and sniffling. Allistor managed to open one eye enough to see a blurry image of her leaning over him, her hands covering her face. "You managed to save William, I think. He's unconscious, but alive, barely. Amanda, she... sacrificed herself. To make sure you could save him." Allistor felt more heals wash over him, and managed to open his other eye.

As his vision cleared, he turned his head to the side. Looking up from the floor and past Helen, who was kneeling beside him, he blinked away tears and saw the jagged opening in the station's hull. The force field that had sealed the breach glowed faintly. Laying between him and the hole was the tiny body of William. Ramon and two others were kneeling next to him, all three of them casting repeated healing spells.

Allistor tried to roll over, but his muscles didn't respond. And the attempt caused his abused nerve endings to scream even louder, making him groan in pain.

"Don't try to move!" Allistor thought the voice was Cogwalker's. "Ye were exposed to the vacuum of space. The motes inside ye kept ye alive, but yer body was nearly frozen, and needs time to warm up. Ye just lay there and recover! Any movement right now could do more damage. Here, drink some o' this if ye can." Allistor saw a flask move into his field of vision, then felt a small amount of liquid dribble into his open mouth. He couldn't taste it, but he felt a warmth in his throat and chest when he swallowed it down. "Yer friends be healin' ye as fast as they can. Let em do what they're doin for a bit."

Allistor wasn't in the mood to listen. He closed his eyes and pictured Amanda floating away from him as he reached out. His pulse hammered in his ears, and he could feel more tears run freely down his face. When he tried to speak, his voice sounded slightly better.

"What... happened?"

This time it was Harmon who answered. "The griblin's vest was wired with explosives. When it went off, the blast opened a breach in the hull. There have been other explosions as well. We're still trying to gather information. I will handle this, my friend. You rest. We very nearly lost you."

"Stupid fool!" Helen grumped at him, causing him to open his eyes and see her face pasty white and her eyes red and puffy. "Brave, but stupid! Don't you ever do that again!" She smacked his shoulder, causing a new flair of pain. Allistor gritted his teeth and tried not to show it.

Instead, he took a few deep breaths, the pain in his lungs slightly less now. Another wave of heals washed over him, and the pain lessened further. He licked his lips before asking, "Anyone else?"

"What?" Helen blinked at him, momentarily confused. "Oh! No, some injuries, but nothing serious. And no one else was killed, thankfully. Well, none of our people." Allistor saw her glance briefly in William's direction, a look of doubt in her eyes.

"I'm fine, go help William." He rasped at his best friend.

"William is getting plenty of attention. And I'm not so sure you're out of the woods yet. So shut up and let us help you." Another wave of healing magic. Allistor coughed, and a splatter of blood sprayed into the air, some of it coming back down to land on his face. Strangely, there wasn't much pain. "See! You're all messed up inside. Your body tried to decompress out there. You're lucky you didn't burst like a water balloon."

Harmon's voice came from somewhere outside of Allistor's field of vision. "Actually, when a body is exposed to space..." Allistor saw Helen's gaze rise above his head, and the look on her face silenced the ruler of the entire orcanin race.

Allistor lay there for what seemed like an eternity. While the pain in his body faded, the pain in his soul deepened. He thought back to moments shared with Amanda, little things like a mischievous smile, the sound of her snoring in his ear, the twinkle in her eye as she came at him with a scalpel in hand. And lastly, her hesitation at walking onto the space station.

"She was right." He mumbled to himself.

"What was that?" Helen leaned closer in order to hear him better.

"She was right. She was afraid of this place, and it killed her."

Helen shook her head, having no words for him. Somewhere behind him, Harmon answered. "This place did not take her from you, Allistor. Some ONE was responsible for this. And when we discover who that is, you and I will seek retribution together. This I swear upon my throne, and the lives of my people." Allistor gasped as the swirling glow of a binding oath enveloped his body.

"Ah, I'm sorry my friend." the orcanin stepped into sight and bowed his head.

"Ye'll have to get to em before we do." Cogwalker had ceased issuing orders into his comms and rejoined them. "This be our responsibility." He bowed deeply to Allistor. "On behalf o' me clan, I offer our deepest apologies, and acknowledge the life debt we owe ye. I dunno yet what has caused this, or who be behind it. But know that the Stardrifter clan meant ye no harm. It be our great shame to have this happen to ye on our watch, and *we will* make it right."

Allistor found himself unable to find words to respond. He acknowledged with a nod of his head, which seemed good enough for the dwarf who bowed deeply once more before turning away.

Allistor closed his eyes again, and was wallowing in his grief, sinking into a dark place, contemplating revenge. He was beginning to embrace that darkness when he heard several gasps, then some quiet cheering. He opened his eyes and turned his head just in time to hear Ramon say, "He's waking up! He's gonna be okay!"

Two of the bodies between Allistor and William stood up to hug each other, clearing a path for Allistor to see his squire's eyes blink a few times as he lay on the station floor. A moment later, they opened fully, and Allistor saw the boy's confusion and pain. Once again his heart wrenched, and he gritted his teeth against the physical aches as he moved an arm to reach out toward William.

More heals washed over both of them, and he heard a tiny, rhaspy voice ask, "What happened?"

Still kneeling on the other side of the boy's prone body, Ramon leaned closer. Eyes filled with tears, he spoke softly, his voice thick with grief. "There was an attack. You and Amanda were pushed out into space." He paused, then shook his head, unable to continue. His eyes fell to the floor, and cleared his throat.

Allistor's eyes found Harmon's. "Please, I need to be the one to tell him. Would you…?"

"Of course." Harmon crouched down and effortlessly lifted Allistor off the floor. He turned and took two steps, placing Allistor so that he was sitting upright next to William, his back against the bulkhead. Allistor took a few deep breaths, both to deal with the physical pain, and to give himself a moment to prepare. He saw William's questioning gaze fixed on him, and almost lost it. One more ragged breath, and he began.

"Hey, buddy. I'm so glad you're still with us. That was a scary thing." He paused for another breath. "I want you to know that Amanda saved you. I tried, but I wasn't close enough to grab you. She pushed you to me so that I could bring you back in here. She loved you so much, and her last thought was of you." His voice cracked, and he had to swallow a few times. The look of horror on William's face as he remembered what happened and processed the loss of Amanda nearly broke Allistor. All around them people were openly sobbing, watching the young squire's heart break.

All the dwarves in the corridor with them took a knee and bowed their heads. Allistor noticed that more than a few of them were shedding tears of their own.

Helen broke the silence, kneeling next to the boy and placing a gentle kiss on his forehead. "She will always be with you, William. Her love for you, her quick thinking and acting to save your life... that was her gift to you. She'd want you to think of her and smile, to remember the good times you shared. She'd want you to live a long and happy life."

William face crumpled as he cried, but after a few moments, he managed to whimper, "Okay, I'll try."

*****

Within the hour, all of Allistor's people had been rounded up and escorted back onto the *Phoenix*. Helen had broken the news to the others as Allistor and William were carried to the ship's infirmary. Allistor felt like a coward for not telling them the bad news himself, but he just couldn't face them right then. He was mentally and physically exhausted, and just wanted to hide in a dark room and grieve.

William had fallen asleep, thankfully, and the only other person in the infirmary with them was Meg. He had asked her to leave them alone, and she had responded with threats and insults that were so Meg that Allistor wanted to hug her. Then she went quiet and just stared at him for a moment, before bending to kiss his forehead. He heard her mumble "Stupid boy" before she'd turned and grabbed a chair to pull over next to his bed.

Harmon had them hold orbit for a while, an escort of a dozen orcanin ships surrounding them for protection while his people cleared all the airspace for a thousand miles in every direction. When it was clear that the path from the station to Invictus was secure, the *Phoenix* took them home.

Allistor wanted to walk from the parking garage back to the tower, but Meg forbid it. He and his squire were both transported on hover pads, his people gathered around him, and a small army of heavily armed and angry orcanin surrounding them. Sydney and Addy walked on either side of William, each holding one of his hands as he slept. The girls were humming a sad tune that sounded like a lullaby, and Allistor hoped it would keep William asleep for a good long time.

Back at the tower, most of his party broke off to share the news and answer questions. Sam organized people to send to each of the Strongholds to relay the information in person. Meg and Helen accompanied Allistor, William, and the girls up to their quarters. Meg tried to tuck Allistor into bed, but he just couldn't face the bedroom he and Amanda had so recently shared. Meg eventually agreed to let him sit quietly on the sofa with his feet up and half a dozen blankets covering him. Helen and the girls put William to bed, then returned to sit with Allistor and Meg.

"Can you eat?" Meg asked. "I can have some food sent up. Whatever you want. I... I don't know what to do for somebody that nearly froze and exploded at the same time. Maybe some warm soup?" the woman chattered, clearly rattled.

"Meg, I'm okay. Really. And if you don't quit being nice to me, I'm gonna get off this couch and try to kiss you." He gave her a small smile as he said it, which grew a bit wider when she snorted at him. The smile faded quickly when he saw more tears forming in her eyes and she looked away. Her moment of weakness triggered something in him, and he cleared his throat.

"She loved you, Meg. Just like I do. You've been a friend and mother to us since day one, and now that she's gone, I'm gonna need you even more. So let's all have a good cry, and tomorrow or the next day we'll all get together and say goodbye. We've all lost enough people this year to know that we can't dwell on our sorrow. We've got to get up and keep living." He paused, looking from Meg to the girls, then to Helen. "You know that's what she'd want us to do."

The others all nodded their heads, the girls hugging each other tightly. A short time later, the two of them went off to their rooms. Meg muttered something about making sure everyone got fed before lightly slapping Allistor's cheek a couple times and planting another kiss on his forehead. As she stepped onto the elevator, Helen made a show of settling into the armchair she occupied, putting her feet up on the coffee table.

"Don't mind me, I'm just gonna hang out here for a bit. Make sure you don't do anything stupid. You look fully healed, but if you try n get up off that couch I'll smack you so hard you won't remember your name."

Allistor shook his head. "I love you, too. Could you maybe take three or four of these blankets off me now? I feel like Fuzzy's laying on top of me and-" He froze, his eyes widening the same time as Helen's. "Oh no. Fiona!"

"Don't you move! I'll handle this." Helen was already on her feet. She quickly snatched all the blankets off of Allistor as she rushed past him, then threw one back over her shoulder as she realized she'd taken them all. It hit him in the face. A moment later she was on the elevator and gone.

"Nigel, can you tell me where Fuzzy and Fiona are?" Allistor asked the ceiling.

"*Fuzzy and Fiona left the Wilderness Stronghold several hours ago, and have not returned. However, Master Daigath is currently at that facility, and has expressed a desire to speak with you, when you feel up to it. Please accept my condolences on the passing of Lady Amanda, sire. She will be missed by all.*"

Allistor felt a lump in his throat. After a long moment, he managed to swallow. "Thank you Nigel. Please instruct Helen to find Daigath at Wilderness. And let Daigath know he's welcome here anytime. Explain to him that if I tried to go see him now Meg would be very angry.

*"Of course, sire."*

Despite the jumble of emotions and thoughts racing through Allistor's head, he closed his eyes and slowly drifted off to sleep. When he awakened several hours later, he found Daigath sitting in the chair Helen had vacated. On the table between them was a pile of neatly folded blankets. There was also a plate of fruit with a cup of chicken soup sitting in front of Allistor. Daigath appeared to be finishing one of Meg's scones, popping the last bit into his mouth and chewing calmly before swallowing.

"Fiona will be okay, I believe." He smiled at Allistor. "I was nearby when her bond with Amanda was severed. I am sorry for your loss, Allistor. She was a wonderful lady, and I quite liked her." The elf bowed his head slightly.

"Thank you, Master Daigath. I'm sorry I was asleep when you arrived. I hope you haven't been waiting long?"

Daigath shook his head. "When you are as old as I am, 'long' is a relative term. I understand you nearly perished yourself today, saving young William. I know that in the coming days you will doubt yourself, even berate yourself, and feel guilty for not saving them both. I spoke to Harmon, and he told me exactly what happened. There was nothing more that you could have done. In fact, it was a miracle you were able to retrieve William. An act of great sacrifice from Lady Amanda. Yet another reason to admire her."

Allistor shook his head, tears forming again. "I could have saved them both. I teleported myself out there without calculating how fast they were going. I should have known better, If I'd only jumped further out..."

"No!" Daigath leaned forward in his seat. "If you had taken the time to do that calculation, assuming you are even capable of getting it right, they would have been out of range of your *Dimensional Step* spell. By acting quickly, you got yourself close enough that Amanda was able to help you save William. That was the best possible result in the circumstance thrust upon you. You need to get those 'if only' thoughts out of your head. Such unfounded self-doubt might cripple you, and there are many thousands of people out there depending on you."

Allistor sat there in silence. He had grown angry as Daigath lectured him, and had to restrain himself to keep from lashing out. The old elf watched him, his face stoic as Allistor took some deep breaths and considered his words. Despite his anger, and his self-doubts, he found some comfort in his mentor's words.

"I will try." He unconsciously echoed Williams words from earlier.

Daigath nodded once, leaning back in his chair and producing another of Meg's scones. "Helen is with Fuzzy and Fiona. I put Fiona to sleep, to give her time to adjust to the loss of her bond, and to keep her from causing any harm in her grief. I expect she will survive, though I do not know what her mental condition will be. Fortunately, the bond was relatively new."

"Thank you for that. And for coming here." Allistor paused. "When you spoke to Harmon, did he give you any indication of who did this, or why?"

Daigath shook his head. "Our mutual friend is literally scouring the Collective for information. He has applied the full weight and might of the Orcanin Empire to the problem, and has recruited many of your allies as well. Including the Or'Dralon. The Stardrifter Clan is also creating quite a stir already. They will not rest until they have punished those responsible and restored their honor." The old elf paused to take a bite of his scone, chewing thoughtfully for a moment. "I must say, I would not wish to be the one responsible for this cowardly attack. They now have some very powerful forces aligned against them."

Chapter 10

Loki sat in his new home atop the Hawaiian volcano, his dark mood causing the mists around him to swirl with agitation. Two facts contributed to this mood. First, the human prince had been attacked, his mate killed. Second, Odin and Baldur were going to punish Loki for that, though he was not behind the attack.

Baldur's warning replayed in his mind as he awaited his arrival. It would not be long, he knew. And Loki would, of course, attempt to convince Baldur that he was innocent. He had, in fact, discovered and eliminated several threats to the young prince. Each time it had galled him to do so, but his fear of Odin's wrath was greater than his pride. So he had protected the human.

Loki had been working on expanding his territory on Earth when he received notification of the attack. His aim was to thwart the human's plan to expand his holdings on the planet and become Emperor. Having fully claimed this island and the surrounding Hawaiian islands, Loki had moved westward. He now owned the entirety of an island nation formerly known as New Zealand, and large swathes of a nearly empty continent known as Australia. Most of the continent had already been sparsely populated prior to the Assimilation. During Stabilization the population centers were quickly overrun, as few of the humans possessed any weapons with which to defend themselves. The larger population centers still held several Strongholds, and even a couple Citadels constructed by human survivors. But Loki had claimed more than ninety percent of the land mass. He'd been standing atop a large reddish colored flat plateau and surveying his new property when his comms bracelet alerted him to the attack.

With a thought he activated his private teleport system, returning his body to his base atop the volcano. His initial thought was to barricade himself inside, and fight Baldur when he came. But as strong and as skilled as he was, Loki was no match for the combined wrath of Baldur and Odin. And though he could be on his flagship in an instant, and could flee the system within seconds, he knew there was no place he could go that Odin could not follow.

So he spent his remaining time attempting to ascertain whether Hel was behind the attack. If his daughter was the cause of this, he had taken steps to ensure that her demise would precede his own. The simple push of a button on a device implanted in his chest would vaporize her along with her entire lab complex. That same device was designed to trigger if his heart ceased beating. He could, of course, have eliminated her in this way at any time. But it would be a crude act of vengeance, and that was not his style. The two of them had spent eons attempting to best each other, to find devious and unexpected ways to murder each other, or steal power from the other. He wanted his final victory over her to be elegant and slow, with her being fully aware of the means of her defeat as she perished. Not a quick and brutal explosion.

Getting up from his seat, Loki approached a holo-display and used four of his tentacles to adjust the multiple feeds. His eyes widened slightly as he noted a communication from one of his trusted agents. Another quick adjustment, and he was observing Hel in her own communications center. She appeared to be trying just as urgently to discover the identity of the humans' attackers.

"Interesting." He mumbled to himself.

"What is so interesting?" Baldur's voice echoed through the mists from behind Loki, who resisted the urge to spin and face his brother.

"I know you will not believe me when I say this, Baldur. But I was not responsible for the attack on your pet human. I was just attempting to discover if my daughter was the culprit, but my sources, and my own eyes, tell me that she is also investigating. Which may mean nothing." Loki sighed, the mists swirling in an elegant and almost mournful pattern around him.

Baldur took a step toward Loki, the mists transferring the righteous anger radiating from him. "Surprisingly enough, brother, I believe that you did not order this attack. Not that it matters. I warned you that any harm that came to Allistor would mean your end. Failing to protect him condemns you just as surely as attacking him yourself."

"I *have been* protecting him, Baldur. See for yourself." Loki waved toward his holo display, then moved to activate a file. The entire display filled with a multitude of images and data that flashed so quickly no human mind could have absorbed them. But Baldur's eyes glowed as he took it all in, his head nodding once. The information revealed nearly a score of plots against Allistor and Invictus that Loki had discovered and put an end to.

"Assuming this information is not fabricated, I commend you for these actions, brother. But none of this changes the fact that you ultimately failed to protect him. The blast that killed his mate could easily have taken him as well, and in fact very nearly did so. You will come with me, now. Do not resist, brother. As much as I would enjoy ending your mortal existence here and now, Odin has decreed that we see to some business first. Will you cooperate?"

Loki took only a fraction of a second to think it over. If he were to fight Baldur, he would certainly lose. Whatever business Odin had in mind, remaining alive a while longer might afford him an opportunity to somehow save his own mortal existence. Or to ensure that Hel took the blame and shared his fate. His agents would continue to gather and relay any useful information he might use toward those ends. He nodded his head once, all of his tentacles lowering in submission.

A moment later both Loki and Baldur disappeared, the vacuum left by their sudden absence causing the mists to swirl violently for a moment before settling.

*****

Allistor awoke on the sofa just as the sun was rising. Sitting up and yawning while stretching, he enjoyed several seconds of peace before the memory of the previous day's events hit him. He leaned back as if hit by a physical blow, closing his eyes and covering his face with his hands.

"Amanda. I'm so sorry." He whispered to himself. He sat there for several minutes, trying to reconcile his feelings of guilt with Daigath's insistence that there was nothing he could have done.

Eventually he caught wind of his own body odor, and got to his feet. Heading through the master bedroom to the bath, more tears fell down his cheeks. This was her place. Hers and his, together.

As he stripped down and stepped into the shower, he told himself what he'd told the others last night. He needed to accept that Amanda was gone, deal with the grief, then suck it up and move on. Daigath had been right about his people depending on him. As much as he wanted to curl up in a ball on the bed and lay there in the dark, he couldn't.

Leaning against the wall of the shower, he let himself cry. He sobbed under the warm spray of the water, pounding his fists against the tile a few times. Looking up, he let the water wash away the snot leaking from his nose along with the tears. Clenching his teeth and his fists, he held in the scream of grief and loss he wanted to let loose.

The young ones were still asleep, and he didn't want to alarm them.

A minute later he stepped out of the shower and quickly dressed. As quietly as he could, he left the master suite, then the residence. Taking the elevator to the roof, he stepped out past his smithy and the lounge area. Standing at the very edge of the roof, he spread his arms wide, looked up at the first of the rising suns, and took a deep breath.

He screamed as loudly as he could, pushing all of his sorrow and guilt into the sound. Trying his best to shatter the sun with his pain. When he ran out of air, he took a deep breath and did it again. He felt slightly better when he was through. Looking down at the street far below, he entertained a brief urge to simply fall. To end all his sorrow, to lift the burden of all his responsibilities.

But the urge was short-lived. All it took was imagining the look on William's face upon learning Allistor had taken the easy way out. He couldn't do that to his squire, his son. Or the girls, Helen, Meg, and the rest of his loved ones.

Stepping back from the edge, Allistor returned to the sitting area in his quarters and waited for his kids to wake up.

As he sat there, he spoke quietly to the air in front of him. "Nigel, quiet mode, please. I would like you to notify all of my advisors to arrange a memorial service. We'll hold it at noon today, at the Bastion. Any citizen who wishes to attend is welcome."

Nigel's reply was barely above a whisper, as requested. *"Of course, sire. Preparations are already underway, and I shall inform all necessary parties of your instructions."* There was a pause, as if the AI was uncertain whether to continue. *"Also, sire, I have received several messages of condolences from various parties and factions. Would you like to hear them now?"*

Allistor shook his head. He wasn't ready for that just yet. He needed to be strong for the kids this morning, and wanted to focus on that. "Not now, Nigel. Unless... do any of them require an immediate response?"

*"I am... uncertain, sire. None of them state a request for a response. However I am not fully familiar with the social conventions that apply. I am sorry."*

Allistor smiled slightly, despite his mood. "Maybe with the next upgrade, eh Nigel?"

*"I can only hope, sire."*

"Please relay all those messages to L'olwyn and ask him to see me if there is any urgent action needed."

*"Very good, sire."*

Allistor zoned out for a while, expecting William and the girls to sleep for a few more hours. He thought about the upcoming service, and what he might say. He didn't think he was capable of finding the words to properly describe Amanda and how he felt about her. But he'd do his best.

He was contemplating what he might do when they figured out who had attacked them, when he was distracted by the sound of the elevator doors opening. After shaking himself awake, he was surprised to see Sydney and Addy stepping off the elevator, each carrying a tray of food.

"I thought you two were still asleep."

Addy shook her head. "We got up early to help Meg and Sam. We knew there would be a lot of people gathering today, and we'll need to be ready to feed them all."

Sydney set a tray on the table in front of Allistor. "Meg alerted all the kitchen staff everywhere in Invictus to start preparing last night."

Allistor was touched, and it took him a moment to be able to speak. "Thank you, girls." He looked down at the breakfast spread that included large quantities of pancakes, bacon, eggs, cereal, fruit, coffee, and juice. "This looks amazing. I'm not sure when William will wake up, so let's eat. Just be sure and save some for him."

He and the girls grabbed plates and served themselves. They ate quietly for a while, each of them focused on their plate, not meeting each other's eyes or speaking. Eventually Allistor cleared his throat and quietly asked, "How are you doing?"

Sydney looked up first, tears in her eyes. She sniffed loudly, wiping her nose with her sleeve. "I miss her so much already. I… it's hard to believe she's really gone."

"Yeah, me too." Allistor set down his fork. "We just need to stick together extra close for a while, help each other accept it."

Addy got up and moved to sit on the sofa next to him, wrapping him in a tight hug, which he gently returned. When she let loose, she looked up at him with red, puffy eyes. "I just don't understand. Why would anyone want to hurt Amanda? She only ever helped people!"

Allistor gathered her against him with one arm, then motioned for Sydney to come sit on his other side, and hugged her close too. "Listen, guys. I think whoever did this wasn't trying to hurt Amanda specifically. I think they were after me, as the leader of our people, but mostly I think they just wanted to hurt all of us in general. Amanda just happened to be the one they got. We should be thankful that she was the only one. That bomb could have taken William, or anyone else there with us. And the other bombs could have done the same."

Addy growled. "We're going to kill them, right? Whoever they are? They deserve it!"

Allistor squeezed her again. "You just leave that to me. For now, I need you both to focus on helping me watch over William." He lowered his voice to a whisper. "He's going to be dealing with some pretty rough feelings. He'll blame himself for her death, because she sacrificed herself to save him. We need to show him all the love and support we can, okay?"

Both girls nodded their heads, wiping their eyes. Sydney poked him in the ribs. "Of course we will. You didn't even need to ask."

"Ask what?" William's sleepy voice caused them all to turn. He was standing in the doorway, scratching his head as he yawned. "I smell pancakes."

The girls jumped up and mobbed him, burying him in hugs before leading him over to sit next to Allistor on the sofa. They immediately went to work dishing up a plate for him as Allistor put a hand on his shoulder.

"How are you feeling, buddy? All healed up?"

William didn't look up at him, staring instead at his hands, which were folded in his lap. "All but my heart. I think that's broken forever." he whispered.

Allistor bit his lip as both girls froze and looked at William. Addy sobbed, setting down the plate she'd been dishing up and lunging at the little boy, wrapping her arms around him. Sydney just stared, fresh tears trailing down her cheeks.

Allistor took a deep breath, squeezing William's shoulder. "I know it feels like that, William. We all feel that way, because we all loved her. And she loved us. Especially you." He reached down and put a finger under William's chin to lift it up. "You know, she used to tell me sometimes, when we were getting ready to sleep, that she was rooting for you to bonk me on the head with your staff. She'd say she was going to find a way to distract me so that

I didn't renew my barrier in time, and you'd get to smack me."

William sniffed, giving Allistor a slight smile. "That would have been cool."

"For you, maybe." Allistor snorted, giving William a wink. "You wouldn't be the one getting bonked." He turned to look at each of the girls. "We talked about you two quite a bit as well. She was looking forward to the first time one of you brought home a boy you like. Warned me several times not to be too hard on them, or scare them away." He paused and did his best to smile for both of them. "I make no promises!"

The girls both rolled their eyes at him, and a moment later they were all buried in a group hug that almost tipped the sofa over backward. After several seconds William's muffled voice drifted out of the pile. "Pancakes?"

*****

Breakfast consumed, they each retired to their rooms to dress for the memorial service. Allistor was dressed and waiting on the kids when L'olwyn entered the apartment. "Good morning, Allistor. My most sincere condolences for your loss. Lady Amanda's beauty and kind heart will be sorely missed." He bowed his head and held the pose for several seconds.

"Thank you, L'olwyn. Are the preparations underway?"

"They are nearly complete. That is actually why I have been required to come and disturb you this morning. I have reviewed the various and several incoming messages, and more than a few of them are requests from friends or allies who wish to attend, if you would not consider it an intrusion."

Allistor considered it. He wasn't sure he wanted to share their pain with relative strangers. "Like who?"

The Or'Dralon, Stardrifter Clan, a few others you've met and who were fond of Lady Amanda. And..." the elf paused and looked uncomfortable. When he didn't speak for several seconds, Allistor glared at him.

"Out with it, L'olwyn. And... who?"

"Emperor Harmon has relayed a request from High Lord Baldur to attend and offer his condolences, sire."

Distracted, Allistor didn't immediately make the connection. "Baldur?"

The advisor cleared his throat. "One of the Ancient Ones, Allistor. Of the race responsible for Earth being inducted into the Collective."

Allistor was immediately furious! "You... what!? How dare they? What kind of assholes... No!" He jumped to his feet and stomped back and forth across the room.

L'olwyn waited uncomfortably as Allistor vented his anger. When he'd calmed enough to retake his seat, the elf sighed and continued. "Emperor Harmon warned that you'd be unwilling and angry. He bade me ask that, in the name of your friendship, you allow him to speak to you before denying Baldur's request."

Allistor's eyes flashed with anger as he turned his gaze on L'olwyn. "Oh he did, did he?"

Straightening his posture, which Allistor wouldn't have believed could get any stiffer, the elf held up one hand. "This is no small request, sire... Allistor. I advise you to take a few breaths and consider what I've just told you. The leader of an entire race, and the non-human who has perhaps shown you the most friendship of any being you've encountered, has made an earnest and solemn request that you simply speak with him before making a rash and emotional decision that could have *dire consequences for you and your people.*"

The elf's tone, and the emphasis at the end of his statement, were enough to make Allistor pause. He did as L'olwyn suggested and took several long, deep breaths, trying to calm himself. When his heartrate had slowed to some extent, he nodded at his advisor, who instantly said, "Nigel, please ask Emperor Harmon to join us." Looking at Allistor, he added, "He's waiting down in the lobby."

Allistor got to his feet again and paced for the minute or so it took for Harmon to arrive. As soon as he stepped off the elevator, he spoke. "Thank you for agreeing to discuss this with me, Allistor."

Feeling peevish and manipulated, Allistor barked back. "There had better be a damned good reason for you to think I should accept this." L'olwyn sighed at his rudeness, but Harmon just shrugged it off.

"There are several, in fact. Please, let us sit, and I will explain."

Allistor took a seat, and Harmon claimed a nearby armchair, completely filling it with his orcanin bulk. "I have told you before that I have been in contact with the Ancient Ones over the years, and more importantly, since Earth was inducted ahead of schedule. I have also told you that Odin and Baldur suspected that Loki was the one behind that tragedy."

"I remember." Allistor growled.

"I have just learned several things that you should know. First, they have informed me that they have solid suspicion of Loki's guilt in the Induction. Also, they suspect he is behind several of the unfortunate events that have befallen you and your friends since then. Either Loki, or his daughter, Hel. Baldur confronted Loki after the harvester incident and the close call with the hatchlings. At that time he not only forbid Loki from attempting to interfere with or harm you again, but tasked him with *making sure no further harm befell you.*" He paused for a moment to let that information sink in.

When he saw Allistor was considering the implications of what he'd shared, Harmon continued.

"Odin himself has assured me that he believes neither Loki nor Hel were responsible for the attacks that took Lady Amanda from us. However, Loki did fail in his task of protecting you. For that failure, in addition to a long list of other misdeeds, his life is forfeit. Baldur has, upon Odin's command, requested that he be allowed to bring Loki here. Not only to apologize, but to offer you the chance to claim Loki's life."

Allistor froze.

This was what he'd been pushing for. Pushing not just himself, but all his people. Trying to make them strong enough to not only survive in their new world, but to take the fight to the ones responsible for all of this. The ones who nearly eliminated the human race and left the survivors fighting for every breath, every morsel of food.

It was too good to be true.

"What's the catch?" Allistor watched Harmon's face closely. He hadn't known the orcanin long, but he thought he had a pretty good handle on his friend's expressions.

"The catch?" Harmon appeared confused for a moment. "Ah, I see. What you would call the catch is that Baldur will ask that you hear him out, listen to what he has to say. About Earth's induction, all of it. And my guess is that he will offer you the chance to show mercy."

"Why would I do that? If what you're telling me is true, Loki is responsible for billions of deaths just on this planet. The deaths of my family, and so many friends who have become family. And regardless of whether or not Amanda's death was the direct result of his orders, Loki put us in this situation in the first place. She'd be alive if it weren't for him!" Allistor was breathing hard, his fists clenched. He could feel tears forming in his eyes again, but they were tears of anger and frustration this time.

Harmon held up both hands in a calming gesture. "I am not advocating for mercy, Allistor. You should know by now, that's not my style." He flashed a wicked grin at his human friend. "I'm saying that from what I know of Baldur, his inclination is toward mercy. He is slow to anger, and always tries to see both sides of an issue. His demeanor, his beliefs, are the basis for the concepts of justice on many worlds that he and his people have fostered over the eons. Including, I suspect, this one." Harmon looked to L'olwyn, who nodded his agreement.

"As to mercy for Loki, I suspect that Baldur will offer you a significant reward for not taking Loki's life when it is offered. Amanda's death has... altered the timeline Odin and Baldur were working from. Loki is quite skilled at what he does, gathering information, using it to further his own purposes without drawing attention. It was expected he would be more successful in protecting you. Honor demands that Loki's failure be met with the punishment Baldur had already proscribed. And the public, widely viewed nature of her death has its own consequences. Still, Baldur would likely prefer to keep Loki around for some time yet, for investigative purposes and... let's call it intelligence gathering, before carrying out his ultimate punishment."

L'olwyn cleared his throat, obviously wishing to add something. Allistor nodded for him to speak. "I feel it only prudent to point out as your advisor, Allistor, that taking the life of an ancient being such as Loki would grant you a nearly unfathomable amount of experience. Thus making you many times more powerful than you already are."

"Like, how many levels are we talking?" Allistor thought back to when Helen accidentally promoted him by granting him parklands, and the significant jump in levels he received.

The elf looked to Harmon, who shook his head and shrugged. Tapping his chin, L'olwyn thought it over for a moment. "I'm afraid that's unknown. I doubt someone at your current level has ever defeated a being on par with an Ancient One. I'm sure the System would put some kind of limit on your growth. But it would likely mean hundreds of levels of growth for you."

Harmon leaned forward in his chair. "Loki is one of the most ancient and powerful beings still living within the Collective. Even Baldur would probably not be able to end his life without Odin's help. Or direct action by the System. Most of the Ancient Ones have long ago abandoned their mortal forms and ascended to another form of existence. Taking his life, even with the help of Odin and Baldur, would advance you to a higher level than myself or anyone you've met, with the possible exception of Master Daigath."

Allistor's head began to spin with ideas, imagining what he might be able to accomplish with that kind of power. His eyes unfocused as he pictured himself becoming Emperor of Earth, then expanding the human influence across the galaxy. He'd no longer need to be afraid of factions like the Or'Dralon. He could track down whomever was responsible for the attack on the space station and make them suffer for Amanda's death...

Allistor phrased his next words carefully. "Please inform Baldur that he is welcome to attend the service, Harmon. And if you'll excuse me, I need to call my people together and make sure everything's ready."

The massive orcanin nodded once, lifting his great bulk from the chair with ease, and made his way to the elevator. Just before he stepped through the open doors, Allistor called out, "Harmon, one question." When his friend turned and raised an eyebrow, he asked, "How does one go about killing someone like Loki? I mean, do I need a special magical weapon? Or do we lock him in a room and gas him, or what?"

Harmon shook his head, a definite look of sadness on his face. "I imagine that by the time he arrives, his physical stats and health will have been greatly reduced. In which case, like most living beings, a sword through the heart, or removal of his head, would finish the job." He turned his back on Allistor and entered the elevator, the doors closing behind him.

"Nigel, I need all of my ministers, advisors, inner circle, raid leaders, and stronghold leaders to meet me at the Bastion as fast as they can get there. Also, I want all of our raid teams called back from wherever they are around the world or on Orion. Right now, please." Allistor looked at L'olwyn. "If I'm going to kill the being responsible for destroying our world, and maybe many others, all of our people should be there to witness it."

L'olwyn stared at him for a brief moment, his face completely neutral, as usual. Then he rose gracefully from his chair. "I shall help ensure that your instructions are carried out." He looked Allistor directly in the eyes. "I would advise, Allistor, that you not be hasty in your decision. At least wait until Baldur has spoken his piece before making up your mind. I know revenge is something you desire quite... emphatically. But I beg of you to think of what is best for our people."

Surprised, Allistor simply nodded his head. When the elf was gone, Allistor sat for several minutes with his eyes closed. Thoughts of Amanda mixed with visions of removing Loki's head in front of a crowd of Invictus citizens. His mind replayed the explosion on the station, the look of terror in her eyes as she and William were ejected into space. His heartbeat raced, his desire for revenge flaring bright and as hot as a sun. He wallowed in his anger, then focused it all toward Loki and those of his race.

Then he took a few deep breaths and forced himself to replay Harmon's words, and L'olwyn's, in his head. Revenge would feel great, and would be a huge morale boost for his people, but he knew the feeling wouldn't last. What benefit for his people might he secure from Baldur in return for foregoing his revenge? Then again, how much easier would it be for him to become Emperor of Earth if he could tell each human leader he met with around the world that he was the one who killed the being responsible for wiping out most of the human race?

After a while, he cleared his mind and asked in a voice just barely a whisper.

"What would you tell me to do, my love?"

Chapter 11

Allistor had chosen the Bastion in Denver for Amanda's memorial rather than Invictus or their original Stronghold at The Warren. Mostly because there wasn't room for the expected crowd at The Warren, and she'd liked the park area outside the capitol building in Denver. When he and the kids arrived on the Bastion teleport pad, Allistor found most of his advisors already waiting for him. In addition to his four hired alien analysts, there was his core group, along with Master Daigath, Gralen of the beastkin, and each of the Stronghold leaders. Bjurstrom and McCoy stood with a dozen or so raid leaders. There were still some raid groups scattered across the globe who were being picked up by either Kira or Gene, and would be back in time for the service.

"Thank you all for coming here early." Allistor spoke loudly enough for everyone to hear as he and the kids stepped off the pad. Almost immediately it flashed behind him, and a group of twenty citizens that Allistor recognized from Laramie appeared. Folks were already arriving to pay their respects. Seeing the growing crowd beyond the trees, he added, "Let's head inside and talk. We've got a lot to cover."

He led them through the park and into the old capitol building where they gathered in the rotunda. A quick word to Prime and several droid guards sealed off the building to ensure their privacy.

He spent some time updating them all on what he'd learned about Baldur and Loki, and Harmon's suspicions about what Baldur wanted. It took nearly an hour, as his people had many questions, and there were multiple angry outbursts that Allistor sympathized with. Each time he allowed a little while for tempers to calm before he continued.

"So there you have it." He looked around the room at his most trusted friends and advisors, his people, his new family. Surprisingly, it didn't feel at all odd to him that a good number of them were non-human. In his heart he knew that none of them were responsible for the apocalypse on Earth, or for Amanda's death. He had narrowed his focus and hatred to the race of ancient beings that included Loki, Baldur, Odin, and the rest.

"I have a decision to make. I intend to listen to what Baldur has to say, and once I've heard him out, I'll consider his offer. But I'd like to hear from all of you what you think." He held up a hand as several mouths opened. "I realize you don't have all the information yet. And in this case, this isn't up for a vote. This is my decision to make, right or wrong. I'd just like to hear your thoughts. Do I execute Loki for his role in the near genocide of our race, or do I leave him to Odin's justice and accept some probably epic reward from Baldur?"

Immediately there were several shouts of "Kill him!" and even one "Off with his head!" that he was pretty sure came from the usually quiet and reserved Lilly, of all people. In the back there was a shout of "Gnomes rule!"

and he briefly searched for Selby while shaking his head and holding up his hands.

"Okay, clearly some of you have strong opinions. Let's do this. Raise your hand if you have a comment to make, other than kill or don't kill. When we've heard from everyone who wants to speak, I'll ask you to vote by a show of hands. Who wants to start?"

Bjurstrom was the first to speak, raising his hand and stepping forward into the small open area between Allistor and the others. "I think you need to consider what you'd gain from killing Loki. We've been sort of tippy-toeing around since the aliens," He paused and nodded to Gralen and the others, "Excuse me, the *non-humans* started arriving. You've been worried about accidentally angering some faction and being taken out. Well, now we have strong allies, with agreements to help protect us. And if you yourself were to suddenly gain a massive number of levels, you'd become pretty difficult to take out. We'd be operating from a position of strength for a change."

There were lots of murmurs of agreement as he finished, even a little bit of applause, mostly from the gamers in the group, who always approved of leveling up. Gralen cleared his throat and raised his hand, and Allistor motioned him forward.

"While I do not have the same urge for vengeance that all of you native Earthlings feel, I understand your desire to see Loki dead. But I would remind you that Odin has declared Loki's life forfeit, and has done so, at least in part, because Loki failed in his obligation to protect you,

Allistor. An obligation set upon him by Baldur, a member of the same race, who has apparently been working on your behalf all along. In a sense, whether you physically take Loki's life yourself or not, you will be the ultimate cause of his demise. It is merely a question of timing, and what benefits you reap from his death. As someone with more experience in the ways of the Collective, I strongly recommend you consider Baldur's offer, and allow them to deal with Loki in their own time." He bowed his head to Allistor and stepped back, the crowd around them completely silent.

"Thank you, my friend." Allistor nodded his head slightly at the beastkin. "That was a well-considered and logical argument."

One by one his people stepped forward and made their individual cases, both for and against Loki's execution. Not surprisingly, the majority were in favor of taking the mass murderer's head right there in the park in front of everyone. But it wasn't a huge majority. Many of those who'd been gamers like Allistor, while curious about what Baldur might offer, couldn't resist the idea of racking up a huge number of levels and the stats that went with them. Others were, like Allistor, just thirsty for revenge. Allistor noted that Master Daigath did not step forward to offer his opinion. He just stood off to one side and listened.

After more than twenty of them had spoken, they were tending to overlap in their arguments or just repeat what others had already covered. Finally, there were no more volunteers, and Allistor took over again.

"Thank you all for your input. Regardless of what I decide, I want you to know that I'll be seriously considering all of your advice." He paused and took a deep breath. "Now. We have a little planning to do. This is going to go one of two or three ways, and I want us to be ready for all of them. So… here's what I want you to do."

They spent another hour together, going over Allistor's instructions for each scenario. If for some reason things went badly, he wanted to be able to react immediately. When he dismissed them, some of his people were grinning and chatting excitedly, while others were just shaking their heads.

Harmon and Daigath remained behind at Allistor's request. He had some additional questions for them, questions that the others didn't need to hear the answers to just yet.

*****

When Allistor exited the building just before noon, he was nearly overwhelmed by the sight that greeted him. Standing atop the wide staircase that faced westward across the park, Allistor was looking down at a throng of his citizens, tens of thousands strong. There were humans, beastkin, and dwarves in large numbers, as well as a scattering of elves, gnomes and other races. Standing head and shoulders above the rest, gathered around Droban, were a few hundred minotaurs that Allistor hadn't even known had become citizens. Off to one side was a group of more than a hundred of the trainers they'd hired, come to pay their respects.

Atop the stairway, off to the right and left sides, were the representatives of the elves, dwarves, and others who had asked to attend. Cogwalker was there, along with Melise and her father the commander, among a few dozen others. Allistor nodded to them, silently thanking them for attending, before stepping forward to face his people.

He'd known that his citizenry had grown in leaps and bounds, especially as he added in the non-human contingents. But the numbers in his UI as each group had joined had been just that. Numbers. Seeing the football stadium sized crowd standing before him, Allistor's heart beat faster. If he had to guess, he would say there were more than fifty thousand beings in attendance.

All for Amanda.

Unable to speak, for a moment, he just stood there taking it all in. A brief look up at the clear sky showed the protective dome covering the area. Seeing it reminded him of the day Gralen and his shipmates attacked the Bastion. The fact that the wolverinekin had since become one of his most trusted advisors was not lost on him.

Taking a deep breath, he said, "Nigel, loudspeaker please. Everywhere."

"*Go ahead, Sire.*"

"I want to thank you all for coming here today, to help us say goodbye to Amanda. And to thank those of you who stayed behind to guard your various homes." He paused, a small smile forming as he looked across the park. "I can't believe how many of you, how many of *us* are here. My heart is… full today." There was scattered applause, but Allistor kept going. "Some of you never met Amanda, so I'll tell you a little bit about her. I loved her. It wasn't love at first sight, mind you. Amanda was… stubborn, occasionally rude, extremely capable, and independent. She was there with me from the first days of the apocalypse, when we first claimed and built the Warren. She could shoot better than I could, and saved my butt more than once on scavenging trips!" Some of the humans laughed, mostly those who'd been at The Warren or Luther's Landing. "She took great pleasure in using me as a… guinea pig." His voice caught for a moment, visions of her advancing toward him with scalpel in hand making him tear up.

"She teased me mercilessly, often threatening to trade me in for one of you cowboys out there." Several of the cowboys whooped and whistled at this, making Allistor smile along with most of the crowd. "And she never, ever stopped trying to help people. Many of you were healed by her in those early days, before we all learned how to heal ourselves and each other. She saved hundreds of lives after scavenging missions and during raids. She kept me grounded, often called me prince fancy-pants or something similar to keep my head from swelling."

"She was a terrible cook! Her specialty was peanut butter and jelly sandwiches." This time nearly everyone laughed. "But she was a great mother to William, Sydney, Addy, and everyone who found themselves in her care.

She was a natural and gifted healer, and her last act was to save a life." Allistor looked at William, who was standing between the girls, all of them crying openly.

"I loved her, and wanted to spend the rest of my life with her." Again he had to pause, a lump forming in his throat. After clearing it a few times, and taking a deep breath, he wiped tears from his cheeks and began again.

"Like so many other friends and loved ones, Amanda was taken from us too soon. We gather together here, as we've done too many times before, to share our love for her, to offer support to each other, and to say goodbye."

The service continued for nearly an hour as several people climbed the stairs to stand next to Allistor and share a memory of Amanda. Some were funny, others simple stories of how she'd saved a life or healed a devastating injury. Allistor quietly offered the kids a chance to speak, but they all shook their heads, holding each other and crying. When it was through, Allistor nodded toward Harmon, who spoke into his wristband. Stepping forward, Allistor got the attention of everyone below.

"The circumstances of Amanda's passing have left us without a body to bury. So let's just bow our heads instead, and observe a minute of silence for Lady Amanda." Allistor bowed his head, but quickly looked up again at the sound of rustling below. Starting with those of his inner circle in the front row, the citizens of Invictus all began to take a knee. They lowered themselves in a vast wave moving from front to back, heads bowed and silent.

Allistor stepped behind the three kids and put his hands on William's shoulders, feeling the young boy tremble.

When a minute had passed, he called out. "Thank you. All of you." He waited as they all rose to their feet. He was about to say more, when Addy and Sydney began to sing. At first their voices were rough, but they bravely continued. After just a few words, other voices began to join in. The funeral song that the citizens of Invictus had claimed for themselves was slow, and sad. But the chorus of voices swelling up from the crowd and echoing off the walls was beautiful. Glorious. Somehow it made Allistor sadder, and lightened his burden of sorrow at the same time.

When the last note of the song faded, there was a brief moment of silence as people looked to each other and smiled, or hugged. Then the crowd began to disperse. Seeing this, Allistor held up his hands and called out.

"Please, wait. Don't go yet. I want you all to witness something while you're here. In a few moments, We're going to be joined by some guests." He nodded at Bjurstrom, who spoke into his radio. Throughout the crowd, raiders and raid leaders began to circulate. "Citizens of Invictus, I don't know how much of this you already know, so I'll start from the beginning." He walked down a few steps, then sat on the top one. "This is going to be tough to hear, and you might want to take a seat." As he spoke, the people spread out a bit and sat on the ground where they were. "First of all, Earth was not supposed to be inducted into the Collective yet. We were supposed to have had years, centuries more to develop and grow, to become better prepared. But a being named Loki interfered with the natural order of things..."

Allistor spent the next ten minutes explaining to them what had happened, and who was about to join them. When he was through, there was a flash of light, and two beings appeared atop the stairs. Allistor quickly got to his feet, as did everyone else. There was an immediate roar of angry shouts, threats, and calls for Loki's head. Sections of the crowd tried to surge forward, only to be held back by several rows of higher level raiders and advisors in the front. As his people tried to calm the crowd, Allistor took in the two ancient beings.

Baldur was in a more or less human form. He stood eight feet tall, with tanned skin and golden hair that practically glowed in the light of the twin suns above. Allistor wasn't surprised that his human ancestors saw Baldur and his kin as gods if they appeared like this. He was dressed in pristine white leather armor with a sword in a scabbard at his hip. The only color on his attire was a sprig of green mistletoe embroidered upon his left breast.

Loki, on the other hand, was in his natural tentacled form. He looked much like the octopoids that so many of Earth's people had fought, and fallen victim to, since the apocalypse. Except that each of his legs was bound in a shining silvery metal band, attached by chains that ran up to a similarly shiny collar around his rubbery neck. His multiple tentacles all hung limp at his side, twitching occasionally. His gaze briefly took in the crowd in front of him, then he turned to stare at Allistor with open contempt.

Allistor was busy resisting his own urge to attack Loki as his people finished bringing the crowd under control. When things had mostly settled, the front rows turned back to face Allistor and the visitors.

Baldur turned to face Allistor as well, inclining his head slightly. When he spoke, his voice was deep, and reverberated through the Bastion without any assistance from Nigel.

"Greetings, Allistor, Prince of Earth and Emperor of Orion. I am Baldur, and this is Loki." One hand waved slightly toward the chained prisoner. "I appreciate the grace you and your citizens have shown in allowing us this audience. I shall attempt to be brief, so that you may return to your mourning."

Allistor couldn't find it in himself to welcome the so-called god of his ancestors. Despite being told that Loki was the one responsible, Allistor was not ready to accept that. Or to forgive. The best he could do was nod his head and motion toward Baldur. "Go ahead and speak your mind."

Momentarily taken aback by the lack of civility, Baldur blinked at Allistor, while Loki glared daggers. With a sigh and a nod of understanding, Baldur began.

"I have brought my wayward brother, Loki, here before you today to apologize. We have no direct proof that Loki was responsible for the early induction of UCP... of Earth. If we had such proof, the System itself would instantly punish Loki in the most severe manner. Still, our people took on a responsibility many eons ago to foster

243

developing worlds like your own. We have, in fact, visited this world several times since humankind's early ancestors learned to use tools and walk upright. Each time, we contributed in small but significant ways in your development, with the ultimate goal of preparing you to become viable and successful members of the Collective."

There was some grumbling in the crowd, and Baldur paused to allow it to settle down. Loki glared out at them and mumbled something that included the word "ungrateful". Allistor took a step forward, moving the children so that they were behind him, and placed a hand on the hilt of his sword. Down below, the front liners all produced weapons from their inventories, though they didn't point them Loki's direction.

Seeing this, Baldur gave Loki an admonishing look, which his brother ignored.

"The early Induction of Earth was a terrible failure on the part of myself and my people. Odin and I wept together over the near extinction of the human race, but could not interfere without violating the restrictions of the System ourselves. For that failure, my people and I apologize." He bowed his head, first to Allistor, then to the crowd below. Motioning again toward his prisoner, he continued.

"After a series of suspected misdeeds against you, Allistor, and your people, I personally charged Loki, on pain of death, with ensuring that no harm came to you. As you all now know, the recent attack that claimed the life of Lady Amanda and nearly the life of young William, and

Allistor himself, constitutes a failure of that charge. As a result, my brother's mortal existence in this plane is forfeit. We have come here to offer you, Allistor, the right to end it."

The crowd once again erupted, this time in a mixture of cheers and angry shouts. Baldur held up a hand asking for silence, and it took half a minute or so for the crowd to settle. "There is a reason that Loki is known on this world, and most others, as a god of mischief and deceit. And though he is surely guilty of crimes beyond counting, he may not be guilty of all the crimes for which he is suspected, or has been accused. For that reason, I would ask that you forego your right of vengeance and allow Odin and myself sufficient time to fully investigate the extent of Loki's guilt. So that we may seek out those responsible for infractions that may otherwise be laid upon Loki's head."

There were boos and more shouts accompanied by raised fists from the crowd. Once again Baldur raised a hand, asking to be allowed to continue.

"In return for showing such generosity of spirit, Odin will personally reward you. We have both been impressed with you, Allistor. You have shown great determination, heart, and compassion while at the same time rising to a position of significant power in a surprisingly short time. You are a credit to the human race, and a shining example of what your people might have become, had they been given time. And while we cannot undo the damage that has been done, we can offer significant assistance."

Baldur held up a hand, opening it to reveal a small glowing object that most closely resembled an acorn. When Allistor tried to *Examine* it, all he got was question marks.

"This seed can assist you in your efforts to restore your race. Plant it somewhere safe, and the tree that sprouts from it will bear a fruit that, when ingested by human females, will induce a genetic alteration. Any female that consumes the fruit will be able to bear children after just a three month gestation period, rather than your normal nine months. In addition, their offspring will grow to adulthood at a fifty percent faster rate than normal. Upon reaching physical maturity, their bodies' development will then revert to a rate closer to current human norms."

There were gasps from the crowd even as Allistor's own eyes widened and his mouth fell open slightly. His mind raced to absorb the implications of this offering. The human race could reproduce *three times* as quickly? No, more than that. Because the new generations would reach maturity in half the time, and would then be able to reproduce themselves. The math temporarily boggled his mind. He immediately had questions, like would the new generations also need to eat the fruit, or would they automatically reproduce at the faster rate?

His jumbled thoughts almost caused him to miss Baldur's next words.

"In addition, Odin has purchased all remaining settlement rights for Earth. Any land currently unclaimed by humans or off-world settlers will be awarded to you, to be disposed of as you see fit." Baldur's eyes unfocused for a moment, then refocused on Allistor. "That is currently approximately thirty eight percent of the land area of Earth, and eighty percent of its oceans."

Those numbers knocked Allistor ass over teakettle. Odin and Baldur were offering him ownership of most of the planet. As if to confirm this, Baldur added, "This would be more than sufficient to make you Emperor of Earth."

"Ridiculous!" Loki growled at his brother.

Not taking his gaze from Allistor's eyes, Baldur yanked on Loki's chain, causing his brother to grunt in pain. "This would also include the lands that Loki has already claimed for himself. He won't be needing them."

"You go too far, Baldur! These hairless apes do not deserve such a concession! And what's mine is not yours to give!" Loki spat at Allistor, the slimy fluid falling short and landing on the stone at Allistor's feet.

Allistor blinked twice, his amazement over Baldur's offer giving way to fury. He stepped toward the chained prisoner, drawing his sword. Baldur, a look of regret and resignation on his face, took two steps back from Loki, dropping his end of the silvery chain. At the same time, the entire front two rows of citizens raised their weapons. Some carried rifles, projectile or plasma. Others held bows with arrows knocked. Some held swords or throwing daggers, axes and spears.

Allistor placed the tip of his homemade sword against Loki's throat, resting it on the top of the collar. "This hairless ape could claim your life, here and now!" He roared. "I think that's a fitting end for the great and powerful Loki! I imagine your people, and the rest of the universe, will get a good laugh from that! The so-called god of deception, caught red handed, chained and sliced into sushi by a lowly human!" He pressed the sword forward slightly, causing Loki's skin to dimple but not breaking it.

"Vile insect!" Loki shouted back at him. "You could not kill me with that puny stick if Baldur gave you a year and a day!" He jerked his head forward, causing the sword's point to slide cleanly thru his neck and out the back, then leaned back until the blade slid free again. The wound seemed to cause him no harm, or even discomfort. "You are so weak and ignorant that you don't even know what you don't know!"

Despite himself, Allistor looked to Baldur, who looked distinctly upset.

"Is he right? Can I not kill him? I thought you came here in good faith, to offer me his life."

Baldur nodded. "We did. As usual, Loki aims to deceive. Your sword touched no vital organs just now. Our race is hardy, our weaknesses few. And he is correct that under normal circumstances you would have little hope of killing him with that weapon, even were he to stand there and let you strike him all day."

Allistor was growling and considering another strike, just to be sure, when Baldur added, "However, the restraints Loki now wears were designed to fundamentally alter his physical form, as well as prevent him from controlling the motes. He is currently powerless, and as susceptible to injury as any mortal being. He cannot heal himself, as you can see from the wound you just inflicted."

Allistor looked closer and saw that, although there was no blood, there was indeed a three-inch wide open wound on Loki's flesh.

"Go ahead, insect! Take your petty revenge! I tire of this existence! You, and you as well, Baldur, bore me! I will leave this body and the restrictions of a physical form, and join our brothers and sisters on the next plane!"

Allistor didn't like the sound of that. Lowering his sword, he turned and spoke to Harmon. "I've been thinking. We don't really need those eternity gates. Do you think if I offered to return them to the Archons, they'd agree to use the orb to take Loki's soul?"

Baldur's sharp inhale from behind him let Allistor know he was onto something. As Allistor turned around, Baldur addressed him. "You go too far, Allistor. You do not understand what you threaten."

He was about to say more, but Allistor cut him off. Stepping closer to Loki, he raised his sword again, this time pressing the tip against his forehead. "What do you think, murderer? Would you enjoy an eternity trapped in an orb with thousands of fomorian souls?"

Loki's eyes went red, and two of his tentacles whipped upward, one striking Allistor's face, the other his chest. The force of the blows knocked him backward, reducing his health by half.

Instantly, every citizen in the crowd received the same message.

*Alert! The Bastion is under attack!*
*Quest Received: Defend the Bastion!*
*Loki the Deceiver has attacked Prince Allistor*
*within the boundaries of the Bastion.*
*Defend your home and your Prince!*
*Reward: Variable experience.*

As Allistor got to his feet, the crowd surged forward, advancing toward the steps leading up to where their enemies stood. They hadn't taken more than three steps before Baldur shouted, "*HOLD!*". His voice carried such power that everyone within hearing, including those listening in at other strongholds, froze in place.

Turning to Allistor, he asked in a grave but quiet tone. "I ask you not to allow this, Allistor. I greatly regret Loki's assault on your person, and you would be doubly within your rights to end him now. If that is what you choose, I will not stop you. But understand, what you have threatened, the confining of Loki's essence, would cause even myself to react badly. I do not have time to explain to you here and now the myriad facets of the nature of existence as we understand it. Nor would I if I could. That is something your race will need to discover on your own as you evolve." He stared into Allistor's eyes for a long moment. "Ah, I see. You planned this. Very clever. You manipulated Loki, and me as well. If you kill him now, all of your people will share in the credit, earning significant advancement for each of them. I am impressed and surprised, Allistor, which at my age is a rarity." Baldur bowed his head slightly in acknowledgement, a wide smile on his face. "Still, I would prefer that Loki survive the day, as would my father. Name your price." Baldur blinked, and the citizens below came to life again.

Allistor held up his hands, still holding his sword, and shouted at his people. "Wait! Hold your fire! Don't attack!"

There was a seemingly endless moment when he wasn't sure his people would listen. But they eventually stopped moving and lowered their weapons. Despite being frozen, they'd heard Baldur's words.

Looking first toward Daigath and Harmon, both of whom wore blank looks upon their faces that offered no help, Allistor turned back to Baldur and Loki. This was his third scenario, the one he'd been hoping for. The one for which he'd given his inner circle very specific instructions.

"My price is high, Baldur. I want nothing more than to erase this filth from existence right now. And I truly would gladly give up my new eternity gates to ensure he suffers inside that orb." His voice was half shout, half growl as he pointed his sword toward Loki again.

"But my own desires should take a back seat to the needs of my people." He watched as Baldur let out a long exhale. "So, in return for sparing Loki now, you will give us that seed, all the property rights here on Earth that you spoke of, and more." He waited for Baldur to nod, indicating he should continue. Surprisingly, the godlike being was smiling.

"You will also grant each of my citizens, excluding me, a portion of what they would have received had we completed this defense quest and killed Loki." Baldur's eyes unfocused for a moment, and he nodded in agreement.

"That is possible. The system will allow a peaceful resolution of this conflict to count as a successful defense, thus completing the quest. I think you will find the rewards to be satisfactory."

Allistor grinned, idly poking Loki in the chest with his sword, still not drawing blood. "And lastly, I still get to kill him. Not today, but when you and Odin have had time to question him, or suck his memories from his brain, or whatever you plan to do. Let's say… a week from now?"

Behind him, Harmon coughed and covered his mouth with a massive fist. Allistor saw a glint of amusement in his eyes. Daigath retained his poker face.

"Ha! You continue to surprise, young man." Baldur favored him with a warm and open smile. "On behalf of Odin and myself, I agree to your terms. Though I suggest you use the week you've just granted me to reconsider taking Loki's life. Speak with your advisors. Such an action can have consequences that I doubt you've considered." He held out a hand, palm down, and Loki's chain leapt from the ground into his grasp. "Once again, my apologies for your loss. It has been a pleasure to meet you in person, Allistor."

Without waiting for a response, Baldur and Loki disappeared. The very next instant, everyone in attendance except Harmon, Daigath, and the visiting dignitaries from Or'Dralon, Stardrifter and the others, leveled up.

*Quest completed! Defend the Bastion.*
*You have successfully defended the life of your Prince*
*and his property by repelling the invader!*
*Reward: Experience commensurate with threat.*
*Reputation increase with Baldur, Odin, and the Ancient Ones.*

And not just one level. The average citizen received enough experience to grant them twenty five levels. Several of them dropped where they stood, the effect of gaining so many levels at once overwhelming them. Allistor remembered how that felt from when Helen had done the same to him. The lower level crafters and children received as many as thirty levels, while the higher level raiders earned twenty or less in some cases.

The people began to cheer and congratulate each other, but almost immediately there was an ebb in the celebration as people looked up at Allistor. He quickly realized they were feeling guilty about being happy at Amanda's memorial service.

"Go on! Celebrate! Amanda would be happy for you! Let's all eat and enjoy our good fortune."

He smiled and waved toward the long lines of food tables set up under the shade trees farther back in the park. But his people didn't immediately disperse. A quiet chant began somewhere near the front of the crowd, the voice sounding suspiciously like Sam's. It quickly grew louder as it spread, until all of them were shouting. "Allistor! Allistor! Allistor!"

As the people faded away to partake of what had now become a celebration feast, Allistor's guests approached along with Daigath and Harmon. Allistor sent William and the girls down to Meg, who was waving for them to join her and Sam.

"That was… impressive." Commander Enalion gave a stiff but deep bow from the waist. "I doubt I would have had the presence of mind, or the restraint, to do as you did."

"That is a great compliment coming from you, Commander. Thank you." Allistor inclined his head slightly, as L'olwyn had taught him.

"I am truly sorry about the loss of Lady Amanda." Melise's expression matched her words. "I enjoyed the time I spent with her. She was kind and lovely, and it is obvious from your words today that you loved her."

Allistor found he couldn't speak, instead giving her a sad smile and nod.

Cogwalker was much less circumspect. "Holy shit! Ye scammed the damn gods, Allistor!" his eyes were wide and his grin stretched from ear to ear. "I'll be tellin' this tale to me great grandchildren's grandchildren!"

Allistor chuckled, finding great relief in the dwarf's irreverent enthusiasm. "I hope they're buying the drinks while you tell it, Master Cogwalker."

The dwarf roared with laughter, gathering up his clansmen and heading down toward the celebration. Allistor exchanged pleasantries and accepted both condolences and congratulations from the rest of the visiting dignitaries, inviting them all to join in the feast below.

Eventually it was just Allistor, Daigath, and Harmon. All three took seats on the top step, and Allistor took in a deep breath, held it for a moment, then let it out in a long exhale. "Well, what do you think?"

Harmon chuckled. "Baldur was right. That was impressive, Allistor. Even knowing what you planned, I was surprised at how you pulled that off. And more than a little scared, at times."

Daigath shook his head. "You played a very dangerous game, Allistor. Any other being of Baldur's age and power would have simply erased you for your impertinence. You must learn some respect, or you will lead your people to ruin." The ancient elf got to his feet and departed before Allistor could respond.

Harmon placed a giant hand on Allistor's shoulder. "He's fond of you. You worried him quite a bit today. And he's right, the odds of you living through that encounter after responding the way you did…" The orcanin shook his head.

"I was counting on Baldur being everything our legends said he was. If he's truly the epitome of justice and mercy, then he couldn't, or I guess *shouldn't*, have reacted otherwise. I knew it was a risk, but the potential reward seemed worth it. And really, everybody gets what they want."

"Except Loki." Harmon grinned at him. "Now, let's go get some of Lady Meg's cooking before all the food is gone. Those damned dwarves eat like they're full-sized orcanin!"

"I'll join in you a minute." Allistor waved him toward the food. I've got some notifications to get through.

"Ha! I imagine you do." Harmon set off down the stairs, roaring, "Lady Meg! Save me some of that delicious meat loaf!"

Smiling to himself, Allistor took a minute to watch his people. They were all mingled together, humans and non-humans. Most of them were still high from the ecstasy of earning so many levels at once. They were smiling and laughing, some even dancing. He thought this was a much better tribute to Amanda than the solemn wake that it might have been.

Closing his eyes, he willed his UI to display the notifications he'd waved aside earlier. His entire display filled with them.

The first was the same quest completion notification that everyone else had received. Except that his reward did not include any experience. He did get significant reputation increases with Baldur and Odin, and the seed that would help his people to repopulate was listed as loot.

Next came a long list of faction reputation gains and losses. Unsurprisingly, there were a large number that disapproved of at least one of his actions that afternoon. Though after a quick scroll through, he was pretty sure that the gains outnumbered the losses. He'd ask Selby and the others to go through them later and alert him if there were any serious issues either way.

The content of the next notification was expected, but the form of it was a surprise. The moment he opened it up, he braced himself.

*Congratulations!*
*You have completed the hidden quest:*
*Retribution!*
*For exhibiting both guile and sound judgement in reaching*
*a mutually beneficial agreement with Baldur and Odin,*
*you have been awarded ownership of all remaining property*
*rights of UPC 382. These property rights, combined with your*
*existing holdings, grant you the Noble Title of*
*Planetary Emperor!*

*Reward: Noble Title – Emperor of UPC 382;*
*Experience awarded: 2,100,000,000*

The moment he finished reading that particular notification, another flashed across the screen. One that all his people received as well. There was a resounding cheer of approval from the crowd below, and the party got even louder.

*World First: Planetary Emperor!*
*Planetary Prince Allistor of Invictus has secured sufficient holdings*
*to earn the Noble Title of Planetary Emperor!*
*May he rule long and wisely!*

Immediately Allistor felt the rush of gaining several levels. Though he'd not earned any experience directly from the defense quest, the experience from another *world first* achievement and becoming Emperor was significant. He quickly scrolled through the accompanying level notifications.

*Level up! You are now Level 56 ! You have received two Attribute Points.*
*Level up! You are now Level 57...*
*Level up! You are now Level 58...*
*Level up! You are now Level 65 ! You have received two Attribute Points.*

In total the achievement and title had granted him an additional ten levels. At least now he didn't have to worry about any of his raiders out-leveling him for a while. He took a quick look at his status sheet.

| Designation: Emperor Allistor, Giant Killer | Level: 65 | Experience: 21,100,000/270,000,000 |
|---|---|---|
| Planet of Origin: UCP 382, Orion | Health: 72,000/72,000 | Class: Battlemage |
| Attribute Pts Available: 20 | Mana: 16,000/16,000 | |
| Intelligence: 25 (29) | Strength: 10 (18) | Charisma: 12 (16) |
| Adaptability: 8 (10) | Stamina: 13 (20) | Luck: 8 (14) |
| Constitution: 22 (27) | Agility: 15 (21) | Health Regen: 2,200/m |
| Will Power: 25 (33) | Dexterity: 7 (11) | Mana Regen: 1,400/m |

Allistor decided to leave his stat point assignments for later, when he was alone and could focus. He also wanted to ask Daigath about more Battlemage spells. For now, his people were calling for him to join their celebration. He gave a brief smile and a wave, reflecting on how much Amanda would have enjoyed this party as he walked down the stairs.

Chapter 12

Rajesh was sitting at the head of the long
conference room table in his headquarters, bored and barely
listening to his uncle Agni and Fayed his security chief plan
an attack on the jelly creatures, when the worldwide
notification of Allistor's promotion to Emperor of Earth
appeared in his UI.

The conversation in the room went silent as they all
read the news, the first sound being that of Rajesh's fist
pounding the table. "Damn it! How does he keep doing
this?" he growled. "Now I will never overtake him!"

Agni, ever the voice of reason for his volatile young
nephew, tried to head off the impending tantrum. "This
might be a good thing, Earl Rajesh." He carefully used his
nephew's title in the company of others, soothing his ego a
bit. "This Allistor, he is human. We might have had an
alien Emperor instead. At least this way our diminished
race retains some of the power on our own world."

It was clear that Rajesh was only half listening. "It
should be *ME*!" he pounded the table again, the effect
being less than he probably intended. Since his very first
level-up, Rajesh had focused on a min-max caster build,
putting nearly all of his attribute points into *Will Power* and
*Intelligence*. For a post-Stabilization human, he was
physically a weakling. He held his position of power
mainly by embracing the game-like System of the new
world and keeping a calm façade, using his knowledge to
clear and create the first Stronghold in the area. He then

adopted a *fake it till you make it* attitude, convincing his family and a few score lower caste survivors that he knew how to protect them. He quickly showed them how to improve their attributes, pushing most of them into physical builds that focused on *Strength*, *Agility*, and *Constitution*. He immediately put them to work crafting weapons and clearing the area around his factory Stronghold, letting them take all the risks as he stood in the back and cast the occasional spell to ensure he received experience for the kills.

Word of his safe zone quickly spread, and within a month his population had grown to over one thousand peasants, plus a half dozen members of his family. At that time he turned the day to day management of his operation over to his family, with Uncle Agni in charge, and focused on getting his factory back up and running. With more than a thousand people, their supply of toilet paper was quickly diminishing. He had discovered the System's market kiosk, and began selling the valuable commodity to buy weapons and armor. When he'd accrued enough territory and resources to become an Earl, his struggle for simple survival with a modicum of comfort turned to dreams of his own kingdom.

Each time he gained in power, though, his achievement was overshadowed by the fact that this Allistor person had repeatedly beaten him to the punch. Whoever he was, he must be ruthless to have expanded and grown so quickly. Rajesh often contemplated Allistor's possible methods. He'd reached the conclusion that the man must have at least ten thousand peasants of his own, all of them working hard to provide him with resources. Likely he controlled their food supply and access to basic needs such as healing and safe housing, much like Rajesh himself did.

Agni shook his head, then caught the gaze of Fayed. With a brief and subtle nod, he indicated that the man should take his people and clear the room. Rajesh would not allow any honest conversation that might imply he had any weakness in front of others. The security chief, knowing Rajesh's moods all too well, got to his feet and silently waved his people out, exiting last and closing the door behind him.

"Rajesh, you must be realistic. Allistor is now the planetary Emperor. He has crossed the finish line and won the race, so to speak, and done so far, far ahead of you. It is time for you to accept that reality, and reach out to him. It is better to be proactive and make contact than to wait for him to find you. If you make a good impression, you might be able to secure his support. Maybe even garner a position of power within his court, if he has such a thing."

Rajesh got to his feet and began to pace back and forth, his hands clasped behind his back as he considered his uncle's words. Or some of them, at least. His mind was still distracted with jealousy and thoughts of retribution. How dare Allistor overshadow his achievements?

"Rajesh?" His uncle had patiently let him stew for a solid five minutes before speaking again. "Shall I attempt to make contact?"

"What?" Rajesh stood still and looked to his uncle. "Contact? Yes, I suppose that is inevitable now. Yes, tell him that Earl Rajesh requires his presence for a celebratory feast."

Agni nodded once, taking the yes. Though he had no intention of relaying that particular message. One does not *require* one's superiors to do anything. One respectfully requests the honor of their company, or the privilege of attending them at their convenience. Still, progress was progress, and Rajesh would never know the content of the actual message Agni would send.

"In the meantime, I feel the need to kill something." Rajesh looked around the table, blinking in momentary confusion as he noticed the absence of Fayed and his security team. "Get Fayed back in here! I will join them in attacking the jellies."

Agni resisted the urge to correct his nephew with the proper racial name for the hundredth time. At this point, he suspected Rajesh used the term just to annoy him. "Of course, nephew." He waved through the glass door at Fayed, who was unobtrusively waiting a short distance away. If he were honest with himself, he was glad to have this distraction available to take Rajesh's mind off of his rival's successes.

As the security team reassembled and resumed their discussion with a now enthusiastic Rajesh, Agni quietly excused himself and headed toward the room where they'd managed to set up a short-wave radio transceiver. Along the way he mentally composed a respectful and complimentary message to send to the new Emperor on behalf of his nephew.

Once that message had been finalized and transmitted, Agni warned the radio operator, on pain of banishment, to keep the message and any response to himself. If a response was received, he was to find Agni and report directly to him, and only him.

With that task completed, he next went to the kitchens, where his own mother ruled with a sharp tongue and a long wooden spoon. They would need to begin gathering proper ingredients for a celebratory feast, assuming Allistor would be willing to meet with them.

*****


Allistor's first task on his first morning as Planetary Emperor was breakfast with his kids. He woke early, well before sunrise, and asked Nigel to have breakfast for everyone sent up once the kitchen staff was up and going. He spent some time in his study, making himself a hand-written list of the multitude of things he wanted to accomplish. The list was much longer now, as he was drastically altering his most immediate plans. He no longer needed his raid teams out claiming territory. Anything that hadn't already been claimed was now his. And while he still wanted to have his people reach out to as many other survivors as possible, that mission was now a little less urgent. It had been his plan to gather other leaders together and form an alliance that would allow him to take the lead and be voted Emperor. Thus granting him the right to do things like install a planetary defense system in orbit around Earth.

He had already asked Harmon during the party to order and install the system. Rather than pay for it in klax or gold, he agreed to grant the merchant a commensurate amount of land. He even jokingly offered the orcanin an honorary vassal title to go with it, causing Harmon to roar with laughter, frightening several nearby citizens and causing them to reach for weapons.

Next on his list was locating a safe and logistically sensible location to plant the seed he'd received from Baldur. Getting that tree grown and producing it's magical (*or scientifically advanced?*) fruit into the hands of those who wanted to bear children was a priority. He added a note to ask Nancy and Daigath whether it was wise to use their spells to rapidly grow the tree to maturity.

Allistor's new list included following up with his analysts on all the reputation gains and losses, as well as any protocols like formal expressions of gratitude to those allies who had attended the memorial. He figured that as an emperor he probably had to do considerably less ass-kissing, but it wouldn't hurt to check.

Next on his list was dungeons. He needed to place his dungeon cores and get his people running through them. The massive boost in the average levels of his citizens after yesterday would make that easier. Many of those who had been hesitant to join raids would feel stronger and more confident now. And with the trainers available to help them all take full advantage of their chosen classes, Allistor felt much more comfortable with their chances of surviving dungeon runs. He made yet another side note to ask Harmon and Gralen about the dungeons, whether the newly placed cores would start out at a low level and grow. He also wanted to use the satellite surveys, and question any newly contacted survivors, to try and find any naturally occurring dungeons on Earth.

Next he included a visit to check on Fuzzy and Fiona. Helen had been out there herself, and reported that Fiona was still slumbering, and Fuzzy was watching over her. Allistor felt horrible for not having gone to his bear already, but the prior day's events had taken priority. He quickly drew an arrow from Fuzzy's name up through the page margin to the top of the list. He would take Helen back with him, and afterward the two of them could meet to discuss his new holdings. His minister of parks was about to get a whole lot busier.

With great reluctance, he added the space station to his list. He needed to check in with Cogwalker on the extent of the damage and time required for repairs before he could get the station fully operational. His initial reaction was to ignore the station, and the terrible memories that it held, possibly even trade it away. But that would be depriving his people of a valuable resource for his own personal reasons.

Allistor needed to meet with Daigath. Not only to discuss potential new spells, but to dig deeper into his new mentor's words regarding his interactions with Loki and Baldur. Harmon had said the ancient elf was worried about him, but Allistor got the impression that Daigath was in fact angry with him. If so, he needed to know exactly why, and figure out how to mend that fence.

He wanted to add some crafting time to the list, but realistically he was going to be busy with more important tasks for at least the next several days.

And though he was redirecting his raiders, he still wanted to take the *Phoenix* out himself, along with a team of trainers, to personally meet other groups of survivors. While he could also take along supplies of food and maybe lower grade gear to distribute, knowledge of class spells for combat, defense, healing, and food growth was a much more valuable gift. And his supply of scrolls was limited, with Ramon and his people already overwhelmed just trying to provide them for Invictus citizens.

He was still contemplating his list when William emerged from his room, still sleepy, his eyes only half open.

"Hey, buddy." Allistor got up from his desk and joined the boy in the sitting area. "How are you feeling?"

"I'm okay, I guess." His tone was sad, and his gaze was fixed on the floor near his feet.

"Did you already assign all your new attribute points?" William had quietly informed them the night before that he'd picked up a full twenty five levels from the defense quest reward.

"No." William shook his head, but didn't elaborate. Just the tone of that one word, along with his body language, let Allistor know that there was a serious problem. He sat in silence with his squire for a while as he thought it through, eventually deciding to take things slowly.

"Not sure where you want to put them?"

"No, I know what to do." William's tone was slightly defensive. "I just don't feel like it."

Allistor sighed internally. William was still a bit young for teenage angst, so he had to assume the reluctance was something else. The squire was normally enthusiastic about assigning his points, pursuing his dream of becoming a knight. Allistor tried to think like a young boy, and almost immediately the obvious answer was staring him right in the face.

"This is about Amanda, isn't it?"

William nodded sullenly, not speaking right away. Allistor let the boy think it over, not in any rush, despite the busy day he had planned. There was nothing more important at that moment than this tough little guy who had already suffered so much loss and trauma. A quick look at the clock on his UI told him that breakfast should be arriving shortly, and he was content to give William whatever time he needed.

After a few minutes, he finally spoke. "I don't want the points. Or the levels. They're bad."

"What do you mean, bad?" Allistor already knew the answer, but wanted to hear William work through it himself.

"We all got those levels because Loki attacked you. Baldur only brought Loki here because of Amanda dying. Getting all that experience…" he paused and rubbed at his eyes, his shoulders hitching up as a nearly silent sob escaped him. Allistor let him work through it.

"It's like I leveled up for killing Amanda." William finally looked up at Allistor, his eyes haunted, tears rolling down his cheeks.

Allistor moved over to sit next to him on the sofa, grabbing him and pulling him into a fierce hug, rocking the boy back and forth. "Don't ever think that, William. You are not responsible for Amanda dying. Not even a little bit. You were just as much a victim of that attack as she was. It should have taken your life as well. Amanda would have died no matter what, and there was nothing either one of us could do to change that." He leaned back and lifted the boy's chin so that they were looking into each other's eyes. His voice was thick as he continued. "The fact that she managed to save you by sending you back toward me was a miracle, William. She made sure you'd live to level up, get stronger, and help me protect our people. She'd have enjoyed the way I tricked Loki and got you guys all those levels yesterday. It would have made her laugh. I know she wouldn't want you to feel bad about it."

William nodded slightly. "Yeah, that was pretty smart. She liked it when you did smart stuff. Told me even a blind squirrel finds a nut once in a while." His lips twitched in a slight grin as he said it.

"Ha!" Allistor gathered his squire back into a one-armed bro hug. "That sounds exactly like her. So, what do you think? Put all your points into *Charisma*?"

William snorted. "Yeah, right. I got fifty points. I'm putting ten each into *Strength* and *Constitution*, five into *Agility*. Five into *Adaptability*, cuz Amanda told me that was a big part of how you stayed alive at the start." Allistor nodded, agreeing wholeheartedly while at the same time thinking that Amanda had spent a lot more time talking with William than he'd realized.

"I'm adding eight points to *Stamina*, for when fights take a long time. I'm also putting five points each into *Intelligence* and *Will Power*. And the last two I'm putting into *Luck*. So maybe nothing like that explosion will happen again."

That last comment hit Allistor right in the gut. He was going to need to spend some more time working with his squire, convincing him that the attack and Amanda's death were not his fault in any way. His first instinct was to turn the guilt into anger, which was what he had done himself. But it seemed wrong to encourage that path in someone so young.

"Sounds about right. But are you *sure* you don't want to put some points into Charisma? I mean, have you looked in a mirror lately? You're really kind of ugly..." Allistor grinned at his squire, who stuck his tongue out at him, but then smiled back. Allistor gave him a light-hearted punch to the shoulder, and William put some stank on his return punch, his grin widening.

"Meg says I'm handsome! That when I'm a knight, all the girls are gonna want to marry me." He shook his head. "But girls are dumb, and I'm not wasting good points on getting any handsomer."

Allistor chuckled and roughly rubbed the top of the boy's head. "Meg's right, you're plenty handsome enough for now. I think those are good choices." He watched as William zoned out for a minute, assigning his points. A moment later he could already see the difference that influx of *Strength* and *Constitution* made in the kid's physique. His shoulders were slightly wider, his arms thicker. Allistor guessed that if they'd been standing, he'd be a little bit taller as well.

Just then the elevator doors opened, and breakfast came wheeling in on a cart pushed by one of the kitchen staff. Allistor looked toward the girls' rooms and shouted, "Up and at 'em, sleepyheads! Come get breakfast while it's hot!" He heard some faint grumbling in response as he and William began dishing up heaping plates of food. Allistor took it as a sign of the times that he did not know the name of the young man who had brought the food. Meg was adding staff almost daily to keep up with the demands of the increasing population living in and near the tower. So he simply said, "Thank you, this smells delicious!"

*****

Helen and Allistor stepped off the teleport pad at Wilderness and began walking toward the gate. There were several shouts of greetings and congratulations from the citizens who were out and about inside the walls. Everyone was feeling the benefits of so many additional levels. Seeing a sentry walking the wall above the gate, Allistor made a mental note to find a way to compensate those few citizens that had missed out because they were on duty someplace other than the Bastion. Maybe give them priority dungeon runs, or epic gear. He'd ask Bjurstrom to make sure they were given extra assistance in leveling up if they wanted it.

Helen was chatting nervously as they walked the well-established trail through the woods towards Daigath's home. "The bears are just a quarter mile or so off the path. Not far from the stream. I hope Fiona's awake this time. Poor thing. Daigath explained a little about what happens when a bond is lost. I don't know if she's gonna be okay, Allistor." She bit her lower lip as she finished speaking, looking up at him with concern.

"We'll do all we can for her." Allistor wasn't sure what to say. He had no idea how to help the bear, but he was committed to doing whatever was needed. Just as he hoped someone else would do for Fuzzy if he were to get himself killed and leave his cub behind.

They were just crossing the stream when Allistor paused, a familiar sound causing him to look upstream and reflexively crouch down at the same time, pulling Helen down with him. When she looked at him with raised eyebrows, he pointed.

Maybe fifty yards up on the right-hand bank of the stream stood two full-grown murder chickens. One had its head down and was drinking from the stream, while the other swiveled its gaze left and right, scanning for predators, or prey. It let out one of their signature calls, half chirp, half grunt.

Helen whispered, "So there are more of them out here in the wild. That's good news. We should send a crew out here to trap a few of them. McCoy says the little ones we hatched won't be mature enough to breed for a couple of years yet."

"McCoy?" Allistor hadn't known the airman was working with the murder chickens.

Helen grinned, her eyes sparkling. "Yep. Since that drunken escapade when Goodrich got his junk bitten off, McCoy has taken a liking to that momma murder chicken. I know, kind of twisted, right?"

Allistor chuckled, the sound startling the two creatures upstream. Both heads turned to laser focus on him. Sensing that the noisy two-legged beings were clearly more powerful than themselves, the murder chickens wisely dashed off into the brush, heading away from the humans. Allistor shook his head. "Seems like just yesterday they would have been a serious threat. When we fought the others, and the matron, we almost didn't make it."

"But you won, and they were delicious." Helen smacked him on the back. "Let's go."

Allistor followed her as she left the path and picked her way through the brush, thankful for her friendship, and for the distraction. From the day they'd met, Helen had never treated him like he was special. At least, not seriously. Like Amanda, she enjoyed teasing him about his royal status, and the fact that she was the one responsible for it.

It wasn't long before Allistor heard a greeting chuff from his bear cub. A few seconds later he stepped out of the brush behind Helen and into a small clearing. Both bears were sitting upright, staring at him and Helen as they approached. Fuzzy showed none of his usual enthusiasm at seeing either of them, and made no attempt to beg for treats. A clear indicator to Allistor that something was wrong.

"Hiya pal." He stepped forward and petted his bear's head, giving his ears a gentle scratch. "I've missed you."

Fuzzy butted his head against Allistor's chest, enjoying the treatment. He sent Allistor an image of Amanda's face while making a questioning grunt. Allistor focused on his memory of Amanda being launched out into space. And while he didn't inflict the image on his bear, he did let Fuzzy feel his sense of sorrow and loss. The bear whined softly and pawed at the ground.

"Good morning Fiona." Allistor tentatively reached a hand toward the other bear, but she shied away. Not violently, but enough to keep him from making contact. Helen, on the other hand, had more success.

Walking up to Fiona slowly, she held out one hand while speaking softly to the bear. "Hey baby girl. I know you're hurting. We all loved Amanda, and all of our hearts have a little hole in them right now…" her voice was just a murmur, but more than loud enough for the bears to hear. Fuzzy growled softly and leaned away from Allistor to rub his massive body up against his smaller companion's. Fiona let out a plaintive whine, but leaned forward slightly to lick Helen's hand.

Fuzzy moved his head back under Allistor's hand, demanding more scratches. When Allistor obliged, he got a surprisingly clear visual message from the bear. It showed Helen and Fiona walking together through the Wilderness gate. Allistor was instantly reminded of a similar vision Fuzzy had shown him the day Amanda and Fiona had bonded. Fuzzy had made it clear that Helen was a good backup if Amanda didn't want to befriend the bear.

Instead of asking a question, Allistor just held his tongue, watching Helen try to sooth Fiona's sorrow a bit. She scratched her ears, then her muzzle, moving down to give a vigorous scratching of the bear's jowls, Fiona raising her head a bit to give easier access. Helen kept up her quiet banter the whole time, speaking to Fiona as if she were a human. Allistor guessed that the bear didn't understand most of what Helen said, but did understand the tone and the intent behind the words.

Eventually, Helen moved to sit with her back against a tree. Fiona immediately adjusted so that she lay next to the woman, placing her head in Helen's lap. Fuzzy chuffed once in approval, then moved to the berry bushes and began to nibble, clearly stating that Fiona was in good hands.

"We'll be okay here for a while. Why don't you go see Daigath?" Helen suggested, her eyes slowly closing as she ran her fingers through Fiona's thick fur. "When you get back, we can give Fuzzy a bath in the stream."

Allistor grinned as Fuzzy snorted, shooting Helen a dirty look before resuming his harvest of the sweet berries. He gave Helen a little wave and turned to head back the way they'd come. Once he reached the trail, it was only a short hike to Daigath's home tree.

"Greetings, young Emperor." The elf's voice called down to him as he entered the small clearing. Allistor looked up to see Daigath sitting in a chair that looked like it had grown directly out of the tree on a ledge about thirty feet up. "Please, join me." He motioned toward a stairway that began at the base of the tree and wound around the trunk as it rose upward.

Allistor climbed the stairs slowly, touching the trunk and testing his footing as he went. The stairs were as solid as stone and didn't even creak as he placed his weight on them. Soon enough he was standing on what he thought of as a balcony that extended out about six feet from the trunk, looking down at his mentor. He'd been right about the chair, it was formed from several small branches that had twisted themselves together to form a comfortable looking seat.

"Good morning, Master Daigath." Allistor bowed his head to the elf, who remained seated. "Your tree is really amazing."

"We are making progress, yes." Daigath smiled at the tree, patting the trunk. "Your admiration is appreciated."

Allistor's eyes widened. "He understood me?"

Daigath shook his head. "Not your words. He's not quite that aware yet. He more... felt your appreciation of his alterations, and I felt that he is pleased by it."

Allistor started to reach out a hand to touch the trunk, then paused to look at Daigath, seeking approval. When the elf nodded, Allistor placed his hand gently on the bark and said, "You are the coolest, most beautiful tree I've ever met."

Laughing, Daigath motioned for Allistor to sit, which he did, with his feet dangling off the edge of the wooden ledge. "How is Fiona?"

"I'm not sure." Allistor admitted. "Helen is sitting with her now. She seems quiet, mostly sad. But she's letting Helen pet her. So I guess that's a good sign?"

"It is indeed." Daigath's head nodded slightly. "I will continue to hope for her complete recovery."

Allistor debated with himself for a few seconds, then asked, "Fuzzy sent me an image of Fiona and Helen walking together. I'm not sure if he just meant that Helen was helping, or that Helen should try to replace Amanda and bond with Fiona. Is that even possible?"

"Yes, it is possible. Fiona's bond with Amanda was recently established, and not nearly as deep as your bond with Fuzzy, for example. Having Helen as a surrogate might be a very good idea. Though I would suggest Helen wait a few days before attempting it. Fiona will let her know when she's ready."

"Thank you, master." Allistor let out a relieved sigh. That was maybe one less thing to worry about. Being able to keep Fiona in the family, so to speak, would be a great relief. Allistor paused before changing the subject. "I… wanted to ask you about yesterday. It feels like you're angry with me for the way I handled things."

Daigath took his time answering, staring out across the clearing. Finally, he spoke in a patient tone. "I am not angry, exactly. What you chose to do yesterday was risky. Not just to you, but to your people as well. Consider the possible ways it might have gone wrong. For example, what if your people had actually attacked Loki before you stopped them, and a stray shot struck Baldur instead?"

Allistor's eyes widened. He'd planned their displayed 'hostility' ahead of time, but it wouldn't have been possible to spread the word to the entire crowd of thousands in the short time his people had to get ready, even if he had allowed his raiders to share the plan with everyone.

"Or you might have been wrong about Baldur's character, his level of understanding and patience. Had Odin been standing in his place, you and your people might now be ash drifting through that park."

Allistor opened his mouth to respond, but the elf held up a hand to silence him. "I am not saying your actions were wrong, exactly. What you did was intended to benefit your people, and your state of mind was influenced by your hatred of Loki, which is understandable. You are a young and sometimes foolish member of a young and immature race, with almost no experience in these matters. I am frustrated with myself for sometimes forgetting this, and with the situation in general, just as I am concerned for your well-being. I wish to impress upon you, young human, the dangers you court when you confront such powerful entities."

"I'm sorry to have disappointed you, master. I am..." Allistor stopped, unsure how to proceed. "Since our world was seized, and my family was killed, every day has been a struggle. Nearly every choice I've had to make was life or death. I was nobody before this, with almost no responsibilities, certainly none with the weight I carry today. I've been in survival mode, risking everything again and again to gain whatever advantage I could. I... I guess I'm still doing that. But I'll try to do better."

Daigath nodded. "And I will try harder to properly prepare you for the challenges you face. We'll both do better."

"Does that mean you'll be trying to talk me out of killing Loki in a month?"

The ancient elf's gaze met Allistor's, but was unreadable. "I have been sitting here this fine morning, listening to the birds and contemplating exactly that question. Your actions yesterday showed wisdom and a great deal of wit. You cleverly manipulated Loki into attacking you, thus increasing Baldur's obligation of honor. At the same time, you allowed Baldur and Odin the time they desired to determine the extent of Loki's guilt, and discover how much guilt should be placed on the shoulders of others. And by retaining your claim on Loki's mortal life, you have already garnered the reputation gains and losses you would have received had you killed him then and there. So in essence, much of the damage you might have done to yourself has already been done. Whatever enemies you would have made by killing him, you've already made." He paused and raised a finger for emphasis. "And you *have made some powerful enemies.* Loki employs armies of operatives who make their livings serving him. And has an even greater number of allies who benefit from his machinations. Many of them will see you as the cause of their losses now that Loki is not long for this plane."

Allistor didn't want to anger his mentor by arguing, but he felt he needed to defend himself on this one issue. "But master, that was not my doing. Baldur declared Loki's life forfeit, not me. It's not my fault I was the cause of that. Weren't most of his... minions going to blame me no matter what?"

"You are correct. Loki was caught in his own trap, or one set by his daughter Hel. And even his staunch allies would agree that he has earned his fate many times over. The repercussions involved are in no way your fault. And yes, you were fated to be blamed by those who find it convenient, profitable, or in some way beneficial to do so. I would only point out that the arrogance you displayed in executing your scheme will have made you more enemies than if you had been more... humble."

Allistor sighed. There was no arguing with that logic. He pictured a horde of aliens watching holograms of him tricking Loki and benefiting from it, muttering something like "Who does that little shit think he is?" to themselves. He had learned the hard way dealing with other Stronghold leaders and trespassers over the last year that perception is everything.

"I understand, now." Allistor replied. "Though, had you explained that possibility to me beforehand, I don't know that I would have acted any differently. Powerful people or factions are going to hate me, no matter what. I'm not sure I would have given up the potential benefits to avoid the additional risk. I'm sorry, Master Daigath."

"I know, Allistor." Daigath put a hand on his shoulder and gave it a gentle pat. "As for what you choose to do a week from now, what are you thinking?"

"I'm thinking that I'll kill him." Allistor stated bluntly. "I think my people, and really every human left on earth, need to see the murderer of our race executed. Or at least be able to hear that it was done. Retribution is a basic component of our culture. If, as you say, I've already earned the enmity and paid the price for it, why not do it?"

"Well, for one, it may hasten the retaliatory responses from his allies. Knowing you are the indirect cause of Loki's death is one thing. Witnessing you executing him is quite another."

"But wouldn't taking his life make me extremely powerful, and much harder to kill?"

"Indeed. But if I were one who wished to inflict punishment upon you, I would not act against you personally. I would punish those you have sworn to protect. Your people are vulnerable, Allistor, even with the additional levels they received yesterday."

Allistor's gut clenched, and the color drained from his face. He pictured bombs dropping on his strongholds, his people's bodies littering the ground. "But... the alliances we've made. Aren't those supposed to help protect my people?"

"They are. And they will, to some extent. Anyone bold enough to attack Invictus will pay a heavy price. Your allies will exact retribution, swiftly and mercilessly. But there are those to whom that is meaningless. Emperors send millions to their deaths on a whim. And what good will that retribution do for your citizens who die in the attacks? If Hel destroys Orion and everyone on it, will you feel any better when Or'Dralon destroys a moon with tens of thousands of her servants on it? Or will you be crippled with guilt for the loss of so many more innocent lives?"

Daigath saw the look of horror on Allistor's face, and took pity. "That is an extreme example. And honestly, killing Loki would more likely make an ally of Hel than an enemy. But I hope you see my point?"

Allistor could only nod. Daigath had just shown him that he'd already likely doomed some, or all, of his people. And he didn't see that there was anything that he could do about it.

"You've been thrust into an arena you were not equipped or prepared for. In part because of the choices you've made, and in part through simple luck, both good and bad. Your choices have mostly been wise, if risky and sometimes brutal, and came from a desire to help others more than yourself. They are one of the reasons you garnered so much attention during this world's Stabilization. Now, with the level of power you've achieved, your choices, and your actions, have far-reaching consequences." Daigath's stare moved from the forest to Allistor's face.

"Let us both spend the next week contemplating your choice, Allistor. As things are now, I hold great hope that you will lead your people, and now your world, to thrive within the Collective. And I will certainly assist you as much as I am able. You have a great many friends out there, and I'm positive you will earn many more. Do not give up hope."

Allistor mumbled his thanks as he numbly got to his feet and began to descend the stairs. He was so distracted and horrified that he forgot to ask Daigath about additional Battlemage training. Instead his mind was awhirl with questions and apocalyptic visions, regrets and guilt.

He barely noticed when he passed by the point where he needed to turn off the path to meet up with Helen and the bears. Shaking his head, he focused on where he was going.

Chapter 13


Allistor returned to Invictus having left Helen in the woods with the bears. She had calmed Fiona to the point where the bear had fallen asleep with her head on Helen's lap, and they didn't have the heart to wake her. Allistor was confident that between Helen and the two bears, there was nothing out there in the woods that might harm them.

Heading up to the conference room on the analyst's level, he asked Nigel to have whomever was available meet him. When he arrived, he found all but Longbeard sitting at the table waiting for him. Droban got to his feet, bowed his head and spoke first. "My congratulations, Emperor Allistor."

"Please, sit. And thank you. I meant to ask... I noticed a whole crowd of minotaurs with you yesterday. Were they family?"

"Some were, yes. I passed along your invitation to my family and clan. About half of them elected to join me here, one hundred and eighty all told. They arrived and were sworn in the same morning you left to visit the station. My apologies for not informing you sooner, but I didn't want to intrude."

"No apology necessary. I'd love to meet them all sometime soon. Where will they be living?"

"My immediate family will take up residence here in Invictus City. The rest were hoping to purchase some land. Perhaps some open range with forest nearby for hunting? If that is agreeable to you?"

Allistor chuckled. "I suddenly find myself with quite a bit of available land, my friend. Choose a good spot, and I will grant your clan members the same ten acres each that every other citizen has been given. They can be all together, or separate. And of course if you choose land in or adjacent to one of the parks, they can freely use that land for farming or hunting as well. If they feel they need more, we can talk about it. And if they need a loan to establish a Stronghold, just see Chris."

"That is most generous, thank you." Droban bowed his head again. "I will inform them as soon as we're finished here."

Allistor looked to Selby, then L'olwyn. "Did you have a chance to glance at the faction reputation notices I forwarded to you?"

Selby giggled. "We did more than glance. But the list is longer than my... longer than Droban's leg. You might have set a record, Allistor. I've never even heard of so many entities and factions having an opinion regarding a single person's actions. And a lot, I mean aaaa loooot of them are not happy with you."

Daigath's warnings came back to Allistor, and he grimaced. Selby quickly backpedaled. "Still, there are more that looked favorably upon you. And some of the reputation losses were with folks who already liked you, and just like you a little bit less, now."

L'olwyn took over for the flustered gnome. "We will need significantly more time to perform an in-depth analysis, Allistor. Several days, a week at most. But a preliminary perusal of the list has not revealed any surprises. Nor any obvious imminent threats. However..." He paused to look at the other analysts, who both nodded. "An event of this magnitude, and the likelihood of another in the prescribed week when Baldur returns, we feel it would be prudent to hire some... facilitators. To assist with our analysis by gathering information on various entities."

Allistor didn't immediately understand. "Facilitators? Like, researchers?"

"Spies!" Selby shouted, then covered her mouth, her eyes widening. After a moment she uncovered and gushed, "It's all very exciting!"

Allistor couldn't help but smile at her enthusiasm, even if he didn't share her excitement over the need to gather information on a large number of new potential enemies. Still, it seemed like the smart thing to do.

"What do you need in the way of resources?"

Droban was the one to answer this time. "Several hundreds of millions of klax. Maybe as much as a billion. Some factions will be very difficult and expensive to penetrate and gather information on. Those most closely associated with Loki, and therefore most likely to move against you, are in that position because they are skilled at subterfuge and deceit."

Selby bounced up and down in her chair slightly, clearly wishing to say more. Allistor looked at her and raised an eyebrow. She immediately burst forth in a loud whisper. "We should also hire some spy *hunters* to help us weed out anyone who's infiltrating us on our enemies' behalf." As she finished she looked up at the ceiling and around the room as if searching for listening devices.

"Great. I'll never sleep again." Allistor grumbled to himself. For the benefit of the others, he said, "Do what you need to. I'll instruct Chris to give you access to a billion klax for now. If you need more, let me know. And please be careful. Don't put yourselves at risk while contacting these spies of yours. Maybe ask Harmon if he has a reliable intermediary."

"I have several reliable contacts that I have worked with in the past." L'olwyn assured him. "From before I was unhoused. My... social standing among the elves should help defer any connections being made between us by our foes, at least for a while. No one expects reputable elves to have contact with an unhoused."

"Alright, thank you L'olwyn. And I'm sorry. If it helps at all, I don't believe you are unhoused any longer. You are as much a part of this family, this clan, as anyone."

The reserved elf didn't speak, only nodding his head in thanks.

"Right. So what other business do we have to discuss this morning?" Allistor looked around the table. "Oh! I know. Hold on let me grab my list." He pulled it from his inventory and spread it out on the table. "Do we

288

need to send gifts or, like, thank you notes to the folks who attended the memorial yesterday? The guests, I mean."

"It is not required. As an Emperor, you may assume that any invitation extended to one of a lesser rank is an act of favor, or even an honor bestowed. You may even receive gifts from some of those who attended." L'olwyn provided. "However, there is no harm in sending a brief note or small gift if you are so inclined. I would simply caution you that all gifts should be of roughly equal if not identical value. Otherwise you risk showing favoritism and offering offense."

Allistor was about to tell them to forget the whole thing when Longbeard came bursting into the room. Not wasting time on greetings, he hopped into a chair and said "Nigel, please pull up this mornin's survey data, Invictus City."

As the holo image he requested came to life above the conference table, he turned to Allistor. "Me apologies fer bein' late. I was just leavin the lads workin on the volcano at Yellowstone when the survey team called me about this." He pointed to the aerial survey of Invictus City, formerly the southern half of Manhattan, and the surrounding area. With a few quick motions of his hands, he panned the map eastward, zoomed in on Brooklyn, then moved farther east and north into Queens. "There they be." He zoomed in tighter, then said "Nigel, real time, please." He looked at Allistor and the others. "As soon as they called me, I had em hold the satellite in position above us. Here's why."

Allistor looked at the image as the real time feed kicked in. The ground looked as if it were covered in ants, slowly advancing toward the west. "What is that…?"

Longbeard flicked his fingers once more, and the image zoomed in tighter. Allistor blinked twice, staring at the moving figures.

Zombies.

Thousands and thousands of undead humans shambling along through city streets and alleys. Maybe hundreds of thousands. Some were just skeletons with tattered scraps of clothing hanging from their bones. Others were fresher bodies, leaking juices, pus, even dragging entrails as they walked or crawled toward Invictus.

"There be more." Longbeard panned twice more across the map, showing Allistor two more insanely large hordes of undead advancing from different directions. The last was on an island to the northeast that Allistor vaguely remembered from some movie. It was the island that housed the Potter's field cemetery, where New York had buried its indigent and unidentified corpses for something like two hundred years. The undead were advancing off the edge of the island, falling into the East River. Others could be seen crawling back out of the river up and down the western shoreline, having been scattered by the currents. Every one that he saw was doggedly moving toward lower Manhattan island.

"It has to be that lich." Allistor barely spoke the words as Longbeard widened the view to show all three of the undead armies moving toward their location. "Nigel, sound an alert. We're about to be attacked by a very large number of zombies. Have anyone who wants to fight join us here in Invictus City in… an hour. They're not moving very fast. Ask Prime to double the droid guards on the eastern and northern wall. And tell him to add some anti-personnel weapons batteries up there as well. Focus on fire and explosive damage. He'll need to do it quickly, before the first of them reaches us."

"Of course, Sire."

"How the hell did he raise so many, so fast?" Allistor asked his advisors. "And how can he control them?"

Droban grunted as he studied the map. "He would have had to have been working toward this for some time. A master lich can empower necromancer adepts to raise and control their own undead, bound to him through them. His orders would become their orders, much like a standard military structure. A general giving orders to his officers, passed down the ranks to non-commissioned officers on the ground, who in turn issue commands to common soldiers. An army this size would have to involve many adepts. If I had to guess, I would say this process started several months ago, at least."

"What does he hope to accomplish with this? These zombies don't look like they can climb our walls. And even if they were to dogpile on top of each other and build themselves a ramp, we could just burn it down before they reach the top." Allistor drummed his fingers on the table as he watched the live feed outside.

"Longbeard, please ask the survey team to start checking recent footage of the areas around our other strongholds. Maybe this is some kind of diversion, to make me gather our fighters here while he attacks somewhere else?"

"Aye, will do, yer Emperorship!" the dwarf winked at him, then began talking into his wristband.

"Nigel, remind me... with your most recent upgrade, are you able to detect undead within your sensor range?"

*"Unfortunately, if they are not on the surface and moving, I am not, sire. That ability would require two more system upgrades. And even were you willing to make such an investment now, I fear it would take too long. I may only be upgraded once per planetary rotation. It takes that long for my enhancements to fully process and be implemented."*

"Well, just in case, let's take care of the first one right now." Allistor pulled up the *Nigel* tab in his UI and located the next update, grimacing when he saw the cost. Still, he confirmed the purchase, spending nearly four billion klax worth of his gold reserves. He was going to need to speak to Chris soon about their finances, and potential income streams. Maybe move forward on auctioning some of the land on Orion, now that the new gate had increased the value. "Be sure and notify me when you're eligible for the next upgrade tomorrow. If fighting

292

undead is going to be a thing from now on, we're going to need you to be able to detect them."

*"That is most generous of you, sire. Thank you. I will notify you the moment my current update is complete."*

"Don't thank me. Pretty soon you're going to have two whole planets worth of Strongholds to oversee."

*"It is my pleasure to serve. I now have the capacity to operate quite a large number of facilities."*

Allistor looked to the advisors. "You're welcome to join us for this fight if you like. I know you all received at least a few levels yesterday, except maybe Master Longbeard." He paused to look at the dwarf, but got only a poker face that was momentarily interrupted by a wink. "But it never hurts to gain more experience."

"My clan are still here in the city." Droban answered. "I will bring them to the eastern wall. If the undead should somehow reach the top, our axes will clear them away."

"Aye, ye can count on me brethren as well. There be five thousand or so young dwarves at Lightholm just itchin' fer a good fight to test out their new levels n skills." Longbeard grinned at them.

"Alright, thank you. I'm heading down to the lobby to coordinate with Prime and the raid leaders. You can join us there, or on the wall with your people, as you like. If you're not interested in fighting, my guess is you'll still get experience from a defense quest. In fact…"

Allistor looked up at the ceiling. "Nigel, loudspeaker please. Everywhere." He paused for a moment then spoke in a raised voice. "Hey folks, Allistor here. It looks like Invictus City is about to be attacked by tens of thousands, maybe hundreds of thousands of undead. They're walking toward us as we speak. My guess is that it's the lich that we fought before, come to take another shot. We're gearing up here in the city, manning the walls. But I have a suspicion that this is some kind of diversion meant to bring our fighters here while he attacks a smaller, more vulnerable target. So here's what I'd like to do."

He paused for a few seconds to review his thoughts again, then continued. "For those of you in smaller, more isolated Strongholds, I want you to keep all of your guards and defenders there with you. Keep eyes out everywhere you can, because Nigel won't be able to alert you to the presence of any undead. Last time they attacked, they tunneled up inside an Outpost from below, so keep some patrols watching for that, too. Have a plan to get your people through the teleport pad quickly, just in case. And set up some defenses around the pad, in case you need to hold that position while you escape. For those without teleports, get some vehicles fueled up and ready. Have a plan to retreat to the vehicles and get the hell out if necessary. If possible, make plans to torch your place or call for some bombs to be dropped on it if you have to abandon it, to take out as many of them as possible. We can always reclaim your property and rebuild your Stronghold later. Your lives are the important thing."

"Next, those of you who have kids, or are crafters and support personnel who could use some experience, consider coming to Invictus. Once the zombies attack, there should be a defense quest given to everyone who is physically within the city. Based on the number of enemies coming our way, the experience should be significant. The city has high walls, and multiple Strongholds, and we should be able to hold them back without issue. The kids can wait safely here in the tower. I estimate we've got less than an hour before the first undead reach our walls. For those of you from larger Strongholds that can spare some fighters, or from Orion, you are welcome to join us here to kill zombies. Just don't leave your home bases shorthanded. Snipers will be of particular value in this fight, as well as casters with long distance or AoE damage spells. We want to kill as many as possible before they reach our walls."

"Lastly, show no mercy in this fight. Some of the enemy might still look human, but they're not. They're walking corpses that feel no pain, have no feelings, and want nothing more than to eat your face. Thanks, and good luck to us all."

The advisors followed Allistor into the elevator and down to the lobby. Longbeard and Droban split off to begin organizing their people while Selby and L'olwyn went to help organize incoming fighters. William and the girls were waiting for Allistor, geared up and ready to fight. All three wore custom fitted leather armor made for them by Lilly and her crafters. William had his staff strapped diagonally across his back and a short sword at his hip. He held a hunting rifle in one hand. Addy and Sydney each carried a bow strapped over a shoulder, with full quivers of arrows at their sides. For a moment he considered making them wait there in the tower. His instinct to protect them was especially strong, and he had the perfect excuse to leave them, asking them to watch over and protect any kids that might be brought in.

One look at the grim determination on William's face changed his mind. His squire was nearly level fifty now, just behind Sydney and Addy. They could all be useful, and certainly didn't need to be sheltered from the realities of battle after the year they'd had. Not only had they lost their own parents and friends to this new world, but they'd subsequently lost their surrogate mom just a few days ago.

"You three stick with me. Girls, use your magic to boost the rest of us, whether that be damage or healing. William, your job is to watch our backs. You all move when I move, and follow my instructions without argument. Yes?" He waited as all three nodded their heads. There were no smiles, no words, just a solemn acknowledgement of their agreement. Allistor felt a pang of sorrow at seeing these three kids turned into grim warriors. Any one of them was now stronger, faster, and more deadly than any human had been before their world ended. Right then Allistor thought that he'd take great satisfaction in removing Loki's head. Odin's and Baldur's too, if given the chance.

His three kids formed up behind him in the lobby as he greeted Prime, Bjurstrom, Juanita, Rhonda, Frank,

Remy, and his various raid leaders. Lars was there as well, offering his Stronghold as a forward operating base, since it was a short distance outside the city walls. Helen was notably absent, but being out in the woods with the bears, she'd have no way to know about the attack. Ramon and Nancy were there with Chloe, and had even brought Max along to help entertain the kids. Ramon stepped forward. "I have just over a hundred copies of the *Repel Undead* AoE spell scrolls that you got from Kyle." He handed one to Allistor, then began passing them out to the raid leaders and others. Each of them immediately used the scrolls, learning the spell. Ramon gave the remainder to Bjurstrom to be distributed to those who could best use them.

As Allistor and his leaders planned their defense, citizens streamed through the teleport pad, groups of twenty appearing every ten seconds or so, quickly clearing the pad as soon as they arrived to make room for the next group. The lobby was soon filled, along with the cafeteria, and they had spilled out into the courtyard and the street outside.

Since Remy's Stronghold was situated right near the eastern wall where it followed the shoreline of the river, his people had already moved up onto the wall. Remy assured Allistor that they had a plan to fall back into their Stronghold should the wall be overrun. While he did not have a teleport pad, his people could retreat into the high rises and up to the roofs for evacuation via the *Phoenix* and other ships. A few tanks could easily hold the stairwells while the rest escaped.

Rhonda and the others were already moving their fighters to the northern wall, and would have them in place within thirty minutes. Kira, Gene, and the other pilots were standing ready with ships at the parking garage and Battery Park to shuttle larger numbers of people up to the walls. Once the fighters were delivered, the ships would then take up bomber duty. If they could compress large numbers of undead into small areas and drop bombs on them, it would greatly ease the burden of the fighters along the wall.

Gene and his guys had been diligently working on more of the pressure charges, but in this case Allistor had no desire for finesse. The undead bodies needed to be destroyed. Exploded to bits, burned to ash, he didn't care. If the bombs destroyed the buildings outside the city, or even scratched his walls, that was okay with him too. They could either be rebuilt, or cleared away at a later date. So they raided whatever munition stores they had located around the country for conventional bombs meant to do surface damage. They didn't have a large number of them yet, but hopefully with judicious use, there would be enough.

*****

In less than an hour Allistor thought they were as ready as they could be. Plans were made, his people were being deployed along the wall. Prime's droids were already there, having sprinted there to take up posts during the planning session. Ten thousand of them were now stationed along the northern and eastern walls, one placed every ten feet. In between them the human, dwarf, beastkin, and other non-human citizens were filling in. Snipers and ranged weapons, casters, and melee fighters stood side by side. Behind them were support classes. Healers, buffers, even some with no combat skills who were willing to act as loaders or runners, or to pour gallons of flammable liquid down on the enemy. Each of his citizens had at least a basic healing spell to help keep any wounded alive until better healers could be fetched.

Other groups were assigned to patrol the city, looking for any infiltrations. Twenty raid groups of ten members each were sent down into the subway tunnels with radios. They were instructed to report in and retreat if they discovered any underground breaches. Two of the smaller goblin ships captured on Orion were tasked with patrolling the air over the city looking for surface level incursions.

Allistor had quickly used his City tab to place several ground level weapons bunkers at strategic intersections in a dozen places. Each was round, about fifty feet in diameter, with four plasma weapons that together could cover a three hundred and sixty degree field of fire. The weapons were much larger versions of their hand-held plasma rifles that were tied directly into the structure's power source. Where a plasma rifle blast might burn a hole through a metal door or a body, the larger versions would incinerate the entire body, plus two or three behind it.

He had planned to add more, but after his twelfth bunker he received the notification they'd been waiting for.

The attack had started, and he could no longer build additional emplacements until the battle was over.

*Quest Received: Defend the City!*
*Invictus City has been attacked by an army of undead.*
*Repel the invaders, protect the city and its inhabitants!*
*Reward: Variable experience; Bonus rewards for eliminating*
*one hundred percent of the attacking force;*
*Bonus rewards for achieving victory without loss of allied lives.*

A cheer went up from the citizens along the wall. They were excited for the fight and the resulting level gains. Looking down from atop the massive wall at the undead who were shuffling forward, Allistor had to admit he felt safer than he usually did during a fight. Still, the sheer numbers of zombies moving toward them just in his field of view was intimidating. He was rethinking his previous count. If the same numbers were pressing toward them all up and down the wall, there might be as many as a million undead approaching. New York had been a big city with millions of inhabitants, and millions more buried in its cemeteries.

Droban, who was standing next to Allistor, had clearly been thinking along the same lines. "This is too many. Even with dozens of apprentices, the lich must have started raising this army many months ago. Before you even established this city. It must have had some other purpose, at least initially."

Allistor nodded. "And I went and placed our city right in its way. Lucky us."

More cheers rang out as up and down the line, snipers began firing sporadically, ignoring the targets at or near the base of the wall, taking careful aim at those still farther out. Here and there Allistor saw heads explode and undead bodies drop, only to be stepped on or tripped over by those coming from behind. Allistor didn't try to stop them. It was good for morale, and good practice for his shooters.

A moment later, Bjurstrom reported in via radio. "Boss, this is ugly. Some of these zombies are level twenty to thirty. A few of them are even higher. And some of them look too fresh to have been buried. They have bite marks and blood stains, chunks missing. Some are even wearing armor. I... I think they were probably survivors that got taken down by these zombies, then added to their ranks."

McCoy added, "Yeah, seeing the same thing over here. The lich must have been hitting Strongholds or taking down any scavenging parties they caught out in the open. I'm looking at one dude who's level thirty and carrying a spear that's glowing like it's enchanted."

Allistor was about to respond when he was distracted by a commotion a short distance down the line. One of the shooters began shouting insults at the undead, setting down his weapon and jumping up to stand on the edge of the rampart. Still shouting and shaking his hips, he undid his fly and began pissing on the heads of the undead below.

Unfortunately for him, a strong wind coming off the river, and redirected straight up the face of the wall, sent a good deal of the urine right back onto him. He began cursing and shaking his hands as he gyrated atop the wall. Allistor heard someone near him shout "Watch it, Levi! Dammit. Didn't anyone ever teach you not to piss into the wind?" The man turned his head to respond with a middle finger salute, and wobbled slightly. There were more shouts, this time of alarm, as the idiot lost his balance and tipped forward over the wall. Several hands reached out to grab him, but they were too far away, having cleared the area to avoid being splashed. The man screamed as he tumbled downward, still urinating as he went.

Being nearly level forty, Levi's constitution was high enough that the fall didn't kill him. Instead he landed amongst the undead, crushing and killing two of them, the impact leaving him stunned. He then began to scream and thrash as dozens of others clawed and bit at him, piling atop his body so thickly that the citizens on the wall above couldn't see him, and even with his improved strength he couldn't break free. His armor protected him for a while, the zombies being too weak to penetrate it immediately with broken fingernails and dull human teeth. But his exposed face, neck, hands, and privates were quickly ripped apart. His screams turned into gurgles within seconds, then ceased.

There was a stunned silence atop the wall as the defenders tried to absorb what had just happened. Lars, who had been maybe twenty yards further down the wall, started shouting. "That was the single most moronic thing I've ever seen in my life! Anybody else wanna be a dumbass and get themselves dead? Raise your hand and I'll save you some time, toss you over myself! Get your shit together and get back in the fight!" The giant of a man walked up the line glaring at citizens as he shouted. Each and every one of them turned away and began firing weapons. With a roll of his eyes for Allistor, Lars turned and stalked back to his own spot on the wall.

More and more citizens were now firing their weapons. None of the undead were using ranged weapons to fire at the defenders, so they were becoming more bold, holding their positions and taking time to aim carefully. Nearly every round sent downrange, whether lead, arrow, or plasma, took down its target. Some got back up, but most stayed down. Allistor didn't fire his own rifle. Instead he set up his .50 caliber rifle with its bipod legs on the rampart in front of him. He used the scope to search the area farther away from the wall, looking for higher level undead that might be controlling the masses.

If this worked like it had in games and movies, you kill the apprentices, or ideally the lich himself, and all the animated corpses they controlled would drop as well. Instead of *one shot, one kill,* it might be one shot, a *thousand* kills. As he scanned the streets, alleys, and windows from his high position, something disturbed him. An itch in the back of his brain telling him that something wasn't right. It took a full minute before he realized what it was.

There was no screaming.

His people weren't being hit, weren't screaming in pain or fear. And the undead made no noise other than low moaning or grunting sounds. There were a few shouts of encouragement, celebration, or just plain excitement from his people, but it was oddly quiet for such a large scale battle. Even his radio was mostly silent, no one crying out for heals or calling out target assignments. It was kind of creepy.

Eventually Allistor spotted a lone, unmoving individual standing behind an overturned dumpster about six blocks back from the wall. It appeared human, though its skin was grey and pale. Its eyes glowed green even in daylight, and its white hair was a long, greasy tangle. Allistor took a moment to *Identify* it.

**Undead Necromancer Adept**
**Level 40**
**Health: 19,000/19,000**

As he'd noted before, the undead had fewer health points that a living human of the same level would have. He supposed that was a drawback to the whole being dead thing. Of course, they could also withstand injuries that would cripple a living human and keep going, feeling no pain. They could lose an arm, or two, have their innards trailing behind them, and keep attacking.

Allistor took careful aim, making small adjustments to the rifle's position until his crosshairs lined up with the center of the adept's face. He took a single deep breath, then let it out slowly before squeezing the trigger.

The rifle bucked against his shoulder, the large caliber round causing a significant recoil. But with his improved physical stats he barely registered it as he focused on his target. Its head rocked backward, most of it disappearing into a splatter of congealed blood and brain matter that splashed the wall behind it. Being only a few blocks away, he watched with both eyes instead of through his scope as he scanned the area between the adept and himself. After only a second or two, scattered zombies stopped moving and collapsed by the score. Others kept moving, letting Allistor know that more adepts were nearby. And of those that fell, he couldn't be sure how many were controlled by the adept, and how many had been killed by his people right at that same moment. Still, there were suddenly a few hundred fewer moving corpses in front of him.

Allistor spoke into his radio, giving Bjurstrom instructions to pass along to their snipers to look for the adepts and take them down. He assumed most of them would be better hidden, probably inside or behind buildings. But it wouldn't hurt to keep an eye out for them. The moment he stopped talking, he heard a call on the radio from McCoy.

"We've got a few thousand of them bunched up in a side street. One end is blocked by a burned out garbage truck. This would be a good time to drop a bomb."

Allistor watched the sky as *Opportunity* glided over from a short distance away. He saw them stop moving when they'd located the target area, then quickly gain several thousand feet of altitude as a lone bomb fell from the cargo door. On the radio he heard, "Ordinance away." in a growly beastkin voice. A moment later the ground shook slightly as the bomb struck and detonated, a roiling mass of flames and body parts exploding upward and outward. Thick black smoke obscured the area for a while before the breeze cleared it away.

There was some cheering from folks farther down the wall, those who were close to the target and had a view of the carnage. McCoy reported, "Good hit. Got most of 'em!"

Allistor monitored the radio as he resumed searching for adepts to take down. He heard McCoy observe that the newly arriving zombies were now avoiding that blocked side street, obviously being directed away from the dead end trap. He was wondering to himself just how intelligent the lich's minions might be, and whether they could communicate with each other, when he began hearing screams.

Maybe fifty yards to his left, several people were down, writhing in pain atop the wall and screaming.

Allistor cast a heal on the nearest of them, but it didn't seem to have any effect. He saw Nancy and two other healers moving toward them from both directions, and decided to leave them to it, then cringed as one of the wounded rolled off the inside edge of the wall, falling onto concrete thirty feet below. Their writhing ceased, and they didn't move at all.

As he turned back to look through his rifle scope, he spotted another adept. This one had just stuck its head out from behind a brick building, and was waving its hands. The eyes were glowing more brightly than the one he'd shot, and Allistor quickly understood why. There was a sort of pulse, a visible wave of green-tinted magic that erupted from the adept and washed outward down the street. Within moments of its passing, many of the corpses that had dropped when he'd killed the first adept got back to their feet.

"Oh, hell no." Allistor mumbled to himself as he sighted in on the adept. The spell was ending, and it began to withdraw back toward the alley. Allistor pulled the trigger, not having time to sight cleanly before it disappeared back around the corner. His aim was good, and the adept's body fell, followed shortly by a much larger number of lifeless corpses hitting the ground.

Nancy's voice came through raid chat rather than the radio. The raid channel included Allistor, his inner circle, all the raid and Stronghold leaders.

"We just lost half a dozen people to some kind of necrotic magic. Our cure potions didn't work, nor did our standard heals. We managed to save one with a light magic healing spell. By the time we figured that out, it was too late for the others. We need all light magic casters to be prepared with heals."

"Shit." Allistor grumbled. "We should have thought of that ahead of time. Everybody knows you use light magic against dark."

He didn't transmit this, as his people were already quickly and efficiently spreading the word. The undead clearly had mages that could reach his people atop the wall, and they'd begun attacking. Allistor wasn't sure if it was the adepts, or some other type of undead caster. But he needed to find out, and find a way to deal with them quickly.

Down the line, Allistor heard another group begin screaming.

Chapter 14

Goodrich whistled as he walked through the subway tunnel, not at all concerned about alerting any monsters ahead to his presence. In fact, he was using this scouting mission as an opportunity to clear these sections of tunnel of any remaining mobs. At some point Allistor would probably want to reactivate the underground transport system, and Goodrich figured as long as he was down here with a seasoned raid team, they might as well get some work done.

All of his people were at or near level fifty, and had been in multiple fights as a team. They worked well together, and he was looking forward to taking them on some dungeon runs once Allistor had those new dungeon cores set up. In the meantime, they were all behind him, chatting and teasing each other, completely at ease and confident in their ability to handle anything they found down here.

Goodrich stopped whistling when he heard a familiar sound down a maintenance tunnel to his left. It wasn't something he'd heard in person, but he recognized it from every zombie holo he'd ever watched. The moans of the undead.

The side tunnel had once had a solid metal door with *Authorized Personnel Only* stenciled on it. That door lay bent and dented on the train track off to one side, as if something powerful had pounded on it until it broke free.

The rest of his team went silent out of habit, tilting their heads to listen. Eyes widened, and their healer immediately got on his radio to report possible contact, and their location. Two light globes glided over Goodrich's head and down the tunnel, stopping about twenty feet ahead of him.

"Alright, you've all seen the movies. Head shots, decapitation, and fire. Try to avoid fire if they're in close. I don't want them stumbling in amongst us, or scorching our tanks." As he spoke, the group's two tanks equipped shields and stepped ahead of him, one holding a sword in his free hand, the other a spear. Goodrich and two others equipped bows for ranged damage and moved to the back, while their healer and damage casters grouped up in the center of their formation. It was a narrow tunnel, just wide enough for two people to walk side by side. Those in the center went single file to leave a clear line of sight for the archers to fire on either side.

"Push through as fast as we can, let's find a room or a wide spot where we can spread out." Goodrich thought for a bit, then added, "And don't get bit. If you do get bit, call it out right away. I don't know if these things are contagious, but let's assume it's a worst case scenario."

The tanks began moving at a fast walk, their shields held in front of them as they advanced toward the end of the tunnel. The twin light globes remained ahead of them, illuminating the tunnel a good twenty feet out. They stopped when they reached a pair of doors, one on each side of the corridor. One tank remained facing forward toward the now growing sound of shuffling and moans, while the other tried the door on the right. It was unlocked, and swung inward with a squeal of rusty hinges. Goodrich, right behind the tank, had put his bow away and drawn a spear from his inventory. As the tank advanced into the room, he cast his own light globe and sent it up to the ceiling.

The room was a small office, a set of lockers along one side, a desk and chair in the corner. A quick sweep of the room revealed it to be unoccupied, and the thick layer of dust on the floor and furniture showed it had been empty for some time. Exiting and closing the door behind them, they switched to the left hand door. This one was locked, but the tank, with his greatly enhanced *Strength* stat, easily kicked it open.

There was an immediate screech as half a dozen oversized rats charged forward. The tank planted his shield in the doorway and began slicing at the ravenous creatures with his sword. Behind him, Goodrich stabbed over the tank's shoulder, skewering one of the creatures and lifting it off its feet. He held it in the air and used *Identify* while one of the casters behind him fried it with a fireball.

> **Vermin Scout**
> **Level 21**
> **Health: 0/0**

The rat perished instantly, the high level caster's spell more than enough to finish it off. It took a minute for the others to perish as well, mostly because they were quick and hard to target accurately. The tank stepped over their corpses, pushing into the much larger space. This one appeared to be a mechanical room filled with pipes, gauges for monitoring voltage, amps, pressure and heat, as well as large generators and what looked like boilers. The back wall of the room was a good fifty feet from the door.

More vermin rushed out from behind and beneath the long pipe runs, some dropping from above pipes along the ceiling. The tank shouted, using some kind of taunt ability, and all the rats changed course to charge at him. His teammates fanned out behind him, all except the tank who remained in the hallway with one archer to back him up. In moments, another dozen vermin corpses littered the floor in front of the tank. Their healer hit him with a *Restore* that closed a few minor scratches inflicted by sharp teeth or claws.

The group scattered around the room, checking for any hidden doors or additional mobs. They didn't expect to find any other rats, as the tank's taunt would have drawn them if they were within hearing distance. The healer hung back by the door and looted the corpses, staying nearby the other tank in case he was needed.

Two minutes later they were closing that door behind them and advancing further down the tunnel. In the back, one of the archers whispered, "Man I hope these things are higher level. I got zero xp from those rats."

The entire group froze, turning to look at the man. A woman next to him, one of the mages, reached out and slapped the back of his head. "You did *not just say that.*" she scolded as the others groaned or shook their heads.

"That's it. We're all dead." One of the tanks muttered, throwing the archer a dirty look. "You just cursed us."

The archer did his best to look innocent, shrugging and spreading his hands out to his sides. "C'mon guys. You can't tell me you believe in that supersti-" He didn't get to finish the word as the same woman that had slapped him clamped a hand over his mouth.

"Do *not* finish that sentence. In fact, unless you see a horde of mobs running up behind us, you're just not allowed to speak for the rest of this trip. If you need a bio break, just wave and point to your junk or something." She raised one eyebrow at him, waiting for him to give a slight nod before she removed her hand. He opened his mouth as if to speak, but closed it again. Shaking his head, he motioned for the tanks to keep moving.

With a resigned sigh, Goodrich turned and followed the tanks. The group reached the end of the tunnel where it took a ninety degree turn to the right, then ended at an iron ladder bolted to the wall ahead of them. The ladder led up to a steel grate that was hinged on one side. When Goodrich stood at the bottom of the ladder and looked up, the light from the globes above him showed him only grid-shaped shadows on the concrete ceiling above it. The sounds of undead shuffling about were much louder here.

Looking at his two tanks, he grinned. "Which one of you wants to go first?"

The tanks looked at each other, then back at him. The one who'd grumbled about the curse replied. "Screw that. I can see it now. I climb up there, push up the grate, and get my face bit off. I don't think so." The other tank shook his head as well.

Goodrich didn't blame them. That was exactly what he'd been picturing too.

"Okay, I guess this is where we test this new spell Ramon gave us." He handed his spear to one of the tanks. "I'll climb up. You use this to push the grate open a bit, and I'll cast the spell on the floor in front of it. When the zombies run away, you guys follow me up as fast as you can move." He looked at both of them. "I'm serious. Your heavily armored asses better be right behind me through that hole."

Both tanks shook their heads, grinning widely at him. He knew they were just messing with him, that they'd be right there when needed, ready to protect him and the others. His teammates might joke and tease each other, but any one of them would lay down their lives to save another.

With another deep sigh, and a muttered "Jerks." Goodrich climbed the iron rungs. At the top he turned and put his back to the ladder, holding on with one hand as he nodded toward the tank with the spear. He used his other hand to guide the butt end of his spear as the tank raised it up, placing it so that it was secure enough to push the grate upward without slipping. The tank pushed, and one side of the grate began to rise as the hinges on the other side squealed in complaint.

"Shit!" Goodrich pressed his head against the rising grate and sent his light globe forward through the narrow opening, lighting up the floor in front of it. He quickly cast the *Repel Undead* spell from the scroll, and waited. When he didn't hear anything, he whispered, "Give it a good shove."

Both tanks lent their strength to shoving the spear upward, causing the grate to fly open, clanging to a stop so loudly that everyone in the group ducked their heads briefly. Goodrich scrambled up through the opening, grabbing his spear from the tanks as he did so. He saw them both rushing up the ladder behind him as he surveyed his surroundings.

They stood in another, much wider corridor this time. The ceiling was ten feet above, and the walls were at least six feet apart, lined with concrete. He held his spear ready as he checked both directions for any threats. A few seconds later both tanks were up with him, one standing on either side of the opening with shields up. They each cast a light globe out ahead, sending them twenty feet down the hallway. They held this position as the others climbed up to join them. Once they were all up, Goodrich closed the grate, just to be safe.

Something down below had smashed that metal door by the tracks, and he didn't want it following them up. At least, not without them hearing it coming. He didn't like leaving the subway tunnel without fully exploring their assigned sector, but his main purpose down there was to scout for undead, and they needed to follow the zombie sounds.

Those sounds were hard to trace, as they were echoing off the walls and ceilings and appeared to be coming from both directions. Unwilling to split the party and go both ways at once, Goodrich made a decision. "Gimme something that'll make some noise." He said, pulling a cooking pan out of his inventory and setting it down atop the grate. He then grabbed a can of baked beans he'd been saving for a special occasion and set it inside the pan. The others handed him similar items, cookware, canteens, some silverware. He then took out a spool of fishing twine and wrapped it around each piece as they were laid out across the hallway. When he was finished, they had a makeshift alarm. Any zombie shuffling past this point would hook the line and drag the clattering metal along with them. It had the added feature of being placed atop the grate, so that anything raising it from below would likewise cause a commotion.

That done, the group formed up again, this time in a loose cluster since the hall was wider. The tanks walked slightly spaced apart with Goodrich and his spear between them. He also had a shield in his inventory that he could produce if they needed to form a shield wall. Behind them were the healer and casters walking three wide, followed by the archers.

They moved quickly toward the sound of undead activity, not trying to be quiet. In less than a minute they stepped out into a wide space with a domed ceiling. The walls and ceiling were covered in mosaic tiles, still glossy enough to reflect some of the lights from the several globes the group cast and spread outward in a fan ahead of them.

The room was filled with zombies.

They were shuffling across the room from right to left, entering from one tunnel and exiting on the opposite side. If Goodrich had to guess, he'd have said there were three hundred or more of them within sight. For now, at least, they seemed to be ignoring him and his group, despite their light globes. Tapping the tanks on their shoulders, he motioned for everyone to move back. The moment they were back fifty feet or so down the hallway, he gave the healer a significant look, telling them to call it in. With a nod, they got on the radio and reported the sighting with a loud whisper.

It wasn't long before a reply came back for them to hold their position or retreat if necessary, and wait for reinforcements. Three more raid groups from the tower were on their way.

Deciding they were safe enough in the hallway, Goodrich hunkered down and watched. They'd left their light globes in the room, since they didn't seem to bother the passing zombies. As quietly as he could he whispered to the rest. "Grab a seat, and try to count them as they pass."

*****

Up on the northeastern section of the Invictus City wall, Allistor's people were still easily handling the mobs trying to climb the walls. They were happily dropping

*Flame Shot* spells in columns down upon the undead as they began to pile up at the base of the wall. Those who had received the new scrolls from Ramon were experimenting with the AoE spell. Bjurstrom was amusing himself by casting the *Repel Undead* spell at the base of a pile of zombies. Those influenced by the light magic wailed in distress and did their best to flee the area, taking damage until they did. This had the result of destabilizing the pile, causing the zombies higher up to tumble and fall, landing in the spells area of effect and mimicking their cohorts. The spell had a twenty foot radius, and lasted for five minutes, with a ten minute cooldown. For most of those who were using it, that was more than enough time to recover the mana cost of the spell. Meaning they could refresh it indefinitely without running out of mana.

Still, those with the spell were spread wide apart, and after a while the enemy adepts began avoiding the places where the spells were being dropped, guiding their minions in between. The defenders noticed, and simply adjusted their positions atop the wall, casting the AoE onto new piles of attackers. Few of the zombies actually died from the light damage, mostly the ones trapped too deeply under the pile to escape. But the spell was an effective way to break up the growing piles of undead trying to climb the walls.

Wanting to experiment himself, Allistor had the girls stand behind him and sing a tune that would buff his magic. When he cast the spell himself, there was a drastic difference. For one, the area of effect was maybe fifty percent wider, covering an entire pile just below him. And from the wailing that it caused, the light magic damage per second was more severe as well. As the teenagers continued to sing, Allistor watched zombie after zombie expire before they could shuffle out of the spell's damage zone.

For over an hour his people cast *Repel Undead, Flame Shot, Mind Spike,* and *Vortex* down upon the unending waves of undead invaders. They often combined the spells to great effect. *Vortex* cast upon a group of burning mobs created a tornado of flaming zombies that smashed against the wall, and against each other, breaking them into flaming zombie bits. Those were hurled in a wide spray outward from the wall, doing impact and flame damage to approaching mobs.

The near constant use of the spells allowed his people to increase their spell skill levels, especially with the new *Repel Undead.* By the end of the hour Allistor had raised his own to level three. Each level widened the area of effect and increased the damage per second.

There was still no end in sight when Allistor heard the report from Goodrich's group. He was tempted to abandon the wall and join them, but stayed where he was. They had planned for this tactic after Kyle's attack on the Outpost in Laramie, and he had faith that his people would deal with the underground intruders who were already inside his walls. His one concession to fear was to order Prime to send a hundred droids down to assist the raiders.

Nancy was giving orders in raid chat, telling his people to begin alternating attack spells to conserve mana.

Based on the numbers they were still seeing coming at them, this fight could easily last through the rest of the day and night. Just like Allistor and other leaders, she suspected that this was just a preliminary. A way to drain their resources and tire their combatants before the real attack began.

As Allistor looked down the wall to where Nancy was standing, another of the AoE necrotic spell attacks struck. This one seemed more powerful than the others, as she and a dozen citizens began to scream, dropping to the stone at the top of the wall and writhing in pain. Allistor took off at a sprint as other healers rushed in from nearby. He was too far away to cast *Restore*, and even if he could, he knew it did no good against the necro spell. The problem was that two of those afflicted by the spell were the light magic healers Nancy had gathered to cure the effects of the dark magic spell.

Allistor watched as one of those two casters managed to grit through the pain and heal herself properly. As soon as her gyrations slowed, she had the presence of mind to heal the other light mage, a large man who was convulsing face down next to her. Allistor began to feel relieved, confident that the two healers could help the others, when fate chose to teach him a lesson.

Nancy, still writhing in agony near the two healers, rolled off the back side of the wall. Allistor screamed in wordless terror as he tried casting *Levitate* on her. He was still too far away, and the spell failed. He watched helpless as her body impacted the concrete at the base of the wall, a pool of blood spreading around her shattered skull.

The two healers had seen her fall, and were both casting heals at her. The moment Allistor got into range, he began casting heals of his own, desperately hoping it wasn't too late.

*****

Goodrich and his team were holding their position in the corridor, waiting for reinforcements, when their makeshift alarm by the grate started clattering. Instantly they were on their feet and looking warily back the way they had come. The clattering was followed by a loud clang, the sound of the grate being thrown open fully and crashing against the concrete floor. More rattling of pots and pans, as if something were tangled up on the twine, was accompanied by a roar of rage that echoed off the concrete walls.

The sound reached the cavernous room full of undead, causing the nearest of them to turn their heads in response, shifting their paths toward the tunnel and the group of raiders hiding inside. Their moans grew louder, alerting more of their companions, who in turn alerted even more in a wave that rippled across the horde.

With their full attention focused on whatever had just emerged from the grate, none of Goodrich's group noticed the increased sounds of zombies growing closer behind them.

They didn't have long to wait before discovering what had come through the grate. The sounds of pots and cookware being dragged across concrete was quickly approaching. The monster had obviously been snagged in the fishing line and hadn't been able, or hadn't bothered to clear itself. Two more light globes pushed forward over the tanks' heads and out as far as the casters could maintain them, about a hundred feet. As the approaching monster entered the lit area, every member of the group gasped in fear or revulsion.

**Necrotic Amalgamation #3**
**Level 44**
**Health: 59,000/59,000**

The creature was something directly out of a low budget horror vid. It looked like someone had taken the body of a large cat, probably a lion, and began stitching random body parts to it. Except that each of those body parts was also animated and functioning. It had the thick neck and head of a gorilla, with four-inch upper and lower fangs. Jutting out from the shoulders just above its forelegs were a pair of crab forearms with oversized pincer claws. The lion's tail had been replaced with a massive segmented scorpid tail complete with stinger that glistened with venom. The monster was obviously undead, great patches of its fur missing, exposing dead grey flesh underneath. Large chunks of it were missing, as if it had already been in several fights and was unable to heal any damage it had taken. One particularly deep wound exposed three of its ribs along one flank. Goodrich guessed that some sick bastard had found a zoo full of corpses and used them to create this obscene thing.

"Oh, hell no." Goodrich's voice echoed off the tunnel walls. He flinched slightly, having surprised himself by unintentionally speaking out loud. There were some softer mutterings from those behind him.

The amalgamation roared in reply, stepping forward at a slower pace than Goodrich expected. As it moved, its head bobbed awkwardly, and its pincer arms shifted forward out of sync with its feline legs, twisting its body with each step. Clearly it hadn't adjusted fully to its altered form.

"Put it down!" Goodrich called out, not wanting the beast to get any closer. The two tanks stepped forward, moving closer together and raising shields. Goodrich cast *Flame Shot* at the thing's head even as he equipped his bow and quiver. He and the other archers began peppering the thing with arrows while the casters burned, froze, and electrocuted it.

The mob simply absorbed the damage, shaking off the loss of an eye to a lucky arrow, ignoring the crisping and bubbling skin on its face. The lightning attacks did stun it for a few seconds, causing it to stumble as its legs seized up but its forward momentum continued. Still it advanced toward the group, its health dropping quickly. Goodrich could clearly see it would reach them before they managed to kill it, so he called out, "Slow retreat. Back twenty feet. Keep firing!"

He was just starting to follow his own orders when one of the archers in the back shouted frantically. "Boss! Company on our six! Oh, Shit!"

Turning to look over his shoulder, he saw both the other archers turn and begin firing almost point blank into a wall of undead mere steps in front of them. Panic struck him, the nightmare image of so many undead crowding against his team with no tanks to hold them back causing his heartrate to double and a cold chill to run down his spine.

Dropping his bow, he grabbed his shield and leapt toward the oncoming wave. "Mages! Vortex on their front line! Archers, focus on the big one! Burn it down or cripple it! Tanks, push it to one side if you can, so we can get past it. Put it between us and the horde!"

He turned his five foot tall shield sideways and slammed it into the nearest zombies in the center of the corridor, knocking them back and buying himself a second. He quickly grabbed two grenades from his inventory, pulling the rings with his teeth and spitting them out before lobbing the explosives over the heads of the undead in front of him. A few seconds later two explosions filled the corridor and splattered the walls and ceilings with gore. Goodrich shoved against the front line again, then again, before stepping back to take a few deep breaths.

Two vortex spells came to life in front of him, the small tornadoes forming just behind the first row of undead, who were being trampled after Goodrich had knocked them down. He raised his shield and took more steps back as bits of dead flesh and bone began to be ejected by the whirlwinds. It was not ideal, as his people would take some damage from shrapnel, but it formed an effective barrier to hold back the undead while they dealt with the gorilla-cat-scorpid thing.

A scream from behind caused him to look over his shoulder. He saw one of the two tanks falling backward, his left leg severed below the knee by one of the giant claws. Before anyone could act, the other claw darted forward and grabbed the tank's other leg, dragging him forward even as he slashed at it with his sword. The blade bounced off the hardened claw, small chips flying off with each strike. The tail whipped forward, but the experienced fighter had the presence of mind to block the strike with his shield, causing a splatter of venom.

One of the mages hit the creature's face with another Flame Shot, causing it to roar even louder. The claw holding their tank released his leg, and his counterpart bravely darted forward to grab his buddy and drag him backward. Several heals fell on the wounded man, the blood spurting from his severed leg slowing, then stopping as two of the mages took over, dragging him into the center of the group as their remaining healthy tank took up position in front of the enraged amalgamation.

*Necrotic Amalgamation #3*
*Level 44*
*Health: 17,330/59,000*

They weren't burning it down fast enough. A glance showed Goodrich that scattered zombies were making it past the vortexes, heavily damaged but still moving forward as the hundreds behind kept pushing. He produced two more grenades and lobbed them several rows back, the swathe of destruction they created reducing the pressure for a moment. He moved quickly to shield bash a few of the advancing enemy back into the vortexes. Not being a tank, he didn't have any special bash ability, just his own momentum and body strength.

Once again his attention was split when their healer shouted, "Look out!" Goodrich glanced back to see the monster activate some kind of ability that sent it hurtling forward. Its bulk struck their tank, plowing through him and knocking him back into the others. Both pincers shot forward, one closing on a mage's chest and crushing her, the other taking an arm from their healer. Underneath its body, the lion's claws were attempting to shred the fallen tank, who was doing his best to keep his shield between him and it.

Worst of all, the mage who was being slowly cut in half by the pincer was one of the two who'd been maintaining the Vortex spells. Goodrich groaned in despair as the vortex to his left began to dissipate, more zombies already pushing through it, ignoring the rapidly weakening damage it was dealing. Goodrich cast his own Vortex into the gap, but it was a spell he rarely used, and thus was only at level one. His tiny whirlwind looked pathetic next to the much higher level one, and did little to hold back the horde.

He added in the Repel Undead spell, placing it between the horde and his group, hoping to keep them back.

One of the archers and a mage grabbed the one-legged tank and lifted him to his feet, where he gamely raised his shield and used a taunt ability on the amalgamation. The archer left the mage to support the tank from behind, resuming fire on the apelike face of the creature. The mage, holding up the tank with one hand under each armpit, turned back toward Goodrich and shook his head. His message was clear.

They weren't going to survive this fight.

Their healer, still in the fight despite a missing arm, called out, "Reinforcements two minutes out!"

"Tell them to move their asses! We'll be dead in two minutes!" Goodrich growled, plowing into more zombies along the left side, pushing as many as he could toward his right where the remaining vortex was still spinning. The mage who was still channeling that spell obligingly moved it closer to the center, intending to take some of the pressure off of Goodrich. Unfortunately, that also allowed some of the undead to squeeze past along the right hand wall, with no tank there to oppose them. They were pushed through the Repel Undead area of effect by even more zombies behind them, groaning in pain as they pressed forward.

There was a sickening squelch as the captured mage quit screaming, the pincher finally shattering thru ribs and cutting the body completely in half. Goodrich found himself surprised that it took so long for a fatality to happen. Though all of his people were improved far beyond human physical norms and able to take considerable punishment, his mind still thought in old world terms, where the loss of a limb or crushed ribs would quickly lead to death.

His musing was cut short as four badly decomposed and wind-shredded undead tackled one of the archers from behind, knocking him over and piling on top of him. Goodrich couldn't help him, already pressed to his limits by the zombies grabbing at his shield or attempting to push him back. The floor was getting slick with grime that had been splattered everywhere by the vortexes, and he was having trouble holding his ground. The only thing saving him was that the undead were having the same problem.

"Kill that damned thing!" He roared the command at the top of his voice, huffing with the exertion of trying to tank the horde.

A moment later he heard another yell. The tank still trapped under the monster shouted, "Tell Felicia I'm sorry!" just before a huge blast wave knocked the raiders, Goodrich, and a good number of zombies off their feet. Flames scorched everyone, and Goodrich closed his eyes as he cast *Restore* on himself. When the heat dissipated enough that he felt it was safe to open them again, he saw the monster lay dead to one side of the tunnel, its legs mostly gone and a huge hole in its chest. A brief surge of hope rushed through him, immediately replaced by sorrow as he noticed what was left of the tank's body. He had clearly sacrificed himself for the others, setting off a grenade or two directly under the monster's belly.

Getting to his feet, Goodrich saw that the blast had also finished off their healer. The remaining tank with the severed leg was laying atop the mage that had been supporting him. Both were unconscious and bleeding.

Moans behind him stole the last bit of hope from Goodrich. The second Vortex spell had been interrupted by the blast, and the undead were advancing through the Repel Undead AoE.

"Retreat!" He bashed his shield against the nearest zombies then stepped back, looking over his shoulder. The only ones back on their feet were one archer, two mages, and himself. Pointing to the unconscious but still living tank and mage, he ordered, "Drag them back toward the grate! Move it!"

As his remaining mages stumbled to comply, the archer attempted to help him hold back the advancing horde. He fired an arrow point blank into one zombie forehead, the used his bow as a staff to push back three more, stepping backward as he fought. Goodrich did the same, slashing off limbs and heads with his sword as he bashed with his shield. He nearly tripped over the pile of zombies that were feeding on his downed archer, not wasting time trying to kill them, just moving further back before one decided to abandon its meal and attack him.

"Clear!" one of the mages shouted as they dragged their unconscious teammates past the corpse of the monster and the remains of the heroic tank. Goodrich tossed two more grenades, the last two in his inventory, into the crowd.

"Run!" he ordered the archer, who nodded once and took off, grabbing hold of the downed tank and helping to drag him faster. When the grenades went off, Goodrich gave the front line of undead one last bash, then began to jog backwards. He reached out and slapped the corpse of the monster as he passed, looting it. Two quick *Flame Shot* fireballs into the front of the horde, and he turned to jog away. Grabbing one arm of the unconscious mage, he helped drag them faster. The grate was in sight. If they could drop down and pull it closed before the horde reached them, they might make it out alive.

Nearly exhausted after trying to tank, Goodrich pushed himself to the limit, increasing the speed at which he dragged his friend. The mage was waking up, and began to struggle. Goodrich and the other mage let go, yanked them to their feet, and pushed them toward the open hole in the floor. Goodrich moved to help with the still unconscious one-legged tank, dragging him forward to the edge of the hole and unceremoniously dropping him through. The others leapt down as he cast more *Flame Shots* at the advancing undead, while lifting the heavy grate with one hand. He quickly realized he had a new problem. If he jumped down with the grate standing upright, it might not fall closed behind him. He tilted it mostly closed before dropping to sit on the edge of the hole, holding the grate above his head. With a twist of his body, he scooted off the edge and fell through the hole, letting go of the grate as he fell. He yanked his hands in toward his body, the heavy metal just missing them as the grate slammed shut. Because of the awkward angle of his fall, he hit the floor below flat on his back, knocking the wind out of him, and temporarily stunning him.   All he could do was lay there and gasp, watching dozens of skeletal fingers try to reach him through the holes in the grate.  Bits of undead flesh dripped down onto him, some just missing his open mouth and sticking wetly to his cheek.

To his horror, those fingers gripped the grate in unison, and he heard the familiar creak of rusted hinges as the grate began to rise.

He tried to call out a warning, but was still unable to breathe.

His teammates didn't have that problem, their screams echoing out as undead bodies began dropping on top of them.  The last thing Goodrich saw was a rotted face with yellowed and broken teeth lunging toward his face.

He still didn't have the breath to scream.

Chapter 15


Allistor was sitting on the ground next to Nancy, her head cradled gently in his hands as he carefully felt for wounds. Her skull had been cracked in the fall from the wall, and he suspected her neck had been broken as well. She'd lost a lot of blood, but thanks to the quick heals from above, she was still breathing. He'd jumped from the wall and run to her, sliding on his knees in the pool of blood that surrounded her head. The battle above was forgotten as he focused on keeping his dear friend alive.

Just when he was reasonably sure that she would recover, and beginning to wonder if she'd have brain damage when she woke up, he heard the call on the radio. Reinforcements had arrived to find Goodrich and his crew wiped out. They were pushing back the zombies with the help of Prime's droids, who were impervious to the bites and scratches from the undead. The droids had managed to climb the ladder and secure a beachhead around the grate, and the raiders were pushing the horde back.

Allistor was angry.

This lich had already killed a couple of kids in his first attack. Now he'd wiped out Goodrich and his entire raid group, and nearly killed Nancy. How many more of his people was he going to lose?

Motioning for another healer to take over caring for Nancy, he got to his feet, her blood dripping from his knees as he stepped away, wiping bloody hands on his thighs.

Walking away from the wall, he ducked into a nearby burned out townhouse, the sounds of battle fading slightly as he walked through the structure and out the back into a small courtyard. He needed time to think.

They had taken out several adepts, but others had taken over the uncontrolled zombies almost immediately. Taking out more of the adepts was a priority. That would ease the pressure on the outer walls. They also needed to confirm who was casting those necrotic AoE spells and put a stop to them.

The undead in the tunnels worried him even more. The subway tunnels and connected access tunnels, utility tunnels, sewers… they spread under more than half of his city. The lich could use them to attack almost anywhere, coming up through subway stations, building basements, or manhole covers. He didn't have nearly enough people to cover all the ground within his walls, even if he emptied all his other holdings and left them unguarded.

And now he had thirty of his citizens, along with a hundred droids, trying to hold back and contain an unknown number of undead. They had the advantage of tight spaces, and probably higher levels. But humans got tired, and droids needed to recharge, eventually. Their undead enemies didn't have either problem.

Allistor knew Prime would rotate out his droids when necessary without needing to be asked. His general was efficient and intuitive. A hundred droids could push back many times their number of zombies, and act as a bulwark for his people, allowing them to rest when needed.

He could probably afford to pull some people from the wall to help out underground. The fighters and healers out here with him were handling the undead with relative ease, except for the necrotic attacks, which were taking out a few of his people here and there.

That was what ultimately made his decision for him. He needed to locate and kill the adepts, and more importantly the lich. Without their control, the undead would just be a shambling mass, wandering aimlessly for his people to easily dispatch at their leisure. They would even make good training fodder for new raid recruits to use to level up. He'd heard no reports on what kind of loot they dropped, but if it was decent, he might even consider making his unaligned core into an undead dungeon.

For now, though, he needed a plan to deal with the elites.

"Nigel, please put me through to Ramon." He waited a second, then said, "Hey buddy, where are you?"

"I'm on the wall, north side." Ramon's voice was tense, his words clipped.

"I'm guessing you already heard about Nancy. I'm looking at her right now. She's alive, still unconscious." Allistor paused, swallowing once and taking a calming breath. "I'm not gonna lie, man. We almost lost her. She fell and cracked her head, and there was a lot of blood."

"I know. I heard. She'll be fine. That woman is too stubborn to die." Ramon was tough. They'd all lost people since the world ended, and knew in the back of their minds that they might lose loved ones at any moment. Especially during a battle. "What can I do for you, boss?"

"You can come here, grab Nancy, and go back to your library. I need as many of those *Repel Undead* scrolls as you can make." He paused, his voice turning to a growl. "We're gonna hunt down those adepts, and whoever cast that necrotic spell on Nancy."

"Roger that. I'll get on it. Two of my people are now high enough in their *Inscription* skill to make that scroll as well. That means we can make three per hour. Also, after making all those scrolls I'm close to being able to teach the spell directly. When that happens I should be able to teach maybe four people per hour. It's not a lot..."

"It'll be good enough. And I have a feeling this fight is going to last a while. Maybe days. So crank those things out. Another hundred or so people who can use that spell might make all the difference."

"I'm on my way." Ramon was breathing hard now, probably sprinting along the wall toward him. "Anything else?"

Allistor thought for a second, watching the healers at work. "Yeah, if any of your people know light magic healing spells, get them started making scrolls too." He grinned and waved as he saw Ramon speeding along the top of the wall, citizens quickly moving out of his way. Ramon barely returned the wave before leaping off the top to land in a superhero pose on the ground near where Nancy still lay unconscious. Allistor shook his head at the landing, making a mental note to tease his friend later.

One of the goblin ships landed in the street nearby as Ramon scooped up Nancy and jogged over to it. In half a minute, the ship was in the air and headed toward Ramon's Citadel.

"Nigel, please ask Harmon if he has a moment." He only had to wait about ten seconds for his reply.

"Allistor, how goes the battle?" The orcanin's deep voice rang out from the wall, surprising a few of the nearest defenders.

"We've lost a few people, killed a few hundred thousand zombies. But we're having an issue with one or more of them casting a necrotic attack that is impossible to defend against, and hard to heal. It has killed a few of my people already." He pictured the look that was about to appear on his friend's face. "I was wondering if your orcanin wanted to join me in a little hunting? I plan to go over the wall and take out as many adepts as I can while I hunt for that lich."

Allistor could hear Harmon chuckling, and a roar of enthusiasm in the background. "We have been waiting for you to ask, my friend! I will send you an honor guard of one hundred warriors to deal with the undead fodder while you hunt. In addition, I will contact the Or'Dralon on your behalf. They have no shortage of light mages to assist your people. I'm sure they would appreciate the opportunity to slay thousands of mid to high level undead."

"Damn. I should have thought of that. I'm not used to having allies. Other than you, of course." Allistor shook his head.

"You have earned them, Allistor. Now you must learn when to use them. I'll join you shortly with your escort." Allistor let out a relieved breath as the link was severed.

"Nigel, I need Andrea and Dean next."

*"Go ahead, sire."*

"Hey guys, everything quiet at the Citadel and Silo?"

"All quiet everywhere but where you are, Allistor." Andrea answered. "I've got Redd and the others in communications doing regular check-ins with every property. They've also alerted most of our allies on this continent."

"That's good to hear. Listen, I need some help here. Dean, I need you and that fifty cal, along with as many snipers or sharpshooters as you can safely send me, Andrea. Pull them from wherever you need to. Load them up with ammo and send them to Battery Park as quick as you can. One of the goblin ships just took Ramon and Nancy to their island, and can pick up the shooters on the way back. They're to spread out along the wall or other, higher ground within range, focus on taking down the adepts, and scan for any sign of the lich."

"On my way." Dean replied. "Be there in two minutes."

It took a few seconds longer for Andrea to pass on orders to some of her airmen before she answered, "We're on it. Ten minutes, tops. Those who don't get there in time to hitch a ride can hoof it up to the wall. The exercise will do em good." He could hear the wicked smile he knew so well.

"Thanks guys. And be sure and let me know if anything new pops up. You'll need to radio me through the droids, I'm taking some orcanin over the wall in a few minutes."

Andrea's voice became concerned. "Be careful, Allistor. Don't do anything stupid. I hear there might be a million of those things out there. If they start to hone in on you…"

"The orcanin will have a lot to celebrate!" He imagined her rolling her eyes. "If you join them, whatever you do, don't drink that stuff they make. Trust me." He felt a pang of sorrow as he remembered the morning hangover he'd shared with Amanda. "I'll be as careful as I can be. And don't worry, I'll make it back in one piece."

Any response was drowned out by the sound of more than a hundred orcanin roaring as they leapt from their ship's loading ramp onto the wall. Half of them began jogging left and right down the length of the wall, spreading out to assist the defenders. The other half formed up and saluted as Harmon approached Allistor. The emperor took a moment to lean out and observe the battle at the base of the wall, nodding with approval.

"I see your people are mostly using magic, rather than technology. This is good."

Allistor hadn't really noticed, but taking a quick look around he confirmed a distinct lack of plasma rifles, or even human rifles. Only the snipers were using them. He felt a swell of pride at his people using the opportunity to level up their spells and skills.

Harmon held out a ring, which he dropped into Allistor's hand when it was extended. "A small gift."

Allistor put the ring on and checked the inventory.

### *Arsthenix model G740 x 500*

Having no idea what the item was, Allistor raised an eyebrow at Harmon. "Uh, thank you. What are they?"

Grinning, Harmon replied, "A little something to help you track your foes. Nigel cannot detect the undead at his current level unless they are on the surface and moving within his sensor range. That ring is filled with remote sensor drones that can be placed in tunnels or junctures underground. Nigel can connect to them, and alert you to enemy movement if they wander close enough."

"That's great!" Allistor looked at the ring with a whole new appreciation. "I upgraded Nigel this morning, but we still have one more upgrade before he can do this himself. Thank you, Harmon."

"It is nothing. Simple technology, very inexpensive. And I haven't even told you the best part, yet. Instruct Nigel to connect with the sensors. You'll need to give him access to the ring by placing it in direct contact with the wall." The orcanin pointed to the flat surface atop the wall.

"Nigel, go ahead and connect to these sensors." Allistor ordered. He was already planning how to organize raid crews to distribute the sensor drones. A moment later, his AI answered.

*"Connection established with five hundred remote sensors, sire. These will be quite helpful. Shall I proceed with deployment?"*

"What? Deployment? Uhm, sure." Allistor blinked at the ring as first one, then another, then another tiny disc appeared above the ring and hovered in the air in front of him. When the air was aswarm with five hundred tiny drones, they all bunched into a tight cluster and disappeared over the edge of the wall, heading toward a nearby subway entrance.

Harmon explained. "Each sensor has a small power core that manipulates the planet's ambient magnetic field to hover and move, along with a sensor array and transceiver that allows Nigel to control them. He'll not only be able to distribute them throughout the tunnels and sewers underneath the city, but he'll be able to use them to map the whole area for you. They're small enough to fit into tight spaces, even under some doors. They can detect heat, motion, and sound while being virtually undetectable themselves."

"Awesome!" Allistor wanted to leap up and give the merchant a high-five. "I'm still not used to all the cool technology available to us now. Something like that hadn't even occurred to me. I could have had the entire city mapped already." Allistor shook his head. Then a thought occurred to him. "We could use these to search for the adepts out there." He pointed beyond the wall.

Harmon shook his head. "Nigel can only control them within his area of influence. Outside of that, you'd have to control them yourself, or use a portable AI with a significant range."

"Like... a ship's AI?" Allistor looked up at the sky, searching for the Phoenix.

Harmon nodded. "Yes, though you'd have to hover very low. The drones have a limited range. The ones Nigel now controls will only work approximately one hundred feet below ground level before he loses connection with them. As you map and claim more of the deeper underground structures, that range will naturally increase. But outside the walls, the ship carrying your controlling AI will need to remain within one hundred feet of the drones. Which makes them impractical for that purpose. They can easily and quickly search every room of every building below you, but any targets you see can easily spot and avoid the hovering ship."

Prime, who had been standing unobtrusively off to one side, as usual, offered a solution. "One of my communications droids could control as many as ten of the drones at a time. They could boost the signal, relaying the sensor data over a much greater distance."

Allistor did a little quick math. "Prime, please bring me four of your comms units. Harmon, can you sell me forty more of those drones?  That would give us… a line of sensors eight hundred feet wide, or a tighter globe of about four hundred feet in diameter, that'll reach as much as twenty stories high.  That should let us sneak up on some unsuspecting adepts."

It took a few minutes for Prime to summon the droids, while Harmon simply accessed his inventory and produced the additional drones.  The comms droids were each assigned their capacity of drones to control, and while they were establishing their links, a new visitor arrived.

Its graceful curving lines clearly established it as an elven ship.  Allistor assumed it was the Or'Dralon, which was confirmed as it hovered inside the wall level with Allistor.  A ramp extended from the ship, and elves began walking down to step atop the wall.  The lead elf was none other than Melise herself.  Allistor tried not to stare at the beautiful elfess as she smiled up at him.  Rather than the airy and revealing clothes she'd worn at their first meeting, she now wore tight-fitting armor that appeared to be fashioned from scaled reptile skin.  It hugged her form, accentuating features that Allistor instantly felt guilty for admiring.

"Greetings, Emperor Harmon, Emperor Allistor.  Or'Dralon has come to offer our assistance in your time of need. I hope we are not too late?" She bowed at the waist while speaking, first to Harmon, then to Allistor.

"Right on time, thank you Lady Melise." Allistor bowed his head slightly in return. "You and your people are most welcome."

She flashed him another bright smile that caused his heart to thump a few extra beats. "This is but our first contribution." She waved at the roughly one hundred elves who immediately began to fan out down the wall in both directions. "We have summoned others who will arrive in a few hours. Necromancers are the natural enemy of light mages, and we have many who wish to embrace this opportunity."

Unsure of the protocols involved, Allistor just took a chance. "Would you like me to share the City Defense quest with you, so that you might in turn share it with your people? It might significantly increase their rewards for coming to our aid today."

Melise simply smiled and bowed her head in acceptance. Allistor quickly pulled up the quest on his UI and gave a mental nudge to share it with both Melise and Harmon. The orcanin snorted in acknowledgement. Melise's eyes went blank as she took a moment to read, and then share, the quest. "That is most gracious of you, Emperor Allistor."

"Please, just Allistor." He smiled at the graceful and gracious elfess. "Titles make me uncomfortable, still."

"As you wish, Allistor." She took in the orcanin and droids gathered nearby, as well as the drones hovering around each droid. "You are planning a scouting mission?"

Allistor was surprised by how quickly she had ascertained that from the available information. "Yes. We were just about to leave. There are adepts out there controlling the masses, and someone is hitting our people up here with a nasty dark magic spell that has killed several already. That is why we requested light mages, to help us counteract that spell. I'm taking this group outside the wall to eliminate as many adepts as we can find, and hopefully the lich as well."

"I will accompany you." She stated, eyes flashing and her tone making it clear it wasn't a question.

"I... am not sure that's wise." Allistor blustered a bit. He didn't want to risk the elfess' life on such a risky mission. And by extension risk alienating her clan, again.

"You do not wish my company?" She asked, her lower lip extending into the most adorable pout.

"I do not wish you to come to harm." Allistor corrected. Beside him, Harmon cleared his throat. When Allistor looked over, the orcanin smiled at Melise before turning his gaze to Allistor.

"Lady Melise is an experienced warrior, in addition to being a light mage. She is currently level thirty five, and wearing armor that would easily protect her from any attack she is likely to suffer here today." He paused and favored the elf with a smile. "I should know, I sold it to her myself. With my warriors, and you yourself to protect her, she should be quite safe. And I believe you'll find her skills useful."

Allistor wanted to shoot the orcanin a dirty look for totally throwing him under the bus. He could tell the giant was struggling to contain a grin as Allistor stared. But Melise was watching Allistor quite intently, and he couldn't afford to indulge that urge.

"In that case, you are most welcome to join us, Lady Melise." He nodded her way.

"Wonderful! I shall bring one of my house guards along, so that my father does not lecture me later for being careless or impetuous." The moment she turned away to speak to her guard, Allistor elbowed Harmon in the ribs, causing the merchant to chuckle. Allistor glared up at him, only causing his friend's tusk-filled grin to widen. Harmon gave him a quick wink before he covertly and effortlessly nudged Allistor closer to the elfess.

The elven bodyguard, seeing Allistor stumble closer over Melise's shoulder, bowed and took a step back, thinking the Emperor wanted a private word. Allistor threw him a curveball, asking, "What is your name, honorable guard?"

The surprised elf's mouth opened and closed once before he answered. "I am Rekon, of the Or'Dralon Royal Guard, Emperor Allistor." He bowed again from the waist.

"Glad to meet you, Rekon. I will do my best to ensure Lady Melise's safety during this trip, but I'm counting on your help. I want your promise that you will protect her no matter what, even at the expense of my own life."

The elf looked offended for a brief moment before carefully adopting a neutral expression again. "I have already taken such an oath, your majesty."

"Oh, right." Allistor felt foolish. Why would an elf try to protect a foreign emperor over a lady of his own house? "Great, then I believe we're ready to go."

"I offer my own ship to shuttle us to our destination." Melise was clearly trying to ease Allistor's embarrassment over his faux pas, moving past it without comment.

"Thank you. We're not going far," Allistor took a quick look around. He chose a high rise about thirty blocks to the north outside the wall and pointed to it. "That should be far enough. We can hopefully spot some of the adepts from that roof. If not, we'll continue down to the ground and start hunting."

Melise and her guard led Allistor, the orcanin, and the droids back up the ramp and into her ship.

*****

Down in the tunnels below the city, the battle was raging on two fronts. The raiders that had been too late to help Goodrich and his crew had, with the help of the droids, pushed the undead all the way back through the tunnel and into the domed room where Goodrich had first found them. From there they had split the droids into two groups, one blocking the door where the undead had been entering the room, and the other blocking the exit they'd been streaming into. Only the raid leader in each group had received one of the *Repel Undead* scrolls, but those three individuals were making the most of it. They took turns casting the spell on the area directly in front of the shield-bearing droids, happily burning down the zombies who were unable to flee the light magic zone due to the press of bodies behind them. The others were casting spells over top of the droid tanks, burning through the undead hordes' reduced health pools with ease. The raid groups' tanks and other melee specialists were alternating between leveling up their limited damage spells, and using ranged weapons. Several had produced, or borrowed, bows and arrows, and were working at leveling up those skills.

Two of the raid groups were assigned to the entry, while the third took the exit tunnel. The undead in that direction had mostly continued down their ordered path, with just the rear hundred or so turning to fight. Once they were put down, that raid leader, a bearded midwesterner named Kuhns, ordered the droids to push forward, following the string of marching undead toward whatever their destination was. They reported in every two minutes via radio droid, mapping the tunnel and marking any doors or intersections on their UIs as they went. The going was slow, as they paused at each door to open it and clear the room. At each intersection they left two droids to guard the side tunnel they left behind. The last thing they wanted was to get trapped between enemies coming at them from behind, the way Goodrich had.

An hour into their pursuit, they stopped short. They'd reached a huge chamber that was several steps down from the tunnel they were standing in. At the bottom of the steps, thirty or so corpses were getting to their feet, obviously having tumbled down the steps. As soon as they were mobile, they headed in different directions toward one of eight exits.

The chamber was some kind of switching station for the trains. There was a busy starburst-shaped pattern of tracks laid across the floor, one leading into (or out of) each of the eight tunnel openings. In the center of the chamber was a large wheel that could clearly be used to turn train cars. A car would come in on one track at three o'clock, hold on the wheel while it turned like a clock face, then exit onto a whole new track at six o'clock.

"We can't chase them any further." Kuhns called out. "Kill anything you can hit! Start at max range, bring as many of them to us as you can."

Not needing to be asked twice, his people began casting spells and firing arrows at zombies who were just about to exit the various tunnels nearby. The room was too large to reach all the way across with their magic, so they focused on the two nearest tunnels on either side of them. The droids fanned out to their left and right, and set a shield wall at the top of the steps. This was a great position from which to fight, forcing the enemy zombies to climb the steps to reach them, where they were met with droid shields and spears. Faces grim and mana potions at the ready, the group began the slaughter as their healer reported in their position and requested more reinforcements. They had eight new tunnels to follow the undead into.

Chapter 16

Hel watched the multiple holo displays in front of her, tentacles twitching in irritation. The lich was not following the orders she'd given him nearly a year ago when she placed him on that planet. He was wasting resources by attacking Invictus City. Already hundreds of thousands of common undead and something like a score of adepts were lost. Months of work thrown away for no gain.

Even worse, she had a very real fear that Baldur and Odin would discover that she was responsible for the lich being inserted there during the planet's Stabilization. They had Loki in custody, and would be scouring his mind for information on such infractions. If her father had discovered any actual proof of her involvement in this, or any of several other forbidden actions, and brought the proof to light, the System would deal harshly with her.

As ancient and powerful as her race might be, they were still subject to the System and its punishments. Her punishment would be extreme, as the System would take into account her extensive knowledge of its workings, its rules, and the reasons for them. Factoring in the wide-reaching consequences of her actions, the System would almost certainly end her mortal existence.

She didn't fear that, though it would put an end to much of her fun. No, what she feared was exactly what the human had threatened her father with. The binding of her soul, or even its utter destruction. Those who came before, who created the System to begin with, had long ago ascended. They had the knowledge of how to do so, long before Hel's race crawled out of the mud on their planet of origin. They had passed that knowledge on to the System so that it could prevent those whom they would consider unworthy from ascending.

That had been the single most terrifying thing she and her people had learned in their study of the System. Until that point, they had come to believe that they were all-powerful, beyond the point where they might be held accountable for their actions. Secure in the belief that they could simply abandon the mortal plane at will and explore a new existence as beings of pure thought and energy. The realization that the System could deny them this, could hold them responsible for breaking its rules, had nearly led Hel to abandon her own rebellious and predatory lifestyle.

She contemplated a safer, more sedate, life. She already possessed great power, and nearly unlimited wealth accumulated over millennia, and could live in comfort for eternity.

But what was the point? She thrived on the excitement of breaking the rules. Lived for the danger. If she were to give that up, she might as well ascend. Plus, what greater challenge could she ask for? Her entire life she had competed against her father, the being known as the god of deceit and trickery. The only higher challenge than outsmarting her father was beating the System itself.

Which brought her back to the itch in the back of her mind. As if the System were there, watching. Poised to snap into action, to sever the thread of her existence.

And she couldn't help feeling that the itch had something to do with the lich.

It was supposed to have taken over one of the most heavily populated cities on the planet, packed it full of undead until dark magic permeated the very soil to such a degree that it would naturally spawn a dungeon. She could then use access to that dungeon to her advantage, or take the core and do the same.

The lich had been well on its way to completing that task when she'd diverted it to the west, and the human boy, Kyle. That had been her mistake. She'd done it for simple amusement, to throw another barrier at the human prince. The derailment had changed the lich, given him a desire for vengeance, to repay the prince for the insult of defeating him. Now it was wasting resources on a battle it wouldn't win, while at the same time stirring up powerful forces. Questions were being asked, investigations launched.

Instead of a useful and profitable dungeon on an energy-rich new planet, the lich had given her a nervous twitch and an unending sense of unease. The only thing stopping her from smashing its phylactery and ending its un-life was the fact that the sudden unexplained destruction of the lich would generate even more curiosity. As it was now, there was a slim possibility that the lich could be perceived as acting on its own. Having its string suddenly cut would end any speculation and trigger a search for whomever was holding the scissors.

The intermediary she had used to locate and contact the lich was dead, along with the crew that had transported him to the planet, and anyone else even peripherally involved. She had little fear that any new investigation could lead back to her. But the fear that her father had already made the necessary connections ate at her. He could reveal those connections under compulsion, or just to spite her. And all it would take would be a declaration of the truth witnessed by the System.

Thus she was not in the least surprised when Baldur appeared in her lab, causing the mists to swirl as his anger collided with her alarm.

"Odin wishes to speak with you, child. Now."

*****

Kuhns perked up when he heard laughter echo out from one of the tunnels to his left. His team and their droids had taken down more than a hundred undead in the switching station, and were casually looting the corpses. They hadn't pursued the monsters into any of the tunnels, not having the necessary manpower. More raid groups were on their way, along with more droids. The raiders had been calling out any decent loot they received. As with the old MMO's, the undead were dropping items they never would have carried in real life. Like when you would receive gold coins and maybe a chain belt from a murdered fuzzy bunny. These mobs were dropping scrolls, weapons, and armor pieces as well as klax. Kuhns himself reached down and touched the skeletal corpse of a woman wearing what was left of a Victorian era dress. At least, he assumed it was a woman. He briefly imagined it might have been a man dressed as a woman as part of some scheme to lure and shanghai drunken sailors at the port. Or a casualty of a tragic cross-dressing Halloween party mishap. Maybe a lothario caught in his lover's boudoir by an angry husband, who grabbed what clothes he could before leaping out the window, forced to wear a dress as he slunk home through the dark alleys of 19th century New York City. There was no real way to tell. In any case, the loot granted was decent – an uncommon quality spell scroll called Death's Bane, a thousand klax, and two-handed longsword that glowed faintly green.

He was about to Examine the sword to see what kind of enchantment it held when the laughter rang out.

Instantly, all the humans had weapons in hand, the loot forgotten. The droids began to step toward the sound, shields raised. Kuhns stopped them by calling out, "Everybody back up the stairs! Take the same positions as before." The droids waited for the humans to gather and move up the stairs, following the last of them walking backwards with shields up. As soon as they reached the top they formed two lines and hunkered down behind their matte black shields. The humans readied their ranged attacks and waited.

The laughter ceased, and a dry, raspy voice echoed out of the second tunnel to their left. "Humans. Such primitive creatures. So physically and mentally weak, so easily controlled. You will all make fine additions to my horde."

A single undead emerged from the tunnel, taking two steps into the room before stopping. It wore a surprisingly clean blue robe with several arcane symbols stitched in red and black across the front. In one hand it held a very clichéd sickle with a bone handle and a flat ebony blade. Its other hand was wrapped around a tall, segmented bone staff that appeared to be made by several femurs fused end to end, with a human skull at the top, its eyes glowing green. Kuhns cast Identify on the leathery talking corpse.

*Necromancer Adept*
*Level 48  Elite*
*Health:  67,000/67,000*

The adept opened its mouth to say more, but its head rocked back as an arrow blasted into the open mouth. The raiders cheered as it fell backwards, the arrowhead and several inches of shaft sticking out the back of its skull. One of the archers pumped a fist in the air, shouting "One shot, one ki-" He didn't finish the sentence, his mouth snapping shut as the adept sat up and grabbed ahold of the arrow near the fletching, yanking the arrow free amidst a shower of dusty flesh and bits of bone. Using its staff, it regained its feet, shaking its head.

"You'll have to do better than that." The adept thrust its staff forward, and nearly the entire group of humans began to scream as their flesh and muscles seized and began to rot. Kuhns, though he was feeling the same pain from the necrotic attack, had the presence of mind to cast *Repel Undead* atop his own group as he fell. The light magic AoE didn't cancel out the adept's attack completely, but it did ease the pain and damage enough for the raiders to regain their senses. Magic attacks rained down on the undead creature as its body sprouted several arrow shafts within seconds. The group healer focused on bringing his teammates back up to acceptable health levels, while droids held their position.

An ice bolt the size of a football slammed into the mummified face, shattering a cheekbone before penetrating deep into a brain that had long since gone to dust. Fireballs sped toward the adept as columns of flame dropped upon its head. Two stone spikes shot up from the floor, one in front, one in back, to cross tips as they impaled the creature through its back and gut, trapping it by forming a sort of x through its body. Its health bar was dropping, quickly approaching fifty percent.

> *Necromancer Adept*
> *Level 48 Elite*
> *Health: 39,300/67,000*

Holding its hands out wide to either side, the undead creature laughed loudly at them. "Your puny magics cannot kill me. I am the horde! I am *legion!*" it shouted as both hands made a flicking motion. Instantly two streams of black energy appeared from two of the tunnels, one connecting with each hand. His health bar shot back up to full as two zombies staggered out of the tunnels, following along the streaming dark magic threads. They'd taken only a dozen or so steps before they crumbled and fell unmoving onto the floor. Almost immediately more zombies began to emerge, from every tunnel this time.

"Shit, he can steal their energy to heal himself. There are hundreds, maybe thousands of them to act as batteries for him. We can't fight him like this!" Kuhns growled to his people. After a moment's thought, he added, "Ranged, keep pouring on the dps. See if you can interrupt that self-heal thing. Tanks, melee, with me. Charge!"

The tanks wasted no time, activating a rush ability that sent them across the room in a flash, slamming both of their shields into the adept at the same moment. Kuhns sprinted forward at superhuman speed, two melee fighters right behind him. He was still holding the freshly looted sword, so he raised it over his head as he leapt the final ten feet toward the adept. With a downward chop he severed the arm holding the sickle just below the elbow. The adept screamed, more in anger than pain. With its remaining arm it slammed the butt of its staff on the stone chamber floor. Instantly Kuhns, the tanks, and the melee fighters were afflicted with the necrotic spell again. *Repel Undead* was still on cooldown, and Kuhns had no other ace up his sleeve as he succumbed to the pain of rotting flesh and cramping muscles. His legs failed him, and he fell to the floor. His back arched so severely that only the back of his head and his feet were in contact with the floor, and he could hear his spine creak in protest.

Over the screams of his team, Kuhns could hear the distinct sound of metal on stone as the droids charged forward. Several attacked the adept, slamming shields into its body, striking it with spears. The rest each grabbed a human and lifted them up before carrying them out of the dark spell's radius. Kuhns immediately felt better, or at least no worse. He felt a heal wash through him a moment later, clearing his mind enough to cast a second one on himself.

As the droids slowly dismantled the lich's body, surrounding it and chipping away at its health with physical attacks, the ranged raiders had shifted their focus to the incoming horde. Each of the casters placed a vortex at the mouth of one tunnel, hoping to slow the advance of the undead reinforcements. Fireballs sped down other tunnels, setting corpses on fire and illuminating just how many enemies were packed inside. The tunnel nearest on their right was blocked with three stone spikes that impaled the leading zombies and caused a backup of moaning bodies. Several more pressed in behind and impaled themselves, pushing the lead zombies further onto the spikes until one of them simply burst in half, its separated parts squelching onto the floor. A cone of arctic air blasted into the tunnel, freezing the first several rows of mobs solid, creating an effective barrier for the rest.

The group was playing for time, doing their best to hold back the horde long enough to kill the adept. The necrotic damage had worn off enough for the tanks and melee to recover. The two tanks retreated back up the steps to protect the casters, while Kuhns led the two melee fighters around behind the lich.

Its body was heavily damaged, both legs missing great chunks of flesh, its face half gone, and its one remaining arm gripping tightly to the staff, which was the only thing still holding it upright. One of the melee fighters dashed forward a few steps and dropped into a baseball slide, using his legs to knock loose the staff. He screamed in pain the moment his legs came into contact with the weapon, both of them going ice cold and withering to desiccated flesh underneath his gear.

The adept, now without its support, dropped to its knees. Kuhns wasted no time, swinging the two-handed sword. The green glow of enchantment flashed brightly as it severed the adept's spine, setting the head on fire with green flames even as it fell to one side.

Most of the group leveled up from the adept's demise combined with the many common zombie kills. None of them could manage to reverse the necrotic damage to their comrade's legs no matter which healing spell they used. One of the tanks lifted him gently and carried him back up the stairs, placing him near the back of the group.

Without the adept, the horde pressing in on them from all sides was less motivated. Those in the front who'd already taken damage, or been otherwise aggro'd by the raiders, continued to try to advance. Those further behind at the back of each tunnel began to wander away in small clumps of two or three. Not having the adept to deal with, Kuhns organized his group's attacks to focus on one tunnel at a time while maintaining the ice, fire, and wind spells that were holding back the others. He was surprised when a stone wall suddenly grew up to block one of the tunnel entryways. Looking behind him, he saw a grinning earth mage waving his hands and creating a second wall. Right behind him was a flood of nearly a hundred raiders. Tanks moved down the stairs and formed a wall twenty shields wide in an arc that left room for melee fighters to fill in behind. Casters and ranged dps covered the stairs and the platform above, while the healers watched their rear and took turns trying to restore the injured man's legs with spells and potions. A host of droids filled the tunnel behind them, waiting for orders.

With more than enough firepower, they opened two tunnels at a time, allowing the bottled up zombies to advance into the chamber. Few of them even made it to the line of tanks, a storm of magic and arrows filling the room and burning them down in record time. Less than ten minutes later the room grew quiet again. The droids advanced to loot the corpses and guard each tunnel entrance as the raid leaders put their heads together to form a plan. They now had ten full raid groups, plus Kuhns' group, which was still down a man. Kuhns made the decision to send the afflicted man back to the tower with an escort of four droids, in hopes that one of the regeneration machines would be able to help him.

Kuhns and his raiders would remain in the chamber with two more groups, who would help maintain barriers sealing off four of the tunnels. The remaining eight groups were doubling up, two groups working together to clear each of the first four tunnels. Once they were secured, they'd return and clear the other four.

It wasn't long before the other groups advanced into their assigned tunnels, and the sounds of battle resumed. Kuhns, tired and more than a little worried, sat on one of the steps, munched on a stale granola bar as he stared at a nearby droid that was holding the adepts bone staff. None of the humans had been willing to touch it after hearing what it had done to their comrade. With a sigh, he finished his granola snack, downed a few swigs of water, and took a minute to assign his newly earned attribute points.

*****

Allistor knelt in front of the knee wall on the roof of his chosen high rise. His sniper rifle snug against his shoulder, the bipod stand's feet sitting atop the wall. He let out a long-held breath and kept his finger very still where it rested on the trigger. Through his scope he watched a window in a mid-rise building ten blocks away, waiting for the adept within to show its face again.

He didn't need the sniper rifle and its super long distance scope for such a close target. He could easily have made this shot with a standard hunting rifle. But he wanted his first shot to be a kill shot, and the fifty caliber round that he was about to send downrange would, assuming he hit his target, turn its head into a splash of goo on the wall behind it. One would also never normally fire such a round into a city building, as they had a tendency to go through the target, the wall behind it, and several more walls beyond. The risk to innocent bystanders would be too great.

But in this case, the only living things out there in the dead zone around his city were the non-living. If he managed to pick off an extra zombie or two, bonus!

Allistor was having a hard time focusing. He was uncomfortably aware of Melise sitting, slightly too close for his comfort, to his left. And the bodyguard standing behind him, hand on the hilt of his sword as if just waiting to take Allistor's head if he should accidently brush up against the elfess.

Taking in another deep breath, he held it while he refocused on the crosshairs in his scope. He'd spotted the adept while scanning the buildings, but it had moved out of his line of sight before he could fire. So he scanned that and several nearby windows every few seconds, as well as the building entry below. Though he'd grown up hunting, and had done more than his share of shooting since the apocalypse, he was no professional. He needed the thing to remain in view for a solid five or ten seconds to be sure he hit it.

Melise yawned, stretching her arms above her head, distracting Allistor to an even higher degree. "This is not what I expected from a hunt, Allistor."

He chuckled, still eyeballing the building downrange. "I used to say the same to my father when I was a kid. I wanted to be sneaking through the woods Elmer Fudd style, shoot a deer on the move with a perfect shot right through the heart." He smiled fondly, enjoying the memories of time with his dad even as he felt the familiar twinge of loss. "Instead we climbed up into a tree stand and sat there for hours, not moving, not talking, just waiting. Like we're doing now. For a kid like me, that was almost torture."

"Elmer...?" She questioned.

"Oh, right. Elmer Fudd style. He was a classic cartoon character. Uhm, make-believe. An animated drawing. Used to hunt a very clever bunny. He'd tiptoe through the woods trying to sneak up on the bunny, then fire about a thousand shotgun rounds in all directions without reloading. Not at all realistic, but it was funny."

"Sounds... charming." She was clearly just humoring him, but somehow he didn't mind.

"If we ever get TVs or the internet working again, I'll be sure and show you." He offered.

"I believe I would like that very much." She practically purred at him. He stiffened, afraid that he'd somehow just asked her out on a date. But all social awkwardness was forgotten as his target showed itself.

It was now three windows east and one floor up from where he'd seen it before. The adept was standing before the window, waving its hands at a tightly clustered group of undead making its way down the street below. Allistor wasted no time, sighting in on its face and letting out his breath slowly, then squeezing the trigger. The rifle bucked against his shoulder, the bipod legs leaving small scratch marks on the wall's surface. An instant later the adept's head exploded before its body fell from view inside the room. Down below on the street, the shuffling cluster of zombies slowed their march. Several began to wander off down side streets and alleys.

One down, who knew how many to go?

Allistor continued to monitor their progress, waiting for another adept to notice the uncontrolled group and take charge of them. This was how he'd found the adept he just killed. It had taken over for the one he'd killed before that. Since landing on this roof, they had taken down four more adepts.

The shot had effectively halted Melise's subtle advance. She wasn't pressuring him, exactly. Her touch was much lighter than that. She was making it clear that she was available and interested in him, while maintaining a carefully respectful and precise distance and acknowledging his recent loss, all without actually saying any of those things. Her social skills were flabbergasting, and Allistor imagined her *Charisma* attribute must be about a zillion.

The fact that he was responding the way he was, consciously or not, made him feel guilty and a little bit angry. With himself and with her. He felt like enjoying her attention was a betrayal, and that he should be stronger.

There was a crash below, and Allistor shook his head. The orcanin had quickly gotten bored and asked permission to descend into the building and clear it. When that was accomplished, they'd decided it was necessary to clear all the buildings within a one block perimeter, to ensure Allistor's safety. He privately suspected that they were hungry as well as bored, and hoping for some tasty monsters to cook. A quick glance at the two who'd stayed on the roof with him showed them peering over the edge with envious looks on their faces. When one of them noticed his attention, he quickly straightened up and thumped his chest. "Another excellent shot, another kill!" He flashed a tusky grin at Allistor, who grinned back in acknowledgement.

They'd been outside the wall for four hours, and the suns would be setting soon. Between the bored orcanin and his bored elf companion, he was convinced to give it a rest for the night. "Alright, let's recall all your comrades and head back. We'll come back out tomorrow and change things up a bit. Maybe move along at ground level for a while."

Both orcanin perked up at this. They'd wanted to just bulldoze through the undead on the ground in typical orcanin fashion. While they didn't consider sniping from a rooftop to be dishonorable, it was certainly not their preferred method of killing. One spoke into his wrist communicator while the other opened the roof access door and roared down into the stairwell.

Rekon obligingly called for the elven ship to retrieve them as Allistor got to his feet, then fought the natural urge to offer Melise a hand up. L'olwyn had drilled into his brain time after time that he should never make physical contact with those of other factions. Luckily for him, the nimble elf bounced to her feet and began stretching her legs before he'd had more than a second to feel awkward for not offering.

As if sensing his angst, she flashed a bright smile his direction, then fluttered her eyelashes innocently as she asked. "Can you demonstrate for me this hunting style? This… tippytoe?"

Allistor snorted, then blushed slightly when he realized she was really asking. Looking at the three serious and masculine bodyguards on the roof with them, he shook his head. "Like I said, it's... silly."

"Oh, please. I'm afraid I won't be able to sleep tonight, wondering about this Fudd."

With a quick glance at the guards, and another to see if the rest of the orcanin were arriving through the access door, he shook his head in resignation. "Alright, but just for a second." He closed his eyes, remembering the cartoon as best he could from his childhood. Then, gripping his rifle in both hands, he raised up onto the balls of his feet and took several exaggerated, high-kneed tippytoe steps forward. Laughing to himself as he got into it, he even turned and held a finger to his lips, saying, "Sssshhhh!"

He quickly quit his shenanigans when Rekon snorted and Melise giggled. The two orcanin seemed confused and slightly embarrassed for him.

"That was wonderful!" Melise's smile was wide and honest. "Though I doubt you'd have much luck sneaking up on your prey like that."

"Ha! That was sort of the point." Allistor moved back to kneel next to the hard case for his rifle, removing the scope and securing everything in place before returning it all to his storage ring.

The orcanin arrived shortly before the Or'Dralon ship, and they quickly loaded everyone aboard. Just ahead of him, Melise giggled again as she made a great show of tippytoeing up the ramp. Allistor did his best not to notice the sway of her hips as she did so.

*****

Bjurstrom and McCoy sat on crates in the stock room behind the Invictus tower's main kitchen. They'd gone there to convince Sam to liberate a bottle of goblin brandy and join them in a toast to their lost friend and comrade. The battle with the undead was about to move into its second day as midnight approached. There would be time for formal memorials later. Right now their people were rotating down off the wall to get some rest while others took up the fight against the unceasing waves of zombies.

"To Goodrich!" Bjurstrom raised his glass. "He went out fighting, exactly as he would've wanted."

"Goodrich!" Sam and McCoy raised their glasses as well before all three downed a shot of the brandy. McCoy coughed, then spoke with a raspy voice as he thumped his chest with his fist. "Woo! Good stuff."

Sam refilled their glasses, then held his up. "Good stuff!" They clinked glasses and emptied them again.

McCoy sighed. "Not many of us left from the original gang."

"Yeah." Bjurstrom looked down at his empty glass, then held it out for Sam to refill. "You, me, and Andrea. Redd. A few of the desk jockeys. The rest of the old guild are gone now."

"For your guild!" Sam raised another toast. Though he'd not been much of a gamer in his youth, he recognized that gamer guilds could develop into a sort of family.

As Sam refilled the glasses once more, Bjurstrom shook his head, a grin forming on his somber face. Then he chuckled quietly to himself.

"What?" McCoy eyed him, knowing his longtime friend was likely having some completely inappropriate thoughts.

"I was just... thinking. It's kind of too bad the zombies ate Goodrich. If we'd been able to recover his body, we could have fed him to the mama murder chicken."

"Ha!" Sam roared, setting down the bottle to slap his knee. "You are one sick dude."

McCoy snort-laughed. "Yaknow, I actually think he would have liked that. He'd probably hope he gave her the runs, or something. After that whole junk-biting incident, she was totally his nemesis."

Sam raised his glass, waiting for the other two before downing the liquid. "Amanda told me that Goodrich actually tried to bribe Nancy to make it grow back bigger when she used the regenerator machine thingy."

Bjurstrom nodded. "Oh, he bragged to everyone that she did it. Threatened to smack people around with it. He was totally full of shit, but it made people laugh. We don't laugh enough these days."

The three men sat there in silence for a full minute or so before Sam reached out to refill their drinks with the last of the brandy in the bottle. Raising his glass slowly this time, he clinked it against both of theirs. "Goodrich, his junk, and laughter."

Chapter 17

Agni walked into Rajesh's private quarters with slow, resigned steps. He was not looking forward to speaking with his nephew. Still, anytime there was bad news, he needed to be the one to deliver it. Anyone else would be risking their safety, maybe even their lives, by angering their Earl. As unstable as Rajesh was, he would never harm his uncle. Rajesh depended too heavily upon him.

He found his nephew lounging in an oversized marble hot tub on the balcony of his luxurious suite. There were three young women in the tub attending him, none of them looking happy to be there. Though if Rajesh looked directly at any one of them, they would instantly be all smiles and gracious words. Agni carefully warned all the staff against upsetting Rajesh.

As he stepped out onto the balcony and cleared his throat, all the young women were instantly laser focused on him. With just a raise of his eyebrows and a nod toward the door, he did them the favor of dismissing them. When Rajesh began to object, Agni held up a hand for silence and gave his nephew a stern look, implying that he had information for his ears only.

Slightly mollified by the implication of intrigue, Rajesh settled back in the water and waited impatiently for the women to depart, which they did with alacrity.

The moment the French doors closed behind them, Agni began. "We were able to reach Allistor's representatives via radio this morning." He purposely left off *emperor* as the title was a sure way to annoy Rajesh. "They assured me that he would be interested in speaking with you in the near future. However, more specific arrangements will have to wait."

"What?!" Rajesh sloshed to his feet, his face twisting in instant anger. "This is an insult!"

Agni shook his head. "His city has been under attack for the last three days by a large army of undead. I'm sure that once he has dealt with the problem, he will wish to speak with you, and…"

"Nonsense! He must have thousands, maybe tens of thousands of peasant fighters to deal with the zombies! Surely he could come here himself and leave the fighting to them. Does he not have generals or… captains or something?"

Agni held his tongue. He'd been told that Allistor was in fact on the walls fighting with his people. Sharing this information with his nephew, who had not personally participated in a battle for nearly a year since he secured the Stronghold they now sat in, would only make him feel inadequate.

Then again… it might do him some good.

"Allistor is personally leading his people in the battle. I'm told he does this regularly, preferring to risk his own life in hopes of saving those of his citizens." He let

371

that sink in for a moment, waiting for Rajesh to open his mouth to protest before cutting him off by adding the next barb. "That may be the secret to his rapid rise in power. You have said yourself that fighting and killing creatures is the fastest way to gain experience and levels."

Rajesh was a conniving coward at heart. Implying that his lack of advancement over the rank of Earl, while Allistor had risen to become Emperor of Earth, because he was unwilling to risk his own neck... well that closed Rajesh's mouth with an audible *click*. Agni watched as his fists clenched, his face slowly turned purple.

It was hard for any man to be reminded of his own shortcomings. It was exceptionally hard for Earl Rajesh.

Agni waited patiently for Rajesh to either calm himself, or explode in a fit of rage. The odds were about even, either way. Out of the corner of his eye he spotted one of the young ladies peeking around a corner inside, her own eyes wide with fear. He subtly shook his head and waved at her with a hand placed behind his back where Rajesh could not see. She immediately disappeared.

There was a splash as Rajesh stomped a foot inside the tub, then a larger splash as that foot slipped and he lost his balance, falling clumsily into the shallow water. Spitting and spluttering like a drowned cat, he struggled back to his feet as Agni studiously inspected his own shoes, pretending not to have noticed the fall.

"This insult shall not stand!" Rajesh stepped out of the tub and wrapped a towel around himself before beginning to pace back and forth on the balcony. "We must repay him. Get him here, and make him suffer for his insolence."

Agni sighed, able to guess what was coming.

"Send a call for help! If he's so interested in saving lives, let him think he's coming to save some of *my* peasants. Tell him…" Rajesh stopped pacing and gazed out toward where the gelatinous beings had now killed half a dozen peasants that had been sent against them. "Yes! Tell him that we're being attacked by the jellies! That they will soon overrun us, and we are powerless against them! Beg for him to come and save us."

Pleased with himself, Rajesh dropped his towel and stepped back into the tub. "I shall make preparations for his arrival. Maybe the quickest way to become Emperor is to take the throne from another." His eyes unfocused as he pictured himself sitting atop a great throne, millions bowing at his feet. "Tell Fayed to attend me. We have plans to make."

Bowing his head slightly, Agni took his leave. He would send Fayed to his nephew, let the boy be distracted with his nefarious assassination planning for a few days. There was no doubt in his mind that whatever plan they settled upon would fail. He would personally make sure of it.

As he made his way to the radio room, he walked slowly. His instinct was to compose a more suitable and polite message to send to the new ruler of the planet. But a part of him wanted to do just as instructed. To lure Allistor under false pretenses, let Rajesh make his foolish attempt on the man's life, and suffer the consequences. Which, if Agni were any judge of human nature, would likely result in his nephew's death.

Despite his lifelong love for the boy, he was becoming increasingly aware that his Rajesh had been corrupted by the power he'd been granted. He'd become a danger to his own people. There might even come a day when Agni himself was no longer safe.

He'd need to ensure that day never came.

*****

The frustrated lich slammed his staff against the floor once, twice, and a third time. The sound of bone crunching against concrete echoed through the room. None of the adepts standing in an arc in front of him reacted in the slightest. Out of spite, he raised a hand then clenched it, withdrawing some of his life-giving power from each of them, causing them all to drop to their knees. He leaned forward in his throne, a massive raised seat formed completely of bone and sinew that twitched occasionally with some perverted semblance of life of its own.

"Thirty of your brethren destroyed! Hundreds of thousands of my children gone with them! And still you have yet to even break the surface inside the city? Three days and nights you have had!"

The adepts all remained on their knees, their decayed or mummified faces lowered. None spoke, none even moved.

"One hairless monkey of a pretender to the throne of this world! One human has defeated nearly half of my adepts! Yet none of you has managed to put even a scratch on him?"

Finally, one of the adepts spoke. "He fights without honor, master. He kills from great distances with his primitive weapon. Or surrounds himself with an unbreakable wall of orcanin warriors when he moves closer. He has support from the sky, his ships dropping devastating explosives anytime we gather large numbers together to defeat him. And we have counted several hundred elven and dwarven light mages fighting alongside his people."

Another dared to raise its gaze and speak. "We recommend discontinuing the assault on the wall, master. We will not overcome the forces there. It has failed as a diversion, his people having located our forces underground. Further attacks on the wall merely deplete the numbers of your children without purpose."

The first adept took up the plea. "Let us appear to withdraw. Recall your children from the surface attacks, have them retreat into the river. From there we can send the entire force underground. We need not take the city by force, master. Let us quietly hide your children deep under the city. We shall endeavor to raise many thousands more, and send them below as well. Eventually there will be enough to spawn your dungeon."

The litch thumped his staff again, this time with much less force. His empty gaze took in both speakers as the skeletal fingers of his empty hand drummed on the arm of his throne.

"Yessss…" his unnatural voice echoed out from unmoving lips. "We shall create the dungeon as commanded by our matron. This will ease her anger with me." The lich had been avoiding contact with Hel, but could not continue to do so for much longer. "Once we have established the dungeon, we can grow it stronger and larger until it bursts forth to destroy the city from below! We need only time, and patience."

Every one of the adepts raised their head and spoke in unison. "Patience is the province of the dead. We are timeless. We are eternal."

The lich gave a single nod of his head. "Make it so. Recall my children, send them away. All of them, including those still under the city. We shall make the humans believe they have won." His eyes blazed brighter with an unnatural green light. "Bring me thirty, no… fifty children worthy of joining your ranks. I will need more adepts to raise replacements for my lost children. When we've emptied every burial ground within the old city, we will return. In preparation, wait two days for the humans to let down their guard, then send diggers to begin creating a new tunnel deep under the city."

As one the adepts bowed at the waist and departed. The lich's gaze passed briefly over a brightly glowing crystal embedded in the arm of his throne. The communication crystal was a direct link to Hel herself. The fact that it was glowing so brightly meant that she was demanding to speak with him.

He knew he'd made a mistake. His failure to kill the human prince out west was his first defeat since surrendering his soul and embracing his path as a necromancer. He had overestimated the intelligence and capability of the human, Kyle, and let that failure eat at him. When he'd returned to the east and found that Allistor had placed a city right in his path, his desire for vengeance had overridden his sense of duty to his mistress. A foolish mistake, since she literally held his soul in her possession. One act of anger on her part, and he would cease to exist.

With great trepidation, the lich placed a skeletal hand on the crystal to confirm the connection. He would apologize, and explain his new plan. Hopefully she would see the benefits of allowing him to continue to exist.

*****


*"Sire, Knight Bjurstrom wishes to speak with you."* Nigel's voice echoed down from the ceiling.

Allistor lay awake in his bed, though it was nearly three hours before the first sunrise. He'd slept little the past three days, spending most of his time on the wall alongside his citizens. Even with his improved *Stamina*, the adrenaline of battle and the stress of losing his people wore him down and required him to rest. But when he retired to his chambers, he didn't sleep well. His bed felt wrong without Amanda in it. More than just empty, it felt…

accusing. Almost hostile. He couldn't put words to it, and didn't want to spend time pondering it either. After less than an hour of tossing and turning the previous night, he had moved to the sofa.

Tonight hadn't gone any better. He simply lay awake, a kaleidoscope of thoughts tumbling around in his mind, so that he was actually grateful for the interruption.

"What's up, Bjurstrom?" He sat up and moved to a chair, feeling strange talking while laying down.

"Heya boss. Sorry to call so late. Or, early. I'm not... interrupting any elfy fun-time, am I?" He could hear the grin in his friend's voice, and decided not to take offense, even as tired and grumpy as he was.

"Don't make me come down there." He threatened in his best dad voice.

"Right. So, I called to tell you that they're retreating. The zombies, I mean. They've all pulled away from the wall and are heading back to the river. Kuhns reports the same thing down in the tunnels. The raid groups down there are killing as many as they can as they retreat, but every group says they're leaving."

"What? Why would they do that?" Allistor was suspicious. They had no idea why the lich attacked in the first place, and now even less idea why he was retreating. Had he been searching for something, some relic hidden underground, and found it? Or had he just decided he was losing too many resources?

"No clue, boss. We discussed it a bit amongst ourselves, knowing you'd ask. None of us has a good reason. We say just take the win and keep an eye out."

Allistor blinked a few times, something Bjurstrom had just said was bothering him. He replayed it in his head once, then again, until finally it struck him. *Take the win.*

"We haven't won yet. We didn't get any xp for the defense quest. Which means it's not over."

"Yeah, we thought of that, too. McCoy says it's just because they're retreating slowly. Once they've completely left the city and gotten far enough away, we should get the win."

Allistor nodded his head and sighed. "I should have thought of that. I guess I'm more tired than I thought. Thanks, buddy. I'll see you at breakfast?"

"Sure thing, boss. Try and get a couple hours of sleep."

Allistor let the connection drop, then said, "Speaking of breakfast, Nigel please let the kitchen staff know that we may have a large number of hungry people coming off the wall soon."

*"Of course, sire."* The AI went silent, and Allistor laid down on the sofa. He really did need some sleep. With the weight of the battle at least partially lifted from his shoulders, it didn't take long for him to drift off.

He got a solid three hours of sleep, and was just getting into a dream that heavily featured Melise when he was awakened by a ground-shaking gong. The moment his eyes opened he received the accompanying notifications.

*Quest Complete: Defend the City!*
*The stalwart defenders of Invictus City*
*have repelled the undead invaders!*
*Quest Reward: 100,000,000 experience; Kill*
*experience: 0*
*Bonus Quest Reward! For defeating an army*
*more than ten*
*times the size of your own: 50,000,000 experience.*
*Bonus Quest: Win without losing allied lives –*
*failed*
*Bonus Quest: Eliminate one hundred percent*
*of the attacking force – failed.*

Allistor grimaced at the quest failure reminder that he'd lost some good people during the extended battle. They would need to gather everyone soon for a memorial, but he'd let it wait a few days. His people needed food and sleep, a chance to unwind.

After a second quick read-through of the notifications, he wasn't surprised that he'd personally received no experience for kills. The common zombies had mostly been twenty or so levels lower than him. Even the adepts he'd killed hadn't come within ten levels. The System didn't award much for taking out monsters so far below you. The quest and bonus experience did get him a large chunk of the way toward level 66.

On the upside, he was sure that Melise and the orcanin who had accompanied him had picked up some levels. Both from the quest rewards and from the kills. At level thirty five, maybe half of the common zombies and all of the adepts killed would have granted Melise some experience. He would have enjoyed seeing her face as she leveled up. And despite the early hour, he was sure his own people were already celebrating.

He chuckled to himself when he heard a loud hoot from William and cheering from the girls. Dressing quickly, he abandoned his lonely bedroom and went to congratulate the kids.

He was already mentally composing a way to gently tease William once more about putting some points into *Charisma*. Maybe the girls would catch on and play along.

*****

Breakfast in the cafeteria became a two-hour long victory celebration. Everyone except the highest level raiders and inner circle members had leveled up at least twice. Unlike Allistor, they had all received significant awards of klax as well, corresponding to the number of kills credited to them. The droids had gone out as soon as the retreat began and looted the piles of corpses, and the citizens were receiving their shares. Already there was a significant pile of scrolls on one of the tables to be taken back to Ramon and his inscriptionists. People were showing off newly acquired enchanted armor pieces and weapons. One of the healers was generating laughs off to one side. Having received an ugly looking skull helm as loot, she was stomping around with it on her head, the terrifying thing looking slightly silly with her green flower-embroidered robe and soft green leather boots.

Small groups were gathered around raiders who were sharing stories of nasty fights down in the tunnels, or the pain of being struck by the necrotic spells. The most popular of these was the tank who'd had his legs withered by the adept's staff. The healers had finally decided to amputate his legs above the line where the rot had stopped, then use the regeneration machine to replace them. Several kids who were enthralled by his story kept poking at his legs with forks and table knives, asking if he felt anything.

Allistor was happy to see Nancy accompanying Ramon and Chloe as they arrived to retrieve the scrolls and grab some food. Ramon had reported that she was up and about and feeling normal the day after her injury, but it felt good to see her laughing and smiling in person. He walked up and grabbed her without saying a word, hugging her tightly until Ramon cleared his throat.

"You know that's *my* woman you're squeezing there, buddy. Go find your own!"

There was a collective gasp, then silence in the immediate area. Ramon instantly realized what he'd said and covered his mouth with his hand. "Oh, shit. I'm so sorry, man. I didn't think…"

Allistor let go of Nancy and grabbed hold of Ramon, bringing him in for a bro hug. "Don't sweat it man. I keep forgetting she's gone, too. I turn to say something to her, or reach out expecting to find her next to me. Then I remember, and feel like an ass for forgetting. I know you loved her too." Ramon hugged him back hard, tears forming in his eyes. Allistor let him go when Chloe tugged on his shirt and demanded hugs of her own. He whisked her off her feet and spun her around, causing her to giggle. Max barked and hopped around them with his tail wagging like crazy, thinking a game was afoot.

As breakfast was winding down, Daigath and Helen appeared. Allistor immediately looked behind them, hoping to see the bears. But he had no such luck. Helen hugged him, speaking quietly. "Fiona's still in a bad way, though she's getting a little better. Fuzzy stayed with her."

"Helen!" Chloe jumped into the woman's arms, nearly knocking her over. Though she hadn't aged, the levels that the little girl had earned had altered her body, making her stronger, healthier, and heavier than any girl her age had a right to be. "You missed the big fight! I got eight levels!"

"Yeah, nobody ever invites me to the good stuff!" Helen winked at Allistor as she booped the little girl's nose. "Pretty soon you'll catch up to me!"

"Yup! Ramon says I'm gonna be a real badass when I grow up!" Her eyes widened as she looked toward her mom. "Oop! I wasn't supposed to say that in front of momma." She looked guilty as Nancy smacked the back of Ramon's head, then held out a hand for Chloe. Helen set her down, and the guilty-faced little one shuffled over to stand by her mom.

The little family drifted away, Ramon mumbling one last quiet apology, though Allistor wasn't sure if it was meant for him, or for Nancy. Helen went to grab some food, and Daigath stepped closer to Allistor.

"The time grows near, and I would speak with you, young man. If you have the time?"

"I always have time for you, Master Daigath." Allistor did some quick math in his head. He'd been so distracted by the battle that he'd nearly forgotten his pending encounter with Baldur and Loki. "Shall we go upstairs?"

"The roof will do." Daigath nodded, and the two of them headed toward the exit and the elevators, Daigath taking a quick detour to grab some pastries off a buffet table. Just as they were leaving the room, Andrea approached.

"Hey boss. Sorry to interrupt." She bowed her head to the elven master. "Got something I think you'll want to hear right away." When Allistor nodded, she continued. "We've had radio contact with some folks who work for an Earl Rajesh over in India. Earl as in that's his title, like you had when I met you. Anyway, they just called for help. They're reporting being under attack by this new world's equivalent of slimes. I was going to just send a couple raid teams, but their leader has apparently asked for you personally. Wants to meet you."

Allistor had planned to start making goodwill trips before the attack anyway, and had no objection to helping out this Earl. He looked to Daigath. "Would you mind if we talked on the *Phoenix*?"

"Not at all. I would be interested in seeing this place you called... India?" He looked to Andrea for confirmation and got a smile.

"Alright, Andrea load up two or three raid groups, and fifty droids. Try to pick folks who haven't been on the wall all week. Volunteers only. And please let Kira know we're headed to the Phoenix. Oh, and... see if there are some healers available. And some trainers, too. We might as well make this trip as useful as possible. Have everybody meet at the Phoenix in twenty minutes. Let the folks in India know we'll be there in an hour, tops."

Andrea gave a mock salute and a wink before dashing off, already speaking to Nigel. Allistor shouted for Helen, distracting her from her breakfast and waving for her to join them. She stuffed her half-finished plate into her ring and caught up to them as they left the lobby and began the short walk toward the parking garage and the *Phoenix*.

"Any objection to Helen joining in this conversation?" He asked Daigath.

"I have none if you don't." The elf smiled at Helen. "I will not ask if you've changed your thinking regarding the taking of Loki's life. Instead I seek to better educate you on your options and consequences."

"Alright. Options first?"

Daigath nodded. "First let me remind you that taking the life of an ancient one such as Loki will grant you enough personal experience to become one of the higher leveled individuals in the collective. While there are much older and higher level entities out there, myself among them, you would be within the top ten percent or so. On a level with longtime Emperors and faction leaders. Making such a leap at this time would certainly earn you some powerful enemies. Some from jealousy, others who will see you as a potential threat."

"That sounds like a consequence." Helen smiled at the old elf, who returned the smile.

"Yes, it does. And it is. But I have for you an option that will help mitigate that consequence." He turned his gaze to Allistor as he spoke. "As Emperor, you have the ability to bank experience for later distribution to your vassals or citizens. This option includes your own personal experience, or that gathered by your people. If you explore your Empire tab, you will see that you have the right to tax a portion of all experience earned by your subjects. That experience can then be applied as you see fit. Good Emperors use it to the benefit of their empires, while others use it to selfishly grow their own personal power."

Allistor looked at his UI as they approached the garage. He'd never even opened his Empire tab, and instantly felt foolish for not doing so. It only took a few seconds for him to find the ability Daigath spoke of. Once he'd located it and inspected it briefly to see that the tax was set at zero, he closed his UI again. "I see it there. But... I don't *have to* institute a tax, do I?"

Daigath smiled. "I am very glad you asked. No, you do not. It is simply an option. Put in place by the system for large-scale events. Like the battle you just won. I can see you received one hundred and fifty million experience points yourself. If you had chosen to bank that, you might have used it to level up a favored vassal, or given several levels to a few of your weakest citizens. You could use it for bonus rewards on quests." He watched as Allistor considered his words, nodding along.

"While you faced a significant force in this battle, it was nothing compared to the scale of conflicts that faction leaders and Emperors often engage in. They might involve tens of millions of combatants, entire planetary populations, in their battles. Entire cities and their populations might be wiped from existence. The experience earned could be in the billions, the tens of billions." He paused as they reached the Phoenix and walked up the boarding ramp. Allistor motioned for him to sit on a supply crate, then he and Helen took seats of their own.

"That's... I would never do that." Allistor's mouth was dry.

"I believe you would never instigate a fight on such a scale. But as Emperor of two planets, one of which is a valuable high energy world, and the other having an eternity gate, you may well be forced into a defensive battle of just such a scale."

Helen put in her two cents. "And a wise fancypants ruler would use the big ol' mountain of experience he received from taking Loki's head to make as many of his people as possible as strong as possible."

"My thoughts, exactly, Lady Helen." Daigath relaxed slightly.

"I absolutely will do that. No question. I'm not interested in being the strongest ruler alive. I have always been working to make everyone stronger whenever I could."

"Yes, you have proven that time and again, Allistor. It was a large part of my reasoning when deciding to join you here. I see great potential in you, and hope to guide you through the temptations that come with tremendous and sudden personal power."

"Thank you, master." Allistor silently vowed, for at least the hundredth time, to spend more time reviewing the information in his UI.

The others began to arrive, boarding the ship in groups. The last to arrive were the trainers, many of whom had just awakened as they were a couple time zones behind. Andrea had selected a dozen of them from the most popular classes.

With everyone aboard, Kira and her crew took Phoenix up and headed out across the city. She reported that the trip would take less than an hour. Allistor gathered his people around and used the time to explain to them what he wanted. The raiders would immediately engage the invading slimes while the droids gathered up any wounded and carried them to the extra healers in a designated area in the rear. Trainers could participate in the fighting or not as they desired. Allistor hoped their presence and an offer of free training after the fighting would seal an alliance with this Earl.

When Kira announced over the intercom that they were approaching their destination, Allistor opened the cargo ramp and approached the edge, having total faith in Kira's ability to keep the ship steady. Looking down, he saw a Stronghold wall surrounding a sizeable area, the center of which looked like a factory of some kind. There were people walking in the open spaces and streets between the building, nearly all of them now looking up and pointing at the space ship hovering above.

"Nobody is running. Or fighting. At least not that I can see." Helen observed. Several of the others muttered similar comments. Allistor looked closely, seeing the same. He spotted a few dozen defenders on the wall, but nothing like he would expect of a force defending against an attack.

"Did they already win, and just didn't notify us?" He looked around again. "I don't see any wounded, or dead." Suspicious now, Allistor called up Kira. "Set us down on the roof of that big building, then move away. Don't go too far, in case this is some kind of trap."

"It's a trap!" McCoy shouted from further back in the cargo hold, holding his hands up near his eyes and extending his chin down in his best Calamari admiral impersonation. He grinned unashamedly when several of the others groaned at him. "My people!"

The ship's descent came to a halt roughly a foot above the roof's surface, and Allistor stepped off. The rest of his group, including fifty droids, stepped off right behind him. Though the building looked quite old, Allistor knew that Stronghold buildings upgraded by the System were sturdy, so he was not concerned about the large group crashing through the roof.

Kira lifted the Phoenix back into the air and moved off, and Allistor chuckled to see the weapons turrets on the underside of the ship rotate to cover the group on the roof. He wondered which of the trainees was at the weapons station.

"Welcome!" A voice called out from behind Allistor. He and everyone else turned to see an elderly man in pristine white cotton clothing approaching. His hands were empty and he was waving one of them in a friendly manner, a wide smile on his face. Allistor stepped forward to greet the man, stopping about ten steps in front of him. The old man bowed deeply at the waist. "Emperor Allistor? I am First Minister Agni, and I am most pleased to welcome you on behalf of my nephew, Earl Rajesh."

"Thank you, First Minister. I am indeed Allistor, and I'm a little confused. I don't see a battle here."

The old man straightened up, an uncomfortable look on his face. "Ah, yes. I must beg your forgiveness. May I speak frankly with you, Emperor?"

"Just Allistor, please. And yes, please do."

"My nephew is… he *was* a sweet young man before the apocalypse. Always faithful and helpful to our family. A bright boy who, when the world ended, kept many of us alive with his knowledge. He built this Stronghold to protect us, and saved many lives."

Allistor was getting more suspicious and impatient by the second. He looked over his shoulder and put a hand on the hilt of his sword, indicating to his people that they should be ready. Agni's voice faltered as he noticed them silently spreading out and laying hands on weapons. "Get to the point please, First Minister."

"Please, you are in no danger here and now!" Agni held up both hands in a sign of surrender. "I merely wished to give you some background." He sighed, lowering his arms limply to his sides. "My nephew has become… full of himself. He has taken it as a personal insult that you surpassed his title and achievements. The power he has taken for himself has… changed him. And not for the better. I am afraid he plots to take your throne for himself, and may make an attempt on your life."

Allistor stood still, studying the elderly man's deeply tanned face as he heard mutterings behind him. The droids, who had been standing with Prime near the back of the group, began to move. In seconds they had encircled the group and raised shields, facing outward.

Agni looked terrified, his eyes wide and mouth open. "P-please, as I said, I mean you no harm. I would have warned you via the radio before you arrived, but I did not wish to alert my nephew, or transmit such… sensitive and embarrassing information for the world to hear."

Allistor continued to stare at the man, his stat-boosted intellect making connections. After half a minute of silence during which the old man visibly trembled in his sandals, Allistor spoke.

"You brought me here to kill your nephew for you."

Agni sucked in a surprised breath, placing one hand over his heart. "No, not for that purpose. Though I suspect that this will be the end result of your visit here. I love my nephew, Emper-… Allistor. But with his jealous nature and short temper, he has become dangerous to his own people. I had hoped that you would have a way to remove him from power without ending his life, but I accept that the one may not be possible without the other." He paused, looking out over the edge of the roof. "And we do have a colony of gelatinous beings at the edge of our lands. Attempts to communicate have… ended badly for several of our people."

Allistor followed the man's gaze for a moment, thinking. He found that he believed Agni was being honest. Betraying his nephew still placed a good bit of doubt on the man's character, though.

"What level is your nephew?" Allistor's tone was curt, but short of threatening.

"He is level thirty five, the highest among us, except for his security chief and a few of his fighters. None of them is above level forty."

Allistor looked behind him.  None of his people were below level 45.  Unless Rajesh or his forces were extremely well trained and armed, they posed no serious threat.  He quickly sent raid invites to the group leaders, healers, and trainers, as well as Prime.  Out loud he said, "Fine, I think I understand.  Take me to see Earl Rajesh."  To his people he added in raid chat.  "Don't kill anyone unless you have to.  But if it becomes an *us or them* situation, the answer is us every time."

Agni turned and began to lead Allistor toward the roof access door he'd emerged from a few minutes earlier.  Allistor and his people moved forward, the droids maintaining a perimeter that flowed with them.

Chapter 18

"What kind of weapons are your fighters using?" Allistor asked as two droids descended the stairs ahead of him.

"Automatic rifles with armor-piercing ammunition." The old man gulped, clearly afraid. "They also carry swords, spears, and have a supply of grenades."

"And where do they plan to attack?"

"I am sorry, I do not know. I was not privy to their planning. But I suspect that my nephew will pretend to welcome you in his throne room, and ambush you there. It is what I would do."

Allistor glanced sideways at the man. He quickly cast *Identify* and saw that he was too low level to survive such an attack.

**First Minister Agni**
**Level 30**
**Health: 18,000/18,000**

Allistor tried to remember what his health pool had been like back when he was level thirty. He was pretty sure it had been significantly higher. Which told him that the old man had probably put his attribute points into more mental than physical stats. It made sense for an elderly man who was an advisor, not a fighter.

"You should move to the back of this group when we reach the throne room, First Minister. If they begin firing, Prime will have two of his droids protect you. Don't panic when they move close. Those shields are bulletproof." The old man nodded and gave Allistor a grateful look.

There was an elevator one floor down from the roof, but it wasn't nearly large enough to accommodate their group, so they took the stairs. The building was only eight stories tall, and it didn't take them long to descend. They turned down one hallway, then another, and halted when Agni pointed at a set of large double doors. "That is the throne room."

Allistor nodded and advanced, noting that the old man waited for the rear guard to catch up before following. When he reached the doors, he didn't wait to knock or allow someone else to open them. He cast *Barrier* in front of himself, then kicked the left-hand door off its hinges.

There was a surprised outcry from multiple voices within the room as he stepped through the door. Without pause, he continued forward, taking in the room as he moved. Ahead of him was a young man sitting atop a large chair, two steps up from the rest of the room. On either side of the long room were several thick painted steel columns that held up structural steel beams running the length of the room and crossing it in several places. Allistor assumed that any ambushers would be concealed behind those columns. Several people in attire similar to Agni's stood in the space between Allistor and the throne, or off to either side.

395

Earl Rajesh was on his feet and shouting something at Allistor, who ignored him.

"You summoned me here under false pretenses, Rajesh! Explain yourself!" he shouted at the man.

"How dare you?!" Rajesh practically screamed back at him. "I am *Earl* Rajesh! You burst into my home unannounced, flinging false accusations? I will have you flogged!" Spittle flew from the man's lips as he forced the words out. The courtiers standing between the two men quickly vacated the center of the room, joining the rest standing off to one side or the other. A few crouched down in fear covering their heads with their arms.

Allistor laughed, quickly joined by those behind him. The reaction caused Rajesh to pause, momentarily unsure of himself.

"I don't think so, Earl Rajesh. Even if I were to stand here and let your men attack me, it would take them ten minutes to kill me. And they won't have ten seconds." He paused and looked significantly from one set of columns to the other. "Any man who fires a weapon at me or my people will be dead before he can fire a second round. I am level sixty five, and most of the people behind me are over level fifty. Your bullets won't harm us, even if we let them strike." He took a look at the nervous bystanders. "Hold your fire, and you won't be harmed."

Rajesh hopped down off the throne, taking several steps toward Allistor. He drew an ornamental curved dagger from his belt sash and raised it above his head, snarling as he advanced. When he was just a step away and ready to thrust the dagger forward, his face impacted Allistor's barrier, followed a fraction of a second by the rest of him. The dagger broke free of his grip and clattered to the floor as the rest of Rajesh fell backward.

Allistor stepped forward, bending down to grab hold of Rajesh's neck as the man shouted, "Kill them!"

Two rounds ricocheted off of Allistor's barrier, quickly followed by two screams as the shooters were hit with *Mind Spike* spells, arrows, and stone spikes erupting from the floor at their feet. They were dead in seconds.

Allistor lifted Rajesh off the floor, his enhanced *Strength* easily handling the weight. As he straightened up, he raised the man higher until his feet left the floor, dangling six inches in the air. "Anyone else fires, I snap his neck!"

He waited a solid ten seconds for more shots, or the sound of a grenade hitting the floor. Hearing none, he let out the breath he'd been holding. He had been prepared to toss Rajesh's body on top of any grenade he saw. "Come out and set down your weapons. You won't be harmed if you don't make any hostile moves."

Rajesh struggled weakly, his entire weight supported by his jawbone as Allistor held him aloft. His air supply had been cut off, and he was quickly burning through whatever oxygen he held in his lungs. Allistor's people moved forward, pushing through the bystanders to disarm and search the fighters who emerged from behind the columns. Agni stepped forward when Allistor called to him. "Are these all of his men?"

Agni shook his head, looking sadly up at his suffocating nephew. "No, but the rest are out on the wall, I believe. These are his elite fighters."

Allistor released his grip on Rajesh, dropping the man to the floor where he gasped for air and coughed, rubbing his sore throat with both hands. Snot ran from his nose and his eyes watered. Allistor let him recover for a moment.

"I will kill you for this!" The first words rasped out of the young man's throat. Allistor looked at Agni, wanting to kill the moron on the ground at his feet, but remembering the old man's request.

Allistor hooked his foot under the man's back, then lifted him up, flinging him back toward his throne. His body flew about five feet before landing and rolling to a stop against the dais. "You already tried, and failed. You will not kill me, or anyone else, you arrogant little shit. I'm going to give you a choice. You will right now get up on your knees and swear a vassal oath to me, one that will prevent you from harming my people or anyone else. Or you die here and now, sniveling like a spoiled child on the floor in front of your people. You have ten seconds to decide."

As everyone in the room watched and waited, Rajesh fumbled his way up the dais to his throne. As he took a seat, he glared with pure hatred at Allistor, spit a wad of phlegm in his direction, then flipped open the arm of the chair and drew a pistol. He got off two shots before he was simply erased from existence by a barrage of spells from Allistor's people. Flame Shots, Lightning Strikes, and Acid Sprays landed on him alongside arrows and crossbow bolts. A spear flew over Allistor's shoulder and passed through the man's chest, as well as the chair back behind it.

Five seconds after the second shot rang out, the Earl was little more than a burnt and decaying lump of flesh, partially melted into the metal of the throne.

Allistor turned his back on the smoking ruin and addressed Agni. "I'm sorry. I gave him a chance to surrender." He looked down at his arm, which was bleeding slightly. The first bullet from Rajesh's gun had shattered his barrier, which had already taken hits from the previous kinetic rounds. The second bullet had grazed his arm, leaving little more than a scratch.

Agni nodded, tears streaming down his face. "As I suspected. He left you no choice, Emperor Allistor. Please forgive us."

"It wasn't you. I believe that you had good intentions here, Agni." He turned to face the obviously nervous fighters who'd been set to ambush him, now rounded up into a cluster and guarded by droids. "I'm going to assume that you acted under orders, and had no choice in the matter." Several of them nodded, looking grateful. A few just stared stonefaced back at him.

"For those of you who haven't heard, I'm Allistor, the new Emperor of Earth. I came here today because I was told you were under attack from an alien race, and needed our help. That was clearly a lie perpetrated by

Rajesh. He's no longer in charge here. So let me start fresh with the rest of you, and see if we can't all be friends." He began to walk toward the prisoners as he spoke.

"All of you here, all of Rajesh's people, have a chance to become citizens of Invictus, which is my princedom. Or, I guess, empire now. Whatever. All you need to do is swear an oath, and contribute however you can to the community. The oath is simple, and basically breaks down to promising not to hurt each other, and to support each other."

He waited for that to sink in. For the next two minutes he gave the short version of his recruitment speech, outlining their basic laws, the penalties for breaking them, and the benefits of being a citizen. When he was done, he finished with, "I will give you all one day to consider my offer. Let me be clear. This Stronghold is now mine. If you wish to remain here, you will swear the oath and become a citizen. If you refuse, you'll be given a week's worth of food and water, a weapon, and an escort out through the gates. If a large group of you choose to leave, I'll have my people secure a place for you somewhere nearby. You can build your own Stronghold, and we will leave you in peace. But you'll receive no further support from us. You'll need to be able to fend for yourselves."

Looking at the prisoners, he asked, "Who's your leader?"

A tall man maybe forty years old stepped forward. "I am Fayed, former chief of security" He met Allistor's gaze without flinching.

"Good to meet you, Fayed. I presume that since you and the rest of these men did not fire, you're not exactly heartbroken over the change in management?"

Fayed looked down briefly, an expression of shame flashing across his face. But it passed quickly, and he raised his gaze again. "We are not. Earl Rajesh had become... difficult. As I am sure minister Agni has already explained to you."

Allistor just nodded. "I understand you've had some trouble with non-human neighbors. Would you like to show us where they are?"

Fayed nodded. "I would swear your oath, if you'll have me. And join you in battling the jelly creatures."

Allistor was glad to hear it. He looked around the room, first at the other fighters, then the bystanders. "Anyone else already decided to join us? We can administer the oath here and now."

All but two of Fayed's remaining men stepped forward. As did about twenty of the civilians, and Agni. When Fayed raised an eyebrow at the two holdouts, one of them shrugged. "I wish to hear the words of this oath, and see its effect on you. If it does you no harm, I will follow." The other fighter nodded in agreement, along with several of the civilians.

"Fair enough." Allistor motioned Helen forward, and she had all those who wished to become citizens step to one side. They repeated the oath after her, clearly surprised at its simplicity. A moment after the lights finished swirling around the new citizens, the two fighter holdouts and most of the rest of the others stepped forward, repeating after Helen as she gave the oath a second time.

While Helen took care of that, Allistor opened his UI and took control of the Stronghold. He saw that Rajesh had already added all the basic utilities, along with some luxury upgrades. Allistor added in a defensive dome and weapons along the walls, as well as the sensor system. He activated Nigel, giving him control of the facility.

When that was all taken care of, he addressed all the people in the room. "Those of you who have sworn, welcome to Invictus! Your first job is to spread the word about what happened here, and the opportunity I'm offering. Let everyone know to be... someplace big enough for everyone to gather, let's say noon tomorrow." He looked at the few remaining holdouts. "The rest of you are free to tell your version of today's events as well. I've nothing to hide, and no interest in controlling you, your opinions, or your day to day lives. Take the oath, do what you can to support each other, or choose not to join us, and leave in peace."

Turning back to the group of trainers, all of whom were from other worlds, he asked, "Any of you have any experience with gelatinous beings? We fought some slimes last year in a dungeon, but I don't know if these are the same."

Three of the trainers raised their hands and stepped forward. Allistor didn't know any of them, not having had time to socialize with the new trainers much in the short time since their arrival. "I'm afraid I don't know your names yet."

The first one to step forward bowed his head. He was a gnome, maybe three feet tall and wearing leather pants and shirt with a leather sash over one shoulder that held several small knives and tools. "I am Ruddy, cousin to Selby."

Allistor's face lit up. "The gnomebarian! Survival trainer, right? Welcome to Invictus!" He smiled down at the diminutive trainer.

"That's me. And I've had some dealings with the gelatins, as we call them. They are semi-intelligent, and tend to gather in clusters. Generally slow-moving, but hard to kill. Fire, ice, and lightning work best against them. Projectiles do little damage unless they are explosive. Melee weapons are ineffective against them."

"Pretty much as we expected." McCoy said. "Like the ones we fought in the Silo."

Allistor focused on Ruddy's first statement. "What do you mean by semi-intelligent? Can we communicate with them?"

Another trainer stepped forward, introducing herself as Ak'kash, a beastkin herbalist trainer that resembled a leopard. "When they first spawn, they are dumb as rocks. They act on pure instinct, moving about at random while

403

seeking sustenance. As they grow, they get smarter, responding to various stimuli, including external threats. If they absorb a sentient creature, they also absorb a small measure of its intelligence. If these here have taken several humans, they may indeed have reached a level of intelligence that would allow basic communication." Ruddy and the other trainer nodded their agreement.

"Alright, thank you. I can work with that." Allistor motioned for Fayed and Agni to join him, moving off to one side of the room and sitting at a bench there. He indicated for both of them to sit as well. "Tell me about your interactions with them so far."

*****

Baldur stood outside of a small, nondescript room, watching through a transparent force field as Odin finished his work on Loki. There had been no interrogation as humans would recognize it. There was no verbal interaction. No recording for court records, no polygraph machine to weed out truth from lies.

No, they could not afford to allow any hint of what was in Loki's mind to become known to the System. At least, not yet.

So Odin had bent his powerful mind toward breaking Loki's mental barriers. To scouring his mind for secrets and memories of misdeeds. Loki fought, of course. He fought with the tools he knew best, deception and misdirection. But his tricks were no match for the sheer

404

titanic power of Odin's intellect and will. The eldest and most powerful of their race, the *Allfather* as he was known in Earth's legends, Odin pushed and pushed, giving Loki no rest, no chance to recover his dwindling strength. He mercilessly pulled what he wanted directly from Loki's consciousness. Then he pulled more.

There was no question as to Loki's guilt, now. Odin saw the memories of how Loki had conspired to trigger the early Induction of UCP382, and had purposely done so at a time in human development that would be sure to see them labeled as a contaminant. And while that knowledge saddened Odin, much worse was the realization that he hadn't done it for power, or wealth.

He'd caused the deaths of billions of humans just to see if he could get away with it.

Odin revealed a nearly endless litany of crimes and immoral acts Loki committed himself, or conspired with others to carry out. He'd clearly gone insane eons ago, a common enough ailment among those who lived nearly endless lifespans. Few of his people, possibly not even Odin himself, faced the reality of such longevity and remained completely sane. At some point one ran out of the new experiences that kept life interesting. Routine became both nemesis and comforting friend, adventure a thing of the past. Hope faded into acceptance, then ambiguity and apathy.

For four days neither of them had moved from that small room, and Baldur had waited impatiently outside. His father was taking a significant risk in there. He was striding a fine line, uncovering evidence of Loki's misdeeds while simultaneously keeping that evidence hidden from the nearly all-seeing System.

They had made a bargain, sealed by the System, to allow Allistor to end Loki's life. Should Odin's control ebb for even a moment, allowing the System access to the information he was extracting, Loki would be punished on the spot. Said punishment would result in Loki's mortal death, and prevent Baldur and Odin from honoring their own agreement. There were technicalities they could exploit to avoid punishment themselves, but neither being wanted to have to explore those. Negotiating with the System was possible, but rarely beneficial in the end.

Even worse, the information in Loki's mind implicated others. So many others. Hel was not the only member of their race to have conspired with Loki. His memories could take down whole factions, even empires. The degree of chaos their exposure would seed throughout the Collective might cripple it for millennia. And while those in power who had gotten there via unsavory means deserved their fate, their destruction would potentially impact trillions of more innocent lives.

But this... this one crime, the sheer psychopathic indifference to the genocide, the deaths of billions of members of an entire race that Odin himself favored... the magnitude and senselessness combined to wound Odin's soul.

Loki still fought, grimly holding on to a meager few vestiges of the skeletons in his closet. One in particular he buried deepest of all, resolved to perish before allowing it to be exposed. Not out of fear, no. He embraced the fact that this final secret would be exposed in the end. But it would be revealed at a time of his own choosing.

He retreated into the deepest recesses of his own consciousness, exhausted from his seemingly endless losing battle with Odin. He left most of his mind, his precious secrets, to be scoured and consumed by his foe. While Odin was distracted, he prepared his final stand, building up the mightiest and most subtle barriers he could conjure.

Odin, for his part, had lost heart. His perusing of Loki's misdeeds had become peremptory, mechanical, his mind automatically recording, sorting, and filing away the evidence as it came to him. Loki had ceased to resist except in a token manner, and Odin just wanted to end this whole distasteful process.

Finally, Odin's tentacles fell away from where they'd burrowed directly into Loki's brain. A deep sigh sent the mists swirling about the room, the movement projecting dejection and sorrow.

Loki slumped to the ground, unconscious as Odin stepped through the force field on his way out of the room. Not even looking at his favored son, Odin walked slowly past him.

"Father?" Baldur set a single tentacle on his father's shoulder.

Odin paused, facing away from Baldur, eyes closed. "I wish none of this had been necessary my son. I truly do. Had I the power to reverse time and correct the path... but no. There is no value in contemplating the impossible." He turned to face Baldur. "Do not ask me what I have learned, my son. You would not thank me for sharing the knowledge. You would instead curse me, and rightfully so. Let us honor our agreement with the human boy, and await the fallout that follows. I will... take certain steps in the time remaining to us to mitigate what I can. In fact, come with me. I shall require your assistance in preventing some of the more devastating consequences." Odin shuffled down the corridor without explaining further.

Baldur took another long look at Loki's still form on the floor of the detention cell, then turned to follow his father. Time was growing short, and it seemed they had much to do.

*****

Master Daigath tagged along with Allistor and his entourage as they approached the gelatinous settlement. The elf hadn't volunteered his knowledge of the creatures, leaving Allistor to discover what he could for himself. He was not there to hold the boy's hand through every small challenge, nor to answer every question. Growth came from exploration and struggle, from overcoming adversity and learning from it. Instead he sat back and watched, curious as to how Allistor would approach this particular problem.

"Alright, here we go. I kind of like your feeding idea. Bribing someone with food is hardly ever considered a hostile act, in my experience. But let's not just throw meat at them and hope for the best." Allistor spoke to the group as they stood about fifty yards from the opening to the gelatinous beings' domain.

"You want to send another peasant to deliver meat?" Fayed asked.

Allistor took a deep breath, mentally counting to three before turning on the man. "I'm only going to tell you this once. There are no peasants here. There is no more caste system. No one is more or less entitled than any other person. This is a community of equals, where one's value is derived from one's contribution to the community. You earn rank, trust, and privileges based on your actions, not your family name, or bloodline. Is that clear?" He looked at each of the locals and waited for them to nod their understanding.

"Good. Now, to prove that point, I will be the one to deliver the tasty treats to the wobbly dudes in the caves." He motioned for the rest of them to hold their positions, gave Helen a quick wink, and strode forward.

Behind him he heard Fayed mumble something, then Helen snort. "He does stuff like this. It's annoying, but kind of endearing, too. You get used to it."

Smiling to himself, he continued forward. He wasn't truly concerned about this encounter. The recently arrived creatures were probably too low level to kill him. Though from the sounds of the acid attacks described by

Agni, the pain he might be in for was going to suck. His smile faded as he thought about how much Amanda would enjoy studying his burned flesh and how quickly it healed, or didn't.

He had no idea what he might accomplish here. No clue as to whether these creatures could communicate. He'd seen what he thought of as a slime creature in Harmon's store once, so clearly it could interact in some functional way. But Allistor had no idea if these ahead of him were even the same species as that one.

As he drew closer to the opening, three of the... he was just going to go ahead and call them slimes in his head... approached and held position right at the edge. Allistor quickly withdrew three large steaks and held them in his hands with his arms wide and slightly forward.

"Uhm... hello there. I am Allistor, newly appointed Emperor of Earth. That's this planet, by the way. I've come to welcome you, and offer gifts of friendship." He waited several seconds for a response, but the three entities simply remained where they were, unmoving except for the occasional quiver of their bodies. All three of them were in a roughly cubic form with soft and slightly rounded edges.

Stepping forward, Allistor kept the steaks in front of him. When he was within reach, he extended the hand holding a single steak slowly toward the slime on his left, speaking softly the entire time. "Just going to reach out here, nice and easy. This is not an attack, just me offering you a tasty gift. I'll just hold it right... here..." He stopped when the steak was just a couple inches from touching the slime's nearest surface. "Go ahead, this one's for you. I have one for each of your friends, as well." He raised his other hand to show off the remaining two steaks. "Plenty more where these came from."

He might have peed himself a little when a sort of suction cup shape shot out from the surface of the slime and attached itself to the steak. There was a gentle tug, and Allistor quickly let go. "Ya scared me there, buddy. That's okay. Enjoy the snack. Here we go, other buddies." He took a steak in each hand and slowly extended them toward the other two slimes. Both accepted them, but Allistor was glad to see that the tiny suction cup appendages emerged more slowly. As if they'd understood his surprise, or his comments."

Allistor watched with interest as all three drew the meat into their bodies. Almost immediately the protein began to discolor at the edges, being broken down by their digestive acid. After a few moments, the first one he'd fed moved forward slightly, then stopped and quivered from side to side.

"Is that… you want more?" Allistor asked, grabbing three more steaks. He held one out to the slime he was designating as Alpha, and this time the suction thingy was extended slowly and carefully. It gently accepted the offering, then moved its whole body back to its original position.

"Awesome!" Allistor smiled at all three of them, quickly feeding the other two. He turned back to his people while they ingested the steaks, giving a silent thumbs-up to let them know he was okay.

When he turned around, Alpha began quivering again. A moment later an appendage in the rough shape of an open hand extended out toward Allistor. On it sat a surprisingly clean wristwatch. It was just the watch itself, the leather band it had been attached to having been digested. Allistor reached out tentatively, then halted with his hand a few inches from the watch. "You... want to give this to me? You want to trade?"

The hand extended further until Allistor's fingers touched the watch. He very carefully lifted it with two fingers, doing his best not to touch the slime's flesh and get burned. "Thank you." He smiled at Alpha.

The other two, whom he was now calling Bravo and Charlie, each extended a hand as well, one holding a fancy looking fountain pen, the other a gold men's wedding ring. Allistor accepted them both with polite thanks and careful fingers. As soon as he'd taken them, all three of the creatures flashed a shade of blue throughout their bodies and quivered in what Allistor took to be excitement. A moment later they retreated into the darkness.

"Okay, I guess first contact protocols have come to an end for the day." He grinned and waved at the retreating forms. "I'll come back tomorrow and we can chat again, fellas."

Turning away from the entrance, he began to walk back toward his people. He'd taken maybe five steps when Helen began waving and pointing behind him. He glanced over his shoulder, half expecting to see a slime missile flying at his face. Instead he found a stream of maybe a dozen smaller slimes, all glowing blue, following him in a loose cluster. When he stopped moving, so did they. A wave of blue flashes passed through them, and they quivered much like their larger predecessors had.

"Oh, ho." Allistor grinned. "So it's feeding time?" He began pulling meat from his ring, gently feeding each of the small slimes. "Aren't you just the cutest little fellas?" He had to stop himself from using baby talk. "Or… maybe you're females? The big guys are males?" he continued to speculate out loud in a friendly tone as he passed out lunch. If there were a lot more of them inside, he was going to need to go back to the *Phoenix* and resupply.

When he'd fed the last of them, he realized they'd shifted to form a circle around him. As if on cue, each of them moved back about a foot, leaving some shiny offering on the ground in front of them. "Ooh, loot!" Allistor smiled as he carefully picked them up one at a time, making sure to make a big deal out of each of them. There were a couple belt buckles, another ring, some brass boot grommets, a gold filling from a tooth, and what Allistor thought might be a stainless steel medical pin from an elbow or knee implant.

"So, you little fellas, you ate the humans who got too close, and these are what's left of them?" He paused to see if there would be a response. The little ones still glowed blue, and seemed content to sit still in their circle and quiver happily. "Alright, that's fair enough. I can't blame you for eating. And it was nice of you to return these."

They seemed to understand, all of them moving in unison again as they flowed around him and back toward their home. He waved goodbye, and was amused to see the rearmost of them raise a small hand-like appendage and wave back, if awkwardly.

Allistor strolled back toward his group, head high and quite proud of himself. When he was within normal speaking distance, Helen gushed "Did one of those cute little blue ones *wave* at you?"

"Yeah, I think it did." He looked over his shoulder, then changed the pitch of his voice. "To seek out new life, new civilizations..." He imitated everyone's favorite classic sci fi show.

Helen rolled her eyes, and McCoy burst out laughing. "Even after more than a century, still the best!" He held up a fist for Allistor to bump.

Agni, who was now standing next to Daigath, looked thoughtful. When Allistor raised an eyebrow, he spoke. "I'm sorry, Allistor. We never considered them to be anything but dumb monsters. Our first encounter with them was when one of our gamers charged in there to 'clear the dungeon' and was promptly eaten. We did make a similar attempt to bribe them, but as you heard, that didn't go well. They seem to be at least slightly intelligent..."

"They understand the concept of trade, at least. Or maybe just give and take. And the larger ones clearly protected the smaller until they'd determined I was friendly. I sort of got a... feeling, I guess? A feeling from the little ones that they were sorry about eating your people, and were returning what was left of them." He pulled the items from his ring and held them out for the group to inspect. "Maybe they're a little bit telepathic? Like they could sense my intent, or my feelings, and sent some of their own back at me?"

"You just might be onto something there, Allistor." Ruddy agreed. "We can try to find out more tomorrow." He motioned back toward the factory. "In the meantime, should we see if the folks who've already sworn the oath could use some training?"

"Great idea!" Allistor was in a much better mood than he'd been in an hour ago. He had eliminated an asshat, freed a whole group of people from a dictator who looked at them as peasants. Added several dozen new citizens with the prospect of adding a few thousand more. And possibly made a bunch of slime friends. He could already picture William and Chloe trying to find a way to make them into pets.

Not a bad day's work.

Chapter 19

Allistor and company elected to remain at the Stronghold overnight. That would give the trainers time to work with several of those who'd already taken the oath, and allow prospective citizens to see their neighbors benefitting from Allistor's generosity.

Daigath decided to go on walkabout, saying he wanted to study the surrounding lands. He promised to return the next day, or the one after. Allistor was briefly worried about the elf, until he remembered that there was likely nothing on all of Earth that could harm him.

Rather than put any of the locals out of their housing, Allistor quartered his people on the *Phoenix*. There was more than enough room between crew quarters, guest quarters, and the owner's suite. Kira had long since claimed the captain's cabin, which she shared with her two girls, who were both on the current bridge crew. The raiders and trainers arranged themselves in the comfortable bunks of the crew quarters and shared guest suites. As Harmon had told him that first day, the Phoenix normally had a full crew compliment of thirty, plus guests. With only a training bridge crew of six plus Kira, there was plenty of space.

Allistor, for the first time since Amanda's death, slept comfortably in the owner's suite bed. He'd never shared it with Amanda, so there was no ghost haunting him. Within thirty minutes of hitting the pillows, he was snoring.

The following morning he rose early, well before the suns rose, and took a quick shower. Ten minutes later he was down in the crew mess talking to some of the raiders. McCoy walked in, a wide grin on his face, and plopped down next to Allistor.

"You hit the jackpot boss."

Thinking he meant the *Phoenix*, Allistor agreed. "She's a beautiful ship. Comfortable beds."

McCoy looked confused for a second, staring at Allistor and blinking a few times. "Uh, sure she is. But I meant this Stronghold. Did you look to see what that factory is?"

Allistor had not. He'd been busy most of the afternoon dealing with Invictus business, spent some time blacksmithing in the crafting compartment on the ship just to work out some anger and work his muscles, then gone to bed early. "So it is an actual factory? I thought Rajesh had just converted the biggest building around."

"Oh, it's a factory. About half the people here either work *in* the factory, or out gathering and processing materials *for* the factory. Guess what they make? Go ahead, guess!" McCoy was bouncing in his seat, and Allistor grinned at him. It was good to see him happy after the loss of Goodrich. "Uhm... condoms?"

"Nope!" McCoy clapped his hands together. "Though you're not that far off, geographically speaking. Boss... they make friggin *toilet paper*!"

Allistor snorted. "Oh, man. We gotta go get Meg and bring her back here. She'll lose her mind! Probably just jump into a pile of it and swim around like Scrooge McDuck. Then she'll fill the *Phoenix* cargo hold. She still maintains a hoard wherever she goes. She says it's in case of a second apocalypse." He slapped McCoy on the shoulder. "That's awesome! Yaknow, we've been buying it in bulk from the kiosk all this time. Ever since it became hard to scavenge. Never occurred to me to wonder who was selling it to us."

"Well now you're selling it yourself!" the others at the table chuckled. "And that's a good thing, boss. Nothing worse than running out of toilet paper."

Allistor finished breakfast and exited the ship, and for the next hour he just sort of ambled around, greeting passersby and checking out the Stronghold. It covered a lot of territory, the huge factory building, several warehouses, and other buildings he assumed were residential. Reaching one of the latter, he asked permission to look inside. The local whom he'd asked looked vaguely terrified of him, so he took a moment to speak with her.

"My name is Allistor, what's yours?"

"Sirina, sir." She mumbled, looking down at her feet.

"Sirina, that's a lovely name. You live here in this building?"

"Yes, sir. Myself and nearly one hundred other women."

418

Surprised, Allistor looked at the building. It was two story, roughly the size of a large townhouse building in the former Manhattan. "Would you mind giving me a brief tour? If that's proper, I mean. Are there... rules against men entering?"

She snorted, then covered her mouth as her eyes went wide. When she saw him smiling, she relaxed slightly, shaking her head. "It is not a harem, just a dormitory. And since it seems you now own all of this, I am sure that you can enter as you like."

Allistor sensed a certain amount of hostility in her voice, and assumed she'd been told he was the coldhearted monster who'd killed their Rajesh. He decided not to push it. Instead, he took a few steps back from the doorway. "I see. Well, unless this building is somehow bigger on the inside, it doesn't seem like there would be enough room for a hundred of you. Why don't we see about some better accommodations? Do you have a few minutes to advise me?"

"M-me? Advise you? I am but a simple harvester. A peasant."

Allistor sighed. "I truly wish people around here would stop using that word. You are no peasant, not any longer. Not if you don't want to be. If you choose to take the oath, you will become a citizen. On equal footing with any other, except those few who have earned positions of authority. You'll have the same rights as anyone else. You could even challenge me for the throne, if you think you could kick my butt!" He grinned at her, trying to relax her.

This was definitely one of those times he wished he'd put more points into *Charisma*.

"What would you wish me to advise you about?"

"Well, I assume you're from here, you live here now, and you would know the best type of living arrangements for your people, yes? For example, should I build a high rise? Or is there too much wind here? Would big windows create too much heat? Maybe underground housing would be better?"

She thought about it for a moment. "This I can help with."

"Great! Let's head to the gate. If we're going to create more buildings, we're going to need to move the walls. This place is crowded enough already." Without waiting, he turned and strode toward the thirty foot tall gate on the south side of the compound. When he approached, Nigel opened the doors for him. The moment they stepped outside, the gates closed again.

Allistor was looking around at the terrain for a likely spot when Sirina cleared her throat. When he turned to face her, she shook her head. "Not here."

"Okay, why not here?" He asked, curious.

"We are downwind from the factory here. There are days when the smell of the exhaust is... unpleasant. Better to place housing where the air is fresher."

"You see! You have already saved yourself and your people a bit of unpleasantness. I put myself in your hands. Lead the way." He followed her as she hiked counter-clockwise around the outside of the wall onto a slight rise. Looking around, she said, "I think… here. If you are building a high rise, it will have nice views in every direction. This location, if you remove the wall, will still be a short walk to the factory, and a gate here would save us harvesters a long hike through the other gate to reach the forest." She pointed beyond the rise to the north, where a long stretch of forest showed clear signs of harvesting. Stumps littered the field leading up to the tree line.

"Wait, you're a lumberjack?" Allistor was surprised yet again. The woman was maybe five foot two and couldn't weigh more than a hundred pounds.

She looked indignant. "We call ourselves harvesters. Lumberjack is a silly word! And I am stronger than I look!"

Allistor held up his hands in surrender. "Okay, I'm sorry Sirina. I won't make that mistake again."

She looked at her hands. "I do not actually cut down the trees. I remove the branches and haul them to one side so that the larger logs can be dragged away."

He turned back to her chosen location. "Sounds like hard work. If it is not something you enjoy, I'm sure we could find you something different. Have you heard that as a citizen you could relocate almost anywhere here on Earth, or even to our other planet, Orion?"

"I assumed it was… what is the term you westerners use? Bullshit?"

"Ha!" Allistor found he quite liked this woman. "It is the truth. In fact, how about I make you my ambassador to those who believe as you do? When we're done here, I'll place a teleport pad, and you can visit any of our properties you like. You won't have a lot of time, but you can see several before noon."

"What do you mean?" She looked confused. "You will create a whole building before noon? That is not possible."

"I take it you weren't here when the Stronghold was constructed?"

"I was not. My family and I found this place while running from a pack of mutant hyenas. The fighters here were kind enough to save us. Well, some of us. I have been here ever since."

Allistor nodded. "I'm sorry about the ones you lost. I too lost family in the earliest days. My parents and my sister." He took a deep breath. "Now, watch carefully and you will learn a little about what's possible in this new world."

Allistor opened his UI and selected the tab for that Stronghold. He hadn't renamed it yet, so it just said Factory. Rajesh was not the most original thinker, but then Allistor wasn't one to brag about his naming skills. A few quick mental clicks, and the ground underneath them went clear. Sirina cried out and grabbed ahold of his arm for balance, and Allistor heard similar shouts of surprise inside the wall. He probably should have warned them before he did this. He could only hope his people would help calm the others, and get this adjustment over with as quickly as possible.

Focusing on the rise, he quickly selected twin ten story buildings with an air bridge connecting them on the eighth floor. It was a plan he was familiar with, having constructed several of them at various Strongholds. He made each one roughly half a city block square, with a total capacity of six hundred apartments. Some of the locals might need to share at first, but they could always add more housing later. He added a defensive turret on the roof of each building, and moved the shield generator up there as well. After a few moments' thought, he added a swimming pool with a green glass enclosure in between the buildings. The tinted glass would not only limit the light and heat from the sun, but would act as a solar array.

Finished with the buildings, he altered the footprint of the wall so that it enclosed the new structures as well as a great deal of open space in between. He added a gate facing toward the forest, then an actual road to replace the muddy dirt track they'd been using to transport logs to the factory. Finished for now, he looked at her. "Will this do?"

She stood frozen next to him, her body rigid, a tight grip on his sleeve. Her eyes moved from structure to structure, then down to the seemingly unsubstantial ground at her feet.

"Sirina? Is this okay?" He repeated, moving his arm slightly to get her attention.

"What? Yes. Yes! This is wondrous. I... did not realize such things were possible. Earl Rajesh did not share such things with us peasants." She took in a breath, realizing she'd just said the p-word. "I'm sorry."

Allistor let it slide, finalizing his choices and enjoying the wonder on her face as everything solidified. The wall magically appeared several hundred yards farther out than it had been, the old wall simply melting into the ground. The two buildings appeared fully constructed, and the pool began to fill with water.

"As my consultant, your payment is first choice of the apartments inside. I suggest one of the top floors, with a view you enjoy."

"What? An apartment?" He gently took hold of her elbow and led her into the nearest of the two buildings. There was a small, wide open lobby and a bank of three elevators. Nigel obligingly opened the doors for them as they approached, and Allistor pressed the button for the tenth floor. When they exited the elevator, there was an open apartment door directly in front of them. To the left and right a corridor extended, several other open doors visible. At each end, the corridor made a ninety degree turn and continued on.

"The elevators are in the center of the building, surrounded by apartments on all sides. This way every unit has a view." He nudged her forward toward the open door. "Go ahead, look inside."

She stepped through the door, now moving quickly as she took in the small dwelling unit. There was a kitchen immediately to the right, with an open sitting area. To the left was a door leading to a bedroom with its own bath. The entire thing was maybe six hundred square feet. These apartments were meant for utility, not luxury.

But she looked at it like it was a palace.

"My sister and my mother, they can live here with me, too?" She asked as if afraid of his answer.

Allistor shook his head. "No." He watched as her face tightened up in disappointment, then quickly shifted to acceptance. The woman had clearly lived a hard life, and learned to accept defeat. He instantly felt bad.

"What I mean is, if there are three of you, and you want to live together, then you'll need one of the corner units." He led her back out and down the hall to a door in the corner. This unit was larger, with three small bedrooms, a master on one side and two more on the other that shared a bathroom in the hall. "If you like the view, this one is yours." He pointed toward the floor to ceiling windows in the sitting area. They faced the forest, the view from up here showing a green carpet of treetops stretching into the distance.

She didn't speak, but the tears forming in her eyes told him that the view was acceptable. He tried to imagine what kind of life she'd lived before the apocalypse, and how dismal her existence must have been since. Growing up where he had, it was hard to believe that in the modern world, people still lived such harsh lives. That this rather basic living space would have such an effect on her…

"Nigel, please assign this unit to Sirina and her family."

"*Of course, sire.*"

Sirina's eyes shot up to the ceiling. "Who was that? Can he see us?" Her gaze darted around the room, looking for cameras.

"That is Nigel. He's the AI that runs all of my Strongholds, ships, everything. And it's more like he... senses you. There are no cameras in here. And Nigel is harmless. In fact, anytime you need something, anywhere near one of our structures, you need only call out to him."

Sirina looked up at the ceiling again. "Uh, hello... Nigel?"

"*Greetings miss Sirina. It is a pleasure to meet you.*"

Allistor had a thought. "Sirina, do you mind if I cast a small spell on you? It's called Identify, and it will give me your basic information."

"What would you like to know?" She took a nervous step back.

"Well, what level are you? And do you have a chosen class?"

"I am level eight. And I do not have a class."

"No, at level eight you wouldn't. You choose your class when you reach level ten. Are most of the people here a similar level?"

"We do not discuss such things much, but yes, I believe so. My mother is level six, my sister eight, like me. We do not fight the monsters to level up, but we have been here in the Stronghold when monsters attacked and were defeated. And my sister and I were on a work crew that was attacked by hyenas. We held them off with axes and sharp branches until enough fighters could be summoned to kill them."

"Then you are very brave, as well as intelligent. Tell me, what would you like to do? Given the choice of anything. Would you want to hunt? To cook? Are you good with machines? Maybe heal? Or do you enjoy being a lumber... I'm sorry, a harvester?"

"My mother loves to cook, but I'm afraid I did not inherit her talent for it. My sister and I are very good dancers! But I do not suppose one could earn a living that way anymore." She lowered her gaze.

"Probably not right now, though as we rebuild and grow, that might be a possibility." Allistor did remember a few exotic dancers at the Stadium, but didn't think that line of work was right for this woman.

"I like to garden..." She offered.

"There you go! There are several classes that involve plants. Druids, farmers, herbalists, alchemists... lots of possibilities there." He smiled at her. "And I know just the person to introduce you to. Come with me."

He led her out of the apartment, closing the door behind them. She gasped as the door closed, looking over

427

Allistor's shoulder. When he glanced back, he saw letters appearing as if carved into the door. They spelled out *Lady Sirina.*

Five minutes later they were standing in an open area inside the newly expanded wall. Allistor placed one of several additional teleport hubs he'd purchased from Harmon, and enjoyed the look on her face as it sprang into existence. Several others noticed the seemingly magical appearance, as well as the towering new buildings, and had wandered over to take a closer look. Allistor took the opportunity to make a sales pitch.

"I'm Allistor, new proprietor of this establishment." He smiled at the crowd, but got only blank looks and neutral expressions in return. "This is a teleport pad. It is connected to a whole network of other pads at my various properties here on earth, and our new planet called Orion. I'm about to escort miss Sirina here to meet a few friends of mine, who can teach her about some available classes that fit what she likes to do, which is gardening."

He paused as there was a bit of mumbling. Realizing they might have no idea what classes were, he took five minutes to outline them, describing his own class, and a few others. As well as the spells that came with them. He was realizing more and more that Rajesh had kept most of these people completely in the dark about the opportunities for growth this new world offered. They were so far behind the curve, it made him angry. If Rajesh still lived, he'd kill him again, slowly.

Finished with discussing classes, he changed his mind about the day's schedule. These folks were not informed enough about their world to make an important decision like whether or not to become citizens. Though he was doubtful they would survive otherwise, he wanted to educate them.

"Nigel, loudspeaker please. Through this whole Stronghold."

"*Go ahead, sire.*" The voice echoed out of the pad, causing several folks to step back.

"Attention everyone. This is Emperor Allistor. Please drop what you're doing and join me at the new teleport pad. Just walk toward the two new high rise buildings, and you'll see our gathering. I have some information to share." He didn't want to bully these people, but he needed all of them to hear him. "This is a mandatory meeting. Please make your way to my location now. This includes all my raiders and trainers, please."

While they waited for the others, Allistor answered some questions. They were pretty basic, like who was he, how did he become emperor, did he maintain a harem? That one had come from a hopeful looking teenage boy. After about fifteen minutes there were several thousand locals standing around him. A few were so elderly and frail looking that he had his people produce whatever they had in their rings that could be used as seats.

"Nigel, is everyone here?"

*"There are two elderly residents who are in their beds, and one of them has two young children with her."*

Allistor looked around for one of the healers. Spotting one, he asked, "Please go take a look at them, do what you can? Nigel, have five droids meet her there. They can carry our last few stragglers back here."

A woman stepped forward, an angry look on her face. "The old woman with the children is my grandmother, and those are my children. She is sick, and cannot be moved. You leave them alone!" There were some angry rumbles from the crowd behind her.

"I mean her no harm. I'm sending a healer to her. If there is something wrong with her other than age, she will help your grandmother. The droids will carefully carry her here, so that she can hear what I have to tell you all. No harm will come to her, or to your children."

Sirina stepped forward and placed a hand on the woman's arm. "Trust him, he is a good man." The woman looked uncertain, but must have trusted Sirina to some extent. She nodded once and stepped back. The healer departed at a sprint, knowing Allistor wanted to get things moving. Another healer took off after her, unasked, to see to the other senior.

Allistor took the time to tell the rest of the crowd the short version of his story. How his town had been flattened by the void titan, his family killed. He spoke about when they first formed the Warren stronghold, and of the challenges they faced in the early days. These people were basically still at that stage, not having been allowed to develop, and he thought they could best relate to that period in his life.

Then he spoke about adding more Strongholds, about making allies of other leaders, and his stroke of luck when Helen granted him the parks. He introduced Helen, then some of the others. It was at that point that the droids and healers arrived with the grandmother and children, and an extremely old man wrapped in several blankets. The healer walking alongside the old man's droid shook his head, letting Allistor know there wasn't much he could do for the old man. You couldn't cure old age with a healing spell.

But this gave Allistor an idea.

"Please excuse me for just a moment, I need to check on something." He opened his UI and the tab Daigath had pointed out to him. A quick glance at his own stats showed that he had more than a hundred and fifty million experience points toward his next level. After a bit of exploration, he confirmed what he'd wanted to know, and made an adjustment.

"Thank you folks." He looked at the healers and motioned for them to bring the droids carrying the seniors forward. "I needed to check to see if this was possible. I'm about to do something I've never done before."

He took a deep breath, organizing his thoughts. "I had planned to give each of you until noon today to make a choice as to whether or not to join me and become citizens of Invictus. Unfortunately, I've learned that Rajesh kept a lot of vital information from you. He also kept you stagnant, rather than helping you to grow stronger." He looked around the crowd. "Are any of you, other then the fighters, level ten or higher?"

Maybe fifty hands went up into the air. "And you were given the opportunity to choose a class?" He focused on one individual near the front, whose face he could see clearly.

The man nodded, then shook his head. "I got a message about choosing a class, yes. But Earl Rajesh instructed me, all of us, to ignore it. He said he would instruct us on which class to choose, later."

Allistor was getting angry again. He took a couple deep breaths. "Did any of you ignore Rajesh and choose a class anyway?" He waited several seconds. "It's okay, you won't get in trouble. Rajesh is a melted pile of goo, probably still smoking. He can't hurt you, and I won't hurt you. In fact, I'm hoping to make it so all of you can choose a class."

After several more seconds, half a dozen hands went up. "Please, step forward."

When the six had meekly moved forward through the crowd and joined him up on the teleport pad, he continued. "Thank you, for your courage and for stepping forward. I like people who think for themselves. May I ask, what classes did you all choose?"

The first in line spoke quietly. "I chose farmer."

"Very good! And extremely valuable now, since commercial farms are no longer producing food. Feeding everyone is a high priority."

Encouraged by his reaction, the others shared their classes. There were two more farmers, one blacksmith, a druid, and an enchanter.

"Wonderful. Good choices all around. And we have folks who can help you improve your class skills and spells." He smiled at them all, then motioned for them to rejoin the crowd. "Now, normally I reserve this kind of assistance for my own citizens, for people who have sworn the oath not to harm me or mine. But in your case, you have been so oppressed by Rajesh that I feel I need to put you on a little more level playing field before you make that decision. So as I mentioned before, I'm going to do something I've never done before. I'm going to give you all a very valuable gift. Something that I and the rest of my people had to fight hard for, to risk our lives to earn."

He paused, holding his hands out for dramatic effect. "Nigel, please assign experience points from the Empire's pool to each of these people. Exactly enough of them to raise each person to level ten." He smiled at the crowd full of widened eyes and open mouths.

"*I am sorry, sire. I cannot comply. Recipients must either be subjects of your empire, or must complete a quest to receive experience points as a reward.*"

"Ha!" Allistor began to blush. His grand gesture had just fallen embarrassingly flat. Helen snorted, then laughed loudly beside him, as did most of his raiders. The crowd just looked confused.

"Well, as I said, I've never tried this before. Even your mighty Emperor makes mistakes…"

"A lot of mistakes." Helen added.

"Mistakes that usually end up with him bleeding all over everybody." McCoy called out from somewhere in the crowd. Allistor shot him a bird and moved on.

"Alright, let's try this. Those of you who took the oath yesterday, please step forward."

When they'd gathered around in front of him, the roughly one hundred locals turned at his direction to face the crowd. "Nigel, please use the experience pool to raise each of these people who aren't already there to level ten. For everyone who is already ten or higher, please raise them a single level."

"Of course, sire." The crowd gasped as a glow surrounded each of the local citizens, and their eyes unfocused. One by one they finished reading their notifications and turned to smile at Allistor, or bow, or cry out.

"He did it. He raised me to level ten." One man raised both hands in the air. "I can now choose a class for myself!"

Others began to speak out as well. As they did, Fayed cleared his throat and motioned to Allistor, who nodded his permission to approach. The man stepped next to him and spoke quietly. "Thank you for the additional level, Emperor Allistor. And for the boon."

"Boon?" Helen asked before Allistor could.

"Yes. I received The Boon of the Emperor." He saw that Allistor was confused, so his eyes unfocused as he pulled it up and read it aloud.

*You have received: **The Boon of the Emperor!***
*Planetary Emperor Allistor has looked upon you with favor,*
*and gifted you an allotment of his personal experience points*
*sufficient to increase your level. You receive two additional*
*free attribute points.*
*Experience gains increased by 50% for a period of thirty days."*

"Wow!" Helen exclaimed, again before Allistor could speak. Which was probably a good thing. He needed to act like an emperor, not a surprised kid.

"That is… unexpected." Allistor replied. "But a valuable boost. I hope you make the most of it, Fayed."

By this time, the others had stopped talking and were listening to Fayed and Allistor. Seeing this, he opened his arms again. "All of you who just received the boon. Make the most of it. My people will give you quests to complete, take you hunting, even take you on dungeon runs if you desire. A fifty percent boost to your experience is too valuable to waste."

Every one of them nodded or smiled, grateful for the levels and the boon.

"As for the rest of you… I have a quest for you." He opened up his UI and created a quest, specified it was for anyone under level ten, left the experience as variable knowing that Nigel would handle the numbers, and finalized it.

"Those of you who have children with you, please pick them up. Have someone next to you help if you have more than one. You will have to accept the quest on behalf of your children if they can not read." He fervently hoped that all of the adults could read. When all the kids were accounted for, he sent out the quest.

> *Quest received: Hold Still, Please.*
> *Do not move from where you stand for ten seconds.*
> *Reward: Experience sufficient to reach Level 10.*

Those ten seconds were among the longest Allistor could remember. He hoped no one would move and fail the quest, as that would be both embarrassing and inconvenient. When the clock ran out, swirls of light surrounded each of them, including the children. All of them were now level ten.

The crowd went from dead silent to an explosion of wonder and celebration. Kids cheered, not sure what was happening, but thrilled at all the smiles and laughter. Allistor got the impression this hadn't been a very happy place before.   He let them celebrate and congratulate each other for a while, then held up his hands.

"My friends!  Welcome to a whole new world.  I would ask a few favors of you." The crowd got quiet.  He knew what they were thinking.  Nothing is free.  Now comes the catch.  "First, please don't rush to choose your class.  You have plenty of time to go through your options.  Ask questions of my people and the class trainers that I have here with me.  If you choose to become a citizen of Invictus, you'll have access to more than a hundred different trainers, and can ask any of my people about their classes.  Choosing a class is maybe the most important choice you'll make for yourself, so consider it carefully.  Also, you will have received a bunch of free attribute points.  Don't rush to assign those until you've chosen your class.  You'll understand why soon enough." He paused for effect.  "Next, rather than ask you to make a decision about citizenship today, I'm going to ask you all to take the day off and explore a bit.  This teleport pad can take you to any of our other locations.  This is the only one on this continent, at the moment.  But you can travel to Europe, several dozen spots in America, Canada, the Caribbean, and if you're feeling *really adventurous* you can even travel to another planet called Orion!"

"What about our quotas?" The same woman who had warned him away from her family stepped forward.

Allistor wanted to growl in frustration. "You have no quotas.  As of today, there are no more quotas.  Period.

You are all relieved of whatever production burdens Rajesh placed upon you. If you should choose to become citizens and remain here to work in the factory, you will be paid a fair wage, provided with housing and food, and have all the same rights as every other citizen of Invictus." He looked at Sirina and smiled. "On the other hand, if you should decline to become a citizen, you will be asked to leave. You'll keep the levels I've just gifted you, and we'll give you a week... no, let's make that a month's worth of food and water. We'll even help you clear and claim a Stronghold somewhere else to give you a safe place to sleep, and provide you with decent weapons with which to defend yourselves." He eyed the large factory behind the crowd. "And, uhm, six months' supply of toilet paper." This elicited a laugh from his people, and several in the crowd. "But that's all the help you'll get from us."

"How do we know that if we step through this teleporter, you won't just enslave us in some dungeon somewhere?" Another woman asked.

"That's... no. If I had plans to enslave you, or harm you in any way, I would have already done so. These people I brought with me?" He waved across the crowd, and they all waved back, identifying themselves as if that were at all necessary. "Most of them are level fifty or higher. We just finished fighting off an attack from about a million undead, all of whom were two or three times your level. I could kill every one of you myself in about thirty seconds." To prove his point, he cast *Storm* over the empty field close to the high rises. Clouds formed, and lightning bolts began to slam into the ground. He let it run for about ten seconds, then stopped channeling.

They got the point.

"I came here to help you. I want to help all of the human race that has survived the last year to grow stronger. To take back as much of our planet as we can, and restore our civilization as close as possible to the way it was. There will be no peasants, no slaves, not anymore. I accepted the titles I have because they're necessary under the new System. Somebody has to be in charge and make the rules. To represent the rest of us in dealing with the non-humans out there. But I'm no tyrant."

He waited for more questions. Eventually Sirina helped him out. "How does this teleport work?"

Nigel answered, naturally assuming the question was for him. *"You simply step onto the pad, in groups of no more than twenty individuals, and state your destination. I will send you there. Once you have arrived, please vacate the pad immediately, as others may wish to make use of it."*

"How do we know where to go?" someone from the crowd shouted.

Allistor hadn't thought of that. "I'll tell you what. My people will spread out around the pad to answer questions and make recommendations. Take some time to talk to them. Tell them what you're interested in, and they'll recommend a place to start. I'll give you until noon tomorrow to explore. You can visit as many of our locations as you wish in that time. Wherever you go, feel free to ask the people there whatever questions you like. They can show you around, demonstrate spells, crafting, healing, whatever. And you'll have access to food and drink at your leisure. Just ask whomever you're with, and they'll get you to a cafeteria."

Helen nudged him in the ribs, and whispered "Beastkin."

"Oh, shit! Thanks." He chuckled. "Uhmm... as you move around, you'll notice several non-human beings living and working among us. Don't be frightened, they're citizens, and quite friendly. There are elves, dwarves, gnomes, minotaur, orcanin – those look like storybook orcs, big green muscley guys, but please don't call them orcs, it's an insult to them. They are called orcanin. There are beastkin of various forms – they look part human, part animal. All of them have taken the oath and are fellow citizens. They will not harm you unless you attack them. Even then, they'll probably just restrain you and return you to me. All of them are much more powerful than any of you."

There were expressions of shock and concern. Several people backed away from the pad as if it might bite them.

"Any other questions?" Allistor asked. "If not, I'd like to take care of something. Please, bring our two most senior friends forward. Fayed, Sirina, would you help me?"

The droids brought forth the two frail locals, and Allistor briefly explained what he had in mind to Fayed and Sirina in a whisper. They in turn moved to speak with the seniors, Sirina helping the grandmother, Fayed the old man. It took a few minutes, especially for the old man who was barely lucid. But eventually they achieved the result Allistor hoped for.

Both elders rapidly looked much healthier and stronger. The old man even squirmed to be set down and stood on his own, albeit with one hand on the droid to steady himself. Fayed had coached him into applying attribute points to *Strength* and *Constitution,* as well as a few points into *Intelligence* to help with focus, and *Stamina.* There was no cure for age, but being able to use attribute points to boost yourself beyond human norms was a good substitute.

Having the oldsters suddenly looking much more spry and active went a long way toward reassuring the others. They looked more relaxed and less afraid.

"Now then, I promised to escort miss Sirina here, who you can thank for the brand new high rises, by the way, to meet some friends of mine. We'll be making a quick stop at my capital city on the way. Any of you who wish to visit may join us, or follow."

He moved to the center of the pad and motioned for her to join him. To her credit, she did so with confidence and no hesitation. Agni, Fayed, and several of those who'd already sworn the oath chose to join him, then half a dozen or so from the crowd. Including the grandmother and her family.

With a smile and a wave, Allistor and the others disappeared.

Chapter 20

Master Cogwalker sat behind the desk in his office on the space station. His chair was swiveled so that his back was to the desk and he faced a wide window in the outer wall of the room. Below him was the azure wonder of the planet Allistor and the humans called Earth. Puffy white clouds drifted lazily across vast oceans and land masses alike. To the south a spiral storm system spun westward from one continent toward another. It was beautiful.

Cogwalker had only spent a short time on the planet, but he found he quite liked the environment. It had a much lower gravity than his own homeworld, making him feel like he could leap over buildings without much effort. They had set the gravity here in the station to match the planet's, but everything here was tight spaces and long corridors, no wide open spaces for leaping, except maybe the upper habitat.

Still, he had no time for such boyish foolishness. His clan's honor, his own personal honor, had been badly damaged by the attacks here on the station. He needed to get to the bottom of several questions, and do it soon.

His dwarves had captured and detained all the remaining griblins within minutes of the explosions. Their gear had been searched, and two more explosives found. Each griblin had been questioned extensively, and each had cooperated fully. They too seemed to want to find out what happened. The two who had been carrying unexploded bombs had no idea how or when the explosives had been implanted in their gear. The clan leadership had sent in a full investigative team, including several interrogators, explosive experts, and a mentalist. The mentalist, better than any lie detector, could read the thoughts of its targets, even force them to reveal memories. If the target resisted, the process could become quite painful.

None of the griblins had resisted. They had cooperated fully and without hesitation.

There had been a very limited number of clan members on the station in the days prior to Emperor Allistor's visit. An additional one hundred or so had been aboard during the station's transport to the planet. They had all departed with the tug ships a week earlier. Cogwalker himself had reviewed the crew arrival and departure logs, as well as security feeds, confirming the departure of all clan and crew.

Except one.

A single dwarf, a clansman and fellow engineer, had accompanied the station on its trip to Earth, but had not departed with the rest of the delivery crew as scheduled. Nor had he been detected anywhere in the station in all the days since. He hadn't accessed any doors, trams, or elevators, or appeared in any surveillance feeds. He had not used his ration card to obtain any meals, or sent or received any communications off-station. None of the other clansmen, including the griblins whose gear had been tampered with, remember seeing the dwarf anywhere on the station at any time.

On a hunch, and because he was frankly out of leads and ideas, Cogwalker had requested the clan send a team of snorgs and their handlers. A snorg was a six-legged creature that vaguely resembled a canid in body structure. Its body was short and stocky, heavily muscled like the dwarves that raised them on their home planet. Where it differed most from canids was its head. The creatures had three eyes that could see in several light spectrums and detect heat signatures. In addition, their snouts were three times as long and wide as a standard canid. Giving them olfactory sensing abilities beyond the capabilities of any tech Cogwalker had ever seen.

His engineers had used what tech they had access to. Sensors that could vacuum up discarded skin cells and other biomatter and analyze them at a molecular level. But the station was large, and the process slow. Especially since they had no idea where to search, other than the locations of the explosions. The nature of which tended to destroy biological trace evidence.

A team of six snorgs, on the other hand, could cover the entire station in a day or two. And more importantly, they were the one creature in the Collective that would not be fooled by the beings that Cogwalker now suspected of the sabotage.

Snorgs were trained to track changelings.

It was the only explanation that made any sense to Cogwalker. His theory was that the creature had replaced the missing dwarf sometime during the station's transit to earth. Taking the dwarf engineer's form, it would have had free access to every part of the station in the two solar days between the delivery and the tug ships' departures. Plenty of time to plant the explosives they found, and possibly many more that they hadn't.

When a changeling adopted a form, in this case a dwarf, its DNA when scanned would read as dwarf DNA. The creature in effect became a dwarf in appearance as well as chemical composition. It would be impossible for standard medical and security scanners to detect a difference. Which was why the creatures were so effective as smugglers, spies, and assassins.

But snorgs, with their incredible sense of smell and larger than normal canid brains, were able to detect the scent of a certain waste product produced by the changelings when they morphed. The Stardrifter clan had discovered this when a captured changeling had killed its guards and assumed one of their forms to escape, only to be foiled by a pack of snorgs kept in the prison compound grounds. That changeling, which had only been previously charged with smuggling, was quickly convicted of murder. Never ones to waste valuable resources, it was sentenced to a lifetime of assisting its captors in training more snorgs to detect and track its kind. The clan earned a great deal of wealth by selling the services of those snorgs as security or investigative teams across the Collective. Faction heads and Emperors wanting to prevent changeling assassins from accessing their homes paid well for snorg patrols and guards at access points.

The teams had arrived the day before, and Cogwalker had just received confirmation. Three of the six teams had detected signs of a changeling on board. They were now tracking its scent through the station, accompanied by well-armed guards, both dwarven and griblin. The griblins had begged to be included, wanting revenge for the deaths of their brethren, and a chance to restore their reputations within the clan.

Already they found that the changeling had visited several key locations within vital engineering and life support sections, and three bombs had been located and disarmed. From what the handlers could tell, the changeling was no longer on the station. The scents had all been old, based on the level of interest expressed by the snorgs. They got much more excited over fresh scents.

This was the dilemma that Cogwalker now faced. The ships that arrived with the investigative teams had been sealed the moment the teams departed onto the station. Snorgs were stationed at each ship's access to prevent the changeling from sneaking aboard the ships. All of the station's escape pods and service pods – little one-man utility vessels used for external repairs in the vacuum of space – were still docked in their stations. No other ships had docked with the station… except Allistor's.

He found himself hoping that one of the griblins that had exploded was the changeling in disguise. But that hope was faint, and not at all likely. Which meant, if the snorgs did not locate the changeling in the next several hours as they finished their sweeps of the station, it must have boarded Allistor's ship.

And Cogwalker would have to be the one to tell Allistor that a changeling assassin who had targeted him, killed his intended bride, and might still be planning to kill him, had probably hitched a ride down to the planet on the *Phoenix*.

*****

Allistor escorted Sirina, Agni, and Fayed on a brief tour of the Invictus Tower before taking them through the teleport again to Ramon's Citadel. They were instantly greeted by Max, who seemed to take a special liking to Agni. The elder gentleman obviously returned the affection, actually taking some time to roll around in the grass and wrestle with the dog. He smiled sheepishly and shrugged when he got to his feet.

"I had a dog much like Max as a boy. He brings back fond memories."

Chloe joined them soon after, bowing and politely greeting the newcomers before leading them to Ramon and Nancy. Allistor made quick introductions before nudging Sirina forward slightly.

"Sirina here has been working as a harvester. Helping to strip newly felled lumber of branches so that the wood could be processed for use in their *toilet paper plant*." He winked at Ramon as he emphasized the words. "Also, don't call her a lumberjack. It's a silly word." Both Ramon and Nancy laughed.

"Oh, you have to let me go back there with you and take Meg. I want to see her face." Nancy chuckled.

Ramon saw the confused expressions on their visitors' faces. "Meg is one of our original family and our head chef. She was with us from day one, and was constantly reminding us to scavenge toilet paper wherever we went. When we were running low, if you came back without a roll or two, she might refuse to feed you. It became sort of a thing."

"Ah, I see." Agni smiled, getting the joke. "Yes, we had similar issues before we got the factory up and running."

Sirina added, "We never consider the little luxuries in life until they are taken from us."

Allistor nodded, a long list of pre-apocalypse items running through his head that he'd love to have back. Top among them being chocolate, hot pockets, the internet, and a wireless network.

"Anyway…" he smiled at Sirina. "She has expressed an interest in gardening, and I thought maybe you could coach her on related classes, crafting, et cetera." He motioned toward Nancy and added, "Nancy is a druid class. She's our very best healer, as well as the one who organizes all of our crops. Both food crops and herbs for seasoning and potion ingredients. Nancy and George, who we just recently lost, are the ones who fed all our people through the winter. Plus, she can teach you a spell that I think you'll find very useful, regardless of whether you go back to being a lumber- ehh, a harvester, or not."

449

Nancy rolled her eyes at him, gently shouldering him aside as she gathered up Sirina and led her out the door. "Let me show you my greenhouse…" Her voice faded as the two women, plus Chloe, rounded a corner.

Ramon took up the mantle of host. "I don't suppose either of you have an interest in inscription or related work?" He motioned for them to follow him into the library. Both men's eyes widened at the sight of the bustling facility. The walls were lined with books, with scrolls stuffed in between them here and there. Tables were covered in paper, inkwells, and other implements as dozens of people worked at inscribing magic spells onto special paper.

As they gawked, Ramon produced several scrolls from his ring. "I'm guessing Allistor hasn't given you any of these, yet. All of our people receive several basic spells at a minimum. Stuff to help keep you alive. Here are scrolls for *Restore*, a healing spell. *Light*, which creates a small light globe that hovers near you, and *Flame Shot*, which should be self-explanatory. Go ahead and use them now. Then we can discuss your stats and what class build you're leaning toward, and maybe get you a few additional scrolls." He looked at Allistor, who nodded in confirmation. He also took a third set to give to Sirina when he saw her again.

"These are basic scrolls, which can be made by pretty much any low level *Inscriptionist* class." He spoke while the two men tentatively opened a scroll each and learned the spells. When they'd burned through all three, he smiled and reached into his ring, producing two scrolls and another item, tossing them onto a table. "Please, take a seat." He motioned for them to sit, then sat across from them. With a motion of his hand, the third item he'd dropped on the table came to life. It hopped up and stood upright on two legs, looking much like a foot-tall gingerbread man. "I've raised my *Inscriptionist* class level high enough that I was able to specialize as a *Paper Sorcerer*. Which allows me to do things like this." He stared at the little paper man, who stepped forward and bent down, grabbing a scroll in each hand. It then walked across the table and presented Agni and Fayed with a scroll each.

"This one is called *Mind Spike*. Again, pretty self-explanatory. It causes a great deal of brain pain, and makes a good spell interrupter. Pretty much anyone with an Intelligence stat above ten can use it." Ramon explained as his little paper golem returned across the table. When he reached Ramon, the little guy did a dance, twirling on one foot, waving its arms, and finishing with a hip thrust that made the paper crinkle.

"Ha!" Fayed was enchanted by the little dude. "That's quite interesting. May I?" He held out a hand, and Ramon obliged by sending the golem running back across the table. Allistor watched, expecting it to jump into Fayed's open hand, but instead it ran around to the side and hugged his thumb with both arms. To his credit, the surprised man didn't yank his hand back.

"I think he likes you." Ramon chuckled. A moment later the golem hopped onto the open palm and struck a hero pose as Fayed raised his hand closer to his face to get a better look.

"Wonderful! It actually seems to be alive."

"It's not, at least, not yet." Ramon shook his head. The little golem took a seat and leaned back, lounging in Fayed's palm. "I'm not high enough level yet to give the golems any true sentience. Right now they obey my commands in real time, or they can follow a set of clear and simple instructions. Like 'go pick that up and drop it in the trash can' or 'go find Nancy and bring her back'. That last one did not go well, by the way." He looked at Allistor. "These things already creep her out, and the one I sent with those instructions tried to physically drag her back here."

"Hahaha!" Allistor thumped the table. "Did she say bad words?"

Ramon hung his head in mock sorrow. "So many bad words. Chloe learned a few new ones, even." He winked at Fayed. "I had Max taste all my food for a week, in case it was poisoned."

The conversation turned to classes and spells. Agni had chosen an *Administrator* class, and as Allistor had suspected, focused most of his attribute points on *Intelligence* and *Will Power*. They gave him several more scrolls, including *Mend, Vortex* and *Restraint*. Fayed on the other hand had a very balanced build, with a slight emphasis on *Strength* and *Constitution*, but nearly equal points in *Stamina*, *Agility*, and *Intelligence*. He was given *Erupt* and *Restraint,* not having quite enough points in *Intelligence* to learn *Vortex*. He hadn't chosen a class, which surprised Allistor until he remembered something he'd heard.

"Did Rajesh also forbid you from selecting a class?"

"He did." Fayed nodded. "I think he was afraid that if I had additional class spells I might feel I was powerful enough to overthrow him." The man paused. "Two months ago I would never have considered it. But some of his actions lately made it… difficult to remain loyal."

"Well, what have you been leaning toward as far as a class?" Allistor tried his best to ignore the flash of anger and move on.

"Actually, your own class, as you described it, seems useful. Both offensive and defensive magic. And that lightning storm you called was impressive."

"Ooooh, big fancy storm spell, flashy lightning." Ramon mocked Allistor with a grin, and his golem gave Allistor a deep, mocking bow.

Allistor ignored him. "It has been very helpful in keeping me alive, and protecting my people as well. Master Daigath is our *Battlemage* trainer. If you'd like to speak to him, I'll introduce you. But don't decide on that class yet. Spend some time talking to the other fighter classes among our people, and the class trainers. You might find one you like better. I wasn't kidding when I said picking a class is the most important decision you'll make."

\*\*\*\*\*

Outside in the gardens, Nancy was walking Sirina through the process of converting ingredients into potions. They stood side by side in front of a workbench as Sirina took her first shot at grinding herbs with a mortar and pestle.

"May I ask you something… personal?" Sirina's voice was barely above a whisper.

"Certainly. Ask away." Nancy smiled, dropping a few bits of a healing herb into the ceramic bowl.

"Emperor Allistor. Is he really as kind and gentle as he seems? Or is it an act he puts on for the peasants. His subjects, I mean."

Nancy wiped her hands on her apron and then put her hands over top of Sirina's, adjusting her grinding technique slightly. "Slower, and less pressure. There you go." She let go and smiled. "Allistor is exactly who he appears to be. I knew his mother. She was always talking about him as a child. When the apocalypse happened, despite being so young and having just lost his entire family, he stepped up and used his knowledge to save us all. He kept us alive and safe until we had the chance to improve ourselves and understand how this new world works. He honestly would give his own life without a second thought to save any one of us. And what he wants most is for all of us humans to thrive." She paused to inspect the contents of the bowl, then motioned for Sirina to empty them into a glass beaker.

"All the kindness he's shown you and your people today? Did he mentioned that the woman he loved was just killed a few days ago?"

Sirina's lips tightened and her eyes widened as she shook her head. "Oh, no. I'm so sorry. No, he didn't mention it."

Nancy nodded, pouring a clear liquid into the beaker atop the crushed herbs. "He wouldn't. He loved Amanda, and we had all been preparing for the wedding. She was killed in an attack on our new space station the other day. Right after that, during her memorial service Allistor had to confront two ancient beings who are basically gods as far as power goes. You've heard of Loki and Baldur?"

"I have read the myths about them, yes."

"Well, they're apparently real beings. A race of aliens who visited Earth long ago, so powerful that the humans back then called them gods and based whole religions on them. They're also the ones who caused our apocalypse and killed most of the human race. Anyway, Allistor faced them down and found a way to trick them into granting most of us citizens enough experience to get a bunch of levels. And he has to face them again in a few days. Oh, and in between he spent several days up on the wall of Invictus City fighting about a million zombies."

"He mentioned the zombies. Right before he called down a storm that was quite frightening."

"Heh. He does like to show off that spell." Nancy smiled at her.

Sirina was quiet as she watched Nancy place the beaker over a flame. Eventually, she spoke. "He has been so kind to me, my family, and all of the people in our Stronghold. He gave up some of his personal experience in order to raise us all up to level ten. Thousands of us."

Now it was Nancy's turn to be surprised. She hadn't known that was possible. Still, it was exactly the kind of thing Allistor would find a way to do. She stood quietly next to the woman as they both watched the liquid mixture heat up.

"I think I would like to become a healer, like you." Sirina finally said. "And I would enjoy this Alchemy that you've demonstrated here. Allistor constructed a pool with a glass enclosure inside our Stronghold. There is a little space around the pool where I could grow some herbs…"

Nancy shook her head. "Oh, no. If you're going to become an Alchemist, we'll build you a proper greenhouse. You said there are a few thousand people in your Stronghold?"

"Yes, though I don't know how many of them will stay. Living under Rajesh has left a bad taste in our mouths, and many may not wish to trade one ruler for another, despite Allistor's good intentions."

"Don't worry. Of all the many tens of thousands of people Allistor has given that same choice to, only a handful have declined his offer. Like you're doing now, they'll meet people and ask questions, learn about how things work. Most of them will stay. Which means you'll have a lot of mouths to feed. We'll take some seedlings along, some apple and orange trees. And we'll plant some corn fields too. And I'll build you a greenhouse large enough to grow vegetables and useful herbs inside where they'll be protected from birds and bugs."

She paused when she saw tears running down Sirina's cheeks. Putting one arm around her, she gave the woman a squeeze. "I know, it's a lot to take in. But you're going to be one of us now, and we look out for our own. Our job is helping you grow as quickly as possible, so that you can in turn help others, and so on. We're going to get the human race back on its feet. Only this time, we're all going to be superhuman. Stronger, smarter, generally just more badass!"

Sirina laughed, wiping her cheeks. "You're so wonderful. I'm happy to have met you. Thank you so much, for all of this."

Nancy pulled the beaker off the flame and poured its contents into another receptacle. From there they watched it pass through several tubes and other glass containers, until it finally dropped into a vial held in a round stand filled with empty vials. The liquid had changed color from a sickly green to a vibrant red during the distilling process. When the vial was full, she deftly rotated the stand so that the still-dripping liquid began to fill another. By the time they were done, six vials were filled with the red liquid.

"There, now! You've just made healing potions." She placed stoppers in each vial, then handed them to Sirina. "Each one will restore approximately five thousand health points instantly, and an additional five thousand over thirty seconds."

Sirina's eyes unfocused as she received notifications. A moment later her smile stretched from ear to ear. "I've just learned the profession of Alchemy! And it says I'm already level two, since I've been instructed by a master."

"One of the perks of making several thousand vials of potions over the last year or so. You'll find your skills level up faster if you also grow and harvest your own ingredients."

"Thank you again!" Sirina moved as if to hug Nancy, but nearly dropped the vials she still held in her hands. Looking down at her outfit, she realized she had no pockets and just shrugged, holding the vials in both hands as she beamed at Nancy.

Nancy smacked her forehead. "I'm guessing you don't have a storage ring, right? It sounds like that guy who was running your Stronghold didn't do much to help you out. Come with me." She took the vials and stored them in her own ring before grabbing Sirina's hand and pulling her out of the garden. "Nigel, tell our illustrious Emperor that I'm taking Sirina to use the kiosk, and that he's a slacker. He needs to buy about two thousand more storage rings. And I'm headed to the new Stronghold to spend a whole lot of his build points."

Allistor was still in the library with Ramon, Agni, and Fayed. They were just getting up to retrieve Sirina and head back to Invictus Tower when Nigel relayed Nancy's message.

Ramon guffawed, halfheartedly covering his mouth as he laughed. "You know she's gonna do it, too. She'll build like a ten story greenhouse, a couple orchards, maybe an alchemy lab if that's the direction Sirina chooses to go. Actually, she'll probably build it no matter what, and talk someone else into being an *Alchemist* if Sirina isn't interested."

Not in the least upset, Allistor still forced a grimace onto his face. "Yeah. When are you gonna learn to control your woman, Ramon?"

"Ha! Not in this lifetime, my friend. It's the other way around on this island. She's the boss, I'm just the scroll monkey she enjoys cuddling with from time to time."

Agni smiled at the two of them. "You are a wise man, Ramon. I predict you'll lead a happy life."

*****

The following morning Allistor, Helen, Nancy, William and the girls insisted that Meg and Sam accompany them to the new Stronghold to hear what the majority of the locals had decided. They gave the excuse of wanting to organize a proper kitchen for them, and provide a welcome feast.

Meg leapt to the task with her usual enthusiasm, making comments that Allistor was slacking if there were only two thousand new mouths to feed instead of five or ten thousand. She packed a storage ring full of food and recruited half a dozen kitchen staff to assist her, and they were off.

The moment they arrived, Helen led the group toward the factory building. "I think the main building might be the best place to set up the kitchen. I didn't look before, but I think that's where it is now. Though I'm sure you'll want to expand it…"

Allistor opened the door for them and allowed Helen to lead the group inside. Everyone who was in the know had expectant smiles on their faces. They quickly stepped down a short hallway and through a set of swinging double doors into a wide open space.

Rather than the kitchen, Meg found herself on a factory floor. Everywhere she looked there were pallets of toilet paper stacked six feet high.

"Ta-daaaa!" Helen threw her arms wide as she turned around to face Meg. "Welcome to your happy place, Megster! Allistor went n got you a toilet paper factory!"

"It's about damn time!" Meg fake-grumped, turning to glare at Allistor as Sam roared with laughter. "Smartest thing you ever did, boy!" She turned and hustled over to the nearest pallet, arms wide as she hugged one corner of the toilet paper towers that were taller than her, her eyes closed and a beatific smile on her face.  A moment later she stepped back and held up one hand.

"Think I can fit this whole pallet in my ring?"

Chapter 21

When Allistor made his way to the Factory teleport pad just before noon, he found that one of his earth mages had kindly raised a platform with three steps so that everyone would be able to see and hear him. They'd also been thoughtful enough to place several long stone benches in an arc in front of the stage for the elderly to be able to sit on.

Allistor waited as the locals gathered, along with those of his people who had decided to attend. To his surprise, he spotted a large contingent of the trainers present, gathered in several clusters. Nearly a hundred of them if he had to guess. Curious, he walked over and spotted Selby talking to her cousin.

"Hiya Selby. What's happening?" he asked casually, a smile on his face.

"Allistor! Hi. You mean the trainers? Well, when Ruddy here got back to the trainer compound, he was telling the others about how you raised everyone here up to level ten so that they could get a class." She paused as she looked at her feet, kicking the dirt slightly. "He might have also mentioned how bad off they were, as far as knowing how things work, not learning any spells or anything."

Ruddy stepped in. "We all felt bad for them. What you're doing here on Earth is exceptional, Allistor, and by becoming citizens, we all bought into it. We talked a bit, and decided to come and help these folks catch up a little bit. All of us that didn't already have training sessions scheduled for today are here to help."

Allistor wanted to hug the little gnomes. "That's… amazing! Thank you guys."

Ruddy cleared his throat. "There's something else, if you have a moment?" Allistor nodded for him to continue. "I don't know if you were aware, but one of the skills I teach is *Animal Husbandry*. I've been working with Daniel over at the silo, as well as the other folks who've bonded with drakelings."

"Oh, cool. I know the kids were excited about bonding, but they haven't had much time to visit the drakes the last week or so…"

"The kids and their drakes are doing fine." Ruddy looked uncomfortable. "But the little white who was bonded to Airman Goodrich…"

"Oh, shit." The color drained from Allistor's face. How could he have forgotten that Goodrich bonded with a drakeling on that first day? It had happened right in front of him! And after worrying so much about Fiona, it should have clicked."

Ruddy held up his hands, patting the air. "No, no. It's not that bad. The drakeling is very young and still small. The loss of the bond was traumatic, but not fatal. I was going to suggest that we try and find a replacement companion as quickly as possible."

"Yes. Sure! Of course. There won't be any shortage of people who want to bond with a drake." He paused to think. "I suppose we could ask for volunteers and then do some kind of lottery…"

Ruddy shook his head. "It would be best if the companion was one who has ice magic. Or at least compatible powers like water magic, or air magic." He gave Allistor a lopsided grin. "You and your people just sort of went willy-nilly in picking drakes when they hatched. Normally we would screen candidates and bond them with drakes that are most compatible."

"Ah, well yeah, that makes sense." Allistor scratched his head, feeling a little foolish. "Although, it was mostly the other way around. The drakelings sort of picked their humans. Just one more thing we leapt into without knowing what we were doing."

"No harm done, really." Selby elbowed her cousin, giving him a dirty look for worrying Allistor. "The compatibility just makes the bonded team more effective. Those who've already bonded aren't in any danger or anything. They'll be fine." Ruddy nodded his agreement.

"Good to hear." Allistor shook his head. "Nigel or Longbeard can tell you who has classes that involve the proper magic. I guess reach out to them and see who's interested? Then do a lottery if you have more than one?" He turned to the growing crowd. "That includes these folks. If one of them chooses to be an ice mage or whatever, add them to the list."

Allistor made a mental note to go check on Fuzzy and Fiona when the day's events were concluded. He was just getting back near the stage when there was a commotion on the outer edge of the crowd. People were shouting, several were moving quickly to one side or another. Stepping up on the stage for a better view, he saw the crowd parting as Daigath walked toward him at a leisurely pace. But it wasn't the old elf that had people so stirred up.

Walking next to Daigath was a tiger the size of a small SUV. It padded along next to the elf, sniffing at the crowd and twitching its long tail. Daigath spoke calmly to the crowd as he advanced, telling them not to worry, and warning them against attacking.

Allistor hopped down off the front of the stage and moved to meet his mentor. "Master Daigath! New friend?"

"Allistor! Yes indeed. This is Sher'gal. I found her near the forest's edge just a few miles from here. I'm afraid I wandered into her territory without permission. She was quite grumpy about it, initially." Daigath grinned.

Behind the elf, one of the raiders whistled in amazement. "That kitty is level forty. What has she been eating?"

Daigath, hearing the question, turned to the raider. "There are significant packs of hyenas wandering around this area. Most are under level ten, but I came across an alpha that was level thirty five. I also encountered a constrictor serpent in a nearby lake that had grown to some thirty feet long and reached level thirty two. The wildlife in this area has been quite busy feeding and spawning, it seems." Looking around at the fearful faces of the locals, he raised both hands in the air for silence.

"Sher'gal has agreed to bond with me. She will not harm any of you, unless attacked. You may approach her and say hello, just please do not make any sudden movements. She is not accustomed to large crowds of people. Or, any people, really." He smiled. Several raiders stepped forward to greet and pet the tiger, much more used to the ways of the world and impressive pets like Fuzzy. When they saw that the tiger remained calm, the locals began to step forward as well. Only a few of them, but it was good to see them adjusting.

When the excitement over the tiger settled down, Allistor saw that there were no more locals trickling in. "Nigel, is everyone from this Stronghold in attendance?"

*"Yes, sire. All of the local residents, both sworn and unsworn, are here with you."*

Allistor grabbed Helen, who was still happily jibing Meg about maybe becoming Duchess of the toilet paper factory, and pulled her up onto the stage with him. "Can I have everyone's attention please?" He raised his hand, and the crowd quickly grew quiet."

"I hope all of you have had the chance to satisfy your curiosity about Invictus and myself. Enough time to get your questions asked and answered. And I hope you've all decided to join us. So I'll jump right to the question. Is there anyone here who does NOT wish to swear the oath and become a citizen of Invictus? Just raise your hand."

He and Helen waited for a quarter minute or so, and no hands went up.

"That's great! Helen here will administer the oath. Just repeat after her. If you have little ones who are too small to understand, your oath will apply to them as well. When they grow older they can decide for themselves whether to keep it or be released."

Helen stepped forward, and a minute later nearly two thousand more citizens joined Invictus. She stepped back as Nigel confirmed that everyone present, with the exception of Daigath and the tiger, was a citizen. Allistor's map reflected a sea of new green dots, and no red ones.

"Welcome to Invictus! All of you have some decisions to make, now. First, you can choose to remain here to live and work, or you may choose any of our other locations. If you remain here, there are about six hundred new apartments in those high rises. Nigel can assign you one based on your family size." He waited for the muttering this caused to die down a bit. Someone near the front raised a tentative hand, and he pointed to them. "Yes? You have a question?"

"What is the cost of the apartments? Rajesh did not pay us a wage..."

"There is no cost. As long as you contribute to the community's well being and growth in whatever way you can, your housing and food cost nothing. You'll also be able to earn money. Some of you may do so by joining raid teams and sharing in the loot, others by hunting, or crafting.

Hunters are expected to contribute meat to the community, but can sell the hides and other useful parts they obtain. Crafters will be given materials to help you raise your skills, as long as the items you create with those materials are given back to the community. Or you may sell those items via the kiosk, reimburse us for the materials used, and keep the profit for yourselves. Of course, any items crafted from materials you harvest or purchase for yourself are one hundred percent yours to keep, or sell for profit. We only ask that items sold to fellow citizens are reasonably priced. Feel free to fleece anyone else if you can!" He grinned as several in the crowd chuckled. "I strongly suggest each of you choose to learn a crafting skill of some kind, even if just as a hobby. I myself am learning weaponsmithing and enchanting."

"For those of you who wish to continue working in the factory, or harvesting, or any other of the professions that directly benefit the community, you will be paid a good wage in addition to your food and housing. This includes teachers, cleaners, cooks, administration staff, anyone giving their service to support their neighbors."

He nodded toward Selby, who in turned mobilized a group of crafters and other citizens. They took up places at four long tables set in a row to one side of the stage. "Speaking of support, your fellow citizens have gotten together and rounded up some gifts for you. First, stop and see Selby the gnome at the first table. She will give each of you a small storage device. Most of them are in the form of a ring, though we couldn't purchase two thousand rings all at once. So some of them are bracelets, belts, or pouches.

Each of you will receive a storage device with at least fifty slots. Those of you who will be serving as hunters, scavengers, or crafters will receive higher capacity to accommodate your work. They are simple devices that can store great quantities of goods, like this." He pulled his shield from his ring, set it down on the stage in front of him, then pulled several random bits of meat, fruit, and water bottles to set on top of the shield. Then with a wave of his hand he returned them all to his inventory.

"Once you have your rings, we're going to help you fill them. Citizens from all over have donated weapons and armor pieces that they've grown out of, but are appropriate for your current levels. Just speak to one of the folks at the tables, and they'll provide you with whatever is available. I'm sure you'll continue to grow and quickly make these items obsolete, but for now they'll help to keep you safe." There were cheers and cries of thanks from the crowd.

"Lastly, if you haven't already spoken to them, there are about a hundred trainers here who can help you choose a class, or train you in your chosen class. These folks have kindly volunteered their valuable time to be here today. If the trainer you need is not here right now, don't worry. We have more that couldn't be here today. You can make appointments with any of them soon. And please, I cannot emphasize this enough, if you aren't yet sure what class you want, don't rush it. You are safe here now, and have time to make an informed decision. You don't need a class to contribute to the community, though if you're going outside the walls to fight or harvest, a class will make you stronger and safer."

Allistor looked at Helen and whispered, "Did I forget anything?" When she shook her head, he finished up. "Again, welcome to Invictus! I'm so happy that all of you have chosen to join us. In the coming days, I intend to reach out to as many other humans as we can find, and offer them the same. We have the land and resources to expand across the globe. I hope you'll all join me in those efforts."

With that he stepped down off the stage and watched as the newcomers lined up to receive their rings, then file down the line of tables. Allistor smiled sadly as he watched the first few of them being taught how to equip their gear from inventory with a thought, rather than manually donning and lacing and fastening the items. These people had been kept almost totally in the dark. It was going to be an exciting several days for them.

After watching them for a while, he accompanied Daigath, the tiger, and Helen back to Wilderness to check on the bears. It was interesting to watch the meeting between Fuzzy and the oversized tiger. Fuzzy was a higher level than Sher'gal, and though she stood taller at the shoulders, he had much greater mass. And since Fuzzy was still only a yearling, even if he didn't level up any more, he would still grow a great deal over the next year or two.

The two approached each other across the clearing near the blueberry bushes after Daigath made verbal introductions. Sher'gal's hackles were up slightly, the cat having been feral until very recently. Fuzzy seemed relaxed and curious, chuffing at the large cat with his nose going a mile a minute. Eventually the tiger relaxed, and

Fuzzy grinned at her. He reached out with one forepaw and batted her shoulder, then hopped back playfully. She immediately dove forward and tackled him, and the two of them rolled around in a mock battle that Fiona avoided with wide eyes and snorts of distress. After a few minutes of getting-to-know-you wrestling, Fuzzy brought Sher'gal over to where Fiona sat, and a much more sedate introduction was made. Sher'gal seemed to understand that Fiona was hurt, and gave her ear a sympathetic lick.

With that out of the way, Fiona lay on her belly and looked at Helen, who promptly plopped down to sit with her back against the bear. Fiona rumbled quietly as Helen scratched her sides and belly, speaking softly to her.

Sher'gal gave Daigath a look, and he chuckled. "Of course you may go hunt. But no two-legged creatures. Those are friends." The tiger trotted away with a grunt, quickly and nearly silently disappearing into the brush. Fuzzy, seeing that Fiona was safe with Helen for a while, tackled Allistor and demanded belly scratches.

"Ha! Get off me you giant, smelly fuzzball! You need a bath. Maybe two." Allistor shoved the bear off of him, then tackled him, offering rough scratches. He had to press hard to have any effect on the tough bear hide. Fuzzy went limp, laying on his back with his paws flopping limply in the air as Allistor scratched his chest and belly.

Content to spend time with his buddy, Allistor stayed in the clearing with Helen and the bears for the remainder of the day. They spoke with Daigath, asking a great number of questions, some of which the old elf wouldn't answer. "You must discover this on your own." Was his common reply.

Daigath was proud of Allistor when he relayed the tale of pooling some of his experience and leveling up the new citizens. Which might have been the reason the mentor did not try to lecture Allistor about the upcoming visit from Baldur and Loki. Instead, Daigath had Allistor practice making dimensional storage devices with increasing numbers of slots. He used some ability to watch Allistor cast each spell, and gave a few pointers here and there. By the end of the afternoon his *Dimensional Manipulation* had increased to level six. An unexpected but welcome side benefit was that his *Dimensional Step* and *Levitate* spells each increased by a level as well.

*****

The day had come, and Allistor awoke before the first sunrise, as usual. Baldur would be bringing Loki back to face his fate at noon. Allistor was jittery with both excitement and stress. He decided to head to the roof and do some crafting to calm his nerves.

In the back of his mind, he'd been planning a very specific blade. Taking out the best quality steel he'd been able to steal from Michael, he lit the forge and waited for it to heat up. Moving to the lounge area, he closed his eyes and pictured the blade he wanted. Breathing slowly and deeply, he calmed himself and focused on the dimensions of the blade, the weight, the sound it would make as it lopped off Loki's head.

When the forge was heated, he slid the steel into the flame and began to arrange his tools. He was going to use all the limited knowledge and skill he had obtained to make this into a proper genocidal-asshole-fake-god-killing weapon.

Pulling the heated metal from the forge, he began to hammer it out into its initial rough shape. His hands did the work, practice and muscle memory combined with the System's odd crafting mechanics to do the work while his mind wandered. He hammered until the metal began to cool, then placed it back into the forge to reheat time and again. The blade took shape while Allistor imagined the finished product, his mind already mulling over enchantments as the twin suns rose higher above the horizon.

Two hours later the girls appeared on the roof with a tray of food. He set down both sword and hammer and motioned for them to join him in the lounge. As they sat, Sydney reached out and offered a handful of seed in her open palm to the swallow nested in the potted shrub next to the sofa. The odd bird had landed there with its coconut companion some time ago, and never left. Helen, upon first seeing the bird, had laughed long and loud, and instantly named it Monty. Addy and Sydney had taken to feeding it every day, so the bird had no real reason to leave.

And it guarded the coconut with ferocity. William had tried to pick it up once, just to get a closer look. The bird had pecked his hand hard enough to draw blood, scaring the boy into dropping the coconut. Allistor had quickly retrieved it and set it back in place, leaving the angry bird and its ruffled feathers in peace. William had since made several grumbling comments about how the bird might taste, fried with some honey mustard sauce.

The three of them shared a quiet breakfast, Addy asking what Allistor was making. When he told them, both girls nodded their heads, as if it were only proper to create such a weapon for the occasion. They asked if they could do anything to help, and when he declined, they quietly left him to his work.

The blade now properly shaped and nearly finished, Allistor heated it once more and pounded out the last few details. He whistled to himself as he ground out some impurities and sharpened the blade, then took some time to work on the handle. He decided on using some of the ancient shellback's shell as the grip, wrapping it with a layer of drake hide. He set a diamond the size of a grape in the pommel, one of the best quality stones he had in his inventory.

A quick glance at his UI told him he had about an hour before he needed to go and prepare for the meeting. He pulled out his enchanting tool case, a gift from Michael, and began to channel his mana into the engraver as he worked. When he was done, he had drawn symbols up and down the full length of the fuller on both sides of the blade. He carefully checked each symbol for a third time, running some steel cloth up and down to remove any remaining scraps of metal. Then he closed his eyes and focused.

His mana pool was many times larger than the first time he'd tried to enchant a weapon. And his skill had improved quite a bit as well. He imbued the metal of the sword itself with its most important attribute, *Sharpness*. Then he focused on the gem in the pommel, and tried a new enchantment he'd been considering all week. As he pushed his energy into the gem, he pictured what he wanted the spell to do. When he felt it lock into place more than a minute, and thirty percent of his mana pool later, he named the enchantment *Retribution*.

Allistor held the completed sword up in front of him. He'd purposely based its design on old photos and movie holos he'd seen that featured the mythical Excalibur. A European style sword with a wide blade and straight edges that tapered toward the point. A wide fuller on both sides cut down on the weight of the blade, though Allistor could easily have wielded one ten times as heavy. In addition to the runes within the fuller, Allistor had etched some decorative scrolls and vines into the metal near the base. The guard was simple and clean, and the drake hide handle gleamed in the sunlight. Though not as much as the diamond in the pommel.

He'd used Excalibur as his model because he wanted this to be a sword of justice, a symbol to his people. The sword that would take the life of Loki, who had taken so many human lives, and taken so much more from the survivors. He wanted the sword to stand as a symbol as he gathered and reunited what was left of the human race, and propelled them out into the universe.

"You're not perfect, and not very powerful in the grand scheme of things." He spoke to the sword. "Then again, neither am I." He tested the sword's weight and balance, swinging it a few times at imaginary foes. "But I think we suit each other well. I'm going to call you... *Unification*."

*****

Once again, Allistor and his people gathered at the Bastion. Nearly all of his citizens were in attendance, all of them wanting to witness the end of Loki. It was an event they could tell stories of in bars and family gatherings for the rest of their lives.

Lilly had, as she always did, crafted and gifted Allistor what she considered proper attire for the occasion. He stood atop the capitol steps wearing drake skin armor from head to toe. Every inch of it had been dyed a creamy white, with white stitching. When Allistor had asked why she'd chosen the light color rather than the previous crimson she'd given him, her answer was simple, straightforward, and surprising.

"It will show the blood splatter better."

Joining him on the upper level were Harmon, Daigath, his inner circle and analysts, as well as the non-human guests who had attended before. L'olwyn had informed him that literally thousands of others had requested permission to attend. But Allistor had decided, with the help of his advisors, to invite just those guests who had been there for the first visit. They were his closest allies, and though he did not want to offend others, he also didn't want to turn the event into a circus.

His people weren't likely to get another defense quest out of this, but Allistor had already set his UI so that only five percent of the experience granted for killing Loki would go toward his personal level increases. The rest would go into the emperor's pool for distribution to his citizens at some later date. Based on rough estimates from Harmon and Daigath, even five percent would grant him several levels.

The crowd grew quiet when Baldur and Loki appeared out of thin air. Baldur was once again in his human form, tall and muscular and glowing slightly with power. Loki remained in his true form, bound in chains from neck to ankles. This time when he glared at Allistor, there was less hatred and more resignation in his eyes. Allistor guessed that whatever Odin and Baldur had done to Loki had taken much of the fight out of him.

Baldur wasted no time. "Emperor Allistor, I have returned at the agreed upon time and place to deliver Loki to you. His mortal life is yours to do with as you please." He nodded his head almost imperceptibly and stepped back, dropping the chain lead to the ground.

Allistor bowed his head briefly to the ancient being, gritting his teeth as he did so. It infuriated him to show any degree of respect to one of this race. "As agreed, I claim Loki's life on behalf of the human race, all those who perished, and all of us who still live. The suffering he has caused cannot be put into words. I hope that knowledge of Loki's death will ease some of the pain for Earth's survivors as we move forward."

Allistor stepped closer to Loki, who did not react at all. He stared at the murderer's face as he slowly drew his new weapon and held it up. He noticed Baldur take in the weapon, though his face betrayed no opinion of it one way or another. The ancient being simply said, "The restraints have blocked his access to the motes, and with it all of his magic. His health pool has been drained to a fraction of normal, so that your execution may be swift. That weapon will suffice."

Allistor raised the sword into the air with one hand, facing his people gathered below. "For Earth! For all of you! For the lost!" His people roared back at him, their own weapons raised.

*"FOR THE LOST!"*

Without hesitation Allistor turned and thrust *Unification* through Loki's chest where an octopoid's heart would be. The unnaturally sharp weapon slid into the flesh with ease, slamming hilt deep so that the point of the blade exited Loki's back.

The ancient screamed in agony as his eyes flashed with hatred and pain, and the sword's enchantment did its work. A burning sensation filled Loki's existence as some of his life essence was absorbed through the blade into the diamond on the pommel.

When the blow didn't outright kill Loki, whose scream had dwindled into a growl, Allistor yanked the blade free and, spinning his body to increase the momentum of his swing, powered the edge of the blade easily through Loki's neck, and spine, cleanly severing the head.

He waved aside the expected flood of reputation notifications as he held his pose for a moment, sword out in front of him dripping blood, as he joined everyone else in watching the head tumble to the ground. It bounced once on the stone surface and rolled a short distance, the hatred gone from the dead eyes. The crowd was still as Loki's body tipped to one side, then slumped to the ground next to the head.

When Allistor took in a fresh breath and raised the bloody sword into the air again, his pristine white armor now bloodstained, the crowd erupted in a wordless roar that shook the buildings and trees around them. Feet began to stomp in rhythm, and the roar became a chant.

*"Invictus! Invictus! Invictus! INVICTUS!"*

Ignoring the crowd, Baldur stepped closer to Allistor, towering over him. "This fulfills our accord, Emperor Allistor. I hope that this display will quench your thirst for vengeance." Without waiting for a response, Baldur disappeared, as did the silvery chains from Loki's corpse.

A moment later, as Allistor watched the blood cease to pump from Loki's neck, another series of notifications flooded Allistor's vision. This time, he didn't have a chance to wave them away, as the euphoric feeling of leveling up overwhelmed his senses and he fell unconscious.

*****

Baldur appeared in front of his father's throne within seconds of leaving Earth. His father, who had been observing the proceedings, was getting to his feet even as Baldur saw the holo image of Allistor dropping insensate to the ground next to Loki's corpse.

At the same time, several other holo displays flashed red, and Odin began to curse.

"I knew it! I knew I should have pushed harder, drained Loki of every last iota of knowledge. I let him keep his last, darkest secrets, not wanting to burden my soul any further. It seems I have made another mistake." Odin spoke quietly as he took in the information displayed. Baldur shook his head as he too absorbed it all.

"We should have expected this. They were always hated rivals."

"So much loss of life for petty rivalry. Such a waste." Odin's eyes were moist with unshed tears. He turned away from the holo displays and looked down upon Baldur. "What was that enchantment?"

Baldur's tentacles twitched. "The boy named it *Retribution*. It had three functions. First and foremost, it drained a bit of Loki's essence into the gem. Not a large fraction, but enough to give the sword sentience, eventually. It will grow as he uses it. The other purposes of the enchantment were to impart pain, and the knowledge of what it was doing. In effect, he designed the weapon to send a message to Loki, and to us. *I can hurt you.*"

Odin nodded. "Smartly done. The boy realized after his threat to capture Loki's essence in the orb, that this was the one thing he feared. Letting Loki know that the sword was stealing some of his essence would indeed have caused anguish." There was concern in his eyes, and a question, as he looked at his son.

"The boy is still a beginner. He has no way to know it, but the power he took was the tiniest fraction of Loki's essence. Not nearly enough to prevent his ascension. Had it been otherwise, I would not have allowed him to use the weapon. As it is, he believes he has his revenge, Loki was deservedly chastened but not truly harmed, and Allistor has earned himself a powerful weapon." He paused and glanced briefly at the displays before continuing. "As for the... other consequences? We will simply have to wait and see."

"Let us hope that this measure of revenge will be enough to cool his temper and give him time to grow out of his hatred for us." Odin sat back in his throne, the tears in his eyes still unshed.

Chapter 22

Hel watched with breath held as the human boy emperor approached Loki with the sword. Like Baldur, she had taken the time to *Examine* the weapon the moment Allistor had drawn it, and her vast powers of perception had told her what the enchantments would do. She took a perverse pleasure in that. Obviously, Loki had not bothered to study the weapon, or he would have had more of a reaction to it. So the enchantment's effects were going to come as a painful, and at least briefly horrifying, surprise to him. Hel took pleasure in that, as well.

The boy made his short speech, then wasted no time carrying out the execution. He stabbed Loki through the chest, causing exactly the pain and horror she'd hoped for. Then with a second swift motion Allistor took the head of his tormentor. *Well, one of your tormentors, you little fool. I'm at least as responsible for your troubles as my father is. Was. He's actually gone. I finally got the best of him once and for all.* She projected the thought at the holo display.

It was the last thought she would experience on the mortal plane.

For at that same moment, Loki's heart ceased to beat. The device he'd implanted sent a signal that triggered the hidden explosives in Hel's lab to detonate. Her body disappeared in a white-hot flash that was the first in a chain of detonations that utterly destroyed the entire moon where she'd hidden her base. Loki had no way to be sure exactly where she'd be standing at the moment of his death. His assumption was that she'd be in her lab, her favorite spot and communications hub. But he was nothing if not thorough, so he'd literally gone nuclear. A dozen devices planted deep within the mantle of the moon detonated within milliseconds of each other. The planetoid burst apart, killing every living thing on or near it.

Across the entire galaxy the very fabric of the Collective was altered. Two of the most devious and active members of their ancient race died within seconds of each other. Eons of sworn oaths and contracts were nullified. Debts were eliminated, and incurred. Thousands who had sworn to protect either of the two beings with their lives perished for failing their oaths. Millions of possessions in the form of object, property, and living beings, were suddenly up for grabs. Within the hour, wars would begin among those looking to take advantage.

And the System took note of all of it.

*****

In a mostly intact building near the north end of what had once been Central Park, the Lich was standing with arms held high, chanting in a low tone. The words that spilled from his mouth would have made any living being's skin crawl, causing them terror beyond tolerating. He was calling on the power of the dead, gathering it to himself in order to transfer a small measure of it to each of the adept candidates standing before him. Their undead forms writhed in pain, floating several feet off the floor as the dark magic imbued itself within their rotted and desiccated bodies.

Partway through his spell, the Lich's voice ceased with a death rattle. The light of magic went out of his eyes as if a switch had been flipped. His arms dropped, followed quickly by the rest of his body hitting the floor. Around him, the floating candidates screamed briefly before dropping to the floor, once again fully dead. The detonation in Hel's lab had brought about the utter destruction of the phylactery holding the lich's soul.

The previously established adepts trembled, some of them falling to their knees, others leaning against a post or wall as they felt their master's shared power leave them. The loss of that power did not destroy them, only diminish them greatly. They were once again on a level with the common zombies outside. Gone was the ability to raise more of the dead. As was the ability to control their fellow undead.

Several simply forfeited the mockery of life that animated them, having no desire to continue without their master's power and will to motivate them. Others slowly wandered away, uncaring of their direction, seeking only to feed.

One adept, the first and most powerful, stood looking down at her master's corpse. A faint glow still smoldered within her eyes, flickering briefly before nearly extinguishing. With a nod and a raspy exhale, she bent down to loot her former master. When she was through, she walked away, his ebony staff thumping on the floor with every other step.

*****


Allistor awoke to pain in the back of his head. Opening his eyes, he blinked several times as the twin suns shone directly into them. His vision was filled with notifications that disappeared with a hazy thought. Reaching up with his left hand to block the light, he saw the blood of his sworn enemy splattered on the pristine armor, as well as his skin.

Several faces loomed above him as he groaned, trying to sit up. He was dizzy, and nearly fell back to a prone position before several helping hands grabbed hold and lifted him to his feet. Directly in front of him, Helen stood next to Meg, each of them helping to steady him by holding one of his elbows and hands.

"What the hell happened?" He managed to speak easily enough before taking several deep breaths, trying to shake the dizziness.

"You passed out, fell down, and hit your thick head." Meg stated bluntly, squeezing his hand to offset the gruff tone.

"That explains the elephant romping around in there wearing cleats." He nodded his head and immediately regretted it.

Melise, who had apparently been standing ninja-close behind him, leaned in and spoke in a hushed tone. "They're worried about you. You must let them know you are well."

"What?" A confused Allistor looked at the elfess, then followed her gaze down the stairway to his gathered citizens. The crowd was hushed, looks of fear or expectation on their faces.

Allistor gritted his teeth and let go of Meg's hand, raising his own to wave at the crowd. There was a roar of relieved cheers, and a renewal of the chant. *"Invictus! Invictus!"* He took a few more breaths, moving his hand to rub the back of his head. He felt a sore spot where his melon had clearly impacted the ground.

Helen moved so that her face was directly in front of his. "You hit the ground pretty hard. I think your fat head actually bounced. We healed you right away, so there shouldn't be any more pain..." She looked worried.

Allistor blinked at her, remembering the notifications. "I don't think my head hurts from the bump. This feels more like when Daigath taught me a new school of magic. Maybe it's from leveling up too much? But I don't under..." He broke off as the question caused his UI to pop up and show his character sheet.

"Holy shit. I'm level ninety seven! How the hell did that happen?" He blinked several times at his UI, not trusting what his aching brain was showing him. "I don't understand."

Allistor had prepared for the experience rush from killing Loki. He had set things up so that he would personally receive just the five percent of the xp awarded by the System. The rest should have redirected into the empire pool. A quick check of that tab showed him an xp number that boggled the mind. He wasn't even sure what that many digits represented. Trillions? He found he didn't have the focus to count them and figure it out. It was too much.

"M-master Daigath? Harmon?" he looked around for his two most senior and knowledgeable advisors. Both stepped forward, but before Allistor could ask a question, Harmon placed a hand on his shoulder.

"Let us retire someplace private. I believe there is much to discuss." The giant orcanin urged Allistor toward the door of the building behind them.

"Hang on a second." Allistor turned back toward the crowd. "Nigel, loudspeaker please." He waited a moment then continued. "It's okay, everyone. I mean, I'm okay. I'm not sure what happened, but I leveled up *a lot*. I just need a few minutes to shake it off. Thank you all for coming." He waved again, then turned and allowed Harmon to guide him inside.

Allistor, Harmon, Daigath, Helen, Meg, and Sam all stepped into the elevator that quickly delivered them to the suite Amanda had created for them in the capitol building. Meg tried to make Allistor lay down on a sofa, but settled for him sitting with an extra cushion behind his head. As he was getting situated, both Harmon and Daigath were speaking quietly into their communicators and listening intently to the replies. At one point, eyes wide, Harmon triggered a holo display from his wrist device, and both he and Daigath stared at it.

"Somebody want to fill us in?" Allistor asked his advisors.

Harmon cleared his throat. "Well, information is still coming in. But the current theory is that by killing Loki, you somehow triggered a failsafe that also killed Hel. As well as a great number of their servants and those in their employ. An entire moon owned by Hel was destroyed, with her on it. The death toll has surpassed one million and is still growing as reports come in."

Daigath nodded, taking his eyes from the display. "Beings of such power and influence leave behind quite a void. And the consequences of their passing ripple outward into the Collective." He paused, giving Allistor a look of sympathy. "Though I did not anticipate it would reach such a scale, I did warn you there would be consequences."

Allistor's gut clenched and he could hear his own pulse ringing in his ears. He had to fight not to vomit on his boots. "I'm... did I just commit genocide? Am I a mass murderer?"

"There will be some who consider you to be so." Harmon's face was hard to read. "Your intentions, while not exactly pure, were directed solely at obtaining justice as you see it. And you were not aware that taking Loki's head would result in the deaths of others. Even those of us who expected some collateral loss of life had no idea it would happen to this extent."

Daigath nodded as the orcanin spoke. "I expect you have received a large number of faction notifications, as well as experience notifications. It will take some time to analyze all of them. I suggest you summon your analysts and have them begin immediately."

Allistor nodded, numbly asking Nigel to do so. The speed at which Droban, Selby, Longbeard, and L'olwyn appeared suggested they had anticipated his need and were hovering close by. Allistor quickly pushed all of the several sets of notifications to all four of them.

When he heard the gasps of surprise and astonishment, he raised his eyes. "Yeah, tell me about it."

After just a moment, Longbeard thumped the coffee table in front of him. The least flustered of the four advisors, he had cut straight to the experience and level notifications. "I see what happened. Ye told the system ta give ye five percent o' the experience fer Loki's death, which it did. But when his death triggered a bunch o' others, it gived ye experience fer those deaths as well. Not a full measure fer each one, as it would if ye killed them directly yerself, but enough that it raised ye more'n thirty levels at once. Ye got the five percent o' the total ye set up fer yerself as personal experience, and..." He gazed at the number for a moment. "several trillion experience points went into yer Emperor's pool."

"You've made an unfathomable number of enemies, Allistor." L'olwyn was actually weeping as he read through the faction reputation notifications."

"And a similar number of new friends or reputation increases." Selby gave him a weak smile, her body trembling. Allistor couldn't tell if it was from fear or excitement. "It will take us weeks to go through and analyze all of this."

"We shall prioritize trying to identify any immediate threats." Droban added.

Harmon chuckled. "You really stepped in it, my friend. I've already ordered a small army of my own analysts to begin gathering and processing as much information as possible. Also, and this might be good news for you, several factions and empires are leaping at the opportunities opening up at the deaths of Loki and Hel. Multiple planets, in a few cases whole solar systems, are now up for grabs. Not to mention power grabs within corporate entities previously under their control. All that excitement might distract new enemies from focusing on you for a while." He winked at Allistor. "The Orcanin Empire is already seizing some useful assets for itself."

"Glad I could help." Allistor deadpanned.

Longbeard cleared his throat. "There be a set of notifications here awarding ye some o' Loki's holdings as well. Most be from last week when Baldur awarded ye Loki's property here on this planet. But a few o' these are from today." He snorted, then chuckled to himself. "Ye now own two more planets, three more space stations, and..."

Allistor held up a hand and cut him off. "Please, not now. I've had enough for one day. I just killed a million or more people, whether I meant to or not. I really don't want to hear what rewards that brought me. Can... can you guys handle it? Or assign some of our people to handle it? Like, check on those worlds and make sure they're not in immediate danger? I just need a little time to process all this."

Longbeard nodded. "We'll be hiring ye some more analysts like ourselves ta help carry this new burden. Don't ye worry, we'll hold things together till ye be prepared to take the reins."

"Thank you, all of you." Allistor looked at Daigath and Harmon. "Is there anything else I need to know right now?"

Harmon looked to Daigath, who shook his head and replied, "Nothing that can't wait a few hours. Get some rest, boy." He produced a vial of softly glowing pink liquid. "Drink this. It will allow you to sleep for several hours. When you awaken, though, you'll need to be prepared to address the most urgent of your new responsibilities."

"Right. No problem. Thank you." Allistor's sarcasm was impolite, but at that moment he was beyond caring. He accepted the potion and drank it down quickly, then allowed Meg to mother him into stretching out on the sofa. She pulled off his blood-spattered boots and propped his feet up on a cushion. When he shivered and she

491

reached for a blanket, he waved her off. The cold he was feeling inside had nothing to do with the temperature of the room. The potion did its work, and he quickly drifted off to sleep despite the desperate vortex of thoughts whirling through his mind.

*****

Allistor dreamt he was standing in a large, empty space. Dimly lit except for a beam of sunlight that shone down from above directly onto him, and a similar spotlight that illuminated a giant of a man atop a massive golden throne. He felt puny next to this being who, even sitting down, was several times Allistor's own height. He imagined that if the man stood, he'd be fifty feet tall.

"Greetings, Emperor Allistor. I am Odin, the Allfather." The giant's voice boomed out, causing Allistor to wince slightly. He took a step back from his imposing enemy and put one hand where the hilt of his sword should have been. When he didn't feel it, he cursed quietly to himself.

"Fear not, young one. You are in no danger here. Your physical body is quite safe where you left it. I am merely speaking to your mind as you sleep. And while I could certainly erase you with a thought, I have no such intention."

Not sure he believed Odin's statement of intentions at all, Allistor also knew there was nothing he could do about it either way. So he simply straightened his back and stared up at the godlike being. "Why am I here?"

"You are here, impertinent child, because I wished to speak privately with you. I wish to share some knowledge, a little wisdom, I hope, and a warning."

"Let me guess." Allistor nearly spit on the floor at the base of the throne. "You want to tell me to be satisfied with the deaths of Loki and Hel, and let go of any plans for further vengeance?"

Odin chuckled. "Well, ultimately yes, I would appreciate that. But it will be many years before you could even locate me, let alone grow powerful enough to come against me. My warning has to do with your much more immediate future." Odin motioned with one hand, and a chair appeared underneath Allistor, forcing him to sit. "But before the warning, let us discuss the day's events."

Curious despite himself, Allistor waited patiently for Odin to continue.

"Your ancestors named me a god, one who is all-seeing and nearly omnipotent. The truth is, though I do possess power beyond your understanding, I am neither all-seeing nor all-powerful. My own race has its limits, just like any other. That is why I must admit that I failed you today." He looked irritated for a moment, shaking his head. "Not just you individually. By not anticipating the depth of Loki's pride, insanity, and hatred, I failed the entire Collective. You were merely the trigger that brought that failure to light."

Odin began to shrink physically, stepping off his throne as he did so. Within seconds he was roughly the same size as Baldur had appeared to be on Earth earlier in

493

the day. A table and another chair appeared in front of Allistor, and Odin took a seat across from him.

"Unfortunately for you, being the trigger has propelled you much further along, much deeper into the game than you are prepared for. You and yours will face opposition you haven't truly earned, and consequences that can not yet be fully foreseen."

Odin sighed. "Let us begin at the beginning. I have always favored the human race. Since you were little more than upright apes living in trees and caves, my race have fostered your development. We visited your world many times throughout your evolution. And even before that. There was another dominant race on your earth that predates your own. They were wiped out by a natural disaster long before... Ah, but that doesn't matter now. You need only know that we assisted in your growth, providing small nudges here and there to motivate and enlighten your ancestors. All so that you might someday become viable and valued members of the Collective."

"Baldur, myself, and a few others took a special liking to humans. You have great potential, combined with deep flaws that make you unpredictable and interesting to watch. You are rash, and quick-tempered, but also creative and loving. You're rarely satisfied with what you have or who you are, and seem driven to explore and understand. We, most of us, have worked to encourage all of those aspects of the human race. We have been like your gardeners, fertilizing and pruning rough weeds so that they might flower and bear fruit."

"You can't possibly take credit for everything we are." Allistor snapped at him. "We have free will, and the intelligence to learn and choose for ourselves."

"I'm not here to argue the extent of our influence, Allistor. I merely wished you to know that we meant you no harm, that we wished to help. And would have continued to do so for many more centuries, at least. Had Loki not interfered."

Allistor fidgeted in his chair, anger warring with his sense of self-preservation.

"Loki's actions were the beginning of my people's debt to you. He should not have been allowed to interfere by triggering your world's Induction ahead of schedule. And today's events have, due to my own failure, increased our debt to you. And to the Collective, which has now been unbalanced. We will do what we can to restore that balance in small ways, but the Collective is very old, and very complex, and will largely balance itself out on its own in time."

"What does that mean for my world?"

"You now own four worlds, Allistor. But I get your meaning." Odin smiled gently at him. "You are like a tiny mouse who, while poking his nose where it doesn't belong in search of a tasty morsel, has shorted out a vital circuit and caused a power outage across a whole city. You did not intend that result, nor would you have any way to have known that it was even possible. Yet, as that tiny mouse would have been fried to a crisp, you will have to face dire consequences. Loki, his pride unable to accept that he might be outmaneuvered, created a failsafe system to ensure that his daughter and main rival would follow him into death. In his zeal, he caused her entire moon and everyone on it to be utterly destroyed. The additional ripples of consequence from their simultaneous deaths will be unpredictable and significant. In my sorrow after learning of so many misdeeds that burdened Loki's soul, I failed to pull that final bit of information from him. That is now my debt to shoulder, and part of that debt is owed to you, little mouse."

"Stop calling me that." Allistor thumped the table with his fist. "I get it. You're super-smart and powerful, and I'm just a hairless monkey about a million levels of evolution below you. Pointing it out repeatedly doesn't help."

Odin stared at him for a moment. "Fair enough. But be aware, your impertinence also does not help." His gaze held Allistor's until the human nodded once in acceptance of that statement.

"I will not give you details now, as things are still very much in flux. But know that Baldur and I will work to lessen the consequences that fall upon you and your people. Still, you will need to proceed with caution, and speed. Learn what enemies you've made this day, and allow your friends to help you prepare for them. Continue on the path you've chosen, gather your people together and make them stronger. So that even if you yourself do not survive the coming trials, they may continue on without you."

"As you said, that was always my mission. To make humans strong enough to reclaim Earth."

"And to venture out among the stars with vengeance in your hearts. Yes, I know." Odin chuckled. "Well you have your wish. You have the resources now to venture far out into the universe. One of the two planets you won today is much nearer the center of the Collective than your Earth. I recommend you take special note of that fact as you plan your people's future." The giant winked at Allistor. "In the meantime, gather your friends to you, and study your enemies. You can learn much from both. And though I may not contact you directly for some time, know that we will be looking out for you, doing what we can under the restrictions of our role within the System. Rest well, Emperor Allistor."

With a flick of his finger, the light in the room around them went dark, and Odin went with it. Allistor found himself back on the sofa in Denver, Helen snoring in a nearby chair. The sky outside was dark, and all was quiet as he sat upright. His head no longer ached, which he suspected might be thanks to Daigath's potion, or Odin's interference in his mind.

Not wanting to wake Helen, he simply sat there with his hands on his knees. With a resigned sigh, he opened up his UI and began the hours-long process of reading all of his notifications.

End Book Five

## *Acknowledgements*

Thanks as always to my family for their love and support. They are my alphas, my sounding board, and the ones who aren't afraid to tell me when something sucks! A simple thank you doesn't seem adequate, but here we are. A shout out to John Ward for drawing the cool space station on the cover.

For semi-regular updates on books, art, and just stuff going on, check out my Greystone Guild fb https://www.facebook.com/greystone.guild.7 or my website www.davewillmarth.com where you can subscribe for an eventual newsletter.

And don't forget to follow my author page on Amazon! **That way you'll get a nice friendly email when new books are released**. You can also find links to my Greystone Chronicles, Shadow Sun, and Dark Elf books there! https://www.amazon.com/Dave-Willmarth/e/B076G12KCL

## *PLEASE TAKE A MOMENT TO LEAVE A REVIEW!*

Reviews on Amazon and Goodreads are vitally important to indie authors like me. Amazon won't help market the books until they reach a certain level of reviews. So please, take a few seconds, click on that (fifth!) star and type a few words about how much you liked the book! I would appreciate it very much. I do read the reviews, and a few of my favorites have led to friendships and even character cameos!

You can find information on lots of LitRPG/GameLit books on Ramon Mejia's LitRPG Podcast here https://www.facebook.com/litrpgpodcast/. You can find his books here. https://www.amazon.com/R.A.-Mejia/e/B01MRTVW3O

There are a few more places where you can find me, and several other genre authors, hanging out. Here are my favorite LitRPG/GameLit community facebook groups. (If you have cookies, as always, keep them away from Daniel Schinhofen).

https://www.facebook.com/groups/LitRPGsociety/

https://www.facebook.com/groups/LitRPG.books/

https://www.facebook.com/groups/GameLitSociety/

https://www.facebook.com/groups/541733016223492/

Made in the USA
Las Vegas, NV
08 June 2023

73127413R00273